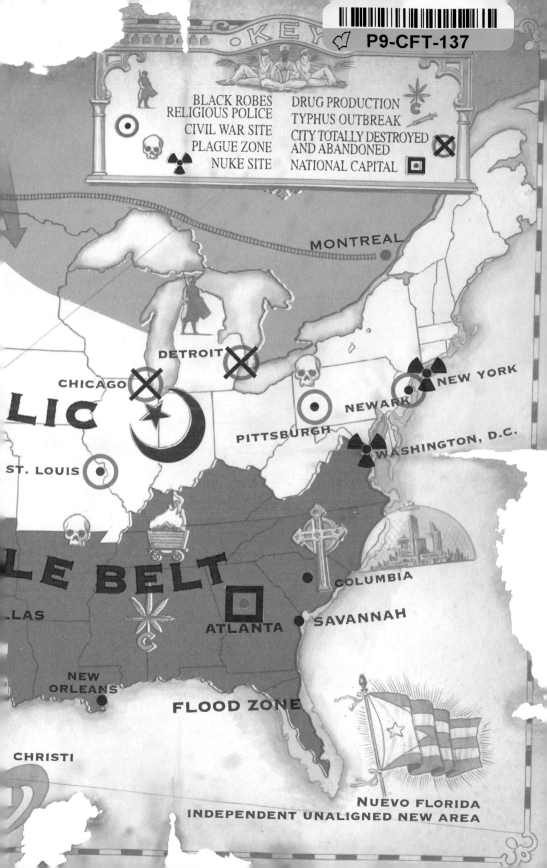

ALSO BY ROBERT FERRIGNO

Prayers for the Assassin

The Wake-Up

Scavenger Hunt

Flinch

Heart Breaker

Dead Silent

Dead Man's Dance

Cheshire Moon

The Horse Latitudes

Sins of the Assassin

A NOVEL

Robert Ferrigno

SCRIBNER

New York London Toronto Sydney

SCRIBNER
A Division of Simon & Schuster, Inc.
1230 Avenue of the Americas
New York, NY 10020

First Scribner hardcover edition February 2008

SCRIBNER and design are trademarks of
Macmillan Library Reference USA, Inc., used under license
by Simon & Schuster, the publisher of this work.

For information about special discounts for bulk purchases,
please contact Simon & Schuster Special Sales:
1-800-456-6798 or business@simonandschuster.com.

Designed by Kyoko Watanabe
Text set in Electra

Manufactured in the United States of America

1   3   5   7   9   10   8   6   4   2

Library of Congress Control Number: 2007048101

ISBN-13: 978-1-4165-3765-6
ISBN-10: 1-4165-3765-1

To Sgt. 1st Class Paul R. Smith,
Corporal Jason L. Dunham,
Lt. Michael Murphy,
and to all the other the warriors who sleep badly,
so that the rest of us can sleep well.

"One kills a man, one is an assassin. One kills millions, one is a conqueror. One kills everybody, one is a god."

—Jean Rostand
(French biologist and philosopher)

SINS OF THE ASSASSIN

CHAPTER 1

Moseby needed to slow down. His haste stirred up a gray confetti of silt, disintegrating paper, and pulverized glass from the neon sign that once flashed OYSTER PO' BOYS, TREAT YO MOUTH. The tiny halogen beams on either side of his face mask bounced back from the confetti, the light made useless by his excitement. Moseby drifted in the warm water of the Gulf, waiting. Plenty of time, no need to rush. He easily got four hours out of a three-hour tank. More if he stayed calm and clear.

Mama's Home Cookin' lay crumbling on its foundation, roof gone, the concrete-block walls scoured clean by the tide. A couple of red leatherette stools still sat upright, the floor carpeted with gently waving sea grass. He thought of the crowd at the LSU homecoming game last month, Annabelle on her feet beside him, pom-poms shaking as she cheered louder than anyone. He smiled around his mouthpiece. The cash register was sprung open on the counter, soggy bills hanging out like fingers from the till. Old money. Worthless. Mama's didn't hold any treasure. The oyster shack was just a marker, an indicator that he was close to what he sought.

Moseby floated in place, listening to the sound of his own steady breathing. Easy to get spooked fifty feet under, a swimmer alone with the dead. It took patience to survive in the drowned city. More than patience, it took faith. Moseby pulled at the chain around his neck, clasped the small gold crucifix between thumb and forefinger. He silently asked the blessing of Mary, mother of God. Asked her to intercede on behalf of all who had lost their lives in the city below. Asked the dead for their permission to take what they no longer needed. A man could never pray too much. Particularly a man like Moseby, who had much to atone for. He let go of the crucifix, drifted again, shivering in the warm water.

Unlike Moseby, most scavengers used electric sleds in their explorations, racing around at full power, churning up debris. Greedy, frightened men chopping their way through the city, so eager to get back to the surface that they ruined most of what they brought up. Dangerous work under the best of circumstances. Rebreathers failed. Floors and ceilings gave way. Walls collapsed. Jagged metal sliced through wet suits, the rush of blood attracting the barracuda and morays that lurked in the mossy grottos of the French Quarter and the collapsed Superdome. More dangerous than anything else to the scavengers was the panic, men disoriented by the darkness, and the fractured geometry of wrecked buildings. Gulping air, swimming frantically, they got lost in the concrete maze, adding themselves to the long list of dead.

The streets below were almost beyond the reach of sunlight, obscured further by thousands of automobiles leaking oil even after all these years. Murkier still in the houses and restaurants, the grand hotels where the easy spoils lay. Afraid of the deep, the scavengers used ever more powerful lights, blinding themselves, losing all perspective in the undersea tableau. Men had died for a crystal doorknob they mistook for a massive diamond, gotten trapped reaching for a sterling punch bowl far from their grasp. Frightened of the dark and the loneliness, frightened most of all by the ghosts. Commuters floating in their vehicles. Lovers in their hotel beds, honeymooners huddling in the lavish bathrooms where they had taken cover. Hard to pluck a gold Rolex off a bony wrist under those watching eye sockets. Hard not to hurry, to drop the goods and fumble to find them again. Easy to breathe too fast, to let the nitrogen build up in the bloodstream, to overestimate the air supply. This year alone sixty-seven men had died or disappeared. Most scavengers focused on the French Quarter—the fancy stores and tourist emporiums had been picked over, but their familiarity offered some illusion of safety. Not Moseby.

His crew worked the untouched areas, the mansions and banks and businesses outside the central core, places where the flood had been most ferocious, leaving behind a deadly jumble of concrete and steel and twisted rebar. They were the most successful crew working the city, bringing up gold coins and jewelry, carved stonework, vintage brandy, and Creole memorabilia. Steering wheels from classic cars had been particularly hot this year—most of them sold to collectors in Asia and South America.

Moseby trained his men himself, taught them as much as they could handle. The men were careful . . . but they still died. Not as often as the men working the supposedly safer parts of the city, but too often, for Moseby. That's why he dove alone today. Men had the right to risk their lives to feed their families, but Moseby wasn't seeking treasure today. At least none that would be sold or bartered.

He switched off his light. Gave in to the darkness. Waiting. Moseby closed his eyes. Patient. When he opened them again, he could see. Not clearly, *even his* eyes weren't that good, but he could see. Now that Mama's had oriented him, the shapes and shadows seemed laid out before him, the messy grid on the city's outskirts, St. Bernard's Parish in the Ninth Ward, where the levee had failed first.

The old government had raised the levees two times after Hurricane Katrina inundated the city. Built them higher and higher, trying to keep up with the rising sea level and the ever more powerful hurricanes spawned by the warming. September 23, 2013, thirty years ago, Hurricane James, a category 6 hurricane, predicted to miss the city, had suddenly veered west in the middle of the night and struck New Orleans at sunrise. The levees gave way as though made of tissue, the waters of the Gulf covering the city under fifty feet of water. Most of the estimated 300,000 dead were stuck in traffic trying to flee. Hurricane James was the most violent storm ever recorded. Until Hurricane Maria two years later.

He glided over the road, his no-wake flippers almost living up to their name. Brightly colored fish ignored him, twisting and turning as they darted past him, weaving in and out the open windows of the barnacle-crusted vehicles strewn below. The houses in the immediate area were small and falling down, but the land rose slightly toward the north, where the homes were larger, many of them surrounded by iron fences and stone walls. This was where Sweeny would have lived.

Annabelle couldn't remember much from her visit to her eccentric uncle's house—she was barely five—but there had been an ancient banyan tree in his backyard dripping with Spanish moss, and a swing set already rusted, squeaking loudly, one leg of the swing lifting off the ground as she had rhythmically pumped away. She remembered Sweeny taking her and her mother to a local po'boy joint, a hole-in-the-wall specializing in oysters drenched in fresh lime juice, bourbon, and Tabasco. Sweeny said he ate two po'boys for lunch every day, proudly watched as his niece devoured one of her own, smacking her lips with pleasure in spite of the blistering hot sauce. Moseby had spent months searching for New Orleans take-out joints specializing in the Cajun delicacy, months of scouring local guide-books and newspaper articles. Last week he got lucky, ran into an old-timer . . . a regular at Mama's in the old days.

Moseby's eyes adjusted even further to the dim light. Annabelle said if it had been him instead of Jonah swallowed by the whale, Moseby wouldn't have needed divine intervention to find his way out of its innards. He checked his watch. Plenty of time. Plenty of air. He passed over a small backyard, a line of laundry drooping but still standing. Shirts and pants and dresses, their colors faded, eaten through with time, ragged pennants rippling in the current. Another yard . . . the screen door thrown open, torn half off its hinges, and Moseby wondered if the family inside the house had made it out alive, had clung to a boat, a skiff, an inflatable swimming pool; he wondered if they had gotten lucky, awakened from a nightmare before dawn, and raced ahead of the raging floodwaters.

Annabelle said her uncle's house had been large, with a high river-rock fence and white pillars; he had become a rich man down on his luck by then, his house the remnant of his fortune as the neighborhood sunk into squalor. She and her mother had never gone back after that first visit. Sweeny had taken offense at something her mother said . . . or maybe it was the other way around. Either way, her uncle and the house were a dim memory.

The marble bust of the woman . . . that was a different story. Annabelle remembered it vividly. The stone queen, that's what she had called the statue. A beautiful woman with a head full of tight curls, her expression distant and dreamy, as though she had seen something that no one else had ever seen, and the sight had changed her. The world would never be quite fine enough for the woman now. Annabelle said she thought the stone queen must have looked into heaven and couldn't wait to go there. Moseby knew better. He and Annabelle had sifted through photos on the Net until she narrowed down what she remembered. If she was right, the statue was Greek, probably early classical, in the style of Aphrodite of Melos. Priceless. Moseby was going to surprise Annabelle with it for their anniversary tonight. For weeks he had been searching for it, not even telling his daughter, Leanne.

A grove of trees had been flattened by the flood, thrown together in a tangle. Beyond the fallen trees, a huge banyan squatted in place, leaves long gone, its branches still sharp. A crumbling stone wall . . . Moseby angled lower, straining to see.

The wall was made from smooth river rock. Spiky, brightly colored sea anemones festooned the stones, completely covering the south wall where the offshore flow brought the densest stream of nutrients. He jerked back as a sea snake poked out from a hole in the crumbling wall, the creature tracking him with its tiny eyes, working its fangs as it undulated toward him. Yellow with red stripes, four feet long . . . five feet, six feet at least as it wiggled out of the wall. Moseby drew his knife as he watched the snake, playing with it now, the flat of the blade making lazy rotations around his index finger. The spinning blade gathered the faint light, flashed in the darkness, and the snake inched closer, attracted. Moseby kept the blade moving, calling it closer. Sea snake venom was more deadly than a cobra's, that's what the old-timers said. All Moseby knew was that three divers had died last month from snakebites, died ugly, puffed up until their skin split. Fifty years ago there hadn't been sea snakes in the Gulf, none like this anyway, but the water was warmer now, the snakes migrating toward rich pickings . . . just like Moseby. The snake stopped, faced off with him, and then slowly retreated back to its grotto in the stone wall.

Moseby waited another minute, then slipped his knife back into its sheath, moved on to the house. He slipped gently through a picture window that had been blown out, scattering fish with his presence. The fish returned just as quickly. He switched his face mask lights to the lowest setting, bounced the beam off the ceiling. He saw well enough to navigate.

Tables and chairs were jumbled below, the carpet thick with mud, tiny crabs scuttling through the saw grass. Paintings on the wall hung askew, their surfaces occluded by a dull blue-gray fungus, gilt frames eaten by woodworms. Fish nosed around him, but Moseby ignored them. He lightly wiped a gloved hand across the surface of the largest painting . . . the paint rolled off in tiny droplets, spun lazily around him as the fish gobbled them down. He kicked on through the house, limpets dotting the walls and ceiling. Stingrays burrowed into the debris, hiding themselves.

He hovered in the doorway of the master bedroom. A huge bookcase had fallen, scattered volumes. Pages swollen, the books gaped on the carpet. The Greek bust lay among the books, toppled off its display stand. He moved inside, eager now; his movements stirred the top layer of mud, but he didn't care. He wrenched the bust from the pile of books, sent the sodden pages fluttering around him, free of their rotten bindings. He cleared away the fine moss that covered the statue's features, taking off his glove to feel the smooth marble, not satisfied until she was clean. Moseby looked into her face. She was everything that Annabelle had described: strong and beautiful, but most of all possessed of secrets that had cost her greatly. The wisdom of time. He ran a finger along her cheek. Even buoyed by the water, the bust was heavy, maybe a hundred pounds, but he tucked it under one arm, comforted by its heft. He swam for the window, his kicks powerful, leaving clouds of pages in his wake. All those lost words . . .

His wrist tracker guided him back to where his boat was anchored 1.3 miles away. He could have tagged the bust and returned for it when he got to the boat. Would have been easier, but the idea of putting aside the sculpture even for a few minutes, after all this time searching for it . . . Moseby couldn't do it.

He swam on, shifting the sculpture from arm to arm, more excited than fatigued. By the time the bottom of the boat came into view, he just wanted to load up and be gone. He carefully placed the bust on the hydraulic shelf at the stern, the stone queen's face gleaming in the sunlight after all those years underwater. Moseby tore himself away from her gaze, grabbed a handhold, and pulled himself quickly onto the boat. Pushed back his face mask. *Trouble.* He turned.

"Nice morning. A little hot maybe . . ."

Moseby stared at the man in shorts and a bright Hawaiian shirt leaning against the command console, cleaning his fingernails with Moseby's boning knife. A muscular bruiser, sweating in the heat. Tufts of short red hair blossomed across his skull. Small, cruel eyes, made worse by the intelligence within, and large, flat, uneven teeth. An albino ape raped by a wild boar would birth something like this man . . . and then abandon it in disgust. Moseby stood on the deck, dripping water. "What are you doing on my boat?"

The man wandered over to check out the statue. Whistled. "You carried that thing by yourself? You're a lot stronger than you look." He grinned with those crooked teeth, idly adjusted the machine pistol slung around one shoulder. "I best watch my manners."

"I asked you a question."

"You know who I am?" the man said softly, working the curved tip of the boning knife deep under his thumbnail. Coarse red hairs on his knuckles waved in the breeze.

"Yeah."

The man flicked something from under his nail with the knife, looked up at Moseby. "Then you know I don't need to give you any explanations."

Moseby had seen the man on video more than once, Gravenholtz . . . Lester Gravenholtz. He was usually standing behind the Colonel at news conferences, rarely acknowledged, but always there. The Colonel was a bona fide war hero, known as the savior of Knoxville for his tenacious defense of the city. "No retreat, no surrender, no prisoners" was his motto. At the height of the battle he had personally executed nineteen deserters, live-broadcasting the slayings to his troops. A local warlord now—plenty of those in the Bible Belt, where any central authority was always suspect—but the Colonel was the most powerful, a law unto himself. Lester Gravenholtz had been a late edition to the Colonel's forces, showed up about ten years ago and made himself at home. The Colonel's imp, hostile preachers had called him . . . until they disappeared. Two years ago, the president himself had signed a federal arrest warrant for Gravenholtz, citing multiple examples of rape, murder, and the sacking of the government armory in Vicksburg. The Colonel had sent home the federal prosecutor who attempted to arrest Gravenholtz, said he'd rein in Gravenholtz himself. The thirty members of the prosecutor's armed detail had defected and become part of the Colonel's private army.

"I don't blame you for being scared," said Gravenholtz.

Moseby didn't answer. In the distance, he saw a stealth helicopter just above the treeline, completely silent, props wafting the branches. He didn't react, turned and watched the water. Not one man in a thousand would have noticed the chopper. Some kind of new silent-running model, probably tricked out with laser rail-guns and optics capable of counting the pores in Gravenholtz's nose. So what was Gravenholtz and this fancy bird doing *here*?

"If you're nice I'll give you a ride," said Gravenholtz.

Moseby pretended not to understand, but realized he wasn't the only one with good eyes.

Gravenholtz tossed the knife, chunked it deep into the teak railing an inch from Moseby's hip. "Heckfire, I'll give you a ride even if you're *not* nice."

Moseby bent down, lifted the stone queen off the shelf, and gently set it down on the deck. "No thanks."

Gravenholtz spit on the deck, wiped his mouth with the back of his hand. "What makes you think it was a *request*?"

Moseby plucked a strand of seaweed off the stone queen's shoulder, kept his attention on her. He didn't need to look at Gravenholtz to sense him closing in.

"The Colonel wants to see you. *Now.* I'll round up your crew later."

"Tonight's my anniversary." Moseby picked tiny bits of sand and moss off the stone queen's marble surface. "The Colonel will have to wait."

Gravenholtz laughed. "You believe in God, Moseby?"

Moseby kept working. "Yes, I do."

Gravenholtz pointed the machine pistol at Moseby's head. "Better to believe in the Colonel, because God can't help you now."

Moseby gently removed a bit of grit from the stone queen's right eye. "You didn't come all the way here to shoot me." He pulled tiny snails from the stone queen's hair, the perfect spiral of their shells one of the infinite proofs of God. He flicked the snails over the side as he worked on the stone queen, his hands steady, unhurried. "You're here because the Colonel needs me for a project of some kind. Something special. Something he thinks only I can do. I wouldn't want to be you if anything happened to me." He looked up at Gravenholtz. "Pick me up tomorrow morning after breakfast. If I like the Colonel's business terms, I'll send for my crew. If not—"

Gravenholtz ripped off a dozen rounds into the stone queen, her head shattering into a thousand pieces. "I know where you live. I'll set my bird down in your backyard." He beckoned and the chopper streaked toward them.

Moseby stared at the shattered stone queen. Stood up. He pulled a shard of marble from under his eye, felt blood trickle toward his lip.

Gravenholtz laughed again.

Moseby promised himself that someday—sooner rather than later—he was going to drown Gravenholtz in the man's own blood and send him to hell still dripping. Christ had commanded his followers to turn the other cheek, to love those that cursed them, but Moseby knew his own limitations.

CHAPTER 2

The Old One cursed his bad luck. First the new German finance minister dies of a stroke—two years' work putting him in place wasted—and now *this*. Was running into Gladwell tonight truly just a coincidence? Or had Allah abandoned him after all this time? Found him an unworthy vessel for the fulfillment of prophecy?

The Old One paced the ornate salon of his suite, feeling a faint vibration underfoot, the mighty engines of the luxury liner *Star of the Sea* churning west across the Pacific, rolling across the bones of monsters. Sandalwood and myrrh burned in the incense brazier, the soothing scents of his boyhood, and all the journeys since. To have come so far, and now . . . The last time he had been this close to success, Redbeard's meddling niece, Sarah, and her renegade Fedayeen, Rakkim, had ruined everything. Decades of work unraveled by that overeducated whore.

At least Sarah and Rakkim's actions against him had been deliberate, but bumping into Gladwell tonight was even more unsettling. He *expected* worthy adversaries, but fortune had always treated him kindly. The Old One wallowed in doubt for a moment longer, then cast it aside as a stone from his shoe. Gladwell's presence on board was not a sign that Allah had turned against him, but was rather a *lesson* given to him by the Almighty. Remain vigilant, for fate can upset even the best plan. That was the teaching. The Old One was far from childhood, but not too old to humble himself before the wisdom of Allah. Bad luck, yes, but not a bad omen.

The Old One kept pacing. His suite was sparsely decorated, mandarin modern, blond wood and titanium, sleek and cool, the essence of Chinese chic. He hated it, but it fit his image as an urbane retiree, a cosmopolitan, high-tech entrepreneur. Swiss three-piece suits, handmade Thai loafers with braided gold-wire tassels. No prayer rug. No mihrab to indicate the direction of Mecca. To all intents and purposes he was a complete modern, an atheist too rich and too smart to honor Allah. When strolling through one of the public areas of the liner, and hearing the discreet call to prayer over the sound system, the Old One had perfected the wan smile of the enlightened as the faithful hurried to their devotions; his smile the same bemused expression he had seen on the faces of the British overlords as a boy when the villagers heeded the call to mosque. The British had rejected Allah then, and now it was too late for them. Alone in his cabin, the Old One prayed, with no witness save Allah. He didn't need a mihrab to point the way to Mecca. He didn't need a clock to tell him the time. Allah understood the necessity for stealth.

He sat on one of the sofas in the stateroom, picked up the wireless tablet he had been studying before his ill-chosen foray onto the upper deck of the liner. Better he had kept reading Sarah's ninth-grade history paper than gone for a stroll in the salt air.

The most contentious question in American history is how the former United States of America became a moderate Islamic nation twenty years after the conquest of Baghdad. Even given the profound spiritual revival that swept across the United States after the Iraq debacle, the suddenness of the transformation was still startling. The televised image of President-elect Damon Kingsley being sworn into office with one hand on the holy Quran while the grand mufti of Seattle administered the oath was a moral triumph that even the most devout could not have predicted.

The history paper had only recently been discovered, lost among the archives of the private madrassa where Sarah had been educated. If he had found it sooner, the Old One might have given the young woman more respect, but he tended to dismiss the female intellect and it had cost him dearly in this case. Sarah had been raised by her uncle, Redbeard himself, head of state security, as fierce and wily an opponent as the Old One had ever faced. She and the orphan Rakkim had been schooled by Redbeard, Sarah in statecraft, Rakkim in the harsh arts. The Old One had concerned himself with Rakkim, but it was Sarah he should have watched.

The Old One studied his reflection in the tablet's screen—a handsome, hawkish older gentleman who appeared to be in his seventies. A false vision. The Old One was far beyond a hundred, very far, possessed of a God-given vitality enhanced by organ transplants and the best science money could buy. He smoothed his gray hair. He had altered his appearance since fleeing Las Vegas. Had shaved his beard, dyed and restyled his white hair, added spectacles he didn't need. His cheeks had been widened, his lips plumped, his ears tucked back. One of his doubles had been trapped outside a safe house in Thailand last summer, committing suicide rather than be captured. Even dead, the man looked more like his former self than the Old One now did.

Though the 9/11 jihadi attacks had little direct, long-term impact on the United States, the martyrdom operation induced the former regime to overextend itself in fruitless military engagements around the world. After their failed attempt to create democracy in the Islamic homeworld, the Crusaders fled, grown weary of war, eager to return to their idle pursuits. This great retreat left the West drained of capital, manpower, and, most important, bereft of will.

The Old One stared at Sarah's words. Most historians considered the transformation of the former United States into two nations, a Muslim republic and a Christian Bible Belt, as preordained by Allah, a separation of the faithful and the faithless prior to Judgment Day. What nonsense. Barely fourteen, Sarah had seen more clearly than any of these so-called experts. Had he known how well she had learned the lessons Redbeard taught, the Old One would have killed her before she bled.

When the U.S. troops trickled home, the former regime was confronted by a prolonged economic downturn that only exacerbated the gap between rich and poor. As the recession deepened and politicians chattered, thousands died in job riots and whole cities were torched. The final straw was the suitcase nuke attacks on New York City, Washington, D.C., and Mecca in 2015, by the Israeli Mossad, which collapsed the former society.

When martial law was lifted two years later, the economy was still unstable, the government distrusted, and the people spiritually starved. Western churches, rather than offering moral guidance, were weak and vacillating, unwilling to condemn even the most immoral behavior. Islam offered a bright light and a clear answer, and the faithful could not build mosques fast enough to satisfy the need. While no force of arms could defeat the armies of the West, it was their moral and spiritual void that ultimately vanquished them.

Sarah couldn't have known—few even suspected—the hand of the Old One at play in the decline of the West. It had been his money, filtered through numerous fronts, that had had financed the academic think tanks and jihadi legal defense teams . . . all the useful idiots. It had been his money that had funded politicians and religious figures, compliant judges and radical journalists, billions of dollars in honoraria, with presidential libraries and foundations in particular targeted. That was the carrot. The Old One stroked his chin where his beard had once been. There was also the stick. Hard-line military leaders discredited. Evangelists mocked. Curious investigators framed or fired. Or worse.

The *Star of the Sea* shuddered slightly. This part of the Pacific was prone to rogue waves kicked up by the super-typhoons that had become so prevalent. Waves and ripples, ripples and waves. He half closed his eyes, fondly remembering the images from long ago—New Orleans flooded, the blacks huddled on their rooftops, waiting for help that never came, while breathless TV reporters spread false stories of murder and cannibalism, of babies raped and women butchered. That was a historic pivot point: the moment when America realized there was no great white father in Washington eager to soothe their woes. All it had taken was a few carefully chosen inept bureaucrats and a dozen small explosive charges placed under the levees of the Ninth Ward. When the great warming permanently submerged the city a few years later, it was almost irrelevant.

He had come so close. Three years ago, his plan to seize control of the Islamic Republic had finally seemed within his grasp. The first step of the greater plan. President Kingsley and his moderate coalition were old and tired, the nation adrift, waiting for a strong man who would lead them forward. In truth, the Old One was the man come to lead the world, the Mahdi, the twelfth imam, the Islamic messiah come to guide the world away from materialism and idolatry. The man chosen by Allah to appear at the End-Time, chosen to create a one-world caliphate under sharia law, and usher in an age of peace and piety. After the nonbelievers were put to the sword.

Then, Sarah and Rakkim had ruined everything. All the Old One's work had been undone when that bitch's research uncovered the truth: The Israeli Mossad wasn't responsible for the suitcase nuke attacks twenty-five years earlier. It was the Old One.

The blood libel exposed, the Old One had fled his citadel in Las Vegas, his bank accounts and assets confiscated. The accounts they could find, anyway. The most-wanted man on the planet, that's what the news reports had called him. The Islamic nations cried loudest for his head, those apostates in Arabia and Iran with their false Islam. Even his oldest son, Ibrahim, had questioned their survival, but then, like most men, Ibrahim had a tiny white worm in his soul, devouring his resolve. With a son like Rakkim, the Old One would have already stood astride the world, but the Old One's bloodline had thinned. He had to make do with the sons he had.

The Old One and his inner circle had taken refuge on the *Star of the Sea*, ensconced on a floor of suites he had purchased when the ship launched five years ago. The liner was a perfect redoubt, always in transit, a nation unto itself, its encrypted communiqués allowing him to maintain at least tenuous contact with his operatives around the world. The vessel itself was under his command—the captain and security team offered him their complete allegiance.

He angrily tapped the tablet with a manicured finger and the screen went black.

Eleven thousand passengers on the *Star of the Sea*, twenty decks of luxury and excess, the largest passenger vessel on the ocean, with dozens of movie theaters, casinos, shopping malls, churches, and mosques. Eleven thousand passengers and the Old One had to encounter Ambrose Gladwell their third night out of Buenos Aires. Forty-five minutes ago, Gladwell had nearly bumped into the Old One, his eyes widening slightly as he made his apology. The Old One had touched his hat, continued on his promenade as though nothing had happened, but he knew that Gladwell's curiosity had been piqued. It wouldn't take long before he realized whom he had met. Leave it to that sharp-eyed bond trader to see what others had missed.

Of course, there was no direct connection between the man who had hired Gladwell fresh out of the London School of Economics and the most-wanted man in the world. The Old One had been already past middle age then, already wealthy beyond any expectation, already secretive too, never quoted, never photographed. Gladwell had been nervous during the initial interview, crossing and uncrossing his long legs as he sat before the Old One's desk. The Old One had been called Derek Farouk then, one of the many names he had used over the long years. One of the many faces he had shown the world. The son of a British mother and an Egyptian father, that was the story. Gladwell couldn't keep his hands off his necktie, adjusting and readjusting his Windsor knot as the Old One peered down his nose at him.

William, one of his young aides, slipped into the salon through a side door. He stopped a few paces from the Old One, lowered his eyes. "Mr. Gladwell is in the anteroom, Mahdi."

"No one saw him enter?"

William shook his head. "The chief steward himself escorted Mr. Gladwell here. Most of the passengers still awake are at the festivities on C deck." He inclined his head. "The communications officer said no calls or communiqués were made from any of Mr. Gladwell's personal devices in the last hour."

The Old One dismissed him with a wave of his hand.

Gladwell bustled into the salon as soon as the door to the anteroom was opened, his joints still limber in spite of his years. Eighty-two last July 17. He wore a herringbone smoking jacket and flannel trousers, deerskin moccasins and no socks. Recommended sailing attire, according to the brochure for the *Star of the Sea*.

"Mr. Gladwell, so glad you could join me," the Old One greeted him, ignoring the infidel's outstretched hand. "I'm Albert Mesta. I think you knew my maternal grandfather."

"I *thought* you might be one of Mr. Farouk's relatives," Gladwell said. "Not immediately, of course, but there was something . . . familiar about you. I didn't realize it until I got back to my cabin." His smile showed yellowed teeth. "At my age, remembering where I left my spectacles is a major endeavor, let alone events that occurred over fifty years ago." He wiped his hands on his trousers. "I used to work for your grandfather." His blue eyes shimmered with moisture, but it wasn't nostalgia that made him tear up.

"He was a slave driver, but a genius with figures. I owe whatever success I've had to the lessons he taught me."

"The odd look you gave me in the passageway aroused my interest." The Old One indicated a purple, tufted silk divan. "It was only when I inquired about you to the chief steward that I realized it was my grandfather you were acquainted with."

Gladwell sat on the far side of the divan. Crossed his legs, revealing the tracery of blue veins in his ankles.

The Old One concealed his disgust. He sat on the other side of the divan, wanting to give the man a good look at him. "I've asked William to bring us drinks. I have some forty-year-old single-malt you might appreciate."

"Oh yes, absolutely." Gladwell plucked at the crease in his trousers. "Mr. Farouk's grandson. You're a lucky man, sir. Very lucky."

"Sometimes," purred the Old One.

Gladwell leaned toward him. "Your grandfather . . . when did he die?"

"Many years ago, I'm afraid."

"I . . . I didn't hear anything about it."

"My grandfather believed in keeping a low profile," said the Old One. "I don't have to tell you that."

"No . . . no, you don't." Gladwell shook his head. "Still, I would have liked to have known." He stared at the Old One. "You . . . you have his eyes."

"So I've been told." The Old One stopped as William entered. The boy set their drinks down on the coffee table—two crystal tumblers of scotch, each containing a single ice cube—then backed out of the room. The Old One and Gladwell clinked glasses.

Gladwell took a swallow, Adam's apple bobbing. "Excellent."

The Old One sipped his drink.

Gladwell glanced around the salon. "You've done well for yourself, sir, if you don't mind my saying so. Your grandfather would be proud." Another swallow. "Very proud."

The Old One swirled his drink, enjoyed the sound of the ice cube hitting the glass. "I think Grandfather would be proud of you as well, Mr. Gladwell."

Gladwell pinked up. "Fast on my feet, always have been. See an opportunity, seize it. When the troubles came with the Americans, well, some gnashed their teeth or dashed off to Australia, and some of us rolled up our sleeves and made a handsome profit."

The Old One raised his glass. "Good for you, Ambrose."

Gladwell bristled slightly at the use of his first name by a man he assumed was younger than he. Always a stickler for protocol. Another swallow of scotch and all was forgiven. "Yes, well, a businessman has to be above politics, above religion. Can't let anything get in the way of the bottom line, that's what I always say. I deal with Muslims as easily as I deal with Christians or Hindus. I dealt with communists, when there still were communists. I even used to do business with Jews, but that was a long time ago." He blinked at the Old One. "Now they say the Hebrews *didn't* set the suitcase nukes, supposed to be some other fellah." He shook his head. "Man doesn't know what to believe anymore." He pulled at his nose. "What about you, sir? Who do you think set off those bombs? You think it was the Jews?"

"No, it wasn't the Jews, Ambrose. It was some other fellah."

Gladwell snorted. "Truth be told, I don't really care."

The Old One clinked glasses with him again.

"I wish my wife was here," said Gladwell. "All the years she spent hearing me talk about your grandfather . . . she would have dearly loved to meet you."

"Dearly," said the Old One.

"We would have been married sixty years tomorrow." Gladwell peered into his glass. "Laura . . . she died three weeks ago. Just . . . keeled over at breakfast and that was that." He looked up at the Old One. Tiny beads of sweat lined his forehead. "My children thought I should cancel the cruise, but it was too late to get a refund. First-class tickets . . . I paid thirty-five thousand Thatchers. Wasn't about to let that money go to waste."

"Of course not."

"Laura would have never forgiven me." Gladwell breathed harder. "Woman used to reuse aluminum foil until it disintegrated. Waste not, want not, that's what she used to say." He tugged at his collar. "I think . . . I think I may be allergic to your incense."

"Sixty years of marriage," said the Old One, "you must have been a very patient man. Or one utterly lacking in imagination."

"Beg . . . beg your pardon?" Gladwell set down his glass. His hand trembled. "Imagination?"

"It's all right, Ambrose. What you lacked in imagination, you more than made up for in clarity. Given enough time, you always made the correct judgment. Pity."

"You . . . you'll have to excuse me. I'm not feeling very well." Gladwell tried to stand. Sat back heavily.

"No apologies necessary." The Old One draped his arm across the back of the divan. "Just relax and have your nice little heart attack."

The sweat beads strung across Gladwell's upper lip shimmered, his face bright red now. "I . . . I don't understand."

"No, but you would have eventually." The Old One finished his drink. Crunched through the ice cube. "I drove you hard, Ambrose, but look what you accomplished with your life. A spot in a first-class cabin. You should be proud."

Gladwell's eyes grew larger as he stared at the Old One. Larger still. He *knew.*

The Old One leaned back and watched Gladwell die, overwhelmed with the sweetness of the man's recognition. So many years since the two of them had shared a drink. The world had changed, been shaken like a snow globe, and here they were, fifty years later, brought together one last time. Laura dead three weeks. The Old One had bedded her for a bit in London after sending Gladwell to tour factories in Indonesia for potential acquisition. Low-end computer chips. He didn't remember Gladwell's recommendation on the factories, but he remembered Laura's creamy breasts and lightly freckled thighs. Most of all he remembered her greedy mouth overflowing with him.

Gladwell slumped against the side of the divan.

The Old One felt the throbbing engines of the *Star of the Sea* through the soles of his large feet, letting its power flow through him. He wiggled his toes. Pleasant to have dealt so smoothly with Gladwell, but there was still al-Faisal's mission in Seattle to consider. Al-Faisal was capable enough, more than capable, but the mission was crucial to the Old One's plan. Even with all the time Allah had granted him, there might not be enough years left if al-Faisal failed.

The Old One steepled his fingers. If Darwin were still alive he would have tasked *him* with the job. A former Fedayeen assassin, Darwin had been the Old One's personal killer, a slim, serene fellow with lightning hands and an ugly sense of humor. Darwin would have handled the Seattle operation easily . . . but Darwin was dead. The Old One shifted on the purple divan, uneasy. He didn't know who had killed Darwin, or how it could have been done, but the assassin was smoldering in the deepest pit of hell, that much was certain.

Gladwell's jaw hung open. Gums bare. His skin so slack that it was as if his skull were collapsing in on itself. The decay of time, the toll paid by mortal flesh . . . The vibration underfoot stopped for an instant, as though the engines briefly hesitated, and the Old One felt goose bumps along the back of his neck. He got up quickly, disgusted. He summoned William, waited until his aide had removed the corpse.

The door to the salon clicked shut, and the Old One thought again of Darwin. Just an average-looking fellow in his late forties, lightly muscled, almost delicate, and the palest, cold blue eyes. *Bland as buttermilk, that's me*, Darwin used to say. Protective coloration, because no predator ever took such delight in killing. The Old One had killed many men in his time, but there was always a rationale to it, a purpose. To Darwin, the killing itself served some deeper function, filling a void known only to himself as he stockpiled the dead. He could still see the man's insolent smirk—Darwin might work for the Old One, but he made it clear he served neither God nor man, only death itself. No one had treated the Old One with anything less than respect in almost a hundred years. Except Darwin. And Rakkim. The Old One had offered Rakkim a position at his right hand, offered him the *world* . . . and Rakkim had turned him down. No wonder Darwin hated him.

He walked to the windows of the stateroom, restless now. Find the one who had killed Darwin and find yet another player in the great game, one the Old One had not factored into his calculations. The Old One had even considered the possibility that Rakkim had killed Darwin, but the idea was laughable. There was a Fedayeen saying: Only Allah or another assassin can kill an assassin, and Rakkim was neither.

Still . . . the Old One had made inquiries. Rakkim, as befitted his shadow warrior training, had disappeared, as had Sarah. In spite of all his spies, all the Old One had were rumors. They had married. Rakkim wandered the Zone, reeking of alcohol. Sarah had been spotted at a university in China. In Lagos. They had gone on the hajj, stayed too long and died of radiation sickness in Yemen. She had gone mad after the death of Redbeard. He had become a modern, with pierced ears and perfumed hair. Sarah had renounced Islam and now lived among the Jews. Rakkim had rejoined the Fedayeen, had the ear of General Kidd. One thing he was sure of, the Old One would not underestimate *either* of them again.

The Old One whistled and the window shields slid open, revealing the stars spilled across the night. He drank in the sight, drunk on the infinite vastness, the limitless gulf of Allah's domain. At this very moment, Tariq al-Faisal was in Seattle, doing the Old One's bidding. Soon, very soon, Allah willing, the Old One would begin to remake the world.

CHAPTER 3

Tariq al-Faisal didn't walk like the Christian he pretended to be. It was the walk that had drawn Rakkim's attention from a block away, long before he recognized the man. Al-Faisal in *Seattle*? Rakkim's palms itched. Money, that's what the fortune-teller outside New Orleans would have said. She'd peer up from her table on the beached *Delta Queen* riverboat, rub his open hand, and say, Beaucoup l'argent *coming your way, child.* Rakkim knew better. Seeing al-Faisal here was worth more than silver or gold. Rakkim sauntered after al-Faisal, moving with a little stutter step as though listening to music no one else could hear.

At least al-Faisal had the externals of his Catholic pose right: high-ride trousers, cuffs rolled, fingerless gloves, even the St. Paul's Academy ear stud, which was a nice touch, but his walk kept reverting to type. He led with his chest as he stormed past the marble statue of Malcolm X on the corner, shoulders set, the gait of a Muslim fundamentalist certain of his place in the universe. A Black Robe, no less, one of the infamous enforcers of public morality. Christians, no matter their station in life, moved from their hips, gliding, heads swiveling, alert for disapproval or harassment. *Kafir-walk*, Rakkim's shadow warrior instructors had called it.

Rakkim eased down the sidewalk, taking his time. You had all the time in the world when you knew what you were doing. Like al-Faisal, he pretended to be a Christian, but the pope himself would have given Rakkim communion without a second thought. Invisible as a stolen kiss, that was the shadow warrior ideal. The Fedayeen were elite warriors, totally loyal to the president, the shock troops of the Islamic Republic—most were combat units, but there were two specialized branches, the best of the best. Shadow warriors and assassins.

Rakkim remembered practicing the kafir-glide for hours, days, weeks, remembered being jerked from sleep by his instructor, beaten if his first step was wrong. Homegrown Christians were easy enough to mimic, but Bible Belt patterns had been much more challenging, and failure had cost more than one shadow warrior his life. Rakkim had ranked first in his unit, able to pivot seamlessly between a Gulf Coast shuffle and an Appalachian hitch-along. He had lived for months in the Belt without rousing suspicion, sung hymns in a tiny church, tears rolling down his cheeks, worked on shrimp boats and done double shifts at a silicone-wafer factory outside Atlanta, guzzling beer and pigs' feet afterward. He had retired from the Fedayeen after his initial seven-year enlistment, but the Fedayeen had never left Rakkim.

Almost thirty-three now, Rakkim was dark-eyed, lean and agile, a tiny gold crucifix bouncing at the base of his throat with every step. He flirted with the Catholic girls who passed, and they responded in kind, putting an extra wiggle in their walk for his benefit. Be a Catholic on a Saturday night, and you'll never want to be Muslim again . . . that's what they said.

Al-Faisal eyeballed a new green Lamborghini curbed in a valet parking area. Ran a finger over the perfect finish as he walked past. Pathetic. A Christian wouldn't *dare* touch a vehicle with a Quranic inscription etched into the windshield. A high-ranking Black Robe like al-Faisal feared nothing. His three bodyguards were better trained—ex-Fedayeen from the look of them, and the way they slipped easily through the crowd. They maintained a shifting perimeter around al-Faisal, a rough triangulation, two ahead, on either side of the street, another trailing far behind, hoping to pick up a tail. No eye contact between them, just three moderate Muslims, seemingly part of the crowd, but the same barber had cut their hair, his distinctive scissors work easy for Rakkim to read. Details, boys, details.

It must be an important mission for al-Faisal to leave the safety of New Fallujah. A mission too important to trust to an underling. Too important to trust sat phones or Net encryption. No, just like the old days, the most important conversations could take place only where no one could listen in. *So what are you here to talk about, al-Faisal? And whose ear will you be whispering in?*

People filled downtown Seattle, streamed out of the office complexes—commuters heading toward the monorail, students jostling toward the sin spots of the Zone, the faithful hurrying to prayers. A crowd of contrasts: moderns and moderates in casual and business attire, the fundamentalists robed in gray, prayer beads clicking away, while the Catholics clustered together, loud and boisterous, delighting in the flesh. While 70 percent of the country was Muslim, most of them were moderate, tolerating the Christian minority. Christians ate in the same restaurants as moderates, but the Christian silverware was disposable to prevent contamination. Modern Muslims rarely went to mosque, worked in high-tech jobs, flaunted the latest styles, and might even have a Christian friend or two. Fundamentalist Muslims were the most dangerous to the nation's stability; rabidly intolerant, they voted as a block and encouraged the worst excesses of the Black Robes.

A modern in a short dress swept past Rakkim in a wave of bright color, her soft hair floating around her shoulders, and a fat fundamentalist businessman glaring at her nearly collided with Rakkim, cursed him as a shit-eating Catholic. The businessman's coarse gray robes billowed as he barreled off for sundown prayers. Rakkim didn't even break stride, the man's wallet cupped in his palm. He dropped the businessman's money into a war-widows alms box a block later, arced the wallet into the gutter, and kept walking.

You'd think Allah hated beauty the way the Black Robes acted.

Rakkim stayed far behind al-Faisal, loose-limbed and easy like a good Catholic funboy, quietly nursing his anger. While Seattle and Southern California were bastions of moderation, even in the capital, the Black Robes enforced their dictates on the fundamentalist population. A devout Muslim woman unescorted by a brother or husband could be whipped on the streets of Seattle, and adulterers and fornicators were stoned to death in the countryside. Fundamentalist redoubts like New Fallujah and Milwaukee and Chicago were worse—governed by the most extreme sharia law.

Rakkim had last seen al-Faisal two years ago at a mass hanging in New Fallujah. Harlots and homosexuals, witches and Jews dangled from the high beams of the bridge, swinging gently over San Francisco Bay as al-Faisal harangued the crowd, called forth the blessings of God. The Golden Gate, that's what it was called in the old days. Its new name, the Bridge of Skulls, suited it better. He flexed his right forearm again as he watched al-Faisal walk down First Avenue. Felt the Fedayeen knife tucked flat against the inside of his forearm, ready to snap forth. For those with memories, there were always scores to be settled. Odd thoughts for Rakkim. Shadow warriors preferred anonymity, killing only as a last resort, but Rakkim wasn't a shadow warrior anymore. He was something else now, and whether it was more or less than before, he hadn't decided.

The air tasted of smog and salt water, hung heavy with the aroma of coffee from the nearby Starbucks, of clam chowder and jerked goat kebabs from the street vendors. Shoppers coughed as they strolled along, and Rakkim felt the grit at the back of his throat too—smoke and ash from the superfires raging across Australia and China, incinerating everything in their path. News kiosks yesterday showed footage of burning kangaroos hopping wildly across a smoldering landscape, the whole sky black behind them. The antiterror blimps ringing the city caught the last of the setting sun, looked to be ablaze, and it seemed to Rakkim that the whole world was on fire.

Two brightly garbed moderns chattered past, and Rakkim inhaled the women's fragrance, grateful for the heady scent of the latest Italian perfume—La Dolce Vita, the sweet life, at eight hundred dollars an ounce. Moderns were so optimistic. Eager consumers enamored of their shiny, pretty things, the constantly upgraded gadgets. The modern's wealth comforted them, made them fearless as dreamers, eyes fluttering as dawn approached.

Al-Faisal threw his arm around a stranger, pretending bonhomie with a fellow Catholic, certain of his camouflage. Al-Faisal another optimist, assured that Allah had already written his triumph in the Book of Days.

Ironic that the two opposites, moderns and fundamentalists, were the only ones in the Islamic Republic certain that the future would be better, that their vision was destined to sweep away all others. The rest of the country, the silent majority of moderate Muslims and Christians . . . they noticed the crumbling freeways and failing energy grid, an infant mortality rate worse than Nigeria's, and the regular outbreaks of cholera in Chicago and Denver. Let the fundamentalists and moderns trust in their hollow gods. Rakkim believed in the warmth of Sarah beside him, and the first halting steps of their son. He believed in unexpected friendships and laughter in the face of the inevitable. Optimism? A man had to close his eyes to remain an optimist, and there was no honor in that.

Optimism was for fools and children, that's what Redbeard used to say. Pray for victory, *plan* for disaster. Redbeard had been Rakkim's mentor.

His tormentor. His taskmaster. His uncle in all ways but blood. Redbeard, the nation's spymaster, lover of bone-crunching football and contraband Coca-Cola . . . ferocious patriot, committed moderate. Redbeard had died as peaceful a death as God granted, sitting in the back of a limo with his niece Sarah by his side. Not a day passed that Rakkim didn't wish Redbeard were still alive. President Kingsley needed him now more than ever. Needed his strength and determination, his cool counsel when the world seemed ablaze. The nation needed Redbeard. So did Rakkim.

News reports boomed from a kiosk, a holographic display showing troop movements along the border of the Mexican empire. Rakkim slowed. A commercial for cling free chadors crawled along the bottom of the display while tanks rolled across the desert, a red crescent emblazoned on their turrets. Rakkim pretended interest, watching the bodyguards reflected in the display. The three of them did a slow pivot, scanning the crowd as al-Faisal hurried on. The Black Robe still walked wrong.

Two college girls approached, moderates, their sheer pink veils only enhancing their beauty rather than masking it. Their eyes lingered on Rakkim—Catholics were forbidden fruit, their lust and volatility whispered about with fascination. Rakkim smiled back, kept walking, embarrassed at the pleasure their interest gave him. He thought of Sarah waiting for him at home, and for the millionth time was grateful for not being Catholic. Those fools so eager to confess. Who could keep up with his own sins?

Al-Faisal cut across the street, oblivious to the horns beeping around him. His bodyguards took their time, peeling off slowly.

Rakkim crossed at the signal, then stopped to buy an ice cream cone. Strawberry mango. He ambled after al-Faisal into the warren of small shops on the outskirts of the Zone, licking ice cream off his fingers.

The Zone was a moral free-fire district, a sector where vice was tolerated and the police minded their own business. Creative, sordid, corrupt, the Zone was filled with dance clubs and foreign-movie theaters, black-market electronics and love hotels. A center of dangerous fun. A safety valve. Americans were still Americans in spite of the new flag, the new regime. No streetlights in the Zone; the only illumination came from the neon signs and the dim interiors. Rakkim had lived in the Zone before he married Sarah. Had owned a nightclub, the Blue Moon. He knew the Zone, but the Zone no longer knew him.

Music throbbed from every doorway, part of the unique signature of the Zone. While most of the city was off-limits to anything other than religious chants and sermons, the Zone took pride in showing off its freedom from any restraints. Russian pop, Brazilian thump, Chinese techno, and Motown overlapped and merged in the Zone, became a dissonant heartbeat. Everyone walking down the street picked up the beat, feet moving faster, hearts racing, heads bobbing. *Rat-a-tat-tat.* Al-Faisal resisted, but even he was forced to give in, swinging his hands as his stride lengthened. He was going to have to ask forgiveness for such spontaneity, pray himself hoarse to atone for his inadvertent pleasure. Perhaps he would even sacrifice a white goat, slit its throat himself, then distribute the meat to the poor. There were always plenty of hungry mouths.

Al-Faisal stumbled on a patch of blackened sidewalk, the concrete cracked and uneven. A suicide bomber had blown himself up on this spot on Easter Sunday a year ago. The bomber had been trying to get into the Kitchy Koo Klub but the place was packed; he had to settle for taking out forty-three people waiting outside. A costly ticket to Paradise. It had been a bad spring in the capital, with suicide bombers targeting the Zone, the death toll in the hundreds. Officially, Bible Belt zealots had been blamed, but the grand mullah of the Black Robes in New Fallujah had been responsible. The president himself visited the Zone after the worst attack, cameras rolling, declaring the nation would not be intimidated. He also quietly ordered a Fedayeen commando team to infiltrate New Fallujah and blow up the grand mullah's personal mosque. The suicide attacks in the capital stopped immediately.

Al-Faisal turned abruptly and Rakkim thought for a moment that he had been spotted, but the cleric turned back, ducked quickly into a tiny storefront, Eagleton Digital Entertainment. That was a surprise. A long-term resident of the Zone, Eagleton was a staunch modern, a Web hacker and freethinker. The tech wizard had spent many afternoons drinking khat tea at the Blue Moon, getting a pleasant buzz on. So what business did ibn-Azziz's emissary have with him?

Rakkim turned into the next alley, lost himself in the darkness. A glance back to the street, and he free-climbed the vertical brick wall, using just his fingertips and the toes of his boots, swiftly working his way up to the roof of the building next door. From this position he could see if al-Faisal left by the front or back door of the store. Either way, he would follow. Later he would have a chat with Eagleton.

Rakkim waited. Watched as the bodyguards took positions nearby, pretending to window-shop. The trailing bodyguard stood in the doorway of the Crocodile Club listening to music, ignoring the three-hundred-pound bouncer who told him either to come in or move on. The bouncer took a closer look at the man and retreated inside the club.

Rakkim perched in the shadows, noted how the bodyguards carried themselves. He caught his breath, feeling the vibration of the transceiver implanted in his right earlobe. Two long, three short jolts. An emergency signal from Sarah. Three shorts was a call to meet her at the Presidential Palace. Two short meant at home. One short at their safe house south of Khomeini stadium. He waited for the repeal call that would validate the signal. There it was. He hesitated, hating to back off from al-Faisal. No, he should go. He clambered down the wall, slid down the last ten feet. Pulled out his cell. Maybe Colarusso could tail al-Faisal. It wasn't a police matter, but Rakkim trusted Colarusso more than State Security. He took a look behind him as the phone beeped, saw al-Faisal hurry from the shop, going against the traffic flow now. The cleric patted his right pocket, reassuring himself. He had gotten more than information from Eagleton.

"What's up, Rikki?" said Colarusso, the detective's voice gruff.

"Later." Rakkim slipped the phone away. Checked his watch. If Sarah was at the Presidential Palace, she couldn't be in any immediate danger. Not likely, anyway. He walked after al-Faisal, slowed as he passed the storefront. The windows were one-way glass. LED CLOSED sign. He had intended to talk to Eagleton after following al-Faisal, but now . . . something had changed hands in the store, something important enough to draw al-Faisal out of New Fallujah. He reached for the door, saw blood on the knob.

Down the street, al-Faisal increased his pace. Whatever he had gotten from Eagleton made haste his primary concern. Two of his bodyguards fell in beside him, flanked him. The third led the way, breaking a path through the partygoers with his scowl and his shoulders.

Rakkim walked after them, keeping to the edges of the street, where he could make faster progress.

The taller of the bodyguards whirled around.

Rakkim shuffled along, hands waving, muttering to himself like another of the human gin blossoms that frequented the Zone, sloppy from bootleg alcohol. He sagged against a lamppost, pretending to breathe hard, sneaked a look toward al-Faisal.

The tall bodyguard stared right at him. Not taking his eyes away, he said something. The other flanking bodyguard stopped while the third bodyguard in front grabbed al-Faisal by the wrist and dragged him down a side street. The flankers followed slowly as Rakkim hurried to catch up, slipping through the crowd with barely any contact.

This side street must have been picked as their rally point beforehand. Narrow as an alley, its few shops closed for the night. A powerful German sedan waited at the end of the street, idling behind a yellow construction barrier that kept out other traffic. The black sedan was a common vehicle in the capital, easily lost among the evening traffic.

Al-Faisal was halfway to the car by the time Rakkim started down the narrow street. The two tailing bodyguards calmly took positions on either side. Their arms hung loose, knives glinting in the dim light. Like all Fedayeen they were trained to be ambidextrous. The one on Rakkim's right kept his blade in his left hand, the one on his left held his knife in his right. That way they covered maximum space. Rakkim raised his own knife in a mocking salute. They didn't react, which spoke well for them. He might have learned something from seeing how they handled their blades.

"What's your hurry?" Rakkim called to al-Faisal. He had no idea where his own sudden good humor came from. "Stay and watch the fun, al-Faisal. I'm all alone."

Al-Faisal stopped. Shook off his bodyguard. He seemed calm.

"That's better." Rakkim smiled broader. The two bodyguards slightly repositioned themselves, but he ignored them. "The last time I saw you it was Eid al-Fitr, two years ago. You were on the Bridge of Skulls." He strolled closer. "There was a boy . . . maybe eight years old. He had broken his Ramadan fast. Ate an orange. Not a whole orange. Just one section." He could see al-Faisal's eyes narrow. "You remember the boy?"

"I remember a blasphemer," said al-Faisal.

"You gave him three hundred lashes." Rakkim rocked slightly forward. "The boy died after the seventy-third stroke of the whip. Must have been quite a . . ." Rakkim raced toward al-Faisal, his knife flicking out toward the two bodyguards as he sped past them. ". . . *disappointment* to you."

Al-Faisal's third bodyguard shoved him into the sedan. Dove in after him as the driver screeched away.

Rakkim grabbed for the door handle. Missed. He watched al-Faisal's annoyed face pressed against the glass of the back window until the car turned a corner. Rakkim walked back to the two bodyguards.

One of the bodyguards lay curled on the pavement. The tall one stood unmoving, still planted in the direction Rakkim had come from.

Rakkim circled him. The bodyguard was in his late thirties, built strong, with dirty blond hair and a scar meandering along one cheek. Sweat rolled down his face. Rakkim marveled at the effort it must have taken not to move. To tense all of his muscles. All of his *being*. Rakkim had stabbed the two bodyguards in the upper abdomen as he passed. Stabbed them deep in exactly the same spot. The fourteenth ganglia, a cluster of critical nerves just above the solar plexus. Instantaneous death. Except in very rare instances, when the victim stayed perfectly still. So still that the nerve impulses still managed to make the leap across the cut tissue, the familiar pathways in service for a few moments longer.

The tall bodyguard blinked furiously, sweat glistening along his eyebrows. Fear bloomed in his eyes, but he kept that in check. His tongue moistened his lips. "*How?*"

Rakkim stayed silent. The bodyguards were combat Fedayeen, some of the best fighters in the world. Only one in a thousand qualified for Fedayeen—that was both a motto and the truth—but only one Fedayeen in a thousand qualified to be a shadow warrior or an assassin. Rakkim's attack had been fast, too fast for the bodyguards to defend against, but that wasn't the answer to the tall bodyguard's question. Rakkim had always been fast, even for a shadow warrior, but it was knowing precisely where to strike that he couldn't explain. Knowledge of the killing ganglia, the training required to deal the fatal blow . . . that was reserved exclusively for assassins. Rakkim hadn't even been aware of what he was doing until he was past the two bodyguards. He had acted instinctively.

A spot of blood appeared on the bodyguard's shirt. A tiny spot . . . but growing. The bodyguard twitched. Impossible to hold still enough. Even if he could, there was no fixing the man.

Rakkim thought of asking him where al-Faisal had gone but didn't. The man wouldn't tell, and Rakkim wouldn't insult him by asking. The bodyguard might not have done the terrible things that al-Faisal had done, but he had facilitated evil, protected evil. He had *chosen*. Fedayeen swore an oath to defend the president and the nation. When the grand mullah had declared the president an apostate three years ago, the great majority of Fedayeen held fast to their vows, but many had resigned, aligning themselves with the Black Robes. No, the bodyguard had made his decision. He alone was responsible.

The tall bodyguard's bright blue eyes were wide now. Hairs in his nostrils waved with every breath. He clamped his jaw tight.

Rakkim held the bodyguard's gaze. He raised his knife in salute and this time he meant it. "*Salaam alaikum*. Go with God, Fedayeen."

Eyelids fluttering, the tall bodyguard exhaled slowly, weary now, as though settling down for a rest after a long race. He sank to the pavement, already dead.

Rakkim hurried toward the Presidential Palace.

CHAPTER 4

The bioscanner beeped, refused Rakkim entry to the secret passage that led into the Presidential Palace. First time for that. Nothing worked right anymore. He stood within a small alcove outside the walled complex, a utility shed concealed by thick shrubbery and the darkness. Seagulls screamed overhead. Trucks rumbled in the distance.

Rakkim kept his heart rate at a steady sixty-five beats per minute as the bioscanner swept over him again. ENTRY REJECTED. Rakkim adjusted the Fedayeen knife nestled against his forearm—carbon-polymer, impregnated with his own DNA, the knife didn't register on any scan. He smoothed it flat anyway. A third failure would set off alarms and armed response. He tried again. ACCEPTED. He stepped inside, the vault-thick outer door sliding shut behind him. Another bioscan required to get past the interior door. He thought of the two bodyguards he had just killed, and the look in the eyes of the tall one as he acknowledged his own death. The bodyguard seemed less troubled by his dying than Rakkim was with his method of killing him. Assassin tradecraft? Where had *that* come from? He heard Darwin's mocking laughter echo in his skull as the security door opened into the president's private corridor, and hated himself for his memories.

Rakkim double-timed down the corridor, wondering why Sarah had called him to the palace. Had the Old One resurfaced? That evil bastard wasn't going to stop causing trouble until someone killed him. Rakkim would happily volunteer. Maybe ibn-Azziz, grand mullah of the Black Robes, was stirring from his stronghold in New Fallujah, Rakkim's sighting of al-Faisal part of some new offensive. Rakkim just hoped nothing had happened to General Kidd—the Fedayeen commander was the president's most loyal, and most important, supporter. Without the Fedayeen backing him, the president was just a well-intentioned figurehead. General Kidd had survived two assassination attempts in the last year. If anything had happened to him . . .

Rakkim opened the door into the president's wood-paneled library. President Kingsley slouched behind his cluttered desk, exhausted, his fine white hair sticking up on one side. Sarah and Spider stood studying a holographic map of North America that covered one wall—the Islamic Republic shaded light green, the Bible Belt in red. Lights pulsed in the current trouble spots in the Mormon Territories, highlighted the incursions into California and Arizona by the Aztlán Empire, the Mexicans attempting to reestablish ancient boundaries. Spider held on to a chair for support—a short, stocky Jewish genius, hair everywhere, twitching from the disease that was slowly killing him. Sarah smiled at Rakkim, then went back to the map.

The president scowled. "Glad you could make it, Rakkim."

Rakkim didn't let his surprise show. Kingsley took pains to maintain a semblance of good humor, even when the cameras weren't rolling. What had *happened*?

"You *are* late, Rikki," soothed Sarah.

"Al-Faisal is in town," said Rakkim. "I tracked him to a tech store in the Zone."

"Al-Faisal *here*?" Spider looked at Sarah. "Have you heard—"

"I don't give a shit about al-Faisal." The president tossed a chunk of jagged, twisted steel from hand to hand, a treasured piece of wreckage from Newark, the climactic battle of the Civil War. "The Black Robes are the least of my concerns."

"What's wrong?" said Rakkim.

"*Wrong?*" said the president, his watery eyes sunk into a nest of wrinkles. "What could be wrong? Allah watches over us, guides our every action, does he not?" He set the paperweight down, then came from behind his desk, a handsome man, formerly robust but slightly stooped now, even with the back brace that no one was supposed to know about. "I want you to go back to the Bible Belt. Save the nation, noble Fedayeen. Be the hero again." He started for the door. "Sarah will fill you in on the details."

The door clicked shut. Deniability, that's what this sudden exit must be about. The president had sent Rakkim on other covert assignments. New Fallujah. The Mormon Territories. Rakkim had air-dropped into Pakistan, to follow up on a sighting of the Old One; slipped into the Aztlán Empire to find out what the Mexicans were up to. The president had always briefed Rakkim himself. Not this time. Tonight Sarah got the job while the president kept his manicure clean in case anything went wrong. President-for-life Kingsley was a great man, a moderate who had almost single-handedly kept the Islamic Republic united, and kept the fundamentalists at bay. But he was still a politician.

"What's al-Faisal doing here?" said Spider.

"Not *now.*" Sarah walked to the wall map, took the remote from Spider's trembling hand.

She was still the same woman Rakkim had fallen in love with, but her responsibilities as secret advisor to the president had taken their toll. So had the covert existence they lived, her rarely going out in public, and the necessity of constant security measures. A brilliant historian specializing in the transition between the former and the current regime, she had been forced to eliminate all contact with friends and colleagues. The strain showed. Sarah was still slender, her eyes just as lively, but her playful instincts were muted now, reserved for moments when they were alone. She had cut her dark hair shorter a year ago, said it was easier. He missed it curling past her shoulders, brushing against him while they made love.

"Rikki?" Sarah nodded at the map. The central region of the Belt—Tennessee and the Carolinas—filled the wall. "You know who Colonel Zachary Smitts is, don't you?"

"Yeah . . . I know the Colonel." Memory carried the smell of bacon and coffee flavored with chicory. Twelve years ago Rakkim had been eating breakfast in a Cracker Barrel restaurant in Gatlinburg, Tennessee. His second insertion as a shadow warrior. The Colonel's picture hung over the counter, not the usual airbrushed glory of the fake warrior, but the Colonel in a filthy rebel uniform, unshaven, an unfiltered cigarette dangling from his lip. Portrait of a young man, hard and handsome under the dirt, a backwoods Elvis with an assault rifle slung over his shoulder instead of a guitar. The Colonel had looked back at him from the picture, tired but unbeaten . . . *look what you made me do.* A trucker had sat at the counter beside Rakkim, tugged at his hat toward the photo. Rakkim had done something similar a few moments later, raising his coffee cup to the photo before he drank—oblique mirroring, a way to bond with a subject without him being aware of it. "His people love him, I know that much. He's a small-time Tennessee warlord sitting on some prime real estate. Civil War hero. Brutal but smart. He stopped our advance along the eastern front. Saved Tennessee and the Carolinas. Did it outmanned and outgunned too."

"He's not small-time now, and he's not outmanned or outgunned anymore either." Sarah scrolled through the map, zoomed in on Atlanta. Closer. The satellite imagery jerked, went to static. She toggled the remote. The image sharpened for a moment, then broke up. She threw down the remote, glared at Spider. "I thought you fixed the digital filter."

"I tried," said Spider. "The chaff's slipping into lower orbits. Reception is getting worse across the board."

"I'm . . . sorry," said Sarah.

"I'll keep working on it," said Spider, "but for now, forget the real-time map."

Last year, a weather satellite had exploded after hitting a chunk of space debris, probably an uncharted leftover from the Chinese fiasco of 2007. The effects of this recent strike were catastrophic—pieces from the weather satellite had struck another satellite, which had disintegrated, causing still more debris, and so on and so on. Within a week, nineteen satellites had been destroyed. Hundreds of remaining satellites had been moved into other orbits, but there was now a layer of fragments circling the earth, a spreading ring of metallic chaff disrupting the global grid. Television and telecommunications still functioned, if intermittently, but spy satellites had been rendered nearly useless.

"The president should be here, not dump this in your lap," Rakkim said to Sarah.

"He had to leave for an emergency session in Geneva," Spider said. "The big boys are getting restless now that they're blind."

"Oh." Rakkim covered his embarrassment. "Fine."

What no one had considered until too late was that the prevalence of highly accurate spy satellites had maintained a semblance of world peace for the last twenty-five years. Once the Russians could no longer read the date on the fifty-yuan coin in the Chinese president's pocket, they had to act accordingly. So did everyone else.

Sarah went back to the large map, circling Tennessee with the laser pointer. "In the last few years, our best estimates are that the Colonel has quadrupled the territory under his control, and increased his army to at least twenty thousand men. A few months ago the Tennessee governor ceded Knoxville to him to avoid a confrontation."

"Too bad we don't have somebody like the Colonel as joint chief," said Rakkim. "The Mormons would be hunkered down in Salt Lake instead of giving the mayor of Denver night tremors."

The Bible Belt was less a nation than a conglomeration of armed individuals with a common enemy: the Islamic Republic. The central government had little offensive capability, but woe unto the attacker foolish enough to invade. The South was a wasp's nest, and every bandit and warlord carried a sting. Unlike the Islamic Republic, where private citizens were forbidden to own guns, in the Bible Belt *everyone* carried weapons. In spite of the danger, Rakkim had been comfortable in the South—there was an ease to life there, a strange sweetness to the days and nights. The Belt was poor, even poorer than the Islamic Republic, but there was the bracing certainty that no despot would have a chance against an armed citizenry. The Colonel might be a monster to his enemies, domestic and foreign, but were he to brutalize his own people, he would not long survive. The Islamic Republic was by nature more autocratic; only President Kingsley's moderation ensured the limited freedoms that citizens of the Bible Belt considered their God-given right.

"The Colonel's up to s-s-something," said Spider, teeth chattering. Leader of an underground network of Jewish tech-geeks, sought by the Black Robes for twenty years, Spider had risked his life to save Sarah and Rakkim in the past. He raked a hand through his tangled beard. "I missed it, but S-Sarah . . . Sarah put the data together."

"I got lucky," said Sarah. "One of our people in-country sent a report about increased heavy truck traffic in the Great Smokies, well beyond any construction projects we were aware of. So I did some checking." She highlighted Thunderhead Mountain in southeastern Tennessee. "The trucks are going *here*. The Colonel's also moved in troops. Not masses of them, and he's moving them in slowly. He doesn't want to draw attention." She looked at Rakkim. "I wondered why."

"The Colonel is excavating a region below the summit of the mountain." Spider coughed into a handkerchief, idly checked the results, and tucked it back into his pocket. "At least a half-dozen test tunnels have been drilled. We thought at first that he was mining coal, or high-grade minerals, but that wouldn't explain the presence of his troops or his secretive actions." His mouth set. "We just got an indication that he's looking for something else."

The map whirled, brought up the Gulf Coast.

"Two days ago the Colonel brought a finder named John Moseby to the site," said Sarah.

"Man and his crew worked New Orleans," said Spider. "Very good, from all reports."

"A beads-and-booze looter?" Rakkim laughed. "The Colonel must be desperate."

"Moseby's not a typical looter," Sarah said carefully. "As I said, he's a *finder*. Lost, missing, he'll bring it back, no matter the risk."

Rakkim watched her. She was trying to tell him something. The presidential office might be secure from outside surveillance, but that didn't mean the president didn't have cameras and laser microphones of his own installed.

"What's the Colonel looking for?" said Rakkim.

Sarah glanced at Spider, then back at Rakkim. "This mountain . . . it may have been a repository for certain weapon systems of the old regime."

"Black ice?" Rakkim shook his head. They had called him off al-Faisal for *this*? Black ice was what the military called the covert programs from the previous regime. Off-the-books projects funded on a scale no current government could match, projects worked on by a scientific elite whose expertise could only be guessed at. The Holy Grail of advanced weaponry. "Bullshit."

"The old regime had so many black-ice programs under way that even the leadership didn't know about all of them," said Sarah. "Not all of them were accounted—"

"I've heard those stories my whole life," said Rakkim. "Mind-control lasers. Antipersonnel nanobots. Prototypes stashed down mineshafts, hidden under lakes, locked away in abandoned missile silos as the old regime collapsed. Thirty years and nobody has found anything. And not because we haven't looked. They're just stories, Sarah. If the Colonel wants to dig up a mountain, let him. It'll keep him out of trouble."

Sarah grabbed his wrist, turned it so the veins showed. "Those cellular injections you got as a Fedayeen recruit, where do you think they came from? Those injections that made you quicker and stronger, that gave you superior vision and hearing, and amped up your rate of healing." Her fingers dug into his wrist. "Did you ever wonder where the research for those DNA boosters came from? *Did* you? It was a black-ice project from the old Americans. The chief scientist was a good Muslim. He died bringing us what he could." She let him go, her face white, surprised by her own anger. "Black ice is *real*."

Rakkim kept his voice level. "Do you have any evidence that weapons were stashed in the mountain?"

"Any evidence would be somewhere in the wreckage of the Pentagon." Spider sat down with a sigh. "Th-th-that's a six-point-five-million-square-foot haystack. Thirty-four acres of radioactive files and fried computer drives. If we don't know exactly where to look, even the best hot suit in the world isn't going to protect somebody sent to find out what's in the mountain."

"So, the answer is no," said Rakkim.

"B-based on the resources the Colonel's committed to the excavation"— Spider's head lolled on the back of the chair—"one would conclude that *he*, at least, is convinced there's something very valuable in the mountain."

"The Colonel is virulently anti-Muslim," said Sarah. "We can't take the chance—"

"He was a patriot last time I was there," said Rakkim, "not a hater."

"He's a hater *now*," said Sarah.

"Why me?" said Rakkim, still suspicious. Sarah was holding something back. "Doesn't the president trust General Kidd anymore?"

"The president trusts the general with his life," said Sarah.

"Then why doesn't the general send one of his shadow warriors to do the job?" said Rakkim. "It's been over three years since I've been in the Belt. Why not send someone with fresh insights, fresh contacts?"

"They *did*." Sarah's lower lip quivered. "They did, Rikki."

"Two-two months ago . . ." Spider stuttered; a tic jerked the skin under his right eye. "Two m-m-months ago the general sent one of his best shadow warriors to find out what was going on . . ." Spider tried to speak, gave up.

"A week later, the man failed to report," said Sarah, her emotions under control again. "So the general sent another warrior. Same result. *Nothing*. No contact at all."

"It's a particularly in-insular region, as I'm sure you know," Spider said.

"General Kidd will brief you whenever you want," said Sarah.

Rakkim walked over to her. Rested his hands on her hips. Looked into her eyes. Waited until her breathing steadied. He embraced her, tilted his head so none of the security cameras could read his lips. Pretended to kiss her ear. Whispered, "Why me?"

Sarah rested her head on his chest. Reached up and drew him closer, her hands cupping his face. They were wrapped in each other's arms, safe from cameras and microphones. She kissed him, whispered, "Because . . . the man the Colonel called on to help with the excavation . . . John Moseby . . . you *know* him. He's a shadow warrior suspected of going rogue eight years ago. You cleared his name. You confirmed his death in action. John Moseby's real name is John Santee."

They swayed in the middle of the room while Spider averted his eyes, the map of the Belt blinking over them.

CHAPTER 5

Rakkim braked as traffic slowed up ahead. Emergency flares fizzed in the darkness, sending out sparks. A semitruck had overturned, spilled its cargo of fresh corn across the freeway. Sarah craned her neck as they passed, ears of corn crunching under their tires, *pop pop pop*. The driver of the semi leaned against the overturned truck, a young guy, blood running down his forehead as he argued with a policeman. Probably going too fast and lost control after hitting a particularly deep pothole. The winter had been hard, the roadbed lousy to begin with, and the repair crews were way behind schedule.

Sarah moved beside him. "I'm glad you're careful."

Rakkim glanced at her.

Sarah laughed. "You know what I mean."

It was just after 2 a.m., light traffic, rain misting in from the Sound. They had barely spoken after leaving the Presidential Palace—Sarah may have suggested him for the mission, but that didn't mean she had to like it. She stayed close, while he maintained security protocols—checking the rearviews, taking a different route and different vehicle each time they traveled, always checking the car for bugs and tracers. Like Redbeard used to say, trust but verify.

Rakkim and Sarah had never been directly connected to the events of three years ago, the unmasking of the Old One as the initiator of the suitcase nuke attacks on New York City, D.C., and Mecca. The official version credited Redbeard for the intelligence breakthrough, but the Old One knew better and he was the only one who mattered. Not that anyone had heard from him. There were rumors that he was dead, murdered by his acolytes or one of the Arab regimes, exposed as another fake messiah. Rumors that he was in exile in the mountains of Pakistan or rendered silent by the infirmities of age, his dream of restoring the caliphate abandoned.

Rakkim and Sarah didn't believe a word of it. Sarah because she was smart enough to appreciate the Old One's cunning, his incredible *patience*. Rakkim because he knew the Old One would never abandon his dream . . . and even more, because Rakkim knew the seduction of hiding in plain sight. The singular pleasure of blending into the background, of setting the table in the house of the enemy and watching him eat dinner. Rakkim had looked into the Old One's eyes, recognized that special delight in floating among the rest of the world, superior and untouchable, there but not there. So Rakkim and Sarah stayed invisible too, unmentioned and unnoticed, just a rumor now themselves. Sarah had quit the history faculty at the university and spent her days privately advising the president and raising their son. A few months ago she started work on a new book. Not done causing trouble? he had asked her. *Never*, she had answered.

"Any idea what kind of weapon the Colonel's looking for?" said Rakkim.

"Not at this point. Spider's still doing what he can with his own sources . . . his own methods."

"I still want to know what al-Faisal's doing."

"Let State Security handle it," she said. "That's *their* job."

He veered toward the shoulder, trying to avoid misaligned sections of freeway. Even with its heavy-duty suspension, their car shook running over the rough pavement. He thought of John Santee, the renegade shadow warrior who now called himself John Moseby. What had it taken for Moseby to throw in with the Colonel? Moseby was a man who wanted only a smooth ride . . . no more hide-and-seek, no more enemies and knives at the throat. Did he even know what kind of bumpy road he was accelerating down now?

Fedayeen forever, that's what they told you at the Academy, and it was true enough for the combat units. Not so for shadow warriors and assassins.

The part they didn't tell you, the dirty little secret, was that given time, shadow warriors *always* went rogue. To survive, shadow warriors had to walk, talk, and think like the enemy. Ultimately, they became the enemy. Before that happened, they were pulled out of the Belt and given a post closer to home. Promoted with honors. Asked to teach at the Academy. Moseby had gone native sooner than anyone expected, with all his Fedayeen knowledge and training intact. Rakkim had been sent in to find him and kill him. A mission for an assassin, but given to Rakkim instead. They said no one knew the Belt like he did. He'd found Moseby, all right, but let him live. Came back with a lie. A year later Rakkim retired and took up residence in the Zone. He became part owner of the Blue Moon, wallowing in sin. It didn't help. It took Sarah to save him from himself.

If shadow warriors always turned renegade, assassins always slipped their leash, became drunk with blood, killing without direction or restraint. No such thing as a retired assassin. Darwin had lasted longer than any of his breed before the order to terminate him was given. They'd sent three master assassins to do the job. The commander of the assassins found their three heads sitting on his desk the next morning, their mouths smeared with red lipstick, cheeks rouged like kewpie dolls, rhinestones stuck in their jellied eyes. Then Darwin stepped out of the shadows . . . the horror show was left on the security cameras for all to admire.

A coyote blinked in the headlights as it tore at something by the side of the road. They were getting bolder every year, coming in closer to the city from the surrounding forests.

Sarah turned her head, watched the coyote as it got back to work.

"Tired?" said Rakkim.

Sarah lowered the window, the sound of rain filling the car. Wind blew her hair, and the smell of her was clean and electric. "A little."

"Why don't you sleep in tomorrow? Let me take care of things."

Sarah rested her hand on his leg. "You have enough to do . . . before you leave."

"I'll be fine." He glanced over at her, then back at the road. After all they had been through, he could still see the little girl in her—she was four the first time they met, Rakkim nine, a streetwise orphan Redbeard brought home after Rakkim picked his pocket. The two of them had grown up together in Redbeard's fortified villa, played and fought, swam and argued, and when Rakkim had left at eighteen, Sarah had seen him to the door. She was thirteen, thin and gangly, but she had kissed him, and spoke with the certainty of a woman. *I'm going to marry you someday, Rikki.* He had laughed but she was serious. Smarter than he was then . . . smarter than he was now.

"What are you thinking?" said Sarah.

"Nothing . . . just, sometimes I wish we had a simpler life."

"I don't," said Sarah.

"I know."

Illuminated by floodlights, the Grand Saladin mosque loomed ahead, the largest fundamentalist mosque in the city, a delicate, turquoise blue domed structure built with Saudi money and the labor of the faithful. The side of the mosque facing the freeway was adorned by an eighty-foot mosaic of a hook-nosed Jew with cloven hooves carrying a nuclear bomb into a New York City cityscape. Ugliest thing Rakkim had ever seen. The mosaic itself formed from Quranic script, neatly sidestepping the prohibition against depictions of the human form. Although in this case the human was debatable. The mosaic had been ordered bricked over after the revelation of the truth behind the atomic attacks. Last month the Supreme Court finally ruled that the mosaic was protected religious speech. The grand unveiling had drawn a crowd of over 200,000 and was broadcast around the country.

Exposing the Old One's responsibility for the suitcase nuke attacks had exonerated the Israeli Mossad, and by extension, all the Jews. Within a year, well-funded scholars published articles challenging the evidence against the Old One, and once again, politicians again blamed Zionists for the ills of the world, claiming that even the crafty Redbeard had been taken in. Six months ago, the top-rated late-night comedian made a joke about the attacks, blaming mermaids and leprechauns. There was silence . . . then wild applause. The international police agencies still searched for the Old One, but the average citizen in the Islamic Republic wasn't even sure he existed.

Rakkim turned away from the mosque. It had been Sarah who first suspected the Old One's role in the attacks, Sarah who persisted in spite of the danger, Sarah who insisted they had a responsibility to history. Rakkim didn't care about history. He had wanted to simply slip out of the country, move to Canada or Brazil and start a new life. Sarah said *he* could leave anytime he wanted. Made him feel like a coward for even suggesting it. He saw the floodlit mosque in his rearviews. "You ever wonder if it was worth it?"

"No."

"All the people who died so we could prove the Old One—"

"I said *no*. That filthy mural is just a setback, a minor—"

"I thought we had changed the world." Rakkim drove faster, the edges of the freeway overgrown with weeds, the asphalt crumbling. "The truth will set you free? What a joke."

"You don't have to go," said Sarah. "General Kidd wanted to send in another shadow warrior team, three of them—"

"I said I'd do it."

"If you feel it's not worth it, just say so," Sarah said gently. "No one would blame you."

"*You* would."

She stroked his arm. "No . . . I wouldn't."

He glanced at her. She was telling the truth. "Nah, I could use a vacation. Besides, after two years of marriage, I'm getting a little tired of your cooking."

"Oh, *really?*"

"Southern food can't be beat. Something as simple as grits and eggs, sunny-side up . . . it's the bacon grease they fry the eggs in that makes all the difference."

"Sounds yummy. Perhaps when you come back you could bring home a *hawg.*"

"Sure. We could put a leash on him, tell the neighbors he was a pit bull."

"Dogs are filthy animals, pets fit only for Christians. We'd have to tell the neighbors we converted to Catholicism." Sarah crossed herself, mumbled something in Latin.

"I really will come back."

"I know."

"I *will*, Sarah."

Sarah looked straight ahead as Rakkim accelerated.

Sarah flopped back on the bed, exhausted, hair lank, their bedroom steamed with sex. She stared at the ceiling, eyes half closed. "Wow."

Rakkim curled himself around her, watched her breathe. Captivated by the steady rise and fall. Her breasts were fuller since the baby. He liked them before. He liked them now. He lightly raked his nails across her belly, and she shivered. His kissed the warmth back into her.

Sarah threw a leg across him, pinched him. Laughed as he yelped.

They still hadn't talked about John Moseby. They had driven through the gates of their fortified home, walked inside, stopping only to peek in on Michael. Sarah had adjusted the baby's covers, and Sarah's mother, Katherine, grumbled from the next room, said if Sarah woke him up, *she* was going to have to put him back to sleep. Rakkim and Sarah kissed their son on the forehead. They lingered, listening to him snore and wondering what he dreamed of.

Afterward, they made love in silence. Time enough for words later. Rakkim lost himself in her as always, lost *himself* in the process, relieved at the absence of his own thoughts, the awful weight of knowing what he had to do. There were times making love with her that he couldn't remember his name, and was grateful for it. He played with her hair while she rested her cheek on his heart. The two of them spent and exhausted, content for a moment, drifting . . . Of course he had to ruin things.

He raised himself on one elbow. "Do I . . . do I seem different to you?"

"Different how?"

"I don't know. Just . . . different."

"You're more playful lately. More fun. Not so serious. I like that." Her fingers traced the scars on his chest. She kissed the biggest scar, a pale, thick knot where Darwin had plunged his knife in. It should have been a killing strike, but Darwin had stopped the blade an eighth of an inch short, wanting to draw out the fun. Another kiss and she looked up at him. "You're a better lover." Her eyes creased, teasing. "Not that you weren't always wonderful, but lately you've been a real maniac." She must have seen his expression. Laughed. "I mean you're just . . . unstoppable." She kissed him. "I'm flattered, if you really want to know. I was worried after we had Michael that . . . that you might not be so interested in—"

"I killed two men earlier this evening."

Sarah pulled back slightly.

"Al-Faisal's bodyguards."

"I'm . . . I'm sure they were trying to kill you."

Rakkim nodded.

"Then they made their choice." She reached for him. "What is it?"

"They made their choice . . . that's just what I said afterward."

She pulled the sheet over them, cooling their bodies as it fluttered down. "Well, they *did*." She yawned. "Are you complaining?"

"No." Since he had killed Darwin, Rakkim had been scanned, poked and prodded, every few months. The doctors said he had been lucky, his recovery miraculous. Most Fedayeen, in spite of their genetic boosters, would have died in that abandoned church in New Fallujah, bled to death from a hundred cuts, or gone into shock. Instead the two of them had circled each other, covered in each other's blood, jabbing and slashing. Darwin chattered away the whole time, pale and rat-faced, but his hands, those beautiful hands, long-fingered as a concert pianist's, and *fast* . . . faster than Rakkim . . . Yet it was Darwin who had died in the abandoned chapel, Rakkim's knife driven into his open mouth, silencing his taunts, severing his brain stem. Darwin was gone, but there were times, late at night, while Sarah slept beside him . . . There were moments when he held up his hands and didn't recognize them as his own. Moments when he closed his eyes and saw Darwin's arrogant leer, heard his voice echoing in the church—*Don't die on me, Rikki. Not yet. Come on, don't you want to play some more?* It was all a game to Darwin. Until Rakkim killed him. Rakkim still wasn't sure which one of them had been more surprised.

This wasn't the first time he had closed his eyes and seen the dead. Heard the voices of men he had killed. Taking a life put one in God's place for an instant, and with that role came the burden of ghosts. Killing Darwin had been different. Rakkim, the shadow warrior, had a new shadow now. Today he had killed two men in the Zone. Trained men flanking the choke points of the alley. At best he should have attempted a series of asymmetrical feints, hoping to draw them out of position, but instead, he had killed them without breaking stride. Killed them so quickly he wasn't even aware of how he did it. Killed them as though they were cobwebs to be brushed aside.

"When you come back from the Belt, I want us to make another baby." Sarah cupped his face. "*Promise* me."

They both knew the pledge she wanted was that he would come back. "I promise."

He drew her close. "How did you find out that John Moseby is John Santee?"

She yawned again. "How did I find out that you gave a false report to the commander of the shadow warriors? Is *that* your real question?"

"You're too smart for me."

"I know." Sarah curled up against him. "Redbeard told me. I don't know how he found out." Her nipples stiffened against him. "It was after you asked for my hand in marriage. *That's* when he told me." She giggled and her nipples tickled him. "He said a Fedayeen who violated his oath had committed a capital offense. He asked me if I thought such a man was a worthy husband."

He pulled her on top of him.

"I told him . . . I told him you must have had a good reason to lie . . ." She slipped him inside of her, rocking gently. ". . . and surely . . . surely a man who thought for himself, without the burden of law or tradition, surely such a man was the *best* of all husbands." She bit her lip, back arched, her eyes locked on him. "I said . . . I said, Uncle, if you hadn't come to the exact same conclusion, surely you would have turned him over to the Fedayeen rather than risk being branded a traitor yourself."

Rakkim groaned, his cries slowly trailing off.

She flattened herself against him, the two of them prickly with sweat. She waited until they got their breath back. "Why . . . why did you tell them Moseby was dead?"

He was still inside her, feeling her pulse as his own.

"This man broke his oath," she said. "What was it about him that made you break yours?"

He remembered the last time he had seen Moseby. The man was a light sleeper, but not light enough. He had opened his eyes, felt Rakkim's knife against his throat, but made no move to struggle or resist. Moseby was a shadow warrior too, he *knew* how skillful Rakkim had to be to sneak up on him. Moseby let out a long sigh, released his fear like a flock of white doves. Rakkim looked down at him and knew he had never felt at such peace with himself as this dead man did. *Go on,* Moseby whispered, not wanting to wake his wife, who lay sleeping beside him. *Do what you have to and go quietly.*

"Rikki? Why did you lie for him?"

"When I met him . . . it was before you and I were together, before I had any hope for us to be together. The way he looked over at his wife when he thought he was going to die . . . I never saw anybody so in love before." Rakkim felt her grip him, enclose him with her heat. "Moseby . . . he was the only man I was ever envious of."

CHAPTER 6

Rakkim and General Kidd washed their hands and feet with clean sand as the muezzin called the faithful to dawn prayer from the minaret. The light brown sand was imported from the general's Somali homeland, its fine grit an accepted way to wash in that arid place. Swathed in white robes, they quickly filed into the mosque with the other men, the only sound their bare feet shuffling on the cool slate.

It had been almost three years since Rakkim had been to mosque with Kidd, and he missed it. Missed sharing meals with Kidd's family afterward, missed seeing Kidd as a father in a more intimate setting. His own father murdered when he was nine, Rakkim had learned from Kidd's stern but loving treatment of his children, his patient guidance, and patterned his own behavior accordingly. Choosing to remain in hiding after the death of Redbeard, he and Kidd had continued to meet privately, maintaining their friendship and Rakkim's back-channel contacts with the Fedayeen. Now though, leaving soon on this mission into the Belt, Rakkim had wanted to pray with him, for perhaps the last time.

Rakkim rested on his haunches inside the mosque, eyes half closed, listening to the imam's sermon, and the sound of the man's voice might as well have been the crash of waves in the distance. He sat in the tiny mosque, packed so close that he could hear the rustle of Kidd's white djellabah beside him, inhale the faint sandalwood oil Kidd rubbed into his anthracite black skin. The only white man in the mosque, Rakkim was half a head shorter than the others, Somalis mostly, with a scattering of Ethiopians and Nigerians, all of them Fedayeen, retired or active-duty. Like Kidd, the older men had journeyed to the former United States when the Civil War broke out almost thirty years ago, men who had left their homes and families behind, risking everything for the chance to conquer new lands for Allah. Fierce fighters, they had died by the hundreds, by the thousands, most of them buried in haste, without proper treatment, their graves unmarked. Still they had come, heeding the call. Rakkim, aware of his own faith only by its absence, felt honored to be among them.

As a newly minted major in the army of the Islamic Republic, Kidd had led a brigade of African volunteers at Newark, Bloody Newark, or the second Gettysburg, as later historians called it. Kidd knew nothing of Gettysburg, he only knew that the standing order never to retreat was madness. To fight to the last man only meant there would be too many warriors in Paradise and not enough on the ground, where they were needed. Hopelessly outnumbered, Kidd had led a controlled retreat, gathering American Muslims with him as they drew the rebels from the Belt deeper into parts of the city still standing, high-rise neighborhoods where the rebel tanks had trouble maneuvering. On the fifth day of the battle, Kidd took control of all the Islamic forces and counterattacked, outflanking the rebels and halting their advance.

Rakkim's eyes were on the imam, but he saw only the footage from the war museum, video of Newark burning, the flames like a tidal wave. The battle raged for three more days, the city wreathed with oily smoke, the streets clogged with the dead. Newark was the deepest penetration into the Muslim republic by the rebels, and while not a victory for either side, it was Kidd who staved off a Muslim defeat and stymied the rebels' plan to head into Pennsylvania and Ohio, splitting the republic. A cease-fire was declared a week later, a cease-fire that had held ever since. Given a battlefield promotion by order of President Kingsley, after the armistice Kidd had created the Fedayeen, a small, elite force of genetically enhanced holy warriors.

The army had fifty times the men under arms as the Fedayeen, but they were poorly led, poorly equipped, and poorly trained, garrison soldiers strung along the border, ill suited for combat. Redbeard had told Rakkim that the army's weakness was no accident. The Fedayeen remained outside the military chain of command, a praetorian guard operating without any oversight, answering only to General Kidd and the president. The calculation had worked well for many years, but the rise of the Black Robes had created fissures in the ranks of the Fedayeen, testing the loyalties of even the most devout. Three months ago, an entire company of Fedayeen, eighty fighters, had defected, taking their heavy weapons with them to a Black Robes' stronghold outside of Dearborn, Michigan.

The imam leaned against the pulpit, white-haired and bent as a stick, his voice echoing, every sound magnified in the stillness, as the faithful nodded in agreement. Unlike the lavish grand mosques scattered across the city, this little mosque in the Fremont district was plain and unadorned, solid as the worshippers themselves. The floors were gray slate, the walls immaculate white plaster, the dome of beaten copper. The mihrab on the east wall, an ancient, wooden crescent indicating the direction of Mecca, had been brought over from Kidd's boyhood village outside Kismaayo. Rakkim felt comfortable here among the old warriors and their many sons, more comfortable than in any other mosque. While the fundamentalist clerics bellowed demands from the pulpit, this Somali imam's sermon stressed traditional values of piety, simplicity, and duty, urging the faithful to avoid the gaudy distractions of the modern world. Study the Quran, the imam repeated, exhorting the brothers to care for their families as Allah cared for them, "in this way shall you find peace in this world, and reward in the next."

Peace in this world. The faithful pressed their foreheads to the floor. *Allahu Akbar.* God is great. Fine thoughts from the imam, but even in this holy place, Rakkim felt no comfort. He had spent his life mouthing the words, declaring his belief in one god, and Muhammad as his last prophet, but he was a Muslim in name only. Like most of the country, going along to get along. The difference was that Rakkim envied the faithful their piety. Their joy in submission. Their *peace.* All of it out of reach to him, a drowning man forever carried beyond the shore. Until he had killed Darwin.

Strange to think that only when facing evil incarnate had Rakkim felt the presence of God. Darwin, the Old One's personal assassin, should have killed Rakkim when he had the chance. Instead he had toyed with Rakkim, gone blade to blade with him in an abandoned church, laughing as he cut his signature into Rakkim's flesh again and again, both their blood flung about like holy water. *Sarah's going to be all alone after I kill you, Rikki. Nothing better than fucking a new widow. Best pussy in the world.* Darwin's face was pale and slack, but his eyes burned in the twilight. *Maybe I'll leave your cock under the pillow for her.* Rakkim remembered the sound of his own labored breathing as he moved across the floor, stained glass crunching underfoot as he held eye contact with Darwin, and Darwin . . . seemingly fresh and free, almost dapper, knife in his long, slender hands, gracefully directing Rakkim's movements like a symphony conductor.

You're not tired, are you, Rikki? We're just getting started. This is just fore-play. Wait until you see what I've got planned for you. Then, as Rakkim teetered, bleeding from a hundred cuts, he had felt soft wings brush his cheek, angel wings, and strength rushed into him as he flung his knife. Darwin staggered back, stood pinned against a wood pillar, Rakkim's blade driven deep into his mouth. Darwin's soft, full lips twitched, trying to speak, as shocked as Rakkim. Not so bad to die, that's what Rakkim had thought as he collapsed onto the floor of the church . . . not as long as that devil precedes me to hell. Angel wings . . . the delirium of a dying man, that's what he told himself as he drifted off. Then he felt the angel's touch again, and lost all doubt, blinded by tears as those downy wings enfolded him, lifted him up from the well of death. While Darwin died, Rakkim lived. Granted the gift of life. And the burden.

Sitting on his heels, hands resting on his knees, Rakkim spoke in unison with the faithful, entreating Allah's blessing. He turned his head to the right, toward the angel recording his good deeds. Then turned his head toward the left, toward the angel on his shoulder recording his bad deeds. *"Assalaamu Alaikum wa Rahmatullah."* Peace and blessings of Allah be upon you. Rakkim stood with the other men, gently embraced Kidd. "May Allah receive our prayers."

Rakkim walked quickly to the door. After that time in the abandoned church, after killing Darwin, he had never again felt the presence of Allah. *Never.* God had slipped away from him like sand through his fingers. Slipped away while Rakkim lay for days where he had fallen, his body slowly healing itself. No matter. That one touch, that glimpse of the infinite, had left its mark. So much for miracles. Rakkim was on his own now. A new creature. Each step a first step. These thoughts had troubled him, but lately . . . lately he had taken a perverse pleasure in his situation. Never had he felt so free. So limitless in his reach.

Kidd walked beside Rakkim as they strode the narrow streets toward the family compound, the apartments already noisy, the air rich with the smell of frying bananas and corn cakes. The Fremont district was almost exclusively Somali, a conservative enclave with tribal mores and extremely heavy security. Kidd was safe here. So was Rakkim. Six of Kidd's sons, all Fedayeen, walked behind them at a respectful distance.

"The mosque did not collapse upon us," said Kidd.

"Allah must have been busy with more important things," said Rakkim.

Kidd smiled for just an instant. "It's been a long time since you've joined me for prayers. Are you all right, Abu Michael?"

Abu Michael. Kidd honored him with the name when they were together. A Somali man lost his given name when he became a father, took on the name of his firstborn. Abu Michael—father of Michael. Kidd told him once that in his grandfather's time, a man whose first child was female would often have the child killed, so as not to bear the shame of being given a woman's name. Strange days then . . . strange days now. Abu Michael. He was *not* on his own. A new creature? Where did such thoughts come from? He had a wife and a son, duties and responsibilities and all the joys that went with them. Father of Michael. Yes, *that* was worth hanging on to. Like all shadow warriors, Rakkim had gone by many names, but Abu Michael was his favorite. If he was ever in the presence of Allah again, what would God call him?

Kidd peered at him, his eyes deep-set over high cheekbones. Light gleamed on his shaved skull as he waited for an answer. "Abu Michael?"

"Never better," said Rakkim.

Amir, one of Kidd's thirty-seven sons, dodged a knife stroke from one of his many brothers, slid under the man's blade, and jabbed his brother in the heart. The two brothers bowed to each other, the loser retreating to the edge of the training room, blood trickling from a dozen minor wounds on his legs and torso. Their veiled mothers, sisters and wives, sprawled on pillows along the opposite side of the room, eating sweets and gossiping.

Amir beckoned to the last of his brothers calmly waiting his turn, the last of his five opponents, and the man trotted out to join him, his bare feet kicking up sand. A light rain started up, beating on the metal roof. Harder now.

"Amir is skilled," said Rakkim. "The news reports did not exaggerate."

"The Lion of Boulder?" Kidd shrugged. "He is twenty-five. A young warrior should not listen to the praise of those who sleep in warm beds every night."

Kidd's youngest wife secretly waved to him, using only her fingertips. It was as seductive a move as Rakkim had ever seen.

"You should have more wives, Abu Michael."

"One is plenty."

"The Quran allows at least four, and for good reason." Kidd leaned closer. "A man with one camel is at the mercy of the camel. A man with a *string* of camels . . ."

"Interesting analogy. I'll try that on Sarah tonight and let you know what she says."

Amir and his brother faced each other, saluted with their knives, and went into a defensive crouch. Amir immediately started to circle his brother, keeping his knife tucked in close. As tall as his father but even more muscular, he had a natural quickness, an innate sense of where he was and where he needed to be in any confrontation.

Seventeen of Kidd's older sons had passed the rigorous Fedayeen training—five had been killed in action, the rest acquitted themselves admirably, but none more than Amir. A junior officer in the strike force, he was already a veteran of campaigns in Panama and the Congo. Two months ago, he had received a field promotion for defeating a Mormon advance into Colorado. Heavily outnumbered, Amir took charge of his troops when four higher-ranking officers were killed, his bold tactics annihilating the enemies' top mountain battalion outside Boulder. His handsome, scarred profile was on every news show for the next week, and a dozen senators offered their daughters in marriage.

"Two of my best shadow warriors lost, a long-term operative on the ground missing . . ." Kidd watched his sons fight as he passed Rakkim a thumb-load with the encrypted file on the Colonel. "I pray you'll have better luck."

"You've got a mole, *sidi*," said Rakkim, using the North African term of respect.

"No more than a half-dozen people knew about the operation," said Kidd. "They've all been tested, complete workup. Nothing."

Rakkim watched Amir move in on his brother. "Test them again."

Kidd nodded. "Redbeard would be proud of you."

Rakkim bowed at the honor. Redbeard had taken him in off the street, had raised him and trained him, taught him always to look for the hidden agenda, the knife behind the handshake. Rakkim had learned the lessons too well.

"Sad state of affairs when I can no longer trust my own." Kidd rubbed the raised scar along the edge of his jaw. "I'll set up a dummy mission back to the Belt. Some covert op that will take weeks to plan. Hopefully our mole, if there *is* a mole, will be distracted."

"Initiate a smaller op too," said Rakkim. "No more than two men, strictly outside the normal chain of command. Tell them to be ready to leave at a moment's notice and then let them wait."

"A feint behind the feint . . . Very good." Kidd nodded. "You should have never retired. I had hoped you might replace me someday."

"You have too many sons for me to replace you," said Rakkim.

"It is not a matter of blood, Abu Michael," said Kidd.

Amir leapt high. His hand darted out as he twisted in the air, knife flicking across his brother's jugular. It was a forbidden sparring move, the chance of a mortal blow too easy, but Amir's cut barely sliced the skin.

"Amir *may* be a worthy successor when my time comes," said Kidd as Amir approached. "A fearless fighter with an aptitude for command, but he needs to control his temper. He was a most difficult child, always demanding his own way." He shook his head. "No matter how hard I beat him, he did not cry. Did not change his behavior either."

"Redbeard used to say the same thing about me."

Amir bowed before his father. "General."

Kidd nodded.

Amir acknowledged Rakkim with his upraised knife. A deep scar ran from under his left eye to the side of his mouth. "I have exhausted my brothers," he said, slightly out of breath. "Care to play?"

"Thanks for the invite," said Rakkim, "but you're too good for me."

Amir's eyes went flat. "Am I a *child* to be told fairy tales?"

"Amir," growled Kidd.

Amir stepped closer still, towering over Rakkim. "Am I not worthy of your attention?"

Rakkim stayed loose. "More than worthy."

Sweat gleamed on Amir's muscled torso. He gripped the knife tighter. A mistake.

Rakkim caught the knife as it came at him, plucked it from Amir's grip. Offered it back to him, handle first. "A fine blade, Amir, worthy of its owner. Thank you for letting me see it." He bowed.

Stunned, Amir slowly took back his knife, bowed to his father, and left.

"I apologize for my son," said Kidd, watching Amir cross the training room.

"Amir meant me no harm, *sidi*, he just wanted to teach me some manners."

"Instead you taught him. A dangerous lesson for the teacher, Abu Michael." Kidd clicked his prayer beads, running them quickly through his fingers, round and round, still watching Amir stalk away. "If you come back from your trip, you must show me how you snatched the blade from him. I've never seen such a thing."

"*If* I come back?"

"I'll walk you out of the neighborhood," said Kidd.

It was raining harder now. Kidd inhaled the fragrance of the open air, his stride lengthening so that Rakkim had to double-time to keep up. "When I was a boy, growing up outside of Mogadishu . . . it didn't rain for a year and a half. Not a drop. Not a cloud in the sky. So dry I could taste dust in my dreams." Kidd raised his face to the sky, the downpour running down his cheeks. "I've been in this country thirty-five years . . . and I still treasure the smell of rain."

Rakkim put up the hood of his robe.

Moisture glistened on Kidd's eyelashes and cropped beard as they walked through the alley. "Redbeard and I were never friends. We were both too hardheaded, too eager to get the president's support for our fiefdoms, but we respected each other. The worst time between us was when you joined the Fedayeen. I don't think he ever forgave me."

Rakkim stopped. "It wasn't *your* idea, it was mine."

"All Redbeard knew was that his dreams for you were over. You were never going to become State Security. You chose another life. A life without him. He couldn't hate you, so he did the next best thing. He hated me."

Rakkim splashed through a puddle. "I didn't know."

"I considered Redbeard's actions weak and petty . . . the mark of a man with too few children." Kidd's skin gleamed in the rain. "Until you left the Fedayeen. Then I knew how he felt. Even with all my sons, I knew exactly how bitter and resentful he felt, how wounded that you had chosen another path."

Rakkim held his head high, listening to the *click-click-click* of Kidd's prayer beads.

"I told myself Allah had other plans for you," said Kidd.

Rakkim looked around, wary now, but they were the only ones out in the downpour.

"Do you think I made a mistake?" said Kidd. "Disbanding the assassin unit . . ." His prayer beads clicked away. "They were dangerous to our enemies, but just as dangerous to us. I thought by subsuming the assassin training into *all* our units, we could have benefit of their killing skills without endangering the souls of our warriors. The assassin trade . . . it's corrosive to even the spiritually strong." He gripped Rakkim's wrist, squeezed. "You know that better than I do, Abu Michael. You saw what Darwin became. Whatever was in him that caused him to be selected for assassins in the first place, whatever moral vacuum made him excel at the killing craft, it perverted him. Destroyed him." He looked into Rakkim's eyes. "I have no idea how you defeated him. Allah must have been beside you that day."

Rakkim looked back into Kidd's deep, dark eyes.

Kidd released him. "Yes . . . yes, that is the only explanation." He blinked in the storm. "Still . . . I find myself wondering if I acted too hastily. If I had a master assassin at my call, I could just send *him* into the Belt, tell *him* to kill the Colonel and everyone else connected to this devil's dig. Instead, my son . . . I must send you." He embraced Rakkim, kissed him on both cheeks. "*Salaam alaikum.*"

"*Alaikum salaam,*" said Rakkim, but it was too late. Kidd had turned his back on him and was walking rapidly away.

CHAPTER 7

Who knew that I-90 was the road to Paradise? Daniel Wilson tried to smile, but he couldn't, pressing down on the floorboard as though that would slow the car down.

"*Allahu Akbar, Allahu Akbar, Allahu Akbar,*" repeated bin-Salaam, one of his brother's many bodyguards, as he hunched over the steering wheel. Bin-Salaam, a glum, beefy zealot missing an ear. "*Allahu Akbar, Allahu Akbar, Allahu Akbar,*" he continued, the words flowing together as he wove the car through morning traffic. God is great, God is great, God is great.

Wilson just nodded, turned around. Far behind, but closing fast, three State Security vehicles chased them, sirens blaring. The other cars on the road moved toward the shoulders.

Bin-Salaam accelerated.

Wilson stared at the detonator wired to his index finger and started to shake. He loved his brother Terry. Tariq al-Faisal, he corrected himself. No, he would always be Terry to him. His older brother. The good brother, that's what his parents called him, and Wilson had to agree. No one outside the family knew that Terry had become a Black Robe. While his older brother now sat at the right hand of Grand Mullah ibn-Azziz himself, Wilson attended mosque intermittently, couldn't keep a job . . . *or* a wife. Delia had left him a year ago, gone to live with some *Catholic* in Los Angeles, flaunting her body in that moral sewer. His mother wept when he finally told her of his shame. His father couldn't look at him. He glanced at bin-Salaam, then back to the road. A failure in every sense, Wilson had been given one last chance to redeem himself. Terry had knocked on his apartment door two nights ago, beardless as a bricklayer. Terry had kissed him on the cheek, said, *Gather your things, brother, I have a great gift for you.*

"The apostates are getting closer," said bin-Salaam. "Expect a roadblock soon . . . and aerosol flypaper to take you alive."

Wilson rubbed his own newly shaven jaw. It *itched.* He patted the device in his jacket pocket. Some construct of wires and chips Terry had given him, a decoy to assure their pursuers that Wilson was the one they sought.

Don't worry, dear brother, Terry had said. *No one challenges a great triumph. State Security will fight among themselves to claim credit for bringing down the great Tariq al-Faisal.* He had inclined his head toward Wilson as though his acknowledgment were a pearl of great price. *You will be laughing in Paradise at their folly, laughing as you frolic with your virgins.* He had smiled then, a smile that Wilson remembered from their youth, Terry beckoning the neighborhood simpleton to pet a vicious dog.

Wilson glanced behind him again.

"*Allahu Akbar, Allahu Akbar, Allahu Akbar,*" mumbled bin-Salaam.

It had taken two days for Terry to convince him. Two days in which Wilson had barely slept, barely eaten, just prayed and listened to Terry tell him over and over what *had* to be done. *You're the only one who can fool them, my brother, the only one.* Wilson should be happy, Terry kept saying. *Dry your tears, little brother, you have a chance to bring honor to our parents, and joy to Allah*—what more could you ask?

"They are very close," said bin-Salaam. "Send us to Paradise."

They have tests, Wilson had told Terry. They will know I am not you. Terry told him not to worry; it had all been taken care of. Bin Salaam had taken hairs from Wilson's brush and a pen with his fingerprints and given them to a high-ranking brother in the police department. They were evidence now, part of the investigation into the murder of a purveyor of black-market electronics. *Trust me, brother,* Terry assured him, *the apostates will believe. Just do your duty.* Terry had called State Security's hotline himself, tipped them that the Black Robe they were interested in was fleeing east on I-90 in a late-model gray mufti sedan.

"It is time." Bin-Salaam nodded at the roadblock up ahead, State Security fanned out around it. A foam truck laid down a wall of adhesive bubbles. "*Allahu Akbar, Allahu Akbar, Allahu Akbar.*"

Duty . . . duty . . . duty. Wilson trembled in the passenger's seat, teeth chattering. "*Allahu Akbar, Allahu Akbar, Allahu Akbar . . .*"

Wilson tore at the tape around his index finger, careful not to trip the detonator. Finally certain of what to do, more certain now than he had ever been before.

Bin-Salaam reached over—*"Allahu Akbar, Allahu Akbar, Allahu Akbar"*—wrapped his massive paw around Wilson's hand—*"Allahu Akbar, Allahu Akbar, Allahu Akbar"*—and squeezed.

For the briefest of instants, Wilson's ears rang from the force of one hundred pounds of C-6 explosives detonating around him. It sounded like the screaming of the damned.

"What, you're not hungry?" Deputy Chief of Detectives Anthony Colarusso held his fork an inch from his mouth, spaghetti dangling onto his plate.

"I like watching you eat," said Rakkim. "It restores my faith in our animal origins."

"Doesn't take a leap of faith, just open your eyes, troop, we're *all* beasts of the field here." Colarusso slurped his pasta, a single strand whipping up into his mouth, spraying red sauce onto the napkin tucked into the neck of his white dress shirt. "Sorry about that."

Rakkim wiped sauce off his hand. "No harm done."

Colarusso hunched over the table, a thickset, middle-aged lawman with a bad haircut and a misbuttoned shirt. One of Rakkim's oldest friends, one of the few who knew what Rakkim and Sarah had done to expose the Old One. One of the few who had helped. He guzzled red wine from his coffee cup. A good Catholic, Colarusso had the best arrest record in the department ten years in a row, but his professional rise had topped out because of his refusal to convert. After the Old One fled and the history books were rewritten, Colarusso leapfrogged to deputy chief. Without giving up his crucifix. Now he recruited from the old neighborhood, fought bureaucratic battles, and oversaw major busts.

Rakkim and Colarusso sat alongside each other, their backs to the wall of the private cop joint located in the basement of St. Ignatius. Ancient music rolled from the sound system: Sinatra, Tony Bennett, Aretha Franklin. Real time-warp stuff, barely audible over the din in the room, gossip and arguments and the clatter of silverware. Father Joe tended bar in his clerical garb, while Father Alberto cooked, a mug of wine always within reach.

Rakkim had been awarded many medals for service to his country, but he was as proud of his standing invitation to this bar as any citation. It had been three years since Colarusso first brought him here. Words had been exchanged that night, jabs and insults, but Rakkim had kept his cool, and even prior to his promotion, Colarusso commanded respect. Three years later, Rakkim was still the only Muslim allowed in, but Father Joe no longer threw out Rakkim's glass when he got up to leave, smashing it into the trash.

"State Security didn't take kindly to me muscling into their investigation." Colarusso twirled spaghetti around his fork. "I told them al-Faisal might be their turf, but when that Black Robe prick kills one of my locals, that's when Homicide gets involved." The ball of pasta grew larger as he wound the fork round and round. "We agreed to disagree."

"Thanks."

"Don't thank me yet. All I've done so far is keep your name out of it." Colarusso slid the fork into his mouth, chewed. "Those two John Does coroner said he'd never seen anybody killed like that. Acted like it was something special."

"I got lucky," said Rakkim.

"Sure you did." Colarusso passed Rakkim his handheld. "Here's something else the coroner thought was odd. Eagleton died from having his neck snapped, but that kind of thing doesn't usually lead to much blood loss."

Rakkim stared at the crime scene images on the screen of the handheld, Eagleton curled up on the floor, blood from his nostrils staining his shirt.

"No other signs of trauma, just the ligature marks around his neck . . ." Another strand of pasta whipped through Colarusso's lips. "Doc seemed to think whoever killed Eagleton must have played with him a while before breaking his neck."

"Al-Faisal wasn't in there very long . . ." Rakkim zoomed in on the back of Eagleton's neck. Saw two precisely spaced indentations.

"Yeah, I noticed that too." Colarusso wiped his mouth. "Haven't seen marks like that since I was a rookie. Looks like the Black Robes got themselves a Bombay strangler."

Rakkim nodded. *Bombay strangler* was an old cop term, partially racist, partially just ignorant. The best stranglers were trained in North Africa, that's what he had heard, anyway. He had never met one, only knew their handiwork. Al-Faisal being a strangler explained his calmness when he saw Rakkim following him.

"So, what I'm wondering, Rikki, is what was it that al-Faisal picked up from Eagleton that was so important that even a strangler *needed* bodyguards?"

"I find out I'll let you know." Rakkim gave him back the handheld. "How's Anthony Junior doing?"

"You know how he's doing." Colarusso rolled up the cuffs of his shirt, his thick forearms knotted with muscle. "Don't pretend you don't get reports from your Fedayeen buddies."

"I heard he didn't get accepted into the shadow warrior program."

"Just as well, if you want my opinion." Colarusso picked up a hot sausage link with his fingers, bit the end off. "He was disappointed, but the idea of Junior being sent into the Belt armed with only his dick don't sit well with me."

"He'll have his blade."

Colarusso belched. "He'd still be all by his lonesome. Just the way you shadow warriors like it." He slowly masticated the hunk of meat, waiting in vain for an answer. "Only one in a thousand makes it into Fedayeen, and only one in a thousand of *those* completes shadow warrior training. That's *so*, isn't it?"

"Something like that."

"I just want him to come home in one piece," said Colarusso.

"Anthony Junior is hardcore."

"Too damned hardcore. That attitude can get you killed."

"Being a coward can get you killed too," said Rakkim.

A black cop and a white cop leaned against the bar, bellowing along to Sam Cooke, slurring the words to "You Send Me," until Father Alberto poked his head out of the kitchen and told them to shut the fuck up.

Colarusso looked into his cup of wine. "I worry about him."

"So do I." Rakkim hesitated. "Anthony Junior impressed a lot of people during the recent action in Alaska. Conspicuous gallantry, from what I've been told. General Kidd himself selected him to lead a forward strike team."

Colarusso glared at him.

"Leading a strike team is an honor," said Rakkim. "You should be proud of him."

"Fedayeen exist to serve and die, right? Heaven awaits and seventy virgins feeding you cherries and pomegranates, right?" Colarusso banged the cup on the table, sloshed wine across his fingers. "I don't believe that horseshit for a moment. Do *you* believe it?"

Rakkim noted the tracery of broken blood vessels in Colarusso's nose and cheeks.

"I asked you a question, Rakkim."

"I believe we have to act as if God is watching. As if God cares," Rakkim said softly. "I believe we have to act as if Paradise awaits the good and the brave, and that the hottest fires of hell await those who do evil in God's name."

"That's your answer? That's the best you got for me?" Colarusso shook his head. "Anthony Junior . . . he's good, isn't he?"

"Very good."

"His mother lights candles for him at St. Mark's every day. Me, I do a lap around the beads before I go to sleep."

"Can't hurt."

"What do you know about it?"

"Same as you. Nothing."

The two of them clinked glasses. Colarusso drained his wine as Rakkim finished his. "You're a poor excuse for a Muslim."

"It's the friends I keep," said Rakkim.

Colarusso watched him. "So what's bothering you?" He narrowed his eyes, the stony look that had elicited a thousand confessions. "What did you want to talk to me about?"

"I need a favor."

"Most times people ask me for favors, they got parking tickets they want taken care of. Or the name of a good attorney who takes time payments." Colarusso ran a hunk of bread around his plate, sopping up sauce. "Something tells me you got a bigger problem."

"I'm going to be gone for a few weeks. Maybe longer." Rakkim watched two vice cops from the waterfront district passing around the latest holographic porn, the air shimmering and pink around them. "I want you to look after Sarah and Michael."

Colarusso chewed with his mouth open. "Where you going?"

"Away."

"You've gone *away* other times. You never asked me to look after Sarah and the boy before. What's different this time?"

"I asked for a favor," said Rakkim. "Not an interrogation."

"If this was an interrogation, believe me, you'd know it." Colarusso wiped his lips with his napkin, crumpled it. "'Course I'll take care of Sarah and the brat. Just don't make me have to. I changed enough diapers to—" He pressed a finger against his ear canal. Listening to the police command alert. He looked at Rakkim. Relieved. "Al-Faisal's gone to the happy hunting ground."

"What does that mean?"

"Means he blew himself up just as State Security was about to arrest him. Hamburger all *over* the highway."

"Stranglers don't die so easily," said Rakkim. "Make sure it's him. Don't take State Security's word for it."

"Don't tell me how to do my job, troop."

Rakkim leaned closer. Close enough that Colarusso backed off slightly. "Anthony . . . make *sure*."

CHAPTER 8

Massakar, the Old One's chief physician, started to help him up from the recovery table, but the Old One waved him back. He felt better after his rejuvenation treatment than he had in weeks, his blood cleansed of impurities, his system restored to its natural vigor by the technicians and their miraculous machines, may Allah be praised. The ocean liner's mighty engines throbbed under his bare feet, the captain running the *Star of the Sea* full speed at the Old One's command. The few passengers who questioned the staff were easily mollified, given tales of tsunamis and rogue waves. In a few days, when the captain told them that there'd been a change in the itinerary, the passengers would merely nod, return to grazing over the buffet, confident that their best interests were the captain's highest priority. Sheep fit only for slaughter.

The Old One thought of Tariq al-Faisal and how close they had come to disaster, wondered again if Allah was testing him with misfortune. He longed for the day when he did not have to work through intermediaries, when he could act directly, without need of cat's-paws. That day was not here, he groused, not yet. He unsnapped his white cotton surgical gown, let it fall to his feet, standing there naked. He gazed at his reflection without shame, his mood brightening again—he still had the bony shanks of an elderly man, but his muscles tingled, his face radiant.

A young nurse bent to retrieve the gown and the Old One felt inspired by the perfectly straight part in her long, black hair, his newly refreshed eyes aware of every glossy hair on her head. She stood up, clutching his still-warm gown to her chest, saw him watching, and lowered her eyes.

"What is your name, child?"

"Alisha, my lord."

The Old One nodded, noting the grace with which she moved.

Women were a blessing from God and the Old One had been blessed beyond all expectation.

He had dressed by the time Massakar approached him again, deferential, head inclined. The Old One had often heard the chief medical officer berate the younger doctors, cursing them for their stupidity and slowness, even saw him once twist the ear of a new endocrinologist so hard that the man wept. First in his class from Harvard Medical and Bombay Neuro-Science Institute, board-certified in five specialties, Massakar had been the Old One's personal physician for almost forty years, but he was starting to slow down. No one but the Old One would have noticed it, but the man's eyes had lost a shade of brilliance, and his cuticles were rough.

Massakar bowed. "Your hormone levels and test results remain strong, Mahdi. All organs operating within anticipated parameters." He stroked his short, gray beard. "Although within a year or so we'll want to consider kidney replacement, just as a precaution. While we're in there, we might as well swap out your adrenals—"

"Fine." The Old One patted him gently on the shoulder, felt the man flinch. "I want you to bring Castle and Gleason up to speed with all your procedures and drug regimens. I'll decide which one will replace you after we consult on the matter."

Tears gathered in the corners of Massakar's eyes. "Have I . . . have I displeased you, Grandfather?"

The Old One smiled at him. "No, little soldier," he said, using the term of endearment he hadn't spoken since Massakar was seven years old. "You have served me honorably and well. I find no fault in you, but time is not the friend of flesh."

Massakar hung his head. A tear dropped onto the toe of his frost-white shoes.

The irony of the Old One's statement was not lost on either of them. Massakar's age had finally caught up with him, but the Old One stayed forever young . . . well, not *young*, there were limits to even the best technology, and the Old One's unique favor in the eyes of Allah merely slowed the wheel of time. Still, while Massakar carried the faint whiff of mortality, the Old One, over sixty years his senior, was infused with a clarity and vitality the younger man could not even imagine.

The Old One kissed Massakar on the forehead and his grandson trembled before him, before backing away. The Old One allowed himself a small sigh, a trace of regret for all those who had passed before him, comrades and lovers, sons and grandsons and great-grandsons, all of them taking their leave while the Old One remained. Surrounded by his most loyal devotees, the Old One was utterly and completely alone. He remembered Massakar's mother . . . she had been a great beauty, an Indonesian princess with eyes dark as obsidian, and an ass as firm as a ballerina's. He could still hear her cries of passion, still see the perfect roundness of her belly . . . but he could no longer remember her face. Nothing. The Old One shook his head at the lapse. There had been so many wives, so many concubines . . . a caravan of lust swaying past, almost out of sight now. Annoyed at this sudden melancholy, he took the elevator to his bedchamber and summoned Alisha.

Alisha, the young nurse, was everything he had hoped for—shy at first, honored and embarrassed by his attraction to her, but the Old One was, if nothing else, experienced. Wise in the ways of the flesh, he drew her out, quieted her fears until she moistened under his caresses, her pleasure sweet as honey, her nipples stiffening to bursting as he kissed her. Awakening the tiger. And what a wild creature she was once roused, wrapping her hot thighs around him, gasping as he drove himself deeper into her, biting his shoulders, urging him on, wild-eyed, wanton, and free as life itself. She was no virgin, but the Old One had long since tired of virgins. The Quran's promise of seventy virgins in Paradise might induce goatherds and students to martyrdom, but not the Old One.

He rolled her over and took her from behind, pulling back on her shoulders, her skin slick with sweat as he hammered into her, riding her hard. She bucked against him, and the sound of her rapid breathing took him back to his youth, hands wrapped in the mane of a fast horse, clinging to the beast as they raced across the hard earth, hooves pounding out sparks. He groaned with memory, released his past inside her as she pressed back against him, the two of them lost in a molten flood. He sank down beside her, his bones turned to porridge, closed his eyes, his heart so loud it drowned out everything else. She curled against him, already dozing in his great, soft bed, peaceful as a child, her small brown breasts riding high as he breathed against the back of her neck. Ah, youth . . .

When he regained himself, the Old One gently disengaged from her, slipped on a robe, and knotted it loosely around his waist. He glanced back at the bed, then walked to the window and looked through the one-way glass onto the main ballroom below.

A black-and-white promenade twisted and turned, touching at their outstretched fingertips, dressed in only those two colors, interlocked, shifting with every step, dizzying from this perspective. The Old One didn't turn away, lost in the sight . . . he might as well have been looking through a telescope or a microscope for all the emotional impact it had on him. Today meant nothing; there was only yesterday and tomorrow.

Ibrahim, his son, his aide-de-camp, had counseled a change in strategy after they were forced to flee Las Vegas. *Your caliphate need not be centered in America, Father. They are weak Muslims at best, their lands and treasure nibbled away by heathens. Better we start in Western Europe or the holy cities of the Middle East, even Nigeria would be preferable.*

The Old One placed his palms on the thick glass, towering above the moving black-and-white jigsaw below, invisible as a promise. Ibrahim was wrong, of course, his suggestion as shortsighted as the rest of humanity. The Old One knew better. America was the *key*, not the perverse satraps of the Middle East and Western Europe: their false Islam was as contemptible as the God of Israel. America was still young and flexible, easily driven toward the truth if the hand holding the whip was strong enough, diligent enough in its application. President Kingsley's limp leadership, his *moderation*, had wasted an opportunity to create a new caliphate, settling instead for a tepid theocracy. The Old One would rouse them from their lethargy soon enough. First the Islamic Republic would fall to his perfect Islam, then the Belt would hear the trumpet, see the sword raised high—convert or die, that was the only choice he offered. The Americans had been the most dynamic people in the world once; they would be so again, even greater than before, under the harsh guidance of the Old One. The rest of the world would follow.

The dancers bowed to each other, slowly returned to the edges of the ballroom, catching their breath as the *Star of the Seas* plowed ever closer to the Old One's destination. He walked to the window overlooking the ocean, bored with the dancers and their petty movements, mechanical and ignorant as cicadas.

Alisha stirred, and he turned, watched her burrow deeper under the coolness of the satin sheets, lips parted, her hair spread out across the pillow, somehow even more wanton in her innocence. The temptations of this world were as vast as the delights of Paradise.

He turned back to the window, the hood of his robe framing his long, angular face. The ocean always gave him strength, its enormity and ever-changing aspect reminding him of the infinite power of Allah, his nature only glimpsed through his handiwork. There had been times in his youth when the Old One doubted that he had been chosen among all others to carry on God's grand design, when he questioned whether his visions were arrogance or madness. He no longer had doubts. No more doubts about his role in Allah's plan . . . but there were still times when he wondered if he would be able to achieve that which God had chosen him for. It wouldn't be God's failing, it would be the Old One's. He watched the dark clouds along the horizon.

Sun streamed through a sudden break in the clouds, gleamed on a speck in the distance, a glistening, massive chunk of blue-white ice broken off an Antarctic glacier. He squinted . . . could barely make out a fleet of tugboats around the ice, probably towing it to Malaysia or Australia. Or Chile, perhaps. The world was thirsty and fresh water scarce. Glacier harvesting and desalinization plants could barely keep up with demand as it was, and someday soon water would become more precious than oil. Then wouldn't those Saudi apostates, those languid Arab petro-ticks scream in their palaces by the sea? Pleased at the thought, the Old One watched the massive iceberg until it moved out of sight and he was forced to think of other things.

He looked down at the thin blue veins running along the backs of his hands. The deep creases in his palms. Allah used time to grow the Old One, to train him, to harden him for the struggle, but so much time had passed. Even he grew weary. Not now . . . not after his treatment, his blood cleansed, his cells rejuvenated. A glance back to the bed, Alisha's hip a soft mound under the sheets, and the Old One felt himself stirred again. No . . . best not to waste his reborn vitality, there were other, more pressing needs. His body felt no weariness now, but there were other signs, indications of a fatigue that no amount of medical procedures could cure. His priorities were clear.

The plan, the game, the Old One's grand design, encompassed hundreds of men across the globe, thousands even, men in all walks of life, commoners and kings, men who did his bidding without even knowing they were in his employ, or, rarest of all, men like Rakkim Epps, surprising adversaries whose challenge to him only furthered the Old One's ambitions. An intricate skein of men and money spread out across time and space, decades of planning, minute shifts in the political landscape, everything designed for a single moment when it would all fall into place.

The Old One saw his reflection in the window, thought of all the faces that had passed before him, the mighty and the seemingly insignificant, all useful tools in proper hands. Sowing seeds, the Old One called it, thousands of seeds spread across the globe, quietly sprouting in the cracks and gutters, waiting to be harvested. A West Point graduate with an ailing sister, a liberal Muslim whose daughter was engaged to an air-traffic controller, a low-level accountant in the Brazilian Budget Office who needed an excuse for his lack of success, a Russian television executive with a taste for young boys . . . weeds and flowers blowing in the wind of time.

He stared into his own eyes and remembered the droopy right eyelid and coarse black hair of Kamal Hakimov, a Tajik tailor he had met just once sixty-five years ago, saw him lying in a medical tent outside Quetta, half his beard burned away from the blast of a Russian mortar. Through his spies, the Old One helped Kamal immigrate to Hamburg, loaned him the money to open a shop. Years later, Kamal befriended Mohamed Atta, an acolyte of Osama bin Laden's, taking him into his home and his mosque. Atta was an idiot, and bin Laden a pampered Saudi dilettante — it had been the Old One who fine-tuned bin Laden's clumsy plan, intercepting the Saudi's communiqués, using Kamal as his go-between. When Atta asked Kamal to make a martyrdom garment, the Old One flew to his house outside Paris and waited — after shorting the American stock market through his proxies. By the afternoon of 9/11, the U.S. economy was staggering, bin Laden was scurrying for cover, and the Old One had made approximately $23 billion. The invasion of Iraq two years later was a bonus.

The U.S. military won every battle, but they had no voice, no message that could be heard. The Old One's servants monitored every TV station and never saw a hero, only the dead. A war without heroes, without victories. Only petty atrocities inflated for all the world to see, clucked over by millionaire news anchors and fatuous movie stars. Their president himself apologized. *We must show that we are more humane than the terrorists,* he said. As though the wolf should apologize for having sharper teeth than the rabbit. Good fortune beyond the Old One's wildest dreams, an enemy who wanted to be loved. Be ashamed of the war and soon you will be ashamed of the warriors—the warriors got that message soon enough. Just as blowing the levees in New Orleans broke the bond between the government and the people, the Iraq debacle broke the nation's spirit, hobbled its ability to defend itself. The former regime never recovered. Those on the Old One's payroll, knowingly or unknowingly, made certain of that.

Alisha called to him from bed, her voice thick and sleepy, but he ignored her, thinking again of his strangler, Tariq al-Faisal, and how close they had come to failure at this most crucial time. A simple pickup, risky to be sure, but . . . Instead al-Faisal had been intercepted, the electronic device almost lost, this whole phase jeopardized. The Old One rubbed his fingertips. The device was safe. The plan intact. Still, he found himself curious about the man who had killed al-Faisal's two Fedayeen bodyguards. Two of his best, al-Faisal had insisted, yet the man had killed them easily. One man. Darwin could have done it in the blink of an eye. So could the man who had killed him, whoever he was. The Old One made a mental note to send word to his agents in Seattle to use all available resources to locate Rakkim or that bitch Sarah. Full surveillance, every informer and covert sympathizer activated. No excuses. Rakkim and the woman were probably not involved in the near intercept of al-Faisal, but the Old One was not going to risk underestimating either of them ever again. Not *now*.

The Old One watched a seagull buffeted by the rising wind, the bird hanging in space directly in front of the window, all its efforts failing to move it forward . . . and the gull slowly, ever so slowly fell behind until it disappeared from view. The Old One felt an ache in his belly, a terrible void, worse than hunger.

There were moments now . . . moments when the plan was too vast, when he lost the tread of the skein for an instant, the faces blurring, connections blurring, before he regained his focus. The duration of his confusion was irrelevant; it was the confusion itself that kept him awake at night. Those lost moments seemed to be occurring more often lately. More than once, the Old One had fallen to his knees, prostrated himself, begging Allah for a little more time to fulfill his divine mission, just a few more years to bend the world to a true and perfect Islam. Many times over the long years the Old One had heard the voice of God, heard it more clearly than the beating of his own heart, but lately . . . Allah had remained silent. Silent as a stone. Time was running short, that much the Old One was certain of. Even for him.

The Old One placed his hands on his hips, faced the gathering storm. Let it come. Let it huff and puff and blow his house down. He didn't blame Allah for his silence. God had been patient enough. So had the Old One.

CHAPTER 9

"Are you listening?" said Sarah. "This is important."

Rakkim played with Michael, holding an index finger in front of the wobbling toddler, pulling it back as the boy grabbed for it. Michael, one of the four archangels, captain of the heavenly host, the angel most beloved of Allah, but this Michael was a chubby infant, not quite two, with his mother's eyes, dark and bright, his gaze steady. He almost fell over, then one hand darted out and pinched Rakkim's finger. Michael squeezed, delighted, and Rakkim kissed his shaggy curls. Michael might have his mother's eyes but he had his father's quick reflexes. Maybe even his guile. Rakkim still wasn't sure if the boy had really almost lost his balance or was just distracting him. It worked, whatever the cause. Michael clapped his hands, wanting to play again.

"*Rakkim?*"

"The Colonel has become more aggressive in the last two or three years," repeated Rakkim, watching Michael as the boy watched them, head cocked. "He's expanding his territory, buying weapons, consolidating his support." He lightly tapped Michael's nose, retreated. Michael giggled. "Tactically brilliant, generous and popular with the locals, threatening to attack the republic . . ." Another tap on Michael's nose. The boy swatted at Rakkim's hand, missed. ". . . although the anti-Muslim invective may be just a recruiting slogan." He looked at Sarah. "I read the data file General Kidd gave me."

Michael lunged at him, flopped in Rakkim's lap. Rakkim lifted him up, tossed him into the air. Caught him. Michael laughed.

"There's currently a power vacuum in the Belt, one that the Colonel could easily exploit—was that in the file?" said Sarah, as Rakkim continued to throw Michael higher and higher. "Their new president was elected with a minority of votes. He's a smart politician, very likeable, but weak and indecisive. There's been talk that his party received massive financial support from the Nigerian Confederation, but no proof. The rumor may have been spread by the Colonel's men for all we know, but . . ." She glared as Rakkim caught Michael by one ankle, the two of them flopping back onto the bed, Rakkim covering his eyes, pretending to cower as Michael launched an attack. "Do you mind?"

"What are you so mad about?" said Rakkim.

"I want you to be prepared."

"I *am* prepared." Rakkim carefully set Michael down on the floor, reached for her. "As prepared as I can be. Sarah . . . all the reports and rumors and projections aren't going to help. They're after-the-fact assessments, outdated five minutes later or dependent on the skill of whoever gathered the information. The only way I can find out what it's really like in the Belt is to go there and sit around talking with strangers, making conversation, listening to what they argue about, what they laugh at. You want me to have a plan in place, some guidebook . . . that's not going to happen."

"You need a plan or—"

"The other shadow warriors sent in, they had a plan, and it got them killed." Rakkim took her hands, pressed them against his heart as tears gathered in her eyes. "I'm going to slip into the Belt, Sarah. I'm going to make my way to where the Colonel is digging up the mountain and I'm going to stop him. Whatever it takes, I'm going to stop him. Then I'm going to come home."

Sarah put on a brave front, but one eye overflowed.

"I know what I'm doing."

She let it lay, watching Michael as he walked hesitantly around the room. "Is General Kidd offering transport?"

"I don't want his help. There may be a mole in the Fedayeen high command."

She stared at him and he could see the effort it took her to stay calm. "I see."

He shrugged. "I also think it was a mistake sending the shadow warrior teams in from the north and the west."

"It's the shortest route," said Sarah. "The most direct and we were in a hurry. We're *still* in a hurry."

"People in a hurry get noticed."

Sarah started to speak. Stopped. Keyed the remote on her earlobe. "Spider's here."

Rakkim didn't ask why. He'd find out soon enough.

The main wallscreen crackled. A car pulled into the armored garage, waited until the blast door closed. Infrared screens showed the outside streets buckled down for the night. No movement. No extraneous electronic activity. Safe. Spider got out of the car, waved to the camera. Someone got out of the passenger side. Big guy . . . no, it was a kid, a soft, doughy teenager wearing khaki trousers that nipped at his ankles and a baggy brown sweater. He didn't wave. Just stood there with a sullen expression while pulling at the seat of his pants.

"Who's Humpty-Dumpty?"

"His name is Leo." Sarah unlocked the door to the house. "He's one of Spider's sons."

"Are they here to brief me too?" He saw her glance away. "What is it?"

"I . . . I wanted to tell you before they showed up," said Sarah. "I'm sorry." Onscreen, Spider and Leo stood in the elevator as it rose rapidly toward the living level. Leo looked like he was going to throw up. "Leo . . . Leo's going with you to the Belt."

Rakkim laughed. "You've *got* to be fucking kidding me."

"Direct order from the president."

"When?" said Rakkim. "*When* did the president issue the order?"

Sarah straightened. "Earlier today. Just . . . just a few hours ago."

"Just a few hours?" he said. "Why not just a few minutes?"

Michael started crying, looking from one of them to the other.

Sarah hurried over to the baby, picked him up. "There had been some talk earlier, but Spider . . . he wasn't sure about sending the boy into the Belt."

"This sudden change of plans sounds like something Redbeard would have pulled," said Rakkim. "Measuring out the mission in teaspoons, not giving me a chance to reject it outright until I'm in too deep."

"I wouldn't do that to you."

He saw the hurt in her eyes, but he didn't back off.

She rocked Michael in her arms, quieting him. "I *wouldn't*, Rikki."

"Anything else you haven't told me? Any other last-minute additions to the mission? Should I pick up a case of Moon Pies and a carton of Marlboros while I'm there? How about a few souvenirs from Graceland? Maybe one of those pillows that sings 'Love Me Tender' when you lay your head down?"

Sarah's eyes flashed. "That won't be necessary."

"You sure? Long as I'm lugging around a civilian, I might as well make myself useful."

"Leo's not just a civilian," said Sarah. "He's smart—"

"All Spider's kids are smart."

"Not like Leo. He's a genius, a true Brainiac. Spider says he's smarter than any of them . . . except for the seven-year-old, Amanda, but she's—"

"Amanda is *not* smarter than—" Leo stood in the doorway to the bedroom, suddenly aware of the blade of Rakkim's knife a millimeter from his jugular. He blinked, a tall, pale, soft-bodied youth with a large head and wispy, dirty-blond hair plastered across his skull.

"Rakkim?" said Spider, hovering nearby. "I . . . I thought we were expected. Please?"

Leo licked his fleshy lips. "My father grossly overrates the intellectual capacity of my baby sister," he said idly, a single drop of blood running down the blade of the knife. He ignored it. "Amanda came up with a more elegant solution than I did for the Riemann hypothesis and he acts as if she's Stephen Hawking. She merely tweaked the zeta function, which I would have done eventually—"

Rakkim pushed him aside. Looked at Spider. "You want to get him killed? Because that's what sending him to the Belt is going to do."

"Rikki, if there was any other option, I'd keep him here," said Spider, "but the truth of the matter is, you need each other."

Rakkim laughed. "What do I need him for?"

"To tell you what's buried in the mountain," said Sarah. "To tell you if it's a decoy, or a failed experiment, or if it's dangerous and needs to be destroyed."

"What are you trying to convince him for?" Leo sniffed, wiped his nose. "*I'm* the key man here. He's just the . . . the travel agent." He sniffed again. "You need to adjust the humidity in here. I've got allergies."

"Leo," soothed Spider, "please, shut up."

"He's got allergies, but no training," said Rakkim. "He's got a face that begs to be slapped, but no useful skills. No survival instincts. First time he opens his mouth in the Belt or doesn't hold his utensils right, we're going to draw attention. *Then* what? How am I supposed to explain him?"

"You'll think of something," said Sarah, rocking Michael in her arms. "You always do."

"Leo's physical attributes may not be impressive, but he stood up well during the hard times when the Black Robes searched for us," said Spider. "He saved the family more than once. He complains, but he doesn't break. And Rikki"—his voice softened—"he really is *very* smart."

"Look, Mr. *Fedayeen*, traipsing around Holy Joe-ville wasn't my idea," said Leo. "Personally, I'd rather be studying plasma physics and let you idiots fight each other until there's nobody left." He blew his nose, shoved his handkerchief into his back pocket.

Rakkim turned to Sarah. "You're right. I have thought of a way to keep Humpty-Dumpty from taking a great fall." He smiled at Leo. "This is going to be fun."

CHAPTER 10

How long are you going to stay mad at me, Rikki?

I don't like being blindsided.

I didn't have a choice, said Sarah. *And neither do you.*

Rakkim turned at the sound of Leo vomiting over the side of the small fishing boat, hanging on to the railing with his chubby fingers as he upended his gullet for the tenth time in the last two hours. There hadn't been anything left for the last forty-five minutes but he kept trying. Rakkim half expected the kid to hurl his intestines into the Gulf.

Leo looked over at Rakkim, the kid still bent over, clothes soaked from the salt spray. Snot ran from his nose, glistened along his chin like an iridescent beard. "You're enjoying this, aren't you? I can feel your brain stem twitching with glee."

"I told you to take Dramamine."

"I'm allergic to it."

"Anything you're *not* allergic to?"

Leo started to respond, grimaced, and lurched over the rail.

"That *pendejo* never been on a boat before?" said Vasquez, captain of the *Esmeralda*, bare-chested, his stringy hair billowing around his grease-stained cap.

"Kid must have had a bad tamale back in Rio Concho," said Rakkim.

"You should choose your companions more carefully, amigo. A strong man tied to a weak man . . . when there is trouble, the strong man's strength counts for nothing."

Rakkim turned his face into the wind. "I don't see any trouble."

Vasquez spit, perfectly timing the wind to carry his burst of tobacco juice away.

Rakkim walked past the wheelhouse. Took a position forward. Bumpier near the bow but he liked watching their progress and catching the full force of the wind. Still no sight of land. He felt the *Esmeralda*'s engine underfoot. Heard the two mates, Hector and Luis, banging around belowdecks. The *Esmeralda* was in even worse shape than ten years ago, when Vasquez had delivered him to Santabel Island in a squall, lightning crackling all around them. Best way to avoid the Belt patrol boats. Vasquez thought he was a smuggler then, thought he was a smuggler now. He told Vasquez that Leo was a diamond cutter, a freelancer on his way to an unnamed client in Atlanta. A lot of the fishermen supplemented their meager income ferrying human contraband in and out of the Belt.

You would have thought the warming of the Gulf of Mexico would have made life easier for independent fishermen like Vasquez, that the waters would be teeming with even more fish than ever. Not so. Global warming had turned the Gulf into a cauldron of sudden storms and a hurricane season lasting six months and rising. Small boats like the *Esmeralda* were forced to remain idle half the year, and the central government of Aztlán, which now claimed most of the Gulf, awarded contracts to massive commercial trawlers who could better handle the storms, and whose miles-long nets swept the waters bare.

Rakkim glanced at the salt-pitted glass of the wheelhouse, then back to the sea. The boat groaned, engine sputtering briefly before kicking in. The best piece of equipment on the *Esmeralda* was a sophisticated new radio/sonar unit. Vasquez said he had spent three months' wages on it, hoping the sonar would allow him to compete with the factory ships in the search for fish. Rakkim checked the stern, saw the kid slumped on the deck, holding his head in his hands. Pathetic. Thanks, Sarah. He tried to remember the last argument with her that he had won.

Did the other teams have a Brainiac along for the ride? Rakkim asked. *Did Spider already lose one of his kids?*

No, Sarah said. *This is the first time he's risked one of his children.*

We're at that point, are we?

We're that desperate, yes, said Sarah.

Desperate enough that you think I need help? Rakkim shook his head. *I don't need Leo to evaluate this weapons system. I could just blow the fucker up. Problem solved. But you don't really want me to hotshot it, do you? You want me to bring the weapon back. That's why the kid's tagging along. So he can tell me if it's worth the effort.*

No . . . bringing it back wouldn't be practical, Sarah said softly. She reached for him but he didn't respond. *You're not supposed to know about this, Rikki. No one is.*

Rakkim waited.

It's not the system per se that's important, Sarah said finally. *It's the science behind it. The schematics. The theoretical leaps the former regime did so well. Leo can evaluate the data, but there's more. Much more.* She moistened her lips. *Leo . . . he's been modified.*

Leo inched his way toward Rakkim from the stern, bent forward slightly, hanging on to the railing for support. The rain gear that Vasquez had loaned him was ridiculously small. He flopped beside Rakkim, tucked in his chin as the storm broke, sheets of warm rain slanting across them. The full force wasn't supposed to hit until tomorrow morning. So much for satellite imaging.

"Is there some *rational* reason why you're standing here and not inside the cabin?" shouted Leo, voice cracking. "Are you even capable of forming a rational judgment?"

"Just working on my tan." Rakkim spread his arms, knees bent, swaying with the rolling of the boat, eyes half closed in the warm rain. "Why don't you go inside? Vasquez makes good coffee."

Leo shook his head. Looked even younger somehow. "They don't like me."

Rakkim noticed a slight change in the engine vibration, started toward the wheelhouse as Leo called after him.

Vasquez turned away from the wheel as Rakkim reached the top of the ladder. Hector, the first mate, slouched in the corner, rain dripping off him as he sucked on a bottle of beer.

"You're turning northeast," said Rakkim. "We at the cutoff point already?"

Vasquez grinned silvery teeth as he cut the running lights. "You have radar too, amigo?"

Rakkim's itinerary called for Vasquez to take them due east from his village of Laguna Madre, then cut toward the Texas coast and drop them off outside Nuevo Galveston in a small inflatable raft.

"Change of plans," said Rakkim. "Drop us off just south of Corpus Christi."

Vasquez peered through the windscreen as the boat shuddered and groaned. "Corpus?" He narrowed his eyes. "Bad idea. Very dangerous currents. Rocks and sandbars—"

"Bery, *bery* dangerous," echoed Hector.

"I'll take the chance," said Rakkim.

"Hey!" Leo called up from the deck. "I don't like being left alone out here."

"We clear, Alejandro?" said Rakkim.

"Gone cost you another five hundred," said Vasquez.

"Fine." Rakkim slid down the railing of the ladder, landed with a splash on the deck. He silenced Leo with a raised finger, scrambled silently back up the ladder. Stopped just below the wheelhouse, listening as the wind howled around him.

"*Cambio de planes,*" Vasquez muttered, giving news of the change of plans to his people onshore, bounty hunters or worse. "*Cerdo americano—*"

Rakkim launched himself up the last couple of rungs, slammed Vasquez's head against the wheel. The radiophone fell to the floor as the captain slumped against the com. Rakkim heard the sound of a shotgun being racked, and grabbed the dazed Vasquez.

"Please, *señor,*" said Hector, pointing the barrel of a sawed-off pump at Rakkim. "Be so kind as to move aside."

Rakkim held Vasquez closer. A friendly embrace.

"*Señor.*" Hector's eyes were the color of mop water. "*Por favor.*"

Vasquez struggled but Rakkim held him tight. With no one at the wheel, the *Esmeralda* lurched through the waves, rolling from one side to the other.

"Rakkim?" called Leo.

Hector's gaze didn't waver at the interruption. He raised the sawed-off slightly, considering a head shot.

Rakkim pushed Vasquez aside, kicked the shotgun as Hector fired. Splinters from the roof of the wheelhouse drifted down. Ears ringing, Rakkim grabbed the sawed-off, clubbed Hector over the head with it.

"What blew up?" shouted Leo. "Are we on fire?"

"Go sit down, kid." Rakkim watched Hector fall to the floor, then grabbed Vasquez, pushed him against the wheel. He jabbed the sawed-off against the back of the captain's fat neck. Hector's blood dripped off the barrel. "North by northwest, *verdad?*"

A knot the size of a robin's egg had formed on Vasquez's forehead. He blinked as he stood at the wheel, knees shaking.

"*Verdad?*" repeated Rakkim.

"*Verdad.*"

"*Capitán!*" Luis's voice crackled over the intercom. "*Qué pasa?*"

"*Nada,*" said Vasquez. "*Nada, vato.*" He switched off the intercom.

"You're a disappointment, Alejandro," said Rakkim, quickly binding Hector's wrists and ankles.

"Please, don't kill me," said Vasquez. "Business . . . this is what the business has become." He breathed heavily, as though he had run a long race and was nearing the finish line. "The Texas Rangers pay hard money for illegals, and my boat needs work . . . so much work. What is a man to do?"

"A man's supposed to abide by his word, motherfucker," said Rakkim.

For the next hour Vasquez steered the boat as best he could, the storm gaining strength behind them while Luis kept busy coaxing the engine back to life. Once Leo poked his head up, saw the situation, and scuttled back below. The *Esmeralda* rode high on the peaks of the waves, then crashed down into the troughs, repeating the process over and over. Hector lay hog-tied in the corner, blood crusting his face. He rolled from side to side as the boat skidded over the waves, watching Rakkim with fiery eyes. The radiophone blinked constantly with incoming calls that Rakkim didn't answer.

The boat listed hard to port, timbers groaning as the bottom scraped along a sandbar. Water poured over the gunwales before Vasquez righted it. The captain threw the *Esmeralda* into reverse, the engines smoking as he finally broke free. "*Señor,* we get stuck here, the storm will tear us to pieces!"

Rakkim could see the lights of Corpus Christi in the distance. Close enough. "Tell Luis to ready the inflatable."

Vasquez did as he was told.

Rakkim pointed the sawed-off at the radio/sonar unit, stopped when he saw the agonized look on Vasquez's face. Had the man begged, made excuses, Rakkim would have blasted it apart. As it was . . . his pained silence was more persuasive. Rakkim opened the unit up with his knife, cut through the wiring harness, and slit the motherboard. The system could be easily fixed when Vasquez returned to Laguna Madre, but he wouldn't be able to communicate with anyone until then.

"G-gracias," whispered Vasquez.

Hector spit on Rakkim's boots. *"Puto!"*

Rakkim tossed the sawed-off over the side and slid down onto the deck. Slung his small, waterproof sack across one shoulder. He saw Luis and Leo struggling to keep the inflatable from sailing into the wind, the two of them drenched and frightened. The wind made it impossible to talk, so Rakkim simply pushed Leo onto the raft and launched it over the side. They hit the water hard, skidding over the surface, the inflatable tumbling end over end. Twice Rakkim had to grab Leo to prevent him being pulled under, the kid gasping and screaming, swallowing water. It was no big deal. Just a matter of hanging on until the wind and waves drove them to shore. You just had to keep your mouth shut and remember to breathe. Which seemed to be more than Leo could manage. Rakkim hooked one arm around the kid, kept a grip on the inflatable with the other, and let Mother Nature take care of the rest.

Ten minutes later Rakkim felt sand underfoot and let the inflatable go, dragging Leo to shore. Leo was unable to walk, kept coughing up seawater, doubled over. Rakkim slung him over one shoulder and walked higher onto the dunes. Dropped him off behind a huge chunk of driftwood, the flotsam providing some shelter from the wind.

"I almost *drowned*," sputtered Leo.

"You didn't." Rakkim walked back toward the water and stood there, catching the full force of the storm, smiling as he struggled to stay on his feet. Sand stung his face, burned his eyes, and his clothes flapped around him so hard it hurt, but he didn't care. He was back in the Belt.

Leo crawled over on his hands and knees. "We got to get out of here!"

Rakkim pulled Leo to his feet. "Spread your arms out," shouted Rakkim, leaning forward into the wind, searching for the balance point. "There . . . right there." He leaned at a forty-five-degree angle, held in place by the wind.

Leo hesitated, tried it. Almost was blown backward . . . tried it again. And again. Until he succeeded.

The two of them stayed there, a couple of scarecrows on the shore, hair beating against their faces. Leo howled into the wind, still nervous, but laughing at his own distorted voice. Probably figuring vectors and parabolas at the same time, trying to decide what scientific journal was worthy of his research.

Rakkim reveled in the power of the storm. In the distance he could see the *Esmeralda* chugging toward the open sea. Vasquez had left his running lights off, but Rakkim's night vision had been amped up, just like the rest of him. Vasquez pressed on, trying to avoid running directly into the storm, wisely choosing an oblique path back south into more familiar waters. Making good progress too, the boat a dim speck among the high waves. Rakkim waved, though no one on the boat could see him, even if they were looking. *Vaya con Dios, Alejandro.*

Vasquez's plan worked fine until the boat ran aground. Like the captain had said, with all the hurricanes, the seabed changed from month to month, sandbars appearing and disappearing overnight. A fisherman needed sonar and a marine echo-location system to know where he was going, and Rakkim had taken care of that. He hadn't meant to sink the boat. He just wanted to make sure that Vasquez didn't alert his contacts on the mainland. Not that Rakkim's intentions mattered now.

Leo kept laughing, arms outstretched, unaware of what was going on around him.

Rakkim saw the boat shudder as the waves boiled around it. He couldn't hear the engine, but knew Vasquez was trying to rock it free—full-throttle forward, then reverse. It wasn't working. The boat seesawed, seemed to be suspended for a moment, then a forty-foot wave crashed down, buried it under tons of water. Rakkim waited. Waited . . . When the waves rolled away, the *Esmeralda* was gone. Torn apart or sucked under and out to sea. Rakkim wondered if Hector had had time to curse him again before he died. Wondered if Luis had died in the engine compartment, down in the dark, trying to coax a little more power out of the ancient diesel. In a week or two Vasquez's captain's cap might wash ashore someplace. Maybe some little girl would pick it up, put it on her head, the oversize hat falling around her ears while she capered on the sand. Until her parents told her to take the filthy thing off. No telling what she might catch just by touching it.

"What is it?" said Leo, squinting. "What are you looking at?"

"Nothing."

"You look upset." Leo sniffed, hitched up his jeans, posing. "This isn't so bad, really." He shivered, watching Rakkim out of the corner of his eye, trying to gauge his reaction. "It's actually . . . kind of fun."

The idiot actually believed he could pass in the Belt with a drawl and a lazy walk. He had no idea. Rakkim stared out to sea. "The fun's just beginning, kid."

CHAPTER 11

Moseby heard Derek fart, groan in his sleep as he rolled over. Moseby waited, listening to Derek and Chase snoring softly on either side of him in the tiny mining shack. Even sleeping they clutched their weapons, locally made assault rifles with speed clips and top-of-the-line Chinese night-vision scopes. The two young hillbillies were still better company than Gravenholtz and the raiders who had packed the Chinese helicopter on the five-hour flight from New Orleans to the Smoky Mountains of Tennessee. The raiders were foul-mouthed drunks who delighted in shooting cattle while the chopper skimmed along at two hundred miles an hour, laughing as the locals dove for cover. Gravenholtz paid his men no attention, watching Moseby the whole way, the red hairs on his arms waving in the draft.

Gravenholtz had assigned Derek and Chase to be his guides around the mountain camp, but they didn't take him anywhere he wanted to go. They were his guards, accompanying him night and day, steering him away from exploring the tunnels honeycombing the mountain. Instead they took him on long walks through the foothills—they shot squirrels with their sidearms gunslinger-style, pelted each other with pinecones, their accents so heavy he could barely understand them at first. Easy duty for them, but Moseby spent the days cataloging the men who roamed the camp, learning their gaits and their speech patterns, memorizing the narrow paths and valleys, making a mental map of the immediate area. He had been invisible before, he would be invisible again.

Three days he had been stuck here waiting for the Colonel to return. Gravenholtz had plucked him from his home, racing back here as though they didn't have a moment to lose. but the Colonel was gone when they arrived, called away to quell some uprising in his rugged domain. Moseby had tried calling Annabelle, but the phone was dead. No signal of any kind on the mountain, took a certain kind of secure phone to call in or out, and access to those was strictly forbidden to all but the select few.

Nothing to do but wait, said Gravenholtz, refusing Moseby's request. *Jeeter will keep your wife and that sweetmeat daughter occupied, you don't have to worry about them being bored without you. Do you good to get away from her anyway. Clean country air and honest work. Might do her some good too.* Gravenholtz's tongue flicked out. *That wife of yours got restless eyes. First time she spied me I thought she was going to suck the clothes right off me. No offense. I just got that effect on the ladies.*

No offense, Moseby had said. Promising himself again that once this was over, he was going to forget Christ's stricture to turn the other cheek. Time enough to ask forgiveness once the redhead had been taught a lesson in manners.

Derek rolled over again, the cot creaking. Pine needles drifted across the corrugated tin roof, the wind rushing past.

Moseby rolled out of bed, rolled out so smoothly that the cot didn't make a sound. He grabbed Derek's camouflage jacket, glided toward the half-open rear window. The first night the two guards had set up a motion detector, but Moseby had taken care of that. Three times that first night he had flicked pebbles onto the floor, setting off the alarm, rousing Derek and Chase while Moseby yawned and asked what was going on. After that third interruption, Derek had turned off the motion detector, kicked it across the shack.

Moseby listened at the window, then hooked his fingers on the top of the frame and pivoted himself out through the narrow opening. He shivered in the cold mountain air, started walking, shoulders hunched, head bent slightly. He missed the warm breeze off the Gulf, the heavy, perfumed air of magnolia and hibiscus. Most of all he missed his wife and daughter. He missed *home.* He sometimes wondered what would have happened if he hadn't met Annabelle on his sixth mission into the Belt. Would he have stayed a shadow warrior, sworn to duty, bound to nothing and no one other than the Fedayeen? All he was certain of was that the moment he met her, there had never been any doubt of what he would do.

Clouds drifted across the crescent moon. It was the time of Salat-ul-Isha, the final prayer of the day. Moseby had converted to Christianity, not just with his mouth, but with his heart—still, even after all these years in the Belt, he wondered if he would ever not hear the call to prayer echo inside his skull five times a day. Ah, well, there were worse things. He nodded at three miners passing a bottle around a campfire, and kept walking. Men were arriving and leaving the mountain every day—miners and soldiers, tradesmen and truckers. No one noticed Moseby.

Violating his Fedayeen oath was a capital crime, but Moseby had willingly taken the risk. It was Annabelle he was worried about. She was considered as guilty as he was. Moseby had covered his tracks well, living quietly, moving every few years . . . until he woke one night with a knife at his throat while Annabelle slept beside him. A young shadow warrior stared down at him in the darkness. Young, but good. Very good. Better than Moseby. Annabelle had moaned in her sleep, turned over, and Moseby had been oddly comforted by her heat, the softness of her skin beside him. He asked the young warrior to kill him quickly, but spare her life. The young warrior hesitated . . . nodded. He had asked the young warrior his name. *Rakkim Epps.* Moseby offered Rakkim his blessing and closed his eyes, waiting to die. A few moments later he opened his eyes, the knife still at his throat. *What is it?* Moseby asked. Rakkim brushed his hand across Moseby's eyes, closed them. Moseby waited for the blade. When he opened his eyes again, Rakkim was gone. Moseby never saw him again.

Moseby heard voices in the distance. Cheering and raucous laughter. He slipped through the trees, heading toward the voices, not making a sound. A ghost. Twice he almost stepped on chipmunks who didn't hear him until the last moment. He wasn't alone in the woods, though, there were other men hurrying in the same direction, loud men charging through the brush, rifles slung over their shoulders as they called out to each other. This was new terrain for Moseby. The trees thinned out, became stony ground. Torches danced atop the next ridge and the sounds were louder now. Moseby moved nimbly over the boulders, leaping from one to the other in his haste, leaving the other men behind.

Small searchlights ringed a deep cleft in the mountain, cast shadows across the natural arena below. Men huddled around burn barrels, drinking and smoking, cheering as they watched the action. Most of them were locals, or soldiers, but there were about a dozen—all of them taking the best spots—with their hair buzzed distinctively short, whitewalls around their ears, hard men. Raiders, that's what Derek had called them, when

Moseby pointed them out. *They's Gravenholtz's boys*, Derek said, voice lowered. *You best not mess with them.* Moseby eased his way through the crowd to get a better look, avoiding the Raiders. The crowd smelled of sweat and coal and sour beer, foul smells, like a dirty copper penny. He stepped back in surprise, then forward again. Gravenholtz was at the bottom of the cleft, but the redhead was too busy to notice Moseby.

Gravenholtz and another man squared off below, both of them bare-chested in the cold air. Gravenholtz's torso was tautly muscled, his skin a pale, freckled fish-belly white. The other man was skinnier, his body covered in bruises, eyes blackened, his dirty-blond hair matted—he moved easily across the rocks in a half-crouch, sidestepping, never taking his eyes off Gravenholtz.

The blond was Fedayeen. A shadow warrior, just like Moseby. No one else moved like that across rough terrain. No one else held their hands just so . . . loose, fingers slightly curled, ready to strike or grasp. Moseby looked pleased. He had no idea how the shadow warrior had been injured, or how many men it had taken to do the job, but one-on-one? Gravenholtz had no idea what he was in for.

Catcalls from the crowd on the rim above, whoops and hollers. The shadow warrior dodged a hurled beer can with a slight turn of his head, not even acknowledging the missile. Gravenholtz closed in, agile himself, more agile than Moseby had suspected, slowly cutting the ring in half.

Gravenholtz threw a punch. The shadow warrior countered, hit him with a solid right just under the heart. Should have shattered Gravenholtz's floating ribs and disabled him, but the redhead just moved in, smiling. A flurry of punches from Gravenholtz. The shadow warrior barely dodged, countered again with a right and a left to no effect. Gravenholtz backed him into a cul-de-sac, but the shadow warrior scampered away. Circled behind him. Launched a roundhouse kick that caught Gravenholtz on the side of the head, sent him sprawling. The shadow warrior rushed in to finish the job, but the redhead was too quick, tripped him, punched him as the shadow warrior scooted away. It was a glancing blow, but the shadow warrior grunted in pain, bit his lips shut.

The crowd whistled. Stamped their feet. One of Gravenholtz's Raiders, a scrawny killer with a broken nose, danced a jig on the rim of the amphitheater, bared his ass to the shadow warrior to a chorus of laughter.

The shadow warrior clutched his side where he had been hit, breathing hard. He moved slightly slower now, and Moseby could see bumps on his rib cage and collarbone where bones had been broken and healed unevenly. Moseby wondered how long the man had been imprisoned here. How many bouts he had fought against the redhead, because clearly they had faced each other before.

Gravenholtz advanced, moving lightly on his feet. His left ear was bleeding from the shadow warrior's kick, but it didn't seem to bother him.

The shadow warrior weaved in the torchlight, made a move that was distinctly Fedayeen—a shoulder feint that was in fact a genuine killing attack, "faking the feint," it was called. Fools the skilled opponent, and the unskilled is dead already, that's what their instructor had taught them. Not tonight. Gravenholtz caught the shadow warrior with an uppercut that sprayed teeth on the rocks.

The shadow warrior backed away, spitting blood. He pressed himself against one wall, seemingly exhausted, only to dodge away at the last moment as Gravenholtz swung again. Gravenholtz's fist hit the wall *hard*, and he whirled around, cursing. It didn't make sense, but Moseby thought it looked like the rock face had cracked under the blow.

The shadow warrior moved in, jerked back, then sweep-kicked Gravenholtz off his feet. He tromped the redhead's ankle, then turned and scrambled up the sheer rock face, faster and faster, pulling himself higher with fingertips and toes, blood running down his chin. It was an amazing feat, even for a shadow warrior, and the crowd fell silent for a minute, then commenced jeering, expecting him to fall at any moment.

The shadow warrior *didn't* fall, but redoubled his efforts while Gravenholtz raged below, beating on the rock walls. As he reached the top of the slope, the Raider with the broken nose pumped the butt of his rifle at the shadow warrior's head. Missed. Missed. Missed. Holding on to an outcropping of rock with one hand, the shadow warrior grabbed the rifle away with the other—he shot the Raider twice in the chest before losing his grip and tumbling back down the ravine. He lay still, one leg twisted under him.

Beer bottles shattered around the shadow warrior, the men on top screaming for the redhead to tear his head off.

Gravenholtz snarled the crowd into silence, then limped across the rocks and stood over the crumpled shadow warrior. The wind howled around them, the flames from the torches sending shadows across the red-head's bare, freckled skin. With his muscled torso and skull tufted with short reddish hair, Gravenholtz looked more like a hyena than a man. He squatted, picked up two of the shadow warrior's teeth, and shook them in his fist. The clicking sound echoed off the rocks. He grinned as he tossed the teeth, snapped his fingers. "Snake eyes!" He scanned the faces along the rim of the arena.

Moseby tucked in his chin, moved out of Gravenholtz's line of sight.

Gravenholtz grabbed the shadow warrior by the back of the neck, held him up for all to see. "He's not dead, don't worry." He beamed as the shadow warrior groaned. "See? Fedayeen are hard to kill. We're going to play with this one for a *long* time."

The crowd cheered.

"Give him a week, he'll be ready again." Gravenholtz tossed the shadow warrior onto the rocks. He wiped his forehead with the back of his hand. Touched his ear and winced. He kicked the shadow warrior, looked up at the rim. "I'm thirsty. Which one of you peckerwoods wants to buy me a drink?"

The crowd *roared*.

Moseby joined the throng moving slowly back through the woods, listening to their happy voices, their obscene glee in the fate of the shadow warrior, their delight in the prowess of their redheaded champion. They were right. Moseby had never seen a shadow warrior beaten like that. Not by anyone other than another Fedayeen, and Gravenholtz was no Fedayeen. What *was* he, though?

Moseby peeled off from the group, shivering now as he remembered his promise to teach the redhead a lesson. The shadow warrior was fast and skillful, deadlier than Moseby had been in his prime, and he was long past that point. Yeah, the shadow warrior was good, but Gravenholtz was better. Clouds slid across the horn of the moon, darkening the night as Moseby made his way back toward the shack. He walked heavier now and there was ice in his guts. He wasn't tired. Shadow warriors didn't get tired. That's what they told themselves anyway. No, Moseby wasn't tired. He was scared.

CHAPTER 12

Leo squirmed as Rakkim shoved his head through the hole in the painted plywood. His Ident collar caught for a second, making him howl.

"Smile," said Rakkim, sticking his own head through a hole.

The camera buzzed. The photographer yawned, handed Rakkim two photo buttons as they stepped from behind the plywood.

Rakkim pinned a button on Leo's chest, pinned the other one on himself. Rakkim and Leo pictured as white-robed angels carrying assault rifles.

Leo wiped his nose. "I think I'm getting a cold."

"Could be malaria," said Rakkim.

"Yes . . . yes, that's possible," said Leo. "Sleeping on the beach . . . all those mosquitoes. This country is a hellhole of disease and poverty and . . ." He pressed a hand against his forehead. "I've got a fever."

"Sounds like elephantiasis. Maybe leprosy."

Leo pursed his lips. You could fool him, but not for long. "How amusing. How *droll*."

They pressed their way through the swarm of tourists surrounding the Mount Carmel memorial, the monument to the Branch Davidian martyrs a bigger draw than the nearby Waco rodeo and cow palace. Late afternoon, the air heavy, sweat cutting trails through the dust on their faces in the East Texas heat. The two of them strolled among suburban families wearing DAMN THE ATF T-shirts, and teenagers with David Koresh masks pushed back on their foreheads as they munched fried Snickers bars. Rakkim led Leo toward Stevenson's Fair Deal Emporium.

All the skin on parade made it hard not to stare: bare arms, bare legs, bare midriffs, short shorts and tube tops and hip-huggers. Hard to tell the harlots from the housewives here. A change since his last visit over three years ago. The Belt was Christian, but evidently the holy rollers had stopped demanding modesty among believers, more concerned with

simply maintaining the faith. Let the Muslims fight to the death over doctrine, the Belt needed whatever unity it could maintain.

Rakkim listened to the twangs and drawls, the low, laconic slur of the
delta, the rapid-fire urban hustle of Atlanta—layers upon layers, the sights
and sounds and smells of a thousand small towns. Young toughs bulled
their way through the crowd, eyeing the cutie-pies as they puffed away on
foul cheroots. Small black remote-controlled helicopters dipped and soared
overhead. A little girl wailed at her snow cone fallen to the pavement as her
father dragged her to a stand selling personalized, gold-embossed Bibles.

A trio of nuns walked past arm in arm, delicately eating individual ker-
nels of kettle corn they plucked from small paper bags. The youngest nun
blushed as she licked her fingers and Rakkim smiled, imagining the exquisite conflict her pleasure must give her. The young nun turned back,
glanced at Rakkim, held his eyes for a moment. He watched her hurry
away, tiny feet kicking up dust, and Rakkim thought of the devout women
back home, faces circled by head scarves, some masked behind veils, hair
tucked out of sight . . . he felt again the erotic charge of those women not
completely of this world.

Leo stood entranced before a holographic info panel detailing the
attack and siege of Mount Carmel by federal authorities that began on
Sunday, February 28, 1993. The panel blended actual news footage with
re-creations that showed the Feds pounding on the door of the compound
attempting to serve David Koresh with a subpoena for illegal weapons. In
the shootout that followed, four federal officers were killed and David
Koresh wounded. The siege began with approximately one hundred
Davidians holed up inside Mount Carmel, surrounded by FBI, ATF, and
army National Guard units. Rakkim dragged Leo away from the panel as
a beatific Koresh lay bleeding, attended by white-robed children.

Leo tugged at his Ident collar. The narrow titanium collar wasn't
tight—it was the idea of it that chafed. Rakkim didn't blame him. The collar was necessary, though. Only way for an outlander like Leo to escape
notice was to hide in plain sight.

Who's ever going to believe I'm a retard? Leo had asked as Rakkim
slipped the collar around his neck.

*You haven't got the skills to pull that off, kid. I'm just asking you to look
like a loser.* Rakkim's hand had darted out, lightly brushed across Leo's

scalp. Clumps of hair drifted down until Rakkim slid his knife back, admiring his handiwork. Leo's hair was gouged, as though cut by someone either indifferent or incompetent. *That's better.*

Plenty of Idents in the Belt. Indentured servants—the poor, the slow-witted, the unlucky, all of them trading years of their lives to learn a trade or pay off a debt. Idents always looked out of place. Even more important, Idents didn't draw attention. Between Leo's baby fat, bad haircut, and the too-small T-shirt Rakkim had bought for him, Leo might as well be invisible.

Rakkim saw another Ident following a family of four, the Ident huffing and puffing as he lugged bags of souvenirs in one hand, holding an umbrella over the mother with the other. The Ident was white, the family black. Sarah said one of the few good things about the second civil war was that race was now irrelevant. Nobody lost a job or a house because he was the wrong color. Things like that only happened because of important differences. Like being the wrong religion. Christians were tolerated in the Islamic Republic, but they were second-class citizens, passed over for promotion, kept out of the choicest real estate. In the Belt, all Christians were equal, but in many places, Catholics were still treated with suspicion. A young man from All Saints High School looking for a college scholarship would do well to start attending the Power in the Blood Tabernacle.

The Ident stumbled, almost dropped a package, apologizing, head lowered. Rakkim spotted a couple of stolid Texas Rangers, a black and white team, each well over six feet tall, their oversize Stetsons seeming to float above the crowd. During the war, the Rangers became a law unto themselves, keeping the peace by any means necessary. The story went that there wasn't a white oak in Texas that hadn't been a hanging tree, but while most of the Belt had been wracked with riots and looting, the streets of Texas stayed safe. Almost thirty years after the truce between the Belt and the Islamic Republic, the Rangers still operated as judge, jury, and executioner.

A group of young Louisiana National Guardsmen emerged from a tattoo parlor, fleshette rifles slung casually over their shoulders, rolled sleeves showing off their new ink. The usual gung-ho tats: flags and screaming eagles, the stone rolled away from the tomb, and Mecca's Kaaba with a mushroom cloud. A muscular Guardsman launched a toy helicopter, guided it around a corn dog stand, then lost control, the helicopter swooping low, knocking the white Ranger's hat askew before cartwheeling into the dirt. The Guardsmen laughed, and the muscular one ambled over, mumbled an apology. As the Guardsman bent to retrieve the helicopter, the Ranger drew his stainless-steel revolver in one quick, fluid movement and whipped the barrel across the Guardsman's head, laid him out. The others shouted, hands sliding along the slings of their rifles. The white Ranger slowly crushed the chopper under his boot while the black Ranger watched the Guardsmen, a toothpick migrating across his mouth.

The crowd gave the Rangers and Guardsmen room, but Rakkim stayed put.

The Guardsmen hesitated, then quickly dragged their comrade away.

"I . . . I don't like it here," Leo whispered to Rakkim.

"I do," said Rakkim, the words escaping him before he was even aware of the thought.

Stevenson's store was in the same spot as the last time Rakkim had seen it, but it was even bigger now, the cross on top state-of-the-art, shimmering with color and so realistic you could see the grain in the wood. SOUVENIRS, ARCANA, RELICS flashed from the wallscreens. A steady stream of dusty pilgrims flowed in and out of the line of revolving doors, air-conditioning leaking out into the heat. A Crusader stood outside in full mock-armor, visor up, sweat streaming down his face, handing out lollypops to the children.

Rakkim pushed Leo ahead of him, into the revolving door. The interior of the shop smelled faintly of frankincense, the smoldering incense barely covering the scent of spilled soda and popcorn. Portraits of David Koresh stared from every wall, including a black velvet painting of Koresh facing Elvis priced at $1,999. Steer horns laser-etched with Bible verses, a bargain at $159.99. Miniatures of the Mount Carmel compound made of everything from cooked macaroni to beaten silver. A Janet Reno voodoo doll with her fangs painted red. Rocks and bits of charred wood from the original compound in bulletproof glass cases with certificates of authenticity. A little girl tugged at her mother's dress, pointed at one of the many kites dangling from the ceiling: Jesus in the clouds overlooking the firestorm, reaching out to welcome Koresh into the heavens, the clouds around them bloodred in the glow.

Leo fingered a display of toy U.S. Army tanks, ignoring the PLEASE, NO TOUCHING sign. He tapped a command into the underside, the tank clanking noisily, treads spinning as hot sparks flashed from the pivoting barrel of the tank cannon. Smoke wafted through the cool air, rippling the small devil's pentagram flag atop the tank.

Stevenson himself barreled over in faded jeans, spangled cowboy shirt, and cowboy boots, scrawny as ever, a hand-rolled cigarette between his lips. "You *buying* that, melonhead?" He noticed Rakkim. Stared. "That *you?*"

Rakkim looked back at him. Leo still hung on to the tank.

"It *is* you." A bit of ash fell from the tip of Stevenson's cigarette, drifted toward the floor. "You look different." He peered at Rakkim, his tiny eyes hard as river rock.

"Must be the new Swedish night cream I've been using," said Rakkim. "Tightens the pores."

Stevenson waved back an approaching security guard. He flicked the photo button on Rakkim's chest. "You could have bought that cheaper here. Three ninety-nine apiece and half off a grandstand ticket to the reenactment. You got taken, son."

"That's what vacation is all about," said Rakkim.

Stevenson snorted. "You ain't never been on vacation your whole life. Same as me." He watched Leo tapping commands into the tank. "Let's adjourn to my office," he said, starting down the aisle. A press of his hand against the wall plate and the heavy door slid open. A tattered American flag was mounted on one wall, its edges singed. Stevenson sat in an overstuffed leather command chair behind a heavy oak desk. He was creased and cracked from the sun, somewhere around fifty, his gray hair buzzed short, a tough, ugly banty rooster, more gristle than meat.

Rakkim sat opposite Stevenson, stretched out his legs while Leo lumbered around the room, touching everything.

Stevenson poured whiskey into a couple of cut crystal glasses, handed one to Rakkim. A glance at Leo. "You want a soda pop, junior?"

Leo ignored him, stood before the flag. He put a hand over his heart. The wrong hand.

Stevenson clinked glasses with Rakkim. "Sorry about Redbeard. Damn shame."

"Yeah." Rakkim took a swallow from his glass, felt fire slide down his throat. He saw Leo slip the tank's remote into his pocket. "You're doing well."

"A man can't make money off tourists, he's too stupid to breathe, but it ain't all gravy." Stevenson sucked his teeth, his incisors as yellow as his nicotine-stained knuckles. "Got ten thousand acres outside of San Antonio about to dry up and blow away, and a car dealership with more salesmen than customers. I'm thinking about buying into a savings and loan in Houston. Banking's near as good as the tourist trade when it comes to easy money." He took another long swallow, his bony Adam's apple bobbing. "Muslims ever get past their stupidity about charging interest, they'll *really* take over the world."

Rakkim sipped his whiskey. "Quran forbids it, that settles it."

"Adapt or die, that's as true for religion as it is for people." Stevenson shook out a cigarette from a pack of Virginia broadleaf. The hand-rolled ones must be for the benefit of the tourists. He watched Rakkim from behind a veil of fragrant smoke.

Stevenson had been State Security during the early days of the republic, one of the few non-Muslims in a position of authority, testament to the respect Redbeard had for him. Stevenson had disappeared around twenty years ago, after a problem with the imam of the largest mosque in Seattle. It wasn't a religious dispute. Stevenson didn't believe in Christ on the cross or virgins waiting in Paradise. Stevenson didn't believe in anything he couldn't taste or touch. The imam had ordered a young woman picked up by the Black Robes. Jewish woman. Esther. Maybe she caught the imam's eye, or maybe someone turned her in. Whatever, she died before Stevenson could spring her. The next day the imam and his two bodyguards were found dead and Stevenson was gone.

Rakkim had run into Stevenson on one of his first reconnaissance missions into the Belt, saw him working a small stand at Mount Carmel. They kept each other's secrets without ever discussing the matter. The Belt paid a million dollars for a captured shadow warrior, and even after all this time, the Black Robes still offered a man's weight in gold and the blessing of the grand mullah himself for the return of Stevenson. Maybe Rakkim and Stevenson both thought they had enough money and enough blessings. The second time they met, Rakkim brought Stevenson a microphoto of Esther's grave. The Black Robes had intended to shove her into one of their mass graves, but Redbeard had intervened, had her placed in a non-Muslim cemetery and paid for a small marble stone. They continued their contact after Rakkim retired from the Fedayeen, after he had turned renegade, helping moral criminals escape from the republic: accused witches and Jews, apostates and homosexuals. Rakkim slipped them over the border and into the Belt. Stevenson passed them along, out of harm's way. Neither of them charged for their services.

Stevenson nodded at Leo. "The Ident collar is a nice touch."

"I've got a businessman up the way needs a Brainiac," said Rakkim.

"If you say so." Stevenson sipped his whiskey. "Always a market for a Brainiac. Don't matter whether it's here or in your neck of the woods, there's never enough smart folks. Not when being smart can get you in trouble. Asking questions . . . that's dangerous in the best of times, and these ain't the best of— Would you take your cotton-picking hands off my things?" he barked at Leo.

Leo jerked, dropped the view globe of the sunken city of New Orleans. It rolled across the desk. Rakkim grabbed it just as it was about to fall.

"What do you want from me?" said Stevenson.

"I'm taking him to Tennessee, and wanted to get the lay of the land. That warlord still running G-Burg? What's his name? The one growing opium for the South Americans."

"Name was Bates, but he's dead now. Him and all his troops." Stevenson swirled his whiskey. "Gatlinburg's deserted, not a soul left. The new honcho runs a ragtag outfit called the ETA. End-Times Army. Bunch of psychos living in the woods like savages."

"What's their game? They want to take over the dope trade?"

"*Hell,* no. They burned every poppy they could find. Burned every opium farmer too, roasted them on bonfires like ears of sweet corn. Their boss is a lunatic named Malcolm Crews. *Pastor* Malcolm Crews. A full-on born-again, and crazier than a shithouse rat." Stevenson took another swallow of whiskey. "I heard Crews survived a night in the Stone Hills, and got the brand to prove it."

Rakkim was impressed with that, if it was true. "I think we should let all these messiahs duke it out. Your guys, my guys, put them all in a steel-cage death match, and the one who walks out alive gets the crown of creation."

Stevenson laughed. "Not used to you talking like this."

"A few years ago I killed a man. A Fedayeen assassin." Rakkim shook his head. "I haven't been right since."

"You killed an *assassin?*" Stevenson squinted over the rim of his glass. "By yourself?"

"No . . . I had help."

"I thought so. Must have taken a whole strike force unit."

"It was an angel," said Rakkim. "An angel, close enough that I could feel its wings against me. Softest thing imaginable . . ." He stopped, embarrassed. "You believe me?"

"You say an angel buddied up, I got no problem with that." Stevenson grinned, shook his head. "It's you killing an assassin that I'm having a hard time with."

"I'm having a hard time with it too."

"*Angels?*" Leo snorted. "The only god I see is the infinite elegance of mathematics."

"The kids's smart, but he's got a lot of stupid in him too," said Rakkim.

"It's good to see you, Rikki." Stevenson chewed his lip. "Things here are going to shit."

"You seem to be doing okay."

"Man like me, you set me down on a desert island buck naked, come back in two years and I'll have hot and cold running water and a machine that gives hand jobs for a couple seashells. I'm not talking about me. I'm talking about the rest of these peckerwoods. Enough people get miserable enough, we *all* got problems."

Rakkim watched Leo unscrew the base of the army tank with a bent paper clip.

"You heard what the Mexicans done?" asked Stevenson.

"I know they've put in all kinds of land claims."

"Claims?" snapped Stevenson. "They're *way* past claims. They diverted the damn Rio Grande six months ago, used the runoff to turn the desert into farmland. Meanwhile, South Texas is about to dry up and blow away. Governor bitched and moaned, president called in the Mexican ambassador, who laughed right in his face." He shook his head. "Never would have happened *before*. Before the war."

"You sound like my wife."

"Your wife sounds like the brains of the family."

Rakkim turned at the sound of screaming from outside.

"Let's get on the roof," said Stevenson, crossing to a small door in the corner of the room. "It's showtime."

CHAPTER 13

Caught in the last rusty light of the sunset, the tanks idled fifty yards from Mount Carmel, diesel engines belching gritty exhaust as the engines revved. The deep, throaty sound almost drowned out the screaming from the nearby sound trucks.

"The noise went on for weeks," said Stevenson over the din. "Feds brought in loudspeakers that blasted the Davidians around the clock for the whole fifty-one-day siege. Evidently the agent-in-charge's personal favorite was the sound of rabbits being slaughtered." He nodded. "If David Koresh wasn't nuts when it started, he sure as fuck was when Janet Reno finally ordered in the tanks."

Stevenson had led them up the stairs from his office to the top floor, the three of them stepping out onto the flat roof. From their vantage point, they had a perfect view of the nearby replica of Mount Carmel, a rambling structure of unpainted boards topped by a steeple. It looked as much like a prison as a church, an impression only strengthened by the presence of a half-dozen tanks, cannons pointed at the front door. Hundreds of tourists clustered around the viewing areas, hands clasped over their ears. Leo stood near the edge of the roof, mesmerized, his fingers taking apart the toy tank without even looking.

The lead tank churned across the flat Texas terrain, kicking up dust. The barrel of its 55-millimeter main gun punched through the flimsy walls of the citadel. FBI sappers in black jumpsuits zigzagged in, attached hoses from the tanks into Mount Carmel, started pumping in CS, a convulsive tear gas. The crowd booed. Children on the viewing areas started crying, their mothers carrying them away.

Rakkim's attention wandered from the assault on Mount Carmel; he had seen the reenactment before and it always turned out the same. Once the little guy drew the attention of the big guy, it was all over. The little guy might fight, might even draw blood, but sooner or later there was going to be a big boot coming down hard on him. Sarah said it was more complicated than that. She said that Koresh bore responsibility for what had happened. Said he could have surrendered. Submitted to a higher authority. Right. Problem was that Koresh thought *he* was the higher authority and was willing to die to prove it. The Belt was filled with people who agreed with him.

"So what are you really here for?" asked Stevenson. "Man like you could find out what was waiting for him in Tennessee a lot easier than coming here to ask me."

"Maybe I came for the company."

"Yeah, and I'm in business for the betterment of mankind," said Stevenson. "So?"

Rakkim turned back to the battle. "I need that thousand-dollar gold piece of yours."

"Why not just ask for my left ventricle?"

"I don't need your heart. I need the gold piece."

"That's the pride of my collection."

"That's why I need it," said Rakkim.

The U.S. Mint had produced thousand-dollar gold pieces just before the Civil War started, but had never distributed any of them. A few prototypes had been released, but the rest were stored in Fort Knox along with the nation's supply of gold bullion. When the army of the Bible Belt overran Fort Knox, they found the vaults completely empty. Not a single gold coin or gold bar in the place. Men had been searching for the treasure trove for the last thirty years.

"Never should have told you I had that thing," Stevenson said. "My own damned fault . . ." He squinted at Rakkim. "I get it." He hitched up his jeans. "My gold piece isn't going to do you any good. Might have been a good plan if Bates was still warlord; he was a greedy bastard, but like I told you, this Malcolm Crews ain't like any normal man. Money don't mean shit to him, it's all about heaven and hell."

"You don't have to look so happy."

"Don't have to, but why resist the impulse?"

Rakkim watched the two Texas Rangers he had noticed earlier clutching a couple of longnecks as they passed effortlessly through the crowd. Their Stetsons seemed to float above the throng as they ambled along, ignoring the people who scuttled out of the way. A father dragged his two children aside, but he was a step too slow, a kick in the ass from the white Ranger sending him sprawling. The children stared up at the Rangers before their father gathered them in his arms, limping away.

"Rangers haven't been paid regular for the last year, and the job hasn't gotten any easier," explained Stevenson. "They're losing control over the border, control over themselves. Can't blame them for taking it out on the citizens."

"You mean the citizens they're sworn to protect?" said Rakkim.

"Yup. That would be the very ones."

Rakkim watched as the Rangers tipped their hats at a couple of teenage girls in short shorts.

"You stay away from them two," said Stevenson. "Don't even make eye contact."

"I don't want any trouble," said Rakkim.

Stevenson squinted at him. "I'm not so sure of that anymore."

Rakkim felt Stevenson watching him, but he didn't turn away from the siege, the flames from the burning church reflected in his eyes. "What is it?"

"You," said Stevenson. "There's something . . . I don't know. You're different."

Rakkim smiled. "I'm married. I'm a father. It takes a toll."

"That's not it." Stevenson hesitated. "Before, when I asked you why you come here, I had the thought . . . I thought maybe you come here to kill me."

"*What?* Why . . . why would you think that?"

"I'm getting old. All kinds of foolish ideas been running through my head lately. . . . Your wife . . . it's good between you?"

"Good enough."

"Good enough is plenty good." Stevenson shoved his hands in his pockets. "I still think about Esther . . . wonder about the life we might have had. All these years, you'd think it would fade, but I still wake up some nights and reach for her." He cleared his throat. "You hold Sarah close when you get home. Put your arms around her and don't let go."

"I'll do that."

Stevenson watched Leo play with the toy tank he had modified, the tank spinning on one end and barking like a dog. "I could make a million dollars with this kid."

"He's already sold," said Rakkim. "This fellah in Nashville—"

"Don't lie to me," said Stevenson. "You don't need the practice and I find it insulting. I seem like a patriot to you? My country right or wrong?" He spit over the side of the building. Watched it fall. "The Belt is like a sack of porcupines, too busy jabbing and poking each other to find their way to daylight. That republic of yours is just as bad. Nothing's gone right since the old regime decided to split the sheets." The light from the fire exposed every seam in his face. "So what are you *really* doing back here?"

"I'm not sure," said Rakkim. "They tell me there's a war on the way, a *new* war, and maybe I can stop it, but . . ."

"If there's a war coming, no one can stop it. Leave it to you to try, though."

"Don't make me into something I'm not. Let's just say I missed the rodeo."

"What's going on?" Leo pointed at the armored bulldozers punching holes through the outer wall of the compound. A heavy truck followed, sent white smoke streaming into the structure through the holes. "Is that real tear gas?"

"Just smoke," said Stevenson. "During the actual raid the Feds pumped CS gas into the living areas. Stings much worse than tear gas. Toxic to children too."

Rakkim couldn't take his eyes off the compound. It was just a reenactment, and there was more than enough blame to go around, but still . . .

"But . . ." Leo turned from one to the other. "But *weren't* there children inside?"

"Twenty-one of them," said Stevenson. "I guess the government thought it was kind of academic, though, since they all burned up in the fire anyway."

Rakkim watched as wisps of smoke swirled in the wind. Sarah said it had never been proven how the fire started; the only thing certain was the government ordering in the tanks and all those dead kids. No wonder folks in the Belt flocked here. To them, Mount Carmel was a clear sign that the United States had turned its back on God, and God had returned the favor by turning his back on the USA. Maybe, but Rakkim wasn't sure if God took things all that personally.

One of the tanks circled around to the rear of the compound, flattening a storage shed.

The compound exploded in a fireball of orange light, windows blown out from the force of the detonation.

"I was just a teenager when the old regime fell," said Stevenson as burning debris drifted down, "and I sure as shit don't like what replaced it, but there's times . . ." He spit over the side again. "Makes a man wonder how something that started out so good could have rotted out like an old pumpkin. Government turning on its own people, murdering kids . . ." He pulled out an auto-pistol and emptied the clip, his face contorted as he howled at the sky.

People in the crowd answered the shots, dozens of rounds fired off into the sky, the gunshots punctuated by rebel yells and shouts of "Amen!" Leo cowered along the edge of the roof, hands over his head, as though that would protect him from gravity. Rakkim stood tall as the crowd blazed away, tried to imagine the sound of gunfire in any city in the Islamic Republic and couldn't. Just *owning* a gun was a capital offense, and even the police almost never used their sidearms. Colarusso had been a cop almost thirty years and had never fired his weapon other than on the pistol range. The National Guardsmen in the crowd opened up now, their rifles on full auto, aiming at the stars. *Good luck.*

"Koresh should have let the Feds arrest him," said Rakkim, the flames reflected in his eyes. "Should have turned the other cheek. If Koresh was the second coming of Christ, that's what he was supposed to be all about, right?"

"First time around, Jesus turned the other cheek. You see where that got him. Next time he's coming as the warrior Christ leading the troops at Armageddon. That's why Koresh named this place Mount Carmel— 'cause the Bible says that's where the battle takes place. Christ and his people going toe to toe with the satanic hordes."

Rakkim scanned the crowd. "Who knew you could buy snow cones at Armageddon?"

"It's not funny," said Stevenson, his gnarly face livid in the rockets' red glare.

The tanks retreated as the flames leapt higher with a *whoooosh*; the steeple upended, falling through the second story. The crowd, which had been restless during the tank assault, almost eager to see the climax of the reenactment, stepped back from the railing and fell silent. The three nuns crossed themselves, bowed their heads.

Stevenson turned away. "I seen this every week for the last ten years . . . you think I'd be used to it by now. Tomorrow morning they'll start building it all over again." He shook his head, his voice hoarse. "Damn ancient history, that's all it is."

Leo stood beside Rakkim, the two of them watching the compound until there was only ashes and smoldering embers.

The crowd dispersed slowly toward the parking lots, people pushing baby carriages along the walkways. A doll fell off a baby carriage as the father pushed past the three nuns, and the young nun Rakkim had made eye contact with earlier bent gracefully down and picked it up. Returned it to the father. The nuns kept up with the crowd, and Rakkim noticed the two Rangers studying them as they passed, then start after them.

Stevenson put a hand on Rakkim's shoulder. "Don't get carried away."

Rakkim watched the two Rangers flank the young nun. The black one pulled away her head scarf, twirled it around a finger. The white one grabassed her while she slapped at his hands. The Rangers laughed as she fled, weeping, after the other nuns.

"Those two are even more out of control than usual," said Stevenson. "Christians get along well enough, but there's still plenty of good ol' boys don't like Catholics. Not near as much as they hate your people, but some folks never forgave the pope for kowtowing to the Muslims the way he did. I understand the situation, two popes assassinated inside of a year, but if the pope can't stand up for what he believes in, who can?"

"What those two assholes did, that had nothing to do with religion," said Rakkim.

"You're probably right about that." Stevenson rocked on the heels of his cowboy boots. "It's just damn criminal stupidity not to pay your centurions. Any fool knows that. You don't feed the guard dog, sooner or later somebody's gonna get bit."

"I've been thinking," said Rakkim.

"*Damn.* Here I thought I was going to skate."

"You got some old Roman coins in that collection of yours?"

"I got a little of everything, you know that," said Stevenson.

"I need a silver coin from around the time of Christ," said Rakkim.

"Like an imperial denarius? I've got plenty of those."

"As long as it's silver. I only need one."

"What are you going to do with that?"

"This Malcolm Crews sounds a lot like David Koresh. You said it yourself—boys like that, money doesn't mean anything to them. It's all about heaven and hell."

"What's that supposed—"

"Forget the denarius," said Leo. "You want a shekel of Tyre."

Rakkim stared at Leo.

"What?" said Leo. "Like I can't correlate the data?" He tapped his forehead. "Me *smart*."

"I don't know what either of you are talking about," said Stevenson, "but a shekel of Tyre is a rare coin. I've only got one."

"One's all I need," said Rakkim, still staring at Leo.

"Stay away from Houston," said Stevenson. "There's typhus—"

"You already told me," said Rakkim.

"Stick to the backroads. You might run into bandits, but there's military press-gangs all over the interstates. And watch out for Mexicans."

Rakkim slid behind the wheel of the rusted-out Cadillac. "I got it."

"You're going to want to take Highway Twenty-seven because it's quicker, but don't do it," said Stevenson. "Rangers coop under the big overpass watching for trouble . . . or folks they can bring trouble to. Had a lot of tourists go missing lately. Women turning up weeks later, kind of condition they'd be better off dead. Best you take the long way around Waco. Rangers aren't the worst that can happen either. You drive down a country lane and see somebody broke down by the side of the road, don't stop. I don't care if it's a sweet-faced blonde holding the baby Jesus."

"Why, hello, miss," cooed Rakkim. "Are y'all in need of assistance?"

"Okay, I deserve that." Stevenson fumbled for a fresh cigarette. "The Caddy's got puncture-guard tires and upgraded body armor. She's fast too. Ugly but fast." Stevenson handed Rakkim a gun. "Here. Nothing fancy. I know you don't want to attract attention, but it's a solid, reliable piece. Twenty-four slims in the magazine."

Rakkim tucked away the gun. Familiarized himself with the controls. A real steering wheel—no autopilot, no verbal controls, no crash-avoidance system. Redneck iron all the way. Perfect.

Stevenson patted the sides of the Caddy—once pink, now a dull red. "Forty years ago, this baby was the most widely produced car in the country. Most of them are still in operation. Can't beat a turbo-twelve for reliability."

"It's crap," Leo muttered. "I'm just glad nobody I know will ever see me in it."

Stevenson inclined his head toward Leo. "You must really need this asshole."

"That's what they tell me." Rakkim started the car, listening. "Me, I've got my doubts."

"Used to be the Chinese made sneakers for us because them coolies worked cheap." Stevenson spit. "Now they build factories in the Belt because *we're* the ones working for peanuts. Cars, clothes, toys, fireworks. Cheap labor, that's all we got to offer."

"Best tobacco in the world," said Rakkim. "That's still true, isn't it?"

Stevenson nodded. "Ozark opium poppies are world-class too. Hell, without tobacco, dope, and Coca-Cola, the Belt wouldn't have any hard-currency foreign trade at all."

Rakkim revved the engine.

"You got the coin, right?"

Rakkim patted his pocket.

"I hope you know what you're doing," said Stevenson.

Rakkim floored it, spraying Stevenson with a rain of pebbles.

"*Now* are we going to Tennessee?" said Leo.

"Not just yet."

CHAPTER 14

Anthony Colarusso parked his car on the shoulder of I-90, got out with a groan, and walked toward the blast site carrying a paper-bag lunch that Marie had packed for him. Five days after al-Faisal's car had detonated at the roadblock and two lanes of the freeway were still roped off, traffic whizzing by in the remaining two lanes. His baggy gray suit flapped around him as a semitruck barreled past. The air smelled of diesel and something worse. Colarusso reached into the bag, unwrapped the peanut butter and jelly sandwich, nibbled on half while he paced off the site.

Must have been some big fucking firecracker. C-6 shaped charge with all the trimmings, according to State Security's official report. About fifteen feet of asphalt had buckled, one whole section melted from the intense heat of the explosion, shards of metal driven deep into the softened tar. Blast killed a couple of SS officers manning the barricade, injured three more. Real geniuses. Like who could have possibly considered that a fleeing Black Robe homicide suspect and his bodyguard might choose to go out in style, and take some company with them. Muslims . . . there were plenty of good ones, but Colarusso had never met a Black Robe he didn't want to kick in the ass.

His tongue probed the space between his right canine and bicuspid. Dislodged a piece of peanut and spit it out. He had only been telling Marie for twenty-seven goddamned years that he preferred *creamy* peanut butter. Probably a sale on crunchy, buy two jars and get one free. Or maybe it was her way of showing him who was boss. If it wasn't for the bowing and scraping five times a day, he'd be tempted to convert and get him a good Muslim wife. One who didn't talk unless spoken to, and didn't make that face when he came home late. He took another bite of sandwich. Strawberry preserves . . . his favorite. Homemade too. Marie picked the berries herself, cooked them up in a big kettle every summer, her face steamy from

the heat, hair lank across her forehead. She was a lousy cook, but her preserves were something else.

He squatted down, examined the blast pattern, trying to sketch out the
debris field in his mind. He ran a hand over the fused asphalt, noted where
it was indented, then looked in the opposite direction. Evidence markers
from the State Security forensics team waved in the weeds beside the freeway, but they weren't planted out nearly far enough for the force of the
explosion. Another reason to question the official finding that al-Faisal and
his bodyguard had killed themselves rather than face arrest. State Security
had been in a hurry to claim jurisdiction over the case. In an even bigger
hurry to issue their report and put the case to bed. Not that police didn't
do the same thing, but Colarusso didn't like being overruled under the
best of circumstances and no way did this qualify. Particularly with a Bombay strangler involved. Sick fucks.

Joints popping, he stood up, scratched his ample belly. Probably best
to keep the wife and religion he had. His knees were in no shape for all
that praying, and besides, Marie might have put on ten pounds with every
kid, but she still had that nasty grin that got to him, got *right* to him no matter how tired he was. She gave him that grin and he still felt like the football hero. All-state linebacker, three years running. Loved to hear the
crunch of a good hit, see the surprise on their faces, like where did *you*
come from? Colarusso would get up, pretend to adjust his pads and helmet, and look for Marie in the stands. She'd wave, not fooled for a minute.
Yeah, save the good Muslim wives for the good Muslim men, Colarusso
would stick with a wild Catholic girl any day.

Gnats floated around his mouth, and he wiped his face with one arm,
got a smear of peanut butter on the sleeve of his suit jacket. He licked it
off. Made it worse. Kept licking until it was gone. Thought he tasted
spaghetti sauce from last week too. About time to get it dry-cleaned.
Almost. He moved slowly toward the weeds, eyes on the ground. *Make
sure, Anthony*, that's what Rakkim had said when Colarusso told him that
al-Faisal had blown himself up. Make *sure*. Good advice under any circumstances.

He looked up as another car skidded up onto the shoulder. Fancy vehicle, opaque, armored windows, reinforced bumpers.

Two men stepped out of the car, shoes shined to mirrors and decked out in tailored black suits. Typical State Security. The short, stocky one looked at Colarusso like he had a bad taste in his mouth; the gangly one walked easier, almost friendly, a farm kid playing dress-up. They each kept a hand inside their jackets.

"Don't hurt yourself, boys, I'm Deputy Chief Anthony Colarusso." He saw the gangly one scan the pin on his lapel, confirming his status. "Just checking out the neighborhood."

"Your rank doesn't mean anything here—all that matters is that you're trespassing," said the shorter one, his hand still inside his jacket. "State Security's got this scene boxed up, so climb back in your ride and haul ass back where you—"

"Relax, Napoléon," said Colarusso, "you're going to give yourself a hemorrhoid."

The stumpy one stepped closer.

"It's all right, Jay," said the gangly one. "We're all—"

"I asked you once, I'm not gonna ask you again," said the stumpy one.

"Just a second." Colarusso fished around in his paper bag, moved the half sandwich aside and looked up. "Nope. I checked, but there's just no give-a-shit in here, not even a little piece."

The gangly one laughed. It sounded like a hiccup.

The stumpy one jabbed Colarusso in the chest. "I could take you down, you fat Catholic fuck. You'll end up in the goddamned emergency ward with a saline drip in your arm and a catheter in your dick."

"Sometimes, when I can't sleep"—Colarusso removed a speck of lint from his jacket, watched it float to the ground—"I think about all the dizzy bastards threatened me over the years, all the tough-guy yak . . ." He yawned, stretched his mouth wide. "Sends me right off to dreamland."

The stumpy one's eyes went dead.

"*Jay*," said the gangly one. "Go on back to the car, I'll take it from here."

"I don't want to go back to the car," the stumpy one said softly.

"Please, Jay," said the gangly one. "I hate filling out paperwork."

The stumpy one glared at Colarusso. "You got no idea how lucky you are." He turned on his heel, stalked back to the car.

"You like to live dangerously, Chief," said the gangly one. "Jay teaches hand-to-hand combat to the recruits just for the opportunity to beat people up."

"I never intended to use my hands," said Colarusso. "Figured I'd go brain-to-brain with him, where I have the advantage."

The gangly one laughed again. He was older than he looked at first, the bones in his face prominent, his eyes steady. "Never met a cop who wasn't a joker. That's the only bad thing about State Security, everybody's so darned serious."

"Not you, though," said Colarusso. "You're a fun guy."

"I enjoy my work, if that's what you mean." The wind from passing cars lifted the blond hairs on the gangly one's neck. A tiny vein throbbed along his jawline. "You really shouldn't be here, sir."

Colarusso sidled back into the weeds, eyes on the ground.

"What are you looking for?" asked the gangly one, keeping up.

"Whatever you State Security boys missed." Colarusso saw a glint in the grass, bent down and picked up a small piece of blackened metal. Tossed it to the gangly one. "See what I mean?"

The gangly one flipped the piece of metal back onto the ground. "We have five or six boxes of debris just like that. No evidentiary value."

"I know," said Colarusso, still walking, "that's why I didn't keep it."

The two of them paced the outskirts of the site for another ten minutes.

"The full report has been sent to all law enforcement agencies," said the gangly one.

"I read it," said Colarusso.

"Then what are you *doing* here?"

"Some folks love going to the movies." Colarusso shrugged. "Me, I just love crime scenes." He heard the buzzing of flies. Followed the sound. Parted the weeds. A swarm of bluebottles drifted up, a couple bouncing against his front teeth before hovering overhead. Colarusso wiped his mouth, reached down and picked up the small, blackened, curled-up thing that the flies had been feasting on.

The gangly one squatted beside him. He used too much cologne. "What is it?"

Colarusso held the blackened thing between his thumb and his fore-finger. Held it a couple inches from his face, and turned it over. "I think . . . I think it's an ear."

"I'll take that," said the gangly one, his voice hard now. Serious as any other State Security officer. He pulled a latex glove onto his right hand. "I'll take it, please." He held out his hand.

Colarusso stood up, still holding the ear. "What's your name?"

"Billings." He snapped his fingers. The glove muffled the sound. "The *ear*? I'm afraid I have to insist."

"You like peanut butter and jelly sandwiches, Billings?"

"What?"

"PBJs. You like 'em?"

"*Yes*. I like them."

"Plain or crunchy?"

"Sir . . ."

"It's a simple question," said Colarusso. "Not like you're being interrogated or—"

"Crunchy. I prefer crunchy peanut butter. Okay? Now may I please have the ear, because it is most *definitely* evidence?"

Colarusso reached into the paper bag, handed Billings the other half of the peanut butter sandwich. Dropped the ear into the bag and stuffed it into the pocket of his suit jacket. He started walking toward his car.

Billings traipsed along beside him. "Deputy Chief Colarusso, it is within my authority to arrest you . . ."

Colarusso kept walking.

". . . and take possession of the item in question," said Billings, voice rising.

Colarusso kept walking.

"Give me the goddamned ear," demanded Billings.

Jay, the stocky one, got out of the car, walked briskly toward them. He had a gun in his hand. Kept tapping it lightly against his thigh with every step.

Colarusso kept walking, neither increasing nor decreasing his pace. Just kept walking. While the two State Security agents conferred with each other, he got into his car, looking straight ahead, and drove away. It wasn't until he reached highway speed that he realized he was soaked with sweat.

CHAPTER 15

"Hey! Stevenson told you not to take Highway Twenty-seven," said Leo.

"We need gas," said Rakkim.

"You got half a tank," said Leo.

"Sit back and shut up," said Rakkim. "Go over the periodic table or something."

"Dad told me you took some getting used to. He didn't tell me how much." Leo pulled computer chips and switches from his top pocket, bits and pieces he had stolen from the toys in Stevenson's shop, examining them in the flex light from the dash, the tip of his tongue poking out of his mouth. "You didn't even ask me if I wanted to go to New Orleans. Don't I get a vote? *Don't* I?"

Rakkim followed Highway 27, checking the darkness on the sides of the road as often as his rearview. The tourist rush from Mount Carmel had thinned out hours ago, but traffic flowed on, mostly truckers, restless teenagers, and families where the dad was too cheap to stop and get a motel. Twice he slowed, approaching gas stations, but the stations were surrounded by flatland and he drove on, Leo too busy working with his tinkering to notice. A few miles farther, a Freedom gas station blinked OPEN ALL NITE near an overpass. Within the shadow of the overpass, Rakkim spotted a Texas Rangers cruiser. He pulled into the station.

The air smelled sweet and syrupy, almost rank. Rakkim looked around. Combines chewed their way through the surrounding fields of sugarcane, headlights gleaming on the bright green shoots. Rakkim undid the gas cap as the attendant hurried over, a middle-aged guy, in a faded but neatly pressed khaki army uniform.

Massive hurricanes from the big warm had pretty much shut down oil production from the Gulf, the few rigs left expropriated by the Aztlán

Empire. Coal and imported oil supplied most of the energy needs of the Belt, but the chain of Freedom stations was owned by retired vets, and sold only ethanol, with every drop coming from domestic sugarcane.

"Fill 'er up?" said the attendant, lifting the hose.

Rakkim pressed his credit chip against the pump, heard it chirp. "Thanks."

"Come from Mount Carmel?"

Rakkim nodded, watching the cruiser over the man's shoulder. PETERS was stitched above his left breast pocket, sergeant's stripes on each arm. A combat infantryman badge was his only decoration. The only one needed. "Where did you serve, Sergeant?"

"Where *didn't* I serve?" The attendant still had the military posture, shoulders back, stomach in. A little stooped, but clean-shaven, his gray hair buzzed. Probably still did a hundred push-ups a day. "How about you, boy? You look like you seen some action."

"Did four years in the Kentucky National Guard, but it was just mostly smoking cigarettes and watching the border. Never even saw a towelie the whole time."

"I don't much like that term," said Peters. "Insults the Muslims and insults the men who died fighting them."

"I apologize, Sergeant."

Peters nodded. "No harm done." He checked out Rakkim's car. "Nice machine. Old but solid. Might run a little rough for a few miles, but she'll adjust."

"I know. Worth it, though, isn't it?"

"Damn right," said Peters, jaw jutting. "Some folks and their fancy new cars won't run anything but gasoline, no matter where it come from or what it cost. I ain't talking just money, either. If we had grown cane a hundred years ago, we might still have the country. The *whole* country."

"Amen," said Rakkim.

Peters grinned. "What did you think of Mount Carmel?"

"Impressive . . . not sure how accurate the reenactment was, but—"

"Accurate? I saw it on the TV with my own damn eyes," snapped Peters. "I was just seven years old, but I knowed there was going to be a reckoning." He shook his head, disgusted. "It's in the *history* books. Don't they teach you Kentucky boys anything?"

"Well, sir, I wasn't much for school," said Rakkim, still watching the Rangers' cruiser.

"Well, here's your lesson for the day, youngblood," said Peters, replacing the hose nozzle onto the pump. "While Muslims were attacking our embassies all over the world, the U.S. government was busy gassing kids in Texas, shooting a nursing woman in the mountains of Idaho, and taking a little Cuban boy at gunpoint and sending him back to practically the last commie on earth. Didn't need a weatherman to tell which way the wind was blowing." He banged the gas cap back into place. "I talk too much sometimes."

"No, sir, you don't."

Peters opened the door to the car, waited for Rakkim to get behind the wheel. He nodded at Leo, but his eyes never left Rakkim. "That overpass up ahead, you can't see them from here, but there's two Rangers holed up underneath there like a couple of hairy spiders. You be careful. Don't give them any excuse to pull you over."

"I'll be careful, Sarge." Rakkim pulled out of the station, driving slowly at first, then gunned it past the overpass.

"What are you *doing*?" shouted Leo.

Rakkim checked the rearview. Saw the cruiser pull out from the overpass, headlights on. The cruiser followed, but kept a distance. The Rangers must be waiting until Rakkim and Leo were near their special spot. Someplace private, where no one would interrupt their fun.

Leo kept glancing behind them as Rakkim continued to accelerate.

A few miles later, Highway 27 narrowed from four lanes to two, the trees thicker as the road paralleled a river. Oncoming traffic continued to thin out at this late hour.

The cruiser's light bar flashed blue-blue-blue behind them, the Rangers coming up fast.

"What do we do?" said Leo, his face bathed in blue light reflected off the windshield.

"We obey the law," said Rakkim, looking for the right spot to pull over. The right spot for the Rangers. They would know the terrain, the perfect place. *There* it was . . . a gap between the trees, only briefly visible from passing vehicles. Rakkim slowed.

"Please don't do anything stupid," said Leo. "Anything *else*."

Rakkim eased into the clearing, tires crunching up dry branches. "Whatever happens, don't react. Stay thick as a brick." He got out of the car, keeping his hands in plain sight as the cruiser came to a stop, headlights pinning him. Rakkim waved, looking sheepish. Leo got out, stood by the side of the car, staring at the ground.

The Rangers killed the headlights, left the blue flasher blinking. They took their time getting out, enjoying the moment, the same black and white team that he had seen at Mount Carmel. They were even bigger close up, hitching up their gear, meaty, wide-shouldered hombres who looked like they wrestled steers when they weren't molesting tourists. Big men, big smiles, their teeth flat and white, almost fluorescent in the blue light as they ambled closer, flanking Rakkim.

They might have been wholesome once, dedicated lawmen risking their lives to keep the peace, but that was a long time ago, and missing a few paychecks didn't have anything to do with it. It was power that had rotted them out, too many years of people paying deference to the badge, lowering their eyes, taking care not to let their shadow fall on them. Every brave man needed a mean streak, a willingness to mix it up, a slight sadism to make the wolves slink away. The Rangers' mean streak had grown year by year, fed by the fear of the citizens who depended on them, fed by the excuses good people made for them. The Rangers were bad clean through now, more dangerous than any other predator loose among the sheep.

"Problem, Officers?" said Rakkim. "I know I was speeding—" He saw it coming, saw it in the white Ranger's eyes before the man reached for the shock stick on his belt. Rakkim relaxed, pretended surprise as the stick jabbed him in the chest. He didn't have to fake his cry of pain as he was jolted backward, thrown against the car. Ears ringing, he slid down the front fender of the car, lay crumpled against the wheel well.

Leo didn't move. Just stood there with his head bowed, mumbling softly to himself. Rakkim was impressed. The kid remembered what he had been taught. Kept his cool.

"You think the speed limit doesn't apply to you, sir?" said the white Ranger, looking down at Rakkim. "You think you're some special case?"

"No . . . no," said Rakkim, tasting blood where he had bitten the inside of his cheek. The tips of the Ranger's boots were so shiny that Rakkim could see the stars reflected in them. "Sorry . . . I'm sorry."

"A sorry son of a bitch is exactly what you are," said the Ranger. "What's the other one's story, Daryl?"

The black Ranger jerked Leo's Ident collar, pulled him close.

Leo mumbled louder but didn't raise his head.

"Some kind of indentured idiot," said the black Ranger, reading the collar. He released Leo. "Got a three-year tag."

Rakkim pushed his way up against the side of the car, got unsteadily to his feet. He smelled burned electricity when he breathed through his nose. "I . . . I didn't know—"

"Ignorance of the law is no excuse, sir," said the white Ranger.

"In fact, sir, we count on that," said the black Ranger.

Rakkim listened to them laugh.

"Three-year term of service," said the white Ranger. "Seems to me we could use us an idiot for the scut work around the barracks." He twirled the shock stick, eyeing Rakkim. "You might be able to get yourself out of trouble by signing the idiot over."

"He . . . he's already bought and paid for, Officer," stammered Rakkim. "There's a farmer in Greensboro counting on him for this year's harvest."

The black Ranger felt Leo's arms, and Leo giggled. Rakkim was more impressed with Leo than ever. The black Ranger sidled over to Rakkim. "Boy hasn't got any muscle to him at all. He's not right for fieldwork. Seems to me, sir, you might have cheated that poor farmer in Greensboro."

"Is that what you did, sir?" said the white Ranger. "You cheat that farmer? You promise him a good strong back and instead plan to deliver this tub a guts?"

"Ten years on the job, Jerry Lee, and I'm still surprised at the duplicity of the human heart." The black Ranger rested one hand on the butt of his pistol as he watched Rakkim. "It's enough to turn even a strong man to violence and drink."

"Do you see what you've done, sir?" The white Ranger kneed Rakkim, doubled him over. "You've gone and upset my partner, and he's a sensitive soul."

"You best turn this boy over to us, sir," said the black Ranger. "We can use someone to scour the floors and swab the toilets. We used to have a beaner for that but he ran off." He flicked Leo's collar. "No problem of that with an Ident."

"How much is the contract on the boy?" said the white Ranger.

"Fifteen thousand dollars," said Rakkim, "but I can't—"

"Fifteen thousand?" The white Ranger shook his head. "That's grand larceny last time I checked. Tell you what, sir, we'll pay you five hundred dollars for the contract. Just submit a bill to the State Bureau of Law Enforcement."

"I can't . . ."

"What's the security code for the collar?" asked the white Ranger.

"Officer, please . . ." said Rakkim.

The white Ranger cuffed him.

Rakkim stayed on his feet. It was probably a mistake, better to hit the dirt, but his patience was about at an end.

The white Ranger cocked his head at Rakkim. He had good instincts, but he wasn't listening to them. The blue light from the cruiser strobed away behind him, his face in partial shadow. "I want the code. *Now.*"

Rakkim swallowed. "Code . . . code's 78455."

The white Ranger tugged at his Stetson. "Thank you kindly."

The black Ranger remote-popped the trunk of their patrol car. Jerked a thumb at Leo. "Climb on in, idiot."

Leo looked at Rakkim.

"Go on." Rakkim flexed a muscle in his wrist, felt the Fedayeen knife slide into his hand. "It's going to be all right. These nice men will take good care of you."

"I don't *want* to get inside the trunk," wailed Leo. "I'm afraid of the dark."

The black Ranger grabbed Leo by the scruff of the neck, dragged him to the back of the patrol car, and tossed him into the trunk.

"Please . . ." said Leo.

The black Ranger slammed the trunk lid down.

"Almost forgot." The white Ranger snapped his fingers at Rakkim. "I need the tracker. Wouldn't want the idiot to run off." He quick-drew his pistol. Fast too. Probably practiced for hours at the barracks. "Hard keeping good help. Don't know why."

Rakkim raised his hands. "Please . . . I'll do what you want."

"*Anything?*" The white Ranger centered the barrel of the pistol on Rakkim's forehead. "You're a right certain accommodating fella, aren't you?"

"What . . . what else can I do?" said Rakkim.

The white Ranger showed those big flat teeth of his again. The cruiser's blue light seemed to be flashing faster and faster. "Yeah, what else can you do?"

"Quit toying with that man, Jerry Lee," said the black Ranger, getting behind the wheel of the cruiser. "Blow his shit away and let's get out of here. Faye's stops serving the buffalo steak special at three a.m."

Rakkim watched the vein along the side of the white Ranger's neck pulse. Looked like about eighty-five, ninety beats a minute. He still had time.

The white Ranger held the pistol steady. "How about you pass over the tracker and I promise to say a few words over you when the deed is done. I'll give you a real sweet send-off. I'm a church deacon." He grinned again, his teeth like chalk in the blue light. "'Course, I'm not saying all my prayers been said over consecrated ground."

Rakkim slowly reached toward the white Ranger, holding the tracker out with two fingers, just as he had been told. His other fingers curled around the Fedayeen knife, its blade resting invisibly against the inside of his forearm.

The black Ranger beeped the horn.

"Daryl's impatient," said the white Ranger. "Me, I'm not all that fond of buffalo steak," he added, reaching for the tracker with his free hand.

Rakkim bumped the white Ranger's gun hand as the man fired, slashed his throat in the same motion, and ran toward the cruiser. The black Ranger fumbled for his pistol, started to raise it when Rakkim drove the blade through the bulletproof window, glass shattering as he slid the knife deep into the Ranger's windpipe.

The black Ranger sighed, the sound filling the stillness. His eyelids fluttered like moths.

Rakkim eased the knife free. The black Ranger's blood splashed across Rakkim's wrist. Warm, but already cooling in the night air. People died so quickly, the heat fleeing from them . . . Rakkim reached in, turned off the light bar. The darkness was soothing. He listened to the rush of the river and the sound of Leo beating against the trunk lid, then walked over and checked on the white Ranger.

The trooper lay facedown in the dirt. Jerry Lee, that's what his partner had called him. Jerry Lee's blood puddled black in the moonlight. A mirror reflecting the stars. Jerry Lee and Daryl. Good to know the names of the dead. Rakkim shuddered. Where did *that* come from? He never needed to know their names before. Killing wasn't counting coup, wasn't keeping score. It was a last resort. Always had been, anyway. He wiped his hands on the grass, washed himself with dirt, still turning things over in his mind. He looked toward the river, his eyes already adjusting to the dim light. Caught in the mangrove roots that bordered the river . . . something . . . a tailfin of a car, only the very tip visible. Rakkim wondered how many other vehicles were piled up under the water, how many others had been carried downstream. He looked back at Jerry Lee and spit.

Leo cried out from inside the trunk.

Rakkim had started toward the rear of the cruiser when the trunk lid popped open. Leo rolled out onto the ground, gasping for air. Wires protruded from one hand. He had bypassed the trunk security lock somehow.

Leo saw the body of the white Ranger. Saw the mess inside the cruiser. His knees buckled. "Rikki . . . what . . . what did you *do*?"

CHAPTER 16

"I can't believe . . . can't believe what you did," said Leo, teeth chattering in the rush of humid air. He rested his head in his hands. "How did I let my dad talk me into this?"

What a crybaby. Rakkim tilted the seat back a little more, steering with one hand. Top down. The Caddy's beams the only headlights on the road. Clear skies, more stars than anyone could count. Acres of alfalfa and sugar beets sweetening the sultry night. Crickets sawing away their desperate love songs, the sound undulating, and Rakkim hummed along with them, part of them now. No limits. No boundaries. He loved the South.

Leo looked up at Rakkim. "You *killed* those men."

Rakkim glanced at him. "You're fucking welcome."

"I didn't *ask* for help. Besides, it was your fault it came to that. You were supposed to take the *long* way out of town."

"I missed the turnoff."

"You think this is funny?" Leo's lower lip quivered. "What's funny about two dead lawmen?"

"Those two weren't lawmen, they were just thugs wearing badges." Rakkim drove on, the big twelve-cylinder engine roaring, steady as a freight train. Easy to ignore Leo's questions, but not his own. Why *had* he done it? Even worse . . . why had he enjoyed it? A peeling sign by the side of the road announced PIGGLY WIGGLY DINER—HOT FOOD, COLD BEER, TEN MILES. "You hungry?"

"Hungry?" Leo's voice cracked. "I may never eat again."

"Wouldn't hurt you to miss a few meals," said Rakkim, "but you'll eat. You'll be surprised how hungry you are the first time you sit down. After seeing what I did, you'll feel like there's a hole inside you and all the food in the world will barely fill it. You'll be shoveling it in with both hands."

"I doubt it."

Rakkim hummed along to the song in his head. He knew the melody but didn't know the words. He wished he could remember where he had heard it before.

"What you did . . . it doesn't bother you, does it?" said Leo.

"I guess I've got a moral deficiency. Maybe I should eat more green leafy vegetables."

"Why do you keep making jokes about it?" said Leo. "Dad said you weren't like that. He said I could trust you."

"You *can* trust me."

"Trust you to do what? Kill people?"

"Yeah, that's right, when it's needed."

"It wasn't needed." Leo sounded like he was about to cry. "You went out of your way to kill those men. You jeopardized our mission."

"*Our* mission? You little shit, this whole thing is on me. You're only here because Sarah said to bring you."

"Murder is a sin. It's a sin in Judaism, it's a sin in Christianity, it's a sin in Islam and every other—"

"I'll decide what's a sin."

"*You'll* decide?" Leo stared at him, mouth open. "You're going to get me killed."

"Don't worry," said Rakkim. "Guys like you always die in bed. Clean sheets and a cup of warm cocoa in your hand, that's how you'll go out."

Leo wiped his eyes. "Liar."

Rakkim turned off onto a still smaller road, unlit and unmarked. Country and western drifted from the radio, love songs even sadder and more plaintive than the crickets. A huge wooden cross tilted by the side of the road. He raced on, pebbles kicking up in their wake. Disturbed by their passing, an owl flapped off from atop a tall pine, wings fluttering briefly across the moon. An omen, that's what most Southerners would call that, a bad omen. Rakkim didn't need an owl to tell him that they were fucked forever. He smiled to himself. Everything seemed amusing lately. It wasn't that his sensations were muted, the fear and pain blurred. Exactly the opposite. The world never seemed more clear, an awful clarity frozen in his heart. *I'll decide what's a sin.* So now Rakkim had added blasphemy to his long list of transgressions.

Leo cleared his throat, afraid to disturb Rakkim's thoughts. "Shouldn't we . . . I mean, after we put some space between us and . . . what you did back there, shouldn't we find someplace to sleep?"

"I'm not tired."

"Right. That shadow warrior thing."

"Why don't you go to sleep? Give your mind and your mouth a rest."

Leo yawned. "I'm not tired either."

Rakkim kept watch for movement in the darkness ahead as he drove down the road, looking for a light, a signal, anything that would indicate an ambush. Leo didn't know anything about death, but he was right about at least one thing: Rakkim had gone out of his way to kill the two Rangers. No real explanation for it either. Sure, they were murderous bastards, but the world was full of murderous bastards with and without badges. Yeah, the Rangers had groped the young nun back at Mount Carmel, but that was no capital crime, and besides, the nun would have been horrified at their deaths, preferring to pray for their forgiveness. No, the killing had been for Rakkim's satisfaction and no one else's, and that bothered him more than anything else.

"I thought shadow warriors *avoided* confrontation," blurted Leo.

"You just can't let it go, can you?"

"I'm just trying to *understand.*" Leo balled his chubby fists. "Shadow warriors are supposed to be invisible, that's what Dad told me. Unnoticed and under the radar. They don't look for trouble. They don't kill without cause."

"I'm not a shadow warrior anymore," Rakkim said.

"Then what *are* you?"

Rakkim didn't answer. Didn't have an answer. All he knew was that he had told Leo the truth—he had changed. Transformation was an occupational hazard for a shadow warrior. And for assassins. Given time, shadow warriors always went native and assassins always went mad dog, but Rakkim was neither.

Like shadow warriors, assassins worked alone, beyond any boundary or authority. No such thing as an old assassin . . . but Darwin had proven them all wrong. He was in his forties when Rakkim tracked him to the abandoned church in New Fallujah, Darwin at the height of his powers, a devout atheist, welcoming Rakkim to his private sanctuary. The two of them cut and bleeding, knives dancing as they gasped for breath.

I recognized you the moment I saw you, taunted Darwin. *I knew what you were.*

Rakkim lunged. Drew blood. *I know who you are too. I know how you think.*

I feel sorry for you then, Rikki. Darwin slipped slightly, but Rakkim wasn't fooled. *Knowing how I think . . .* Darwin's expression sagged—he looked in pain. *Rikki, I wouldn't wish that on my worst enemy.*

Even now, Rakkim wasn't sure if the sadness on Darwin's face at that moment was genuine or another ploy. Ultimately it didn't matter. All that mattered was that Darwin had died, and Rakkim had lived. *Last laugh, motherfucker.*

Rakkim followed a curve in the road, still thinking of Darwin, and the sudden silence in the church as the assassin's mouth had worked around Rakkim's blade, pinning him in place. No last words. Rakkim had stood there watching Darwin's eyes grow wider and wider. He almost missed the man's soft, mocking voice, the way it insinuated itself into their parry and thrust, wrapped itself around him . . . Rakkim slammed on the brakes, skidding.

"What's wrong?" shouted Leo.

Up ahead a mass of vegetation had engulfed the surrounding fields and rolled on, a thicket thirty or forty feet tall now covering most of the narrow road. Rakkim hit the high beams. The light gleamed off the glossy leaves and thick vines, the interior of the undergrowth too dense to see into.

"What *is* that?" said Leo. "Some kind of jungle?"

"Kudzu."

Leo whistled. "I . . . I thought it was just a fast-growing weed."

"Used to be. Before the big warm." Rakkim turned off the headlights, kept the engine idling. "Kudzu was always a problem, but since the weather changed it seems like all our natural enemies got stronger. More tenacious." He stared into the darkness. "Fire ants nesting in the cities, killer bees so bad in Savannah and Birmingham that kids don't play outside in summer. Farmers in the delta calling in napalm strikes to keep the kudzu from taking over the best bottomland, hundreds of people dying every year from poison ivy . . . it's like Mother Nature knows we're on the ropes."

Leo snorted. "Spare me the melodrama." He looked over. "Rikki?" He turned around, peered into the night. "Rikki?"

Rakkim scooted silently across the road and into the underbrush, moving at a forty-five-degree angle from the idling car. The ground felt spongy underfoot. He heard Leo's calls faint in the distance and kept moving. The kid was more trouble than he was worth, just like he had told Sarah. Civilians. She was the woman he loved, the woman at the right hand of the president, but she was still a civilian.

Starlight shone in the eyes of a squirrel watching from a low branch. Rakkim eased deeper into the brush, not making a sound. A deep gully ran along the other side of the road. He walked across a narrow plank half hidden by tall grass, circling around to the treeline, keeping low, staying quiet. He settled in, closed his eyes, let his night vision kick in and then opened them.

From his vantage point Rakkim could see a mile or so in either direction. No lights. No movement. No sound but the wind in the trees and small animals skittering overhead. No one waiting in ambush on the other side of the kudzu. No need to wait. The roadway fronting the kudzu, that narrow half lane of cracked asphalt, had been dug away for ten feet, replaced with a scaffold of wood and black plastic, a false front sprinkled with dirt. Cars approaching from either direction would see the encroaching kudzu and drive onto the shoulder; the embankment would give way, flipping them into the ditch. Next morning, the folks who laid the trap would check for survivors and any other loot that fate had sent their way, then winch out the wrecked car so as not to alert the next victim.

Gnats buzzed around his ears as Rakkim stared into the gully. He picked out a couple of glimmers among the rocks—a piece of shattered windshield maybe, or a hubcap that the locals had missed. Hard to make it on farming alone in this part of Texas, what with the drought and the kudzu sucking up all the groundwater. The survivors probably got ransomed or sold off. People did what they needed to survive. Then went to church on Sunday, said their prayers, and laid it in the lap of God.

Rakkim touched his pocket, reassured himself that the shekel of Tyre was still there. He pulled it out, examined it in the starlight. The silver coin was tarnished and worn, pitted in places, but the profile of the emperor or whoever he was on the front was clear enough. Another sneering, overfed, thick-necked bastard with a crown of laurel leaves on his brow attesting to his divinity. Two thousand years later and nothing had changed. He turned the coin over, tilted it, catching the light. A giant eagle rising up, ready to strike . . . probably trying to get at the suety son of a bitch on the other side.

"Where did you *go?*" said Leo as Rakkim slid behind the wheel.

Rakkim backed up, eyes on the rearview mirror. Faster, accelerating.

"Tell me what's happening," pleaded Leo as they bumped over the rough road.

Rakkim backed into the wide spot in the roadway, turned around, and headed back where they had come. "We're taking another route. This one's too dangerous."

"I'm not scared."

"Right."

Bugs splattered against the windshield like popcorn, the ultrasonics embedded in the glass disintegrating them. The crickets' undulating sound stopped as they approached, started up again as they passed.

"I still don't know why we're going to New Orleans," said Leo. "We need to get to Tennessee as soon as possible, not waste time with Moseby's wife."

"There's no way Moseby would have left without talking to his wife. They would have had to kill him first. We need to know what he told her."

"You could have said something. I'm part of this too, you know." Leo fiddled with the radio, tuning in static more than anything else. "You're lucky to have me with you."

Rakkim flipped him the coin. "How did you know what I was thinking?"

Leo held the coin between his thumb and forefinger, spun it round and round. "It's heavier than I thought."

"That's not what I asked."

Leo hefted the coin, rubbed his fingernail along the raw edge. "This big shot you're interested in is an End-Times Christian. Suddenly you cancel your request for a gold coin, and ask Stevenson for a Roman coin, and it's got to be silver." He lightly touched the surface of the shekel. "Wasn't that hard to see what you were up to. Not like it was non-euclidean geometry. I mean, what good Christian *wouldn't* want one of Judas's thirty pieces of silver?" He handed the coin back. "Your only mistake was you don't really know your history. Judas got bought off by the priests of the temple, and they didn't use Roman silver. The only coins accepted at the Jerusalem temple were shekels of Tyre. That's what Judas walked away with. That's what you've got to show this End-Times gangster in Tennessee."

Rakkim put the coin away. Glanced over at Leo. "Does anybody other than *you* know things like that?"

"Most people are pretty stupid . . . no offense." Leo tuned the radio again, taking his time. Finally found a station. "I figured it was best if you used the right coin, just in case. To fool somebody else, you have to fool yourself first. That's the way it works, doesn't it?"

"That's the way it works." Rakkim laughed. "Thanks."

Leo sang along to the radio, his voice surprisingly strong and sweet. He waited until the song finished before speaking. "Those two Rangers you killed . . . they had guns, but you only had a knife. So, I guess it was kind of fair."

"Fairness had nothing to do with it."

"Just a knife . . ." Leo sniffed. "Could you teach me how to—"

"No." Rakkim hesitated. "I thought the whole thing disgusted you."

"It did, but now when I think about it . . ." Leo chewed a fingernail. "They were bad, weren't they?"

"When I pushed their car into the river, I saw at least two more cars down there. So yeah, I'd say they were bad."

"I learn fast," said Leo. "You could just show me a couple Fedayeen moves . . ."

Rakkim's laughter echoed.

"You're probably just worried I'll get better than you, that's why you don't want to teach me." Leo yawned. "Piggly Wiggly Diner," he said as they passed the sign. "Maybe we should stop and see what they got cooking. I'm *hungry*."

CHAPTER 17

"Mr. *Moseby*." Colonel Zachary Smitts strode across the field-tent that served as a command center, his uniform still dusty from his recent arrival. "A pleasure to meet you," he said, shaking hands. "I apologize for keeping y'all waiting this last week, but I had some shitbirds to attend to." He nodded at Gravenholtz. "Besides, I know Lester here is good company."

The two guards at the entrance chuckled, then stopped abruptly at the expression on Gravenholtz's face.

The Colonel led Moseby into the command center, limping slightly. His high black boots were worn but polished to a bright sheen, his tailored gray uniform hugging his lanky frame. Somewhere in his sixties, the Colonel still cut a gallant, if slightly vain, figure with a pair of ivory-handled automatics on his hips, and his long hair dyed too black. One of those backwoods cavaliers Southerners had venerated for two hundred years.

"While I was busy here, these outlaws swooped down on towns under my protection, stealing and raping and murdering," said the Colonel, handing a videocard to Moseby. "I'm a good Christian, Mr. Moseby, but I won't abide an insult."

Moseby saw a sweep of dismal pine trees on the card, men hanging from every limb, arms tied behind their backs as they swayed in the breeze. Every seam in their grimy faces stood out as the high-def images rolled across the card. Close-ups of unshaven men, hatchet-faced crackers in jeans and jackets, eyes bulging, blood crusted around their nostrils. A blue-bottle fly perched on one man's blackened tongue, gauzy wings shimmering in the dawn's light.

"Attending to such scum is a wearisome business," said the Colonel. "Seems like there's never a shortage of men who need killing."

"You should have let *me* take care of them like I asked," said Gravenholtz, the redhead's voice shaded with insolence. "No need to bother yourself with such chores."

"It's my responsibility," said the Colonel. "Our folks need to see the face of authority. Need to see that authority exact a swift and certain justice. Besides, you would have taken an unseemly pleasure in the accounting. The idea is to give our *enemies* nightmares, not our own people." He winked at Moseby. "In Lester's case, his bite is even worse than his bark."

In the field-tent command center, technicians hovered over video monitors in the rear. The faint crackle of voices floated in the night air. Moseby had tried a few times to sneak into the center on one of his late-night excursions, but it was too well guarded. Since Gravenholtz had him brought here a half hour ago, he had memorized the layout, noted potential weaknesses in the security perimeter. From where he stood, he couldn't see the video screens, but he could hear desperation in the voice leaking from the headset of one of the techs.

"Lester taking good care of you?" said the Colonel.

"Fine," said Moseby. "I didn't realize it was a unit tradition for Lester to give the new man a sponge bath, but he insisted."

The Colonel blinked, then roared with laughter. Banged Moseby on the back.

Moseby saw Gravenholtz rub his knuckles and remembered how the redhead had sledgehammered the shadow warrior.

"Relax, Lester," said the Colonel. "You got to learn to laugh at yourself." He squinted at Moseby. "Sponge bath. You're just full of surprises, aren't you?"

"Yeah, he's a Christmas present with a bright red bow," said Gravenholtz.

The Colonel sat down, propped his boots up on a table. "They say you're a finder, Mr. Moseby. Are you really as good as I've been told?"

Moseby turned his head slightly, tried to see what was on the video screens in the rear, but the angle was off. "I get lucky, that's all."

"That's what they said about me at Memphis, when we sent the towelheads scurrying back to Kansas." The Colonel winked at him. "I'll take a lucky man any day."

Moseby detected an edge to the Colonel's easy banter. The man was worried about something, his eyes sliding away, preferring to watch

Moseby indirectly, taking his measure at his own pace, without himself being examined. A good tactic. Most men wouldn't have even been aware of it, lulled into mistakes by the Colonel's charm.

"You're not the first finder I brought here, Mr. Moseby," said the Colonel. "The others came well recommended too, but the task . . . the mission proved too much for them."

"Useless fucks," said Gravenholtz.

"Some of them have worked out better than others, but none of them have really worked out," said the Colonel, ignoring Gravenholtz. "We've opened up a dozen tunnels, got three that still might yield something. I'm an impatient man, John, it's been my curse, but I've made the best of it. I pay top dollar for success, but I have no tolerance for failure. None whatsoever."

"Don't get your hopes up, Colonel," said Gravenholtz. "This one feels wrong to me."

"Now, now, Lester, no need to insult our guest." The Colonel eyed Moseby. "Still, I do hope I haven't been misled about your abilities." He stroked one of his long sideburns with a thumb. "I heard last year some big Catholic church in Savannah hired you to locate some religious gewgaws swept into a limestone cavern during last year's floods. The underground was a vast honeycomb filled with everything from wrecked cars to drowned cows bloated up like gray balloons. Took you three weeks, but they said you found the Madonna they were looking for. Is that a true story?"

"Colonel, if you want me to find something for you, I'm going to have to be briefed. All I know is your people are opening up a lot of old coal tunnels."

The Colonel looked at Gravenholtz. "You haven't acquainted this man with our situation?"

"I don't trust him," said Gravenholtz. "Thought it best to wait until you got back."

"God*damnit*, Lester . . ." The Colonel ran a hand through his hair. "Fine. I need an update myself." He looked at Moseby. "You believe in God, John?"

Moseby almost laughed but the Colonel was serious, head inclined toward him, waiting for an answer. He was handsome, his long hair slick with pomade, blue eyes hard as turquoise. In spite of all his accolades during and after the war, the Colonel's only decoration was the Congressional Medal of Honor from the former United States that hung from a silk ribbon around his neck.

"Consider yourself a good Christian, do you?" asked the Colonel.

"I do my best," said Moseby. "Figure we wouldn't have needed salvation if we weren't sinners."

"A fine answer," said the Colonel. "What church do you attend?"

"Calvary . . . Calvary Baptist," said Moseby.

"Deep-water Baptist?" said the Colonel.

Moseby nodded. Remembered the preacher anointing his head with a smear of oil before pushing him backward into the Susquehanna River.

"That's good," said the colonel, fixing him with those hard blue eyes. "A deep-water Baptist is just what I need, because, you see, boy . . ." He beckoned him closer. ". . . what you're looking for is under a hundred feet of water at the bottom of a coal seam, a lake of black water cold enough to shrink your pecker to the size of a pinworm."

Gravenholtz laughed.

"Look at him, Lester," said the Colonel. "Look at him. He didn't even flinch. I think we may have found our answer to prayer."

"Speak for yourself, Colonel," said Gravenholtz.

"What am I looking for, Colonel?"

"That's not important, not to you anyway," said the Colonel. "Two or three men should easily be able to raise it. The hard part is finding the right lake. This part of the mountain is mostly limestone and shale, so there's tunnels and plenty of lakes to choose from, but we've narrowed things down. We're getting close."

"If I know what I'm looking for, I'll have a better chance of finding it," said Moseby.

"The Colonel *gave* you his answer," said Gravenholtz.

"Lester said you brought your own equipment," said the Colonel. "Anything else you need, just say the word."

"What's the current status of the digs?" Moseby waved toward the video stations. "Sounded like there was some kind of problem going on."

The Colonel looked at Gravenholtz.

"Number three is still proceeding on schedule," Gravenholtz said to the Colonel. "Number seven was another dud."

"What about number four?" said the Colonel. "They back yet?"

Gravenholtz slouched, scratched at his front teeth with a grimy thumb. "Number eleven's gone to hell. Had a cave-in a couple days ago. Seemed like half the mountain gave way."

The Colonel started toward the video stations. "You should have informed me immediately, Lester."

Moseby was right behind him.

"Didn't see the need for it, Colonel," said Gravenholtz. "Not like we can do anything."

The Colonel stared at the video screen. Turned and glared at Gravenholtz, then turned back to the screen.

"How y'all holding up, boy?" drawled the Colonel.

The man on the video screen sat slumped against a boulder, head resting in his hands. The low-light camera cast a greenish glow on everything.

"Travis?" said the Colonel, louder now.

The video tech switched the sound to the external speakers.

The man's face on-screen glistened with dust, his hair and eyebrows silvery. A young man made old by rock dust and fatigue. He looked around. "Colonel?" He got awkwardly to his feet, dirt falling off his coveralls. Saluted.

"At ease, Travis," said the Colonel. "Save your strength."

Travis licked his lips. Breathing hard. The whites of his eyes stark against his grimy skin. "Sir . . . are you coming for us?"

"We're doing our level best," said the Colonel.

Gravenholtz, standing beside the Colonel, rolled his eyes at Moseby.

"Air's getting pretty bad, Colonel," said Travis.

"Just hang on, boy," said the Colonel. "I'll be back in a few moments. Got to check on the progress of the rescue team." He touched a button, cut the sound. Turned to a technician in the corner of the command center. "Well?"

The technician covered the microphone of his headset. Shook his head. "Whole tunnel is unstable, sir."

"Don't want to say I told you so, but I did, Colonel," said Gravenholtz. "Ain't no big deal. They were on their way out when the roof come down—the lake they found was just a puddle. Nothing there but creepy crawlies."

Moseby peered at the video screen. Watched as Travis sat back down again, panting now. He reached over, flipped the switch. "Travis? I'm John. Could you move the camera? I want to see the rock face where the cave-in occurred."

"Sure," said Travis. "Sure." He got up slowly, picked up the camera. The screen view bobbled as he staggered down the tunnel, the light from the camera bouncing off the walls. The sound of his breathing echoed. "It . . . it was down here."

"Hey!" said Gravenholtz. "That's not your business!"

"Stand down, Lester," said the Colonel.

Moseby leaned closer to the screen. "Travis, could you please hold the camera still?"

"Okay," said Travis. "Hard, though. Can't decide if I'm freezing or roasting."

"Just do your best," said Moseby. The image steadied, and Moseby felt an ache in his stomach.

"I'm tired, sir," said Travis. "You mind if I lie down?"

"No . . . not at all," said Moseby. "You should rest, Travis."

Travis sat back down, slumped forward.

"You should have called me when it first caved in," Moseby said to Gravenholtz. "Might have had a chance drilling a slant tunnel. It's too late now."

"Who died and made you boss?" snarled Gravenholtz.

"Daddy!"

They all turned as a young woman launched herself across the control center, blew past the guards, and wrapped herself around the Colonel.

"Daddy, why didn't you *tell* me you were back?"

The Colonel hugged her, kissed her hair. "I just got back, Baby."

"You *still* should have told me." The young woman stamped her feet, sent her lacy white dress fluttering. "And I'm pissed at you too, Lester God-damned Gravenholtz. You should have let me know he was coming back. Right now you're at the tippity top of my ass-whupping list."

The tips of Gravenholtz's ears flushed.

The Colonel swung her in circles, laughing, and she howled *wheeeeeee* as her feet left the ground. She laid her head back, her long hair flying around them, honey blond, gleaming like warm silk in the camp lights.

Round and round they went, the Colonel laughing along with her. She was barely in her twenties, tall and high-breasted, tan as a pecan, so fine-featured that Moseby couldn't imagine how beautiful the Colonel's wife must be. The Colonel finally put her down, the two of them out of breath, dizzy, still clinging to each other.

"Where . . . where are my manners," gasped the Colonel. He half bowed. "Baby . . . may I . . . may I present John Moseby. Mr. Moseby, may I present my wife, Baby."

Baby grinned, stuck out her hand, her gaze amused and coquettish. "Mr. Moseby," she said, sliding her hand into his, "you better close your mouth before a big ol' horsefly lands on your tongue."

CHAPTER 18

Shit. Rakkim saw the cop car hidden in the shadows just as he pulled into the parking lot behind the Piggly Wiggly Diner, the car up against a storage shed where it couldn't be seen from the road. Too late now. Worst thing to do would be to leave without going inside. Cops were probably inside with a camera remote just waiting for suspicious behavior.

"What's wrong?" said Leo, attuned now to any change in Rakkim's demeanor.

Rakkim drove past a row of haphazardly parked trucks and vans, finally backed into a spot beside a four-by-four diesel with an armored grill and a winch on the back. A barbecue pit smoldered off to one side, the night air heavy with slow-roasting flesh. A huge emergency generator rested under the kitchen. Sun-bleached yellow paint peeled off the back of the diner. Bird shit streaked the walls and windows from dive-bombing crows, crusty under the parking lot fluorescents.

"What's—"

Rakkim backhanded him.

Leo squealed, clutched at his cheek, eyes brimming with tears. "Why did you *hit* me?"

"How do you feel? Angry? Humiliated?" Leo swung on him but Rakkim easily deflected the blow, not taking his eyes off the parking lot. "Helpless? Yeah, that the one eating you up right now? That's what it's like to be an Ident." He grabbed the kid's chin, turned his head. The handprint was still fiery. "These little cafés always use Idents for the scut work. They see you walk in, after you got your leash tugged, they're going to know what that feels like. We may be able to use their sympathy." He stepped out of the car, boots crunching on the gravel. "There's local cops inside too. So mind your manners."

Leo stayed put. "Cops . . . ?"

Rakkim snapped his fingers. *"Now."* He saw the dishwasher peeking out through the slatted windows of the kitchen as Leo scurried out. Leo kept one step behind him as Rakkim walked around to the front, putting on a serious limp, hitching himself forward like a crab.

A grinning terra-cotta pig in bright red trousers stood on its hind legs in front of the diner. Rakkim patted its snout for good luck, the paint worn away from thousands of others who had done the exact same thing. All the people filing into churches and mosques, hoping to curry favor with God . . . Rakkim figured he might as well pat the pig and hope that the heavenly reservoir of good luck still had a few drops left for a thirsty man.

"Sweet Home Alabama" blared from the sound system as Rakkim threw open the front door and stepped inside. Seemed like half the diners and honky-tonks in the Belt had that old song on permanent rotation. Sarah said that during the early days of the Civil War, "Sweet Home Alabama" had been the battle song for the Belt troops. After the armistice there had been talk of making it the official national anthem, but representatives from the other Southern states had balked, and in the end, "Onward Christian Soldiers" had won out. Rakkim would have voted for "Sweet Home Alabama."

The scanner inside the front door beeped, cycling. The clerk seated behind the glass of the gun-check room didn't even look up, busy with his handheld game. Shotguns, assault rifles, and pistols stood stacked and tagged behind him. Rakkim waited. The Fedayeen knife against his forearm was entirely nonmetallic, and didn't register even on scans designed to pick up graphite-composite weapons. The inner door beeped. Swung open.

Rakkim nodded at the flag over the bar, his hand flopping over his heart. Nothing too showy. Shadow warriors on their first mission in the Belt sometimes overdid the patriotism thing. Dangerous mistake. Belt folk loved God and country, loved them so much it was second nature, easy as breathing. Flag wavers drew attention to themselves. The booths were filled, hunters and truckers and college boys. No sign of the cops. The customers craned their necks at the Mudbowl XXXVI rerun on the wallscreen. Good screen too, the image more crisp than anything commercially available in the republic. No wonder the diner drew a crowd, even at this hour of the night. On-screen, young women raced four-by-four buggies, studded wheels spin-

ning rooster tails of mud fifty feet in the air, covering the barely clad con-
testants in a sheath of muck.

The woman pouring coffee at the counter nodded at Rakkim, indicated
a couple of spots. She had mugs of coffee waiting for both of them as they
sat down. Rakkim pushed his aside, ordered a strawberry malt, heavy on
the malt. The request tumbled out of his mouth like somebody else was
talking.

The Mudbowl camera zoomed in on a filthy blonde whose buggy went
airborne over a jump, her hair flying as her feet left the pegs, her body hor-
izontal for a full five seconds.

"I'd eat that three ways from Sunday," said the hunter beside Rakkim,
tall guy with a grimy camouflage jacket, jabbing a thumb at the screen.

"Amen," said his buddy.

The guys in the booths cheered. Before the tit-for-tat in the ionosphere
between Russia and China made the point moot, the republic blacked out
all foreign satellite images. Couldn't blame the religious authorities—half-
naked women riding around full-throttle like they owned the world . . .
people could get ideas. Rakkim leaned forward. The filthy blonde was
Tanya Tyson, three-time motocross champion from Baton Rouge—every
underground club in Seattle had satellite descramblers to pull in forbidden programming, but all that space junk had shut down the global Net,
and no one was willing to say how long it would be before things settled
down. Rakkim wondered what the Blue Moon and the other clubs would
do to keep the customers happy.

Eagleton would have figured a way to filter out the chaff from the trans-
missions. Worst body odor in the Zone, a real curl-your-nostril-hairs stink,
but the guy had vision. Until al-Faisal killed him, Eagleton had sold the
best Swiss and Malayan black-tech out of that hole-in-the-wall shop of his,
zero-grav tech that he tweaked even further. Rakkim still wondered what
Eagleton had put together for al-Faisal—it must have been major, so important that al-Faisal couldn't trust him to live. State Security was certain that
al-Faisal was dead, blown to chunks rather than allowing himself to be captured. He and the device he had picked up from Eagleton. Rakkim would
have liked to believe that . . . another reason he wasn't convinced.

The president of the Belt came on-screen, and somebody immediately
turned the sound down. Laughter rolled from the booths as the new pres-

ident jabbered away, a slick young politician with a mop of carefully tousled hair and too many teeth.

"That grinny-Gus done nothing but sell us out since the day he got elected," said a fat man with a straw hat pushed back on his forehead.

"He weren't elected," said his buddy. "Never met nobody yet who voted for him."

"Brazilians *own* his ass," said the fat man. "How you think they got logging rights on the Carolina state forest?"

Somebody switched the station and the crowd cheered.

The waitress set a strawberry malt in front of Rakkim, the clear glass glistening with condensation. "Got five kinds of barbecue and breakfast's served twenty-four/seven," she said, pointing to the LED menu embedded in the counter. The cigarette tucked in the corner of her mouth bobbed with every word. Melissa McQ was stitched onto the left pocket of her uniform in fraying red thread. She noticed Leo's Ident collar. Noticed the handprint on his cheek too, but didn't say anything.

"Bacon and eggs for me, side a grits too," said Rakkim. "Give him the same, without the bacon. Jew boy here spits out swine. Real disgusting-like."

"Jew boy?" Melissa peered at Leo. The cigarette rose to the one o'clock position. "I've met a few Jewish people in my time. You know a man named Hermann Weinstein? Long drink a water. Big head of black hair. Very clean hands."

Leo shook his head.

Melissa tapped out their orders on the counter keypad. "A Jewish Ident. What won't they think of next?"

Rakkim sucked up his strawberry malt. Loved it. He didn't remember ever ordering one before. Wondered what had taken him so long.

Melissa leaned over the counter. She had a full, soft face, her frosted hair in tiny ringlets like some kewpie doll's. "I was an Ident myself way back when." She absently touched her neck where the Ident collar had once lain. "Spent seven years just outside of Jamesboro. Wasn't so bad. Man holding my contract was a good Christian. Seven children and the poor man's wife died birthing the eighth. I learned my way around the kitchen, I'll tell you that much. *Just* the kitchen; like I said, he was a good Christian. No funny business." She wiped her hands on her apron. "I still get Christmas cards from Darleen. She was the youngest. Ugly child, but nice-shaped feet. You don't appreciate nice feet until you take off your shoes after standing twelve hours a day."

Rakkim nodded, waiting for the cops to show. Matter of time.

"Never had children myself," said Melissa. "Those were good years. Like the good Lord said, seven lean years followed by seven fat years. Yes, sir, lots a wonderful folks been Idents, so you got nothing to be ashamed of." She patted Leo on the arm. "What kind of trade are you going to learn, honey?"

A line of spit ran down the side of Leo's smile.

"Taking him up to the lead smelter at Fayetteville." Rakkim dragged on the straw, sucking up the thick, sweet malt. Amazing stuff. "Got a five-year contract."

The hunters started laughing.

"Mister, you should be ashamed of yourself," said Melissa, "that place is hell on earth." She tried to get Leo's attention. "Honey, you don't want to go to Fayetteville. You won't survive a year. Only folks working there are convicts chose the smelter over the electric chair."

"Relax, lady, he doesn't feel pain like a normal person," said Rakkim.

"They got no safety equipment there, mister, none at all." Melissa shook her head harder, curls flying. "It's a hundred and thirty degrees where he's going to be feeding the furnace, and the fumes peel the rust right off the pipes. This poor soul shows up, all they're going to do is hand him a kerchief to wrap around his face and lock the door behind him."

"Kid's bought and paid for, so save your breath." Rakkim pointed to the kitchen. "How about you fetch my eggs and let me run my business."

"Good on ya, she's a lippy one," the tall hunter said to Rakkim as the waitress started down the counter. "You want my opinion, her owner didn't check out the goods 'cause she was ugly as sin, not 'cause he was some good Christian."

In the mirror behind the counter, Rakkim watched two cops come out of the bar. "Any luck?" Rakkim asked the hunter.

"Got a few ducks," said the tall hunter. "Weird birds, though. Beaks all papery and splintered, half starved."

"There's meat on 'em," said the other one, "that's all that matters."

"They ain't *right*," said the taller one. He leaned closer to Rakkim. "They roost in the wetlands around Houston. Lord only knows what's in the water there."

"I'm tired of hearing you complain about toxic this and toxic that," said the other one, a sunburned yokel with tiny white-tipped pustules covering his cheeks. "You don't want to eat 'em, *fine*, that's more for me."

Rakkim could see the cops chatting with the people in the booths, making everyone nervous as they slowly made their way closer. "I heard there was typhoid in Houston."

The second hunter picked his teeth with a fingernail. "You heard fucking wrong, pal."

"There *is* typhoid in Houston," said the taller one. "And worse shit too."

The smaller scratched the bumps on his face. "Like I said, more for me to eat."

Melissa placed a piece of peach pie in front of Leo. "On the house, honey." She glanced at Rakkim. "Cook burned your eggs. Going to be a while more."

The two cops stood behind Rakkim and the hunters, hands on their stun sticks. Couple of natty lawmen, creases sharp, clean-shaven. A third cop stepped through the front door with a machine pistol against his hip, safety off.

"Evening, gentlemen," said the oldest cop, a bald cracker with plenty of gym time.

The hunters grunted, looked down at their plates.

Rakkim swiveled around on his stool. "Buy you officers a cup of coffee?"

The question seemed to anger the other cop, short fellow with a clipped mustache.

"That your caddy pulled into the lot ten minutes ago?" said the bald cop.

A trick question. They knew what he was driving at. "Yes, sir, it is. It's for sale if you're interested, but I have to warn you, it burns oil."

Leo shoveled in peach pie, chewing with his mouth open.

"This your Ident?" asked the bald cop.

Another trick question. Rakkim took comfort in the blade against his forearm. He could take out the two cops behind him with one slashing movement, but getting to the third one before he ripped the clip . . . that depended on how the cop reacted to the sight of blood. "Yes, sir, he is, but I apologize, he's not for sale."

The bald cop held his hand out and Rakkim gave him the Ident chip with all the fake paperwork. The bald cop slipped the chip into his reader, ran a check. Finally nodded, handed the chip back. "Looks like everything's in order."

The waitress set Rakkim's grits and eggs in front of him. Leo's plate had twice the food on it as Rakkim's. "You sure I can't get you anything, William Lee?"

The bald cop shook his head. He laid a hand on Rakkim's shoulder. "You been to Mount Carmel earlier today?"

"Yup," said Rakkim. "Quite a show too. 'Bout to broke my heart." He looked from one cop to the other. "There some kind of problem?"

The bald cop looked him over. "We got word that a couple Rangers in that area didn't check in. Not like them, evidently. Been some trouble with the Mexes lately, so headquarters put out a three-hundred-sixty-degree alert." He had a soft little smile and Rakkim imagined him at Christmas, drinking eggnog as he watched his grandkids open their presents, making sure they were suitably grateful and correcting them if they weren't. "Seems like half the folks been in here tonight are on their way home from Mount Carmel. Thought you might have seen something."

"Well, sir, I took the interstate even though I was warned against it," said Rakkim. "Supposed to be press-gangs swooping down on folks, but I didn't worry." He rapped his right leg. "With this bum leg of mine, I'm not much good—"

"These Rangers weren't patrolling the interstate," said the bald cop.

"I see." Rakkim mixed yolk with his grits, sprinkled in a little sugar.

Melissa refilled Leo's coffee cup.

"I don't feel so good," said Leo.

Melissa felt his forehead. "You don't have a fever, honey."

"We checked your car." The bald cop waited. "Found your weapon under the front seat."

"Nothing wrong with that, is there, Officer?" said Rakkim.

"Not unless they repealed the Second Amendment when my back was turned," said the bald cop. Rakkim laughed with him.

"Let's take 'em in for questioning until the Rangers turn up," said the other cop. "Everybody's guilty of something."

"The gimp and the retard?" said the bald cop. "Waste of time."

"You want to show up empty-handed at the end of the shift?" said the short cop. "Fine. You listen to the sergeant give that same lecture on casting a wide net and the big one that got away. Not me."

The bald cop sighed, beckoned to Rakkim. "Come along, boys. Duty calls."

Rakkim stood up. His fingertips itched with excitement. No way were they going to the station or anywhere else with these three cops.

"Oh, nooooooooo," wailed Leo, squirming.

"What's his problem?" said the short cop.

"I . . . I pooped my pants," blubbered Leo.

The bald cop grimaced. "Goddamnit, stay here . . . stay here and do something with yourself." He grabbed the tall hunter, jerked him off the stool. "You and your buddy are coming with us." He glanced at the short cop. "Unless *you* want to change the retard's britches."

The short cop reached for the other hunter.

Rakkim watched the cops brace the hunters, banging them around good. Their sergeant would appreciate that. Probably tell them it builds character. As the door closed behind them, Leo went back to wolfing his pie. Melissa McQ returned, humming a happy tune. Rakkim finished his strawberry malt, ordered another one, feeling good. He should check, see if the oceans had caught fire or the earth had spun off its axis, because for the first time since he dragged Leo's ass ashore, the kid was earning his keep.

CHAPTER 19

Leo slapped at the mosquito on his neck. "I *hate* it here."

Rakkim watched the tops of the office buildings sticking out of the Gulf, the remnants of the New Orleans skyline silhouetted by moonlight, the satellite dishes and helipads reduced to aviaries for seagulls, their cries echoing across the water. A hundred years from now the buildings would have crumbled under the waves, and it would have been as if the city had never existed, just a peaceful lagoon with oil slicks. Moseby had chosen a house on the bayou with a dramatic view—maybe he figured he better enjoy it while he could before it was destroyed by the next monster storm. Typical shadow warrior philosophy. Everything in life was transitory, enjoy the moment.

More mosquito slaps. "I can't see *anything*," said Leo.

It was just before dawn, the haze from the burning offshore rigs making the night even darker. Plenty of light for Rakkim, though. More than enough to see the sentry sleeping in front of the outbuilding in the distance, the man curled in the dirt beside a glowing hotbox in the evening damp.

"Stay here." Rakkim moved forward, crawling through the weeds for ten minutes. Elbows and knees, elbows and knees. Gigantic blue land crabs scuttled past, reeking of decay, clacking their claws at him as they thronged toward the mudflats. Rowing over into the bayou, Rakkim had spotted an anaconda close to shore, had to have been twenty feet at least. All kinds of critters were migrating up from South America since the big warm—caimans, piranha, sea snakes, and pure white carnivorous orchids no one had ever seen before. He peeked from the grass.

The sentry didn't move. Closer now. Close enough to hear the man snoring, his chest rising and falling. One of the Colonel's irregulars, probably. No uniform, but he had an insignia of some kind pinned to his collar and a jackhammer shotgun cradled under one arm. Best of the Belt small arms. Gas-operated, drum magazine, 240 rounds a minute at full auto. A man with a jackhammer could take out a charging rhino or a full platoon. The Colonel might forgive a sleeping sentry, but laying the jackhammer in the dirt, that was a firing squad offense. So the Colonel trusted the men left behind to guard Moseby's family, trusted them enough to give them good equipment . . . but a couple weeks of baby-sitting and they were already getting sloppy.

Rakkim and Leo had reached the little town of Kenner yesterday afternoon. Just a speck along the Gulf, filled with dive bars and hangouts for the men who made their livelihood recovering artifacts from New Orleans. Plenty of Idents in Kenner, working the boats and doing the heavy lifting. Nobody paid any attention to Leo. By nightfall, Rakkim was buying beers for some of Moseby's old crew, tough guys with salt-hardened hands and faces. Rakkim said he was looking for Moseby, wanted to hire him and the crew—*I hear you're the best.* The crew nodded, ordered more beer, then said Moseby was out of town, no telling when he was coming back. A few hours ago Rakkim had helped the crew boss stumble home, a skinny Cajun named Hampton, complaining about four armed men staying out at Moseby's place on the edge of Blue Bayou. Four soldiers, they called themselves, and sure as shit not from around here. Might as well be Yankees the way they bitched about the weather and the bugs. Hampton and the rest of the crew would have damn sure done something about it, soldiers or no, damn sure run them out of the barn and off the land, if Moseby's wife hadn't insisted that she didn't want trouble. Said Moseby himself had left instructions for them to keep their distance, promised he'd be back before the hurricanes started up again.

Rakkim skirted the perimeter of the outbuilding, a refurbished barn. He made less noise than the breeze through the banyans. The wind billowed the Spanish moss that hung from the branches, and Rakkim thought of pennants at medieval tournaments, knights charging, lances pointed straight ahead. Ancient war, ancient warriors, ancient tactics. Direct attacks were foolhardy. The circumspect survived. And the deceitful prevailed.

The rear door of the barn hung off the hinges. Rakkim approached, knife in one hand, the pistol in the other. More snoring from inside. He took a position beside the door. He couldn't smell any animals inside, which was good—hard to sneak up on an animal. Glance and back. Three more men inside. Two sleeping on straw. The nearest to the door a muscular hillbilly with half his face blistered. He got the only mattress. Had to be Jeeter. Three inside, one asleep on guard duty, all four accounted for. Assuming that Hampton was right.

A light went on in the house nearby and Rakkim froze. A few moments later he moved forward, retraced his steps, making sure he hadn't left any indication of his passing. Leo was right where Rakkim had left him, shivering with the chill. He didn't see Rakkim. Rakkim left it that way, eased his way to the house.

Rakkim heard the clink of silverware, the rattle of pots and pans. He glanced in the window. Saw Annabelle Moseby alone in the kitchen, busy at the stove. The screen along the side was latched, but the thin blade of his Fedayeen knife lifted it up. The spring on the door was a problem. Everything rusted in the damp air. He listened to Annabelle's movements in the kitchen, learned her rhythm, the unconscious pace she set for herself as she stirred something thick, a wooden spoon going round and round a heavy crock, the rush of water into a metal pot. Rakkim internalized her rhythm, moved with it, opening the door as a cast-iron skillet slid back and forth across the burners. He heard the faint squeak of the screen door spring as he stepped inside the house, but she didn't.

Cypress planking underfoot, and the smell of bacon cooking and sourdough biscuits in the oven. Someone stirred in the next room, stifled a yawn and then turned over, sheets rustling. This was his favorite part of a mission. Insinuated into a subject's routine. Inside their private moment. His solitude. Silent as a kiss. This ability to absorb another person's pattern, to slip between the spaces of his routine, was the essence of shadow warrior training. Impossible to teach, the training was only able to improve an innate capacity to slow down the warrior's own consciousness, to lose one's self for a time.

To graduate the shadow warrior had to infiltrate one of the instructor's own haunts and tap him on the shoulder without being caught. His favorite restaurant or coffee shop. His mosque. His streetcar. Rakkim had watched his chief instructor's home for three days from the house next door, lain atop the neighbor's roof for two days and nights, not moving, watching everything inside through the bulletproof windows. On the third day, the instructor's wife went outside to feed the birds, as she did every morning, and Rakkim slid off the roof, vaulted the fence, and went inside. That night, as the instructor sat down for dinner with his wife and children, Rakkim walked out of the linen closet, tapped his instructor on the shoulder, then bowed and asked for his blessing and a bowl of soup.

Annabelle poured tea, humming to herself as she filled two mugs. A plain crucifix loomed over the stove. Family holograms in the dining nook, Moseby with a shy smile, holding hands with his wife and daughter. The kitchen was furnished with salvage from New Orleans, the ceiling embossed tin, Cajun bubble-glass windows. Brightly colored origami animals were arranged on the soapstone counters, a menagerie of cranes, ducks, deer, and cats. Overhead, three geometric forms dangled from the ceiling, odd origami shapes he couldn't recognize, gleaming as they rotated on the warm air currents. Rakkim stepped out of the alcove of the side door. Her back was still to him, and he saw the creases along her neck, age and fatigue catching up. Time always won the race. She sighed, spooned brown sugar into her tea, the spoon banging against the side.

She had been more delicate the last time he saw her, the twenty-seven-year-old mother of a young daughter, plump and rosy. He had watched her and Moseby from the shelter of the surrounding forest, watched them go about their daily routine while he tried to decide whether to kill the renegade shadow warrior. Trying to decide if he would turn his back on his duty, as Moseby had. She was thirty-five now, lightly tanned, her long, dark hair gathered in a thick braid. Strong hands, the knuckles raw from hard work and not enough time to care for herself. The Belt did that to people, the land poor and played out for the most part, no real industry except what was owned by foreign companies: Chinese and Brazilian auto manufacturers, Swiss food giants, Congolese textile plants. Annabelle had kept her figure; the modest blue dress slid along her slender ankles and he wondered for a moment if Moseby still appreciated her. Foolish question. John Moseby had given up everything for her and the baby. He had abandoned his Fedayeen oath. Turned his back on his country. His religion. He had nothing left but love.

Annabelle turned. Saw him standing there.

"It's okay," Rakkim reassured her. "I'm Rikki. A friend of John's."

The mug of tea trembled in her hands. "I know who you are." Hot water ran down the sides of the mug and over her fingertips, but she didn't react. "You here to kill me?"

"No. *No.* I'm here to help you. To help John."

"I saw you that night," whispered Annabelle. "I woke up . . . I woke . . . and you had a knife at John's throat. I pretended to be asleep, rolled over and reached for something to hit you with . . . when I looked again, you were gone. I thought you were a dream. John tried to convince me that's all you were, but I saw the look on his face, and I knew you were real."

Rakkim took the mug of tea from her hand, set it down before she burned herself worse.

"John told me who you were afterwards. Told me who *he* really was too." Annabelle backed against the counter. "Now, here you are. I suppose I should be grateful to you for letting him go that night. For letting us all go." She slowly shook her head, her braid twitching around her shoulders. "Still . . . I see you and I see death in your eyes."

"You've got me wrong." Rakkim heard the bed creak in the next room. "I'm here to help you."

"Sure you are," she said.

"Mama? What's going on?" The girl stood in the doorway in a pair of red flannel pajamas. She was dark brown, with her daddy's smooth skin, her hair in tight curls. Young . . . she couldn't have been older than seventeen, all her curves in place, a sheath of baby fat just starting to melt away. "Mama?"

"It's all right, Leanne," said Annabelle, "this gentleman is just leaving."

"You don't look like you're all right." Leanne sidled toward the wood-block holding the kitchen knives. "And this *gentleman* doesn't look like he's leaving."

"Annabelle, please." Rakkim sat down, trying to defuse things. "The men who took John . . . they're not going to bring him back. You know that."

Annabelle stared at him, then sat down across from him, her shoulders slumped.

"I'll find him," said Rakkim. "I'll find him and bring him home."

"You're not kin, and for certain you're no saint." Annabelle tore a paper napkin into shreds. Confetti drifted onto the floor. "So what's in it for you, mister?"

Rakkim touched her hand and she pulled it away. "I need his help."

"John's in no position to help anyone," said Annabelle, fingers working away.

"Let me be the judge of that. When exactly did he leave?"

"Twelve days, twenty-two hours, and nine minutes," said Leanne. "Exactly."

"That ugly redheaded toad wanted to leave at dawn, but John made him wait," said Annabelle. "John said we were going to eat breakfast together . . . Together. Like a family." A tear rolled down her cheek and she swatted it away.

"The redheaded bastard, that would be Gravenholtz?" said Rakkim.

Annabelle nodded. "Yes, that would be Gravenholtz."

So the Colonel had sent his number-two man to fetch Moseby. "I've read about him."

"What you read doesn't do justice to the malignant toad that he is," said Annabelle.

"The men that Gravenholtz left behind," said Rakkim. "Is there just the four of them?"

"*Just* four?" said Leanne.

Annabelle watched Rakkim's eyes. "That's right, just four. That's not hardly anything for you, is it?"

Rakkim glanced out the window. It would be dawn soon.

"I bring them breakfast at eight-thirty," said Annabelle. "It keeps them from showing up at the back door."

"It didn't stop Jeeter from peeking in my bedroom window," said Leanne.

"No, it was a pot of hot grits that stopped him," said Annabelle.

"I thought he was gonna kill Mama for burning him, but I guess he thought better of it," said Leanne. "Instead he killed our dog."

Rakkim had seen the small grave at the edge of the woods. "You won't have to worry about this Jeeter—" He heard footsteps, had already flattened against the wall beside the side door when he recognized the clumsy pace. *Knock-knock* on the door. Unbelievable. Rakkim opened the door, pulled Leo inside.

"C-*careful*," sputtered Leo.

"This is Leo," said Rakkim.

Blushing, Leo waved. "Hi."

Annabelle stared at him. Leanne waved back.

"Do Gravenholtz's men check in with him?" asked Rakkim.

"I don't know," said Annabelle.

"Twice a day," said Leanne. "Eight a.m. and eight p.m."

"You've seen them clock in?" asked Rakkim.

Leanne nodded. "It's some special encrypted phone from China that gets great reception. Hardly any chaff. Jeeter won't let anybody else use it, but Pruitt spied the access code one time when Jeeter wasn't paying attention—"

"I told you I didn't want you talking with that Pruitt boy," said Annabelle.

"Pru's not like that, Mama." Leanne watched Leo wander over to the corner of the kitchen, watched him stand there looking up at the three dangling geometric balls.

"Pru?" said Annabelle.

An encrypted phone could work both ways. It allowed the Colonel to keep track of the four men here, but it also might allow someone to eavesdrop on the Colonel's communications. With the phone, Rakkim and Leo wouldn't be operating blind. "What's Pru look like?"

"Tall, blond, and with sweet puppy-dog eyes," said Leanne. "He hates Gravenholtz too. He says they all do . . . all of 'em miserable, except Jeeter."

"Is that right?" said Rakkim. "They argue in front of you?"

"All the time," said Leanne. "Jeeter's always smacking somebody or making fun of Tom Tipton's little chin whiskers, calling him Billy Goat Gruff and saying he's going to slice them off some night."

"I could crack this code you're all excited about," said Leo, watching Leanne out of the corner of his eye. "Won't be any problem at all for me."

"Yeah, you can bend steel in your bare hands too," said Rakkim.

"To a man like you, cracking code must seem like bending steel." Leo fingered the collar around his neck. "I'm not really an Ident, you know," he said to Leanne.

"Wouldn't matter if you were," said Leanne.

Leo lightly stirred the three geometric shapes, set them bouncing against each other. "Who made these?"

"I did," said Leanne.

"Do you know what they are?" said Leo.

"Do *you*?" said Leanne.

Leo touched the largest multifaceted shape. "Giant dodecahedron." He tapped the spiky one. "Great icosahedron. Sometimes known as the Poinsot solids." He spun another, even spikier, like the star on a Christmas tree. "Stellated dodecahedron."

Leanne stroked her curls. Sniffed. "Two out of three isn't bad."

"I *beg* your pardon?" said Leo.

"Count the pentagramic faces." Leanne stepped toward him. "Go on, count them."

"Do you know what she's talking about?" Rakkim asked Annabelle.

"Not since she was ten," said Annabelle.

Leo turned the spiked ornament over and over in his hands. He looked up at Leanne. "This is impossible."

"For you, maybe," said Leanne.

"Fourteen faces instead of twelve?" said Leo. "*Five* pentagrams meeting at each vertex? How . . . how did you do that?"

"I call it a Derbyshire star," said Leanne, "after an old-days mathematician."

Leo stared at her, cheeks pinking up.

"Oh, sweet suffering Jesus, it's *love*," said Rakkim.

CHAPTER 20

Rakkim slowly removed the automatic rifle from beside Jeeter, slid it under a heap of straw with the other three weapons. The sleeping sentry outside had been trickier to disarm, actually using his jackhammer shotgun as a pillow. Rakkim tickled him until he turned over, removed the weapon as the young man sighed, said a woman's name. Jeeter was older than the other three, more muscular, a hardened vet, his face so blistered that one eye was swollen shut. Annabelle had caught him good with the hot grits.

Jeeter stirred as Rakkim watched him. That was Rakkim's fault. Never let your gaze linger if you want to stay invisible. Jeeter might be lying in his own sweat and stink, but there was a good soldier under there somewhere. Gravenholtz knew what he was doing. Rakkim squatted beside the man, watching . . . waiting.

Jeeter opened his eyes.

Rakkim blew him a kiss. "Rise and shine."

Jeeter reached for his weapon, found it gone, and rolled to his feet. Quick too.

Rakkim punched him in the throat. The two others in the barn woke to the sound of Jeeter gagging. Saw Rakkim standing there, hands in his pockets. "Morning, boys," said Rakkim. "Come on over and let's talk."

They got carefully to their feet—Ferris, a chunky, bleary-eyed dullard, and Pruitt, lean and delicate somehow, both of them looking around for their weapons, embarrassed. The sentry stumbled inside, his hair wild, stopped when he saw Rakkim. Scraggly goatee on his chin. Tom Tipton. Billy Goat Gruff.

"Come on in, Tom." Rakkim flashed the penlight video he had taken a few minutes ago. "Wish I could see Gravenholtz's face when he sees this."

They stared at the mini-movie on the wall, right about the axes and chain saws and dive gear—images of themselves snoring, scratching their privates, guns in the dirt, oblivious in dreamland.

"Please, sir . . . you don't have to show this to Gravenholtz," said Tom. "That's not Christian."

"Man wanted me to keep tabs on how you boys were doing," said Rakkim. "Wouldn't be Christian to keep the truth from him."

"*I* didn't do nothing," said Ferris.

"One for all and all for one," said Rakkim.

"What's that mean?" said Ferris.

"Means we're *all* responsible," said Pruitt, working to hold himself steady. "One of us fucks up, we all fuck up."

Jeeter made it to his knees, wheezing, trying to breathe.

Pruitt looked around, as though expecting to see other troops. "Sir, we . . . please tell Commander Gravenholtz that we never let down our guard before. Not *once*."

"Once is kind of enough, don't you think?" said Rakkim.

"This ain't fair," said Tom, small eyes blinking. "It's 'Tipton, do this, Tipton, do that, Tipton, you dumb fuck, wash out my socks,'" he said, voice cracking. "I do everything I'm told, and I still get tagged with guard duty five nights running, no relief. How am I supposed to stay awake? You *tell* me, how am I supposed to do that?"

Rakkim wagged a finger at Jeeter. "You run a sloppy outfit, top dog. I surely would hate to be you when I make my report."

Tom tugged at his wispy goatee. "The women . . . those two women must have put something in our food . . . drugged us out." He looked around for support. "Knockout drops or something."

"I wouldn't put anything past those two bitches," mumbled Ferris.

Jeeter secured the strap of his overalls, looking hard at Rakkim. "I'm not worried. Gravenholtz knows me, knows I get the job done."

"*Please*, mister," said Tom.

"Too late, Tom," said Rakkim. "Already sent it on. I put a three-hour transmission delay on it, give you boys a chance to head out for greener pastures." He smiled at Tom. "Five straight nights of guard duty? You deserve a break. Besides, I hate thinking about what Gravenholtz will do to you if he finds you here. Gives me nightmares."

"Ain't nobody leaving," said Jeeter.

Rakkim checked his watch. "It's up to you."

"Jeeter, hey, man," said Tom, "you can stay, but me . . ." He bent down, started shoving clothes into a backpack.

"I said, stay put," said Jeeter.

"Like this guy said, Jeeter, one for all . . . one for all and we're all fucked," said Ferris. "I seen Gravenholtz crush a man's skull for stepping on his foot. What do you think he's going to do to *us*?"

"He ain't going to do nothing." Jeeter glared at Rakkim with his one good eye. "This turd isn't working for Gravenholtz. He probably don't even *know* Gravenholtz. He's running some game."

Rakkim looked at his watch. Shrugged.

"What kind of a dumb game you think he's running, Jeeter?" said Tom, the backpack overflowing. "He's not asking nothing from us."

Pruitt watched Rakkim

Rakkim spread his arms wide. "It's a free country. You want to stay here and find out who's playing a game and who's not, be my guest. Ta-ta." He started toward the door.

"Where you think you're going?" Jeeter grinned. "By my count, there's four of us and one of you." He scooped a hammer off a workbench. "So *you* hand over that vid and maybe I won't nail your pecker to the wall." He looked around. "Ferris, get your fat ass in gear. Pruitt, Tipton . . . move it."

Ferris hesitated, walked slowly to a corner and picked up a crowbar.

"Maybe . . . maybe we should talk about this first," said Tom.

"Tom's got a point," said Pruitt, still watching Rakkim. "This man here can count as well as you can. He sidles in here, takes our guns, wakes us up. He's not armed . . . might as well be naked as a jaybird. He's *got* to have something else going for him."

"Let's talk," said Tom.

Jeeter hefted the hammer. "Soldier up, Tipton. Fucking Billy Goat Gruff, if you had been standing guard like you were supposed to, none of this would have happened."

"Now, boys, don't argue over me," said Rakkim. "The Good Book says blessed are the peacemakers."

Tom sighed, walked over, and pulled out a single-bladed ax from the stump used as a chopping block. He took a few practice swings, the ax swooshing the air. Dust motes danced in the morning light.

Jeeter nodded at Tom. *"That's* better. Now spread out." He moved forward, tossing the hammer from one hand to the other, his eyes on Rakkim.

Ferris sidled forward, awkward, gripping the crowbar.

Tom closed in. Swung the ax high over his head, drove it down full force into Jeeter's back. Slammed him into the ground.

Rakkim was as surprised as Pruitt and Ferris. All four of them stood there, watching as Jeeter's fingers clutched at the dirt floor of the barn, the ax still stuck in his back as he tore at the dirt like he was trying to hide in the earth. They stayed there watching until the fingers stopped.

Tom spit on Jeeter. Looked over at Pruitt. "No matter what happened, he was going to blame me. You know he was, Pru."

"It's true," said Pruitt. "That's just what he would have done."

Ferris dropped the crowbar. Stepped away from it.

"I ain't facing Gravenholtz . . . I ain't doing that." Tom shook his head. "I'll head out to Florida first, see if Cuban pussy is as good as they say it is."

Rakkim rolled Jeeter onto his side. Patted him down until he found the phone, and then stood up. "You have about ten minutes until your eight o'clock check-in, Pruitt. Make the call and then you can all leave. That'll give you some time before Gravenholtz gets the video. Enough time to put some distance between you."

Ferris and Tom were already packing up their gear, hurrying. It didn't take them long.

Pruitt walked over to Rakkim. "I'm not a deserter."

Rakkim nodded. "I can see that, but it's not safe here anymore. You can stay, but I'm taking the women where Gravenholtz won't find them."

"Does Leanne want to go?"

"They know they can't stay here." Rakkim watched Ferris and the sentry trot out the back door. "She spoke well of you . . . if that matters."

"Yes, sir, it matters." Pruitt looked toward the house. "I should have never joined up. I thought it would be different. The Colonel's a good man . . . but he doesn't know the things that go on. Gravenholtz . . ." He shook his head. "I didn't sign up for—"

"Make the call." Rakkim handed him the phone.

Pruitt ran a thumb across the keypad. "Right . . . yes." He tapped in the access code: 7-8-3-6-0-9-5-3. Waited. A diode on the phone flashed. "It's me. Yeah. Tell Gravenholtz everything's fine." He listened. "I'm stuck on the fucking bayou, that's what's wrong with my voice. Yeah. Talk to you tonight." He closed the phone, handed it back to Rakkim.

"Hurry up, Pru," said Tom from the doorway. "Time to *go*."

Pruitt looked at Rakkim. "You don't really know Gravenholtz, do you?"

"No, but I can't fucking *wait* to meet him."

Pruitt nodded. "Good."

"Pru!"

Rakkim watched them run down the path to the main road before starting back to the farmhouse. He could hear Leo and Leanne chattering away as he approached, going back and forth like there was nobody else in the world. Inside he found Leo in a chair, a towel clipped around his neck while Leanne snipped away at his hair with a pair of scissors. The Ident collar lay on the table.

Annabelle scooped scrambled eggs onto a platter.

"What do you think?" Leanne said to Rakkim.

The kid looked good.

"He wouldn't tell me who cut his hair last, but they sure didn't know what they were doing." Leanne cut a few more spots. Moistened her fingers in her mouth and slicked down a few errant hairs. "I'll have to do a touch-up in a few weeks, but that's the best I can do for now." She whisked off the towel. Her hand lingered on Leo's neck.

"We have to go," said Rakkim. "All of us."

Annabelle glanced back toward the barn.

"They're already gone," said Rakkim. "We'll drive you and Leanne wherever you want. Someplace Gravenholtz won't know about. Someplace safe."

"John expects us to be here," said Annabelle.

"I'll tell him where you are," said Rakkim. He saw her hesitate. "Annabelle, when Gravenholtz doesn't get his eight p.m. check-in, he's going to know something's wrong. You can't stay here."

"We'll bring your father back safe," Leo assured Leanne. "I promise."

Leanne looked him up and down, taking her time. "I believe you."

Leo swallowed, reached into his pocket, and set a tiny metallic object on the counter, another cannibalized creation from the toy tank he had taken apart at Mount Carmel. One of the soldiers from the toy tank hung from a paper-clip trapeze. As the sun hit the soldier's helmet, he started doing lazy flips, then faster and faster.

"We have a lot to do before we leave," said Annabelle.

"Don't take any more than you can carry," said Rakkim.

Annabelle slammed a pan on the counter. "You think this is the first time I've had to leave my home in a hurry?"

"No . . . I'm sure you know what you're doing," said Rakkim.

"That's the smartest thing I've heard you say all morning," said Annabelle. "Now let's all sit down for breakfast. With my good china and crystal and cloth napkins. We're going to eat like civilized people. Then . . . then I'm going to make my bed and lock the door behind me."

Leanne carefully picked up the acrobatic soldier, who continued doing flips while decorative sparks flew from the base.

"At the end of the routine he salutes," said Leo. "I wanted him to be able to do a handstand too, but I ran out of parts."

Leanne chewed her lip. "Maybe I . . . maybe I could help you. I'm good with my hands."

CHAPTER 21

"I wish we could have stayed longer," said Leo.

Rakkim kept driving. They had barely left Annabelle's cousin's house and Leo was already lovesick.

"What would it have hurt to stay another night?" said Leo. "No telling what they might have told us about Gravenholtz."

"Yeah, you're really interested in Gravenholtz," said Rakkim. He had heard Leo creep down the hall from his room last night around midnight, heard him sneak back in around dawn. "Annabelle doesn't know any more than she's already told us. It's time to get moving."

"Why do *you* always get to decide where we go and when we leave?"

Rakkim didn't bother answering.

Annabelle had assured Rakkim that no one would think to come looking for her at her cousin's house. Her daddy's side of the family had cut off all contact after she married Moseby. Racial attitudes in the Belt had softened greatly since the war, but there were still folks who didn't take to mixing things up. She hadn't seen her cousin in a long time, but she and Mary Thurston had been close once. Almost like sisters. Her cousin had been startled to see Annabelle at her front door, but invited her in, then hugged her, the two of them crying like kids over a broken doll. Rakkim and Leo stood around, watching Mary Thurston cry some more over how beautiful Leanne was, and is this your son-in-law? Leo blushed so hard it looked like his cheeks were about to catch fire.

"Mary Thurston said Leanne and I made a fine couple," said Leo. "She does astrology, which is totally ridiculous, I know, but still, she said our signs were a good match."

"Uh-huh."

Rakkim drove on through northern Arkansas, speeding along a fancy strip of eight-lane freeway. Good work too, some sort of computer-assisted roadbed the Japanese had put in to speed goods between their fertilizer-processing plants in Arkadelphia and Little Rock, a ninety-mile stretch that tapered off to the cracked and uneven blacktop that formed most of the roads in the Belt.

"I love Leanne," Leo said quietly. "I love her and she loves me."

"I'm touched. I'm moved. What, you've known her almost twenty-four hours."

"You think you're the only one allowed to fall in love?"

"Why don't you make yourself useful? Check the phone for bugs and tracers."

"I already did."

"Check it again."

"I already *did*." Leo turned around, looked behind them. Leanne was twenty miles away, but you would have thought she was right there, standing beside a white picket fence, waving a lace hanky. "There were two tracers, both of them now disabled." He pulled out the phone, turned it on, and popped open the case.

"I told you not to do that. You were supposed to disconnect the power source until we needed it."

"This is some *very* sweet tech," said Leo, his tongue probing the corner of his mouth as he adjusted the innards of the phone with a piece of bent wire. "Oscillating frequency . . . at least fifty million possible permutations . . . but if you know what you're doing—"

"*Leo.*"

A burst of static from the phone, then, ". . . never found a damned thing, but somebody must be certain. Logged in fifteen dumploads by noon." A man's voice, Tennessee cadence. Leo dragged the wire lightly across an etched circuit within the phone. More static. A different voice now: ". . . chicken for dinner again. Like to tear my guts out. Case you didn't hear, Gravenholtz is on the warpath, so keep your head down."

Leo closed the phone case. Removed the battery.

"They can't hear us, can they?" said Rakkim. "When we're monitoring their calls, they can't hear us?"

Leo snorted. "God, it must be weird to be so dumb."

A caravan of rusted National Guard trucks rolled slowly past, soldiers in the open bed hunkered down, eyeing them from under their helmets.

The men looked sleepy and unshaven, their uniforms caked with mud, but their weapons were clean and well maintained.

"I got a question," said Leo, after the caravan passed. "Don't laugh, though."

"Okay."

"I mean it." Leo cleared his throat. "Leanne and I made love last night."

"No kidding?"

Leo bobbed his head, eyes half closed. "Four times.

"Last night . . . well, it was my first time," he continued, "but it wasn't the first time for Leanne." He looked straight ahead through the windshield. "So . . . what I wanted to know is, how can you tell if it's as good for the woman as it is for yourself?"

"You mean . . . was she faking it?"

"Not exactly. Just . . . was it incredibly beyond-belief astounding for her too, even though she had done it before?" Leo stared at him. "Don't laugh, I'm serious."

"I'm not laughing." He wasn't. "Did Leanne seem like she was having a good time?"

"Yes. I think so."

"So leave it alone. You don't need any more proof than that."

A triple-rig Matsushita trailer truck loaded with tanks of fertilizer blew past them, had to be doing a hundred.

"The first time . . ." Leo hesitated. "The first time we made love . . . it didn't last very long."

"That's pretty normal."

Leo shifted in his seat. "I went off as soon as I got inside her."

"First time . . . a woman's a scary thing. Wonderful, but scary."

"You're not scared anymore, though, right?"

"Oh, I'm still scared a little bit." Rakkim laughed. "That's part of the wonderfulness."

An abandoned shopping center loomed off the side of the road, a gigantic Wal-Mart store with the windows broken, the roof caved in. There were ruined Wal-Marts all over the Belt, stripped of their goods, covered in graffiti.

"Is there a secret trick?" said Leo. "So I don't . . . so I don't lose it so quick?"

"You should ask your father. I'm not really—"

"My father's not here and I couldn't ask him anyway. You're my friend, aren't you?"

Rakkim glanced over at him. Leo's eyes were bugged out waiting for an answer. "Yeah, Leo, I'm your friend."

"Well?"

"I don't know what to tell you. Just . . . try to line up with the woman. Feel like you're part of her. No, like you're each part of something new . . . Or maybe just have fun and let things work themselves out. Come on, the fourth time had to take longer than the first."

"I was calculating the value of pi in my head. That's how come I lasted longer."

"Pi? Like part of a circle or something?"

"The ratio of a circle's circumference to its diameter."

"So you were doing geometry while you were making love?"

"I calculated pi to two hundred and fifty-eight decimal places, then I . . . then I lost my place. Hey! It's not *funny*."

"I'm sorry." Rakkim shook his head, trying not to laugh. "Really. It's just . . . losing your *place*?"

"Okay . . . I get it."

"Give yourself a break, Leo. Sex doesn't have to be perfect. Sometimes it *is* funny."

"I want it to be perfect."

"Sorry, kid, welcome to the monkey house. Ain't no perfect here."

They rode in silence for a few miles, going with the flow of traffic, a few car lengths behind a chromed-out blue sedan with a ONE NATION UNDER JESUS bumper sticker. The Jesus on the sticker carried an assault rifle.

"Thanks . . . for before." Leo raised his window up and down, up and down. "How long until we get to your friend's farm?"

"If we're lucky, we'll get there in time for dinner. You haven't lived until you've tasted one of Florence Tigard's buttermilk biscuits."

Leo pulled out the phone. Stared at it.

"When things are over, we'll bring Moseby back to join them," said Rakkim. "Imagine the reception you'll get from Leanne. You'll be the guy who kept his promise."

"I wish I could talk to her, that's all." Leo slipped the phone back in his pocket. "I miss her. Is that dumb?"

"No."

"You miss your wife too, sometimes. I can tell. You get quiet. Not your normal quiet, but more of a deeper thing where you hardly move but your eyes are happy. Like when we saw that couple holding hands at the little grocery store, the guy carrying the kid on his shoulders . . . you were thinking of Sarah, weren't you?"

Rakkim nodded. Impressed.

"Do you worry about Sarah too? 'Cause I worry about Leanne. She's smart, but we both know that's not much protection. There's too many morons out there."

"More of them than you can imagine, Leo."

CHAPTER 22

Coming here today might have been a mistake, but Sarah's mother needed a break from their apartment, and Michael needed some fresh air. Best place to hide was in a crowd, that's what Rakkim said. Sarah wished he were here. She would have felt safer.

"Your father loved the Saint Sebastian Day street fair," Katherine Dougan said to Sarah as the merrymakers eddied around them. "Even after we converted, we always used to sneak out to one of the smaller fairs for chili dogs and beer. He said he liked them better than the elaborate ones, but I think he also thought they were safer—not so many prying eyes. A man in his position . . . he was supposed to be a moral example, but he had too much life in him for that."

Maybe a thousand people milled around the intersection in the middle of the Ravenna district, one of the many Catholic neighborhoods in Seattle—the festival was a chance for Christians, moderates, and moderns to mingle, one of the few instances outside the Zone where such social interaction was accepted. Sarah watched the juggler in the old Uncle Sam suit walk past, tossing a cantaloupe, a banana, a ball-peen hammer, and a large kitchen knife in the air, the four items fountaining round and round.

Michael, perched on Sarah's shoulders, clapped his hands at the juggler, cried out, "Faster, faster."

Sarah and Katherine were dressed as moderns, in head scarves and brightly colored veils, but wearing baggy trousers and athletic shoes in case they had to make a run for it. The only people looking for Sarah would be the Old One's spies, but anyone with a long memory might recognize Katherine, and that would be a real problem. President Kingsley had quietly removed her from the most-wanted list a couple years ago, and Spider had hacked the central computer system, expunging her biometric profile along with Sarah's and Rakkim's, but that merely protected against surveillance cameras and border-control checks. Idle curiosity could still be disastrous. Sarah rearranged her own veil, made sure her features were obscured.

Relax, Sarah; the only police in evidence were a couple of Catholic patrolmen wandering around, stuffing their faces with sweets and smiling at the women. A lone Black Robe elbowed his way through the revelers. *Relax, Sarah, enjoy the day.* Moderns were beneath the notice of the Black Robes, considered already damned.

Michael chirped happily, as though reading her thoughts.

The streets were lined with booths selling sausages, burgers, ravioli, deep-dish apple pie, cotton candy, pecan rolls, ascension candy, and other treats, plus games of chance like balloon darts and random-access bingo. Under the counter, homemade beer and wine, flags of the old USA, and satellite decoders were available. Forbidden-image vendors and magicians milled among the gawkers, local musicians playing on every corner. Dogs ran wild. The fair was loud and raucous—unstructured, uninhibited, and slightly wicked fun.

Above the throng floated banners picturing Saint Sebastian himself, a handsome youth, naked except for a white loincloth, his perfect body pierced by arrows. One of the most popular treats at the festival were Holy Blood Drops, hot cinnamon candy blessed by one of the priests in attendance. A rotund vendor offered a bag of the cinnamon drops to the Black Robe, who cursed him, threatened him with a flail. The vendor laughed and the crowd laughed with him, some of them chanting the rosary, and the Black Robe pushed on to harass someone else.

Katherine lifted an edge of her pale green veil, nibbled at a huge ball of pink cotton candy. Her hijab had been pushed back in the insouciant modern style, exposing her lustrous red hair, shot with silver. "I'm so glad you suggested we come here today. The people, the music, the dancing . . ." She looked around. "It's . . . almost perfect."

"You're still thinking of Daddy, aren't you?" Sarah felt Michael playing with her hair.

"We used to bring you here," said Katherine. "You rode on his shoulders just like Michael is riding on yours."

"I . . . I have a vague memory of that," said Sarah.

"You could see the whole world from his shoulders," said Katherine. "That's what you used to say."

Sarah's father, James Dougan, had been the first chief of State Security in the new Islamic Republic. A fine, handsome man, a former Olympic athlete, his moderation and good looks did much to assuage the Christians during the transition. When he promised to safeguard their liberty, just like that of other citizens, they believed him. When the fundamentalists demanded that idolaters and homosexuals be hung from lampposts, Dougan stepped in, arrested the troublemakers, and threatened to jail the leadership of the Black Robes if they didn't rein in their followers. Safeguarding the home front from enemies domestic and foreign had been equally challenging.

A hijacked jumbo jet still jutted out of Elliott Bay twenty-five years later, a near miss on the Presidential Palace by a group of rabid Christians. The Space Needle had been toppled in a terrorist attack. The Mormons had continued to make mischief, carpeting the outlying areas of their territory with IEDs. The successes of State Security had been rarely touted for fear of inflaming the populace—three attempts on the president's life thwarted, a plan to blow the Grand Coulee Dam broken up, an incendiary attack on the main gas refinery in Los Angeles averted. Still a young man and wildly popular, Dougan had been talked about as the next president, when Kingsley decided to step down.

It might have happened too, but twenty-four years ago, James Dougan had been assassinated by members of his own security detail on orders from the Old One. Dougan's second in command, his brother Redbeard, had narrowly escaped death himself. After assuming control of State Security, Redbeard ruthlessly hunted down the perpetrators, rolling up much of the Old One's network. Many innocents were killed in the hunt, many falsely accused. Katherine, framed by the Old One as a conspirator in the murder of her husband, had been forced to flee. Sarah, still a toddler, had been left behind and reared by Redbeard. Raised a Muslim, Sarah remained a Muslim, but in her twenty-year exile in a nunnery, Katherine had converted back to Catholicism, a reconversion that in and of itself would have warranted a death sentence for apostasy.

A man on stilts dressed as the pope walked unsteadily through the crowd, trailing incense in his wake. Michael reached up for him and the man blessed him, pretended to pull a chocolate out of Michael's ear and gave it to him. Michael stared at him, then popped it in his mouth, applauding.

"Great thing about being Catholic is that you're allowed to make fun of everyone," Katherine whispered to Sarah, the noise and bustle around them shielding their words from any listening ears. "Paupers to pope, we're all equal in God's sight, all of us equally sinful and foolish." She blessed the man on stilts with her half-eaten cotton candy, using it as a miter. "Try doing that with one of your ayatollahs."

A young Catholic couple walked past, holding hands, feeding each other rolled crepes filled with strawberry jam. Sarah watched them out of the corner of her eye and missed Rakkim even more.

"A good Muslim woman should avoid passion or desire," recited Katherine. "Isn't that right? A good Muslim woman does not make her own decisions. Her goal is to become quiet on the inside."

"I don't want to talk about religion, Mom," said Sarah.

"Do you feel quiet on the inside, Sarah? I never did; even when I wanted to believe, I never felt quiet," said Katherine. "A woman like you, smart and strong and independent . . . don't you find even your moderate Islam suffocating?"

"Did *you*? No one forced you to embrace Islam. Yet you did."

"Things were different then," said Katherine. "We were suffocating in something worse . . . a false liberalism in which nothing was a sin, and everything was tolerated."

"I've studied the prewar days, Mother—"

"You've *studied*, but you weren't there," said Katherine, green eyes flashing. "You don't know what it was really like. They made movies in those days, movies that were shown in every town and shopping center, movies in which women were hung upside down, tortured with power drills, saws, and blowtorches, and the strangest thing of all, people were not ashamed to be seen walking into the theater. No one was ashamed. Shame itself was the only thing shameful."

"*Mother?*" Sarah indicated Michael listening from atop her shoulders.

"I'm just saying"—Katherine slipped her arm into Sarah's—"after what we were living with, Islam seemed like an answer to prayer. The pope was a ditherer, and the Protestants . . . Your father used to say, *When a religion loses sight of what true evil is, it's no longer a religion, it's a bowling league.* Islam offered the clarity of right and wrong, good and bad, and I embraced it eagerly. I make no excuses . . ." She squeezed Sarah's arm as the Black

Robe pushed his way through the crowd, a tall, scrawny man with a sharp nose and a mouth full of crooked teeth. "We were happy to trade away a little freedom for the comfort of a clear set of rules." She eased them out of the path of the approaching Black Robe, a tall, scrawny ascetic. "We just didn't count on who would be *setting* the rules."

Sarah slightly inclined her gaze as the Black Robe passed, as did her mother.

"Aii!" shrieked the Black Robe, clutching his bare head.

Michael giggled, shook the black turban that he had snatched from the Black Robe.

"Insolent bastard!" barked the Black Robe, snatching his turban back, the fabric unrolling onto the ground.

Michael laughed, clapped his hands.

The Black Robe raised his flail, whipped the long, flexible wooden rod back and forth, then swung at Michael.

Sarah caught the blow on her raised arm, gasping at the pain. She clawed at the Black Robe's eyes and he hit her even harder, enraged now.

"Give me the brat, you harlot!" the Black Robe sputtered, flailing at her.

Sarah stumbled to the ground, shielding Michael with her body, taking the blows that rained down on her back. Everyone around them made room, silenced by the Black Robe's fury, unwilling to try and stop him. Christians did not lay hands on a Muslim cleric. Ever. She cried out as the Black Robe's whip lashed across her kidneys. Her stunner was in her pocket, a palm-size device with enough juice to zap the Black Robe or anyone else into unconsciousness. Illegal for a woman to possess, of course. She reached for the stunner, felt it, but the Black Robe's flail kept thrashing her. Like being stung by a swarm of wasps . . .

"Mercy!" Katherine approached the Black Robe, palms pressed together in supplication. "In the name of Allah the Merciful!"

The Black Robe spat in her face, raised his arm to strike Sarah again, and Katherine kneed him in the groin, the force of her knee lifting him off the ground, his robes fluttering around him like the petals of a black lily.

The Black Robe collapsed, lay there groaning beside a crushed snow-cone cup, his mouth making feeble movements as he tried to breathe.

Katherine pulled Sarah to her feet. Sarah's veil had come undone.

Clutching Michael to her, Sarah ran through the crowd, Katherine right behind her.

"S-stop them!" The Black Robe stood partway, then fell back down, clutching himself. "*Stop* them!"

The crowd closed ranks after Sarah and Katherine, so that the fleeing women and child were lost from the Black Robe's sight.

CHAPTER 23

Rakkim watched Bill Tigard heft a trash can full of slop, must have weighed two hundred pounds at least, and dump it into the pigpen. Watched him toss the empty can aside and reach for another one, Tigard grinning as the hogs rushed in, squealing. He lurched slightly as he moved down the fence, an old bullet wound in his hip, a souvenir from Tigard's wilder days, he had told Rakkim once—a wink to his wife—before he found Florence and the Lord. Another wink—*in that order*. Sweat rolled down his bare arms as he worked, his skin shiny and black in the sunset, bulging with muscle. It had been ten years since Rakkim had last seen him. Tigard was still a powerhouse in faded overalls, but his short hair was sprinkled with gray and he had a tire around his middle.

Tigard sang to the pigs as he fed them, urging them on, as though they needed encouragement. Most of the big pork farmers used one- and two-acre concrete pens and automated food delivery systems, but Tigard was a small farmer, proud and independent, a traditionalist out of need and preference. His fat hogs wallowed in mud, his slops came from his fields, his kitchen, and bags of Indian Jack sorghum. He and his family fed the hogs with their own hands, butchered them with their own hands when the time came.

Tigard moved down the wire fence surrounding the pen, humming softly to himself. Rakkim moved closer, silent as a shadow. Step by step, closer still. Near enough now to see Florence's precise stitching on his overalls. Near enough to see a single drop of sweat nestled behind his right ear. Near enough to recognize the song he hummed, a gospel tune . . . "The Old Rugged Cross." Rakkim hummed along with him, insinuating his sound into Tigard's deeper bass. Oblivious, Tigard hoisted up another trash can. Rakkim reached out a hand—

"Step away from him, mister, or I'll blow yer balls off."

Rakkim turned slowly. He heard the trash can drop but kept his eyes on Florence in the doorway, holding an assault rifle. He glanced down. Saw a tiny red dot centered on his crotch. Rakkim spread his arms wide. "Easy target, Florence, blessed as I am. You get more points for a brain shot."

Tigard grabbed Rakkim by the front of his jacket, lifted him off the ground. "Who the . . ." He stared. A smile slowly arced across his broad face. "Rikki?" He wrapped his arms around Rakkim, half smothered him in his warm embrace. "Don't shoot, Mother, it's Rikki."

"*Rikki?*" Florence walked quickly over to them, a slender woman whose high cheekbones seemed carved from mahogany. "Is that really you, boy?"

Tigard set Rakkim down.

Rakkim kissed Florence on each of her high cheekbones. "Yes, ma'am, it is."

Florence laughed. "You still kiss like a Frenchman."

"You hungry?" said Tigard.

"Does a Muslim have calluses on his knees?" said Rakkim.

"Come in the house and wash up," said Florence. "I'll have dinner on the table soon as Bill's done with the hogs." She trailed a hand across her husband's broad back. "I'll tell the boys Rikki's here."

"I'll stay out here a little bit." Rakkim walked ahead of Tigard, picked up a sack of corncobs, and poured them into the trough. "Old man looks like he could use some help."

"Just don't hurt yourself," said Tigard, scooting past him. "You probably haven't done an honest day's work since you left here."

Florence went back to the house, shaking her head, the assault rifle across her shoulder. The house was two stories, small but well kept, with white sideboards and green trim. Flower beds ran down the sides, red and yellow tulips ablaze with color. Antique farm tools flanked the back porch: hay rakes, shovels, a huge scythe that only Tigard could have ever wielded.

Rakkim waited until the kitchen door slammed behind Florence. "Since when does she greet visitors with a gun?"

Tigard grunted, shifted the trash can to the other shoulder. "Been some trouble lately with raiders. Livestock taken, buildings burned. Next county over a farmer and his whole family were found shot dead, wife raped beforehand. City folk probably—wore out their welcome in Birmingham or Decatur and decided their country cousins were fair game. They come here, they're going to wish they never left home."

"You still have your dog?" said Rakkim.

"Jeff died a few months ago." Tigard poured out the last of the slops. "I still get weepy when I think about it."

"You should get another dog. It's cheap security. Or, if you want, I could set up a basic system tomorrow. Nothing fancy. Heat-activated solenoid on the main access road would be better than nothing. We'll go into town tomorrow and get what we need."

"When did you get so smart?"

"I'm still waiting, but I've got help." Rakkim beckoned to the edge of the barn.

Leo appeared from hiding, started toward them, high-stepping, trying to avoid cow pies.

"He walks like he's trying to do the ground a favor," said Tigard.

"He's a good kid, a little out of his element, but when it comes to tech gear he can turn water to wine." Rakkim waved to Leo. "Hurry up! Dinner's ready."

Leo picked up the pace, half slipped, face wrinkling in disgust. He hurried on, wiping one foot as he hobbled toward the house.

A half hour later, they all sat around the dinner table with their heads bowed. "Would you say grace, Rikki?" said Florence.

"Heavenly Father, we give thanks tonight for good friends and good food," said Rakkim, head inclined, eyes closed. "Please watch over all of us in this house and keep us safe from harm. Amen."

"Amen," said Florence and Bill.

"Amen," said their two sons, James and Matthew.

Leo mumbled something, reached for the mashed potatoes.

"I like a healthy eater." Florence beamed as Leo piled on the mashed potatoes, creamed corn, and jerked pork. She nodded with approval as the kid poured gravy over it all.

"Thanks," said Leo, food falling out of his mouth as he chewed.

Matthew cut his meat into neat, even chunks, watching Leo with obvious distaste. James seemed amused by the table manners of their guest, peering into Leo's open mouth like a spelunker. The fraternal twins differed in almost all ways. Matthew was tall and lean, soft-spoken and intellectual, while James was shorter and more muscular, quick to anger, quick to love. James had just gotten a scholarship to the Atlanta School of Economics, the most prestigious business university in the Belt. James had enlisted in the Marines and was shipping out to basic training in a week.

"You ever drove a tractor?" asked Tigard.

It took Leo a moment to realize he was being addressed. He shook his head.

"Neither did Rikki before he showed up at our front door," said Tigard. "That's how we got to be friends. He saw me and the boys plowing late at night, and asked if he could help." He made a depression in the mashed potatoes with his spoon, carefully half filled the depression with gravy. "Not many folks would stop to help a stranger. Regular Good Samaritan."

"The twins couldn't have been more than nine years old," said Rakkim, smiling at the memory. "Matthew steered while James worked the controls."

"We had a couple hired hands, but the press-gangs came by one day and that was that," Tigard explained to Leo. "Don't know what we would have done if Rakkim hadn't come along. No way we could have gotten the planting finished. We were already a week behind."

"You would have done it," said Florence, watching the family eat. "You and the boys. We might have only gotten half a crop, but we would have tightened our belts and made it through. The Lord will provide."

"The Lord provided Rikki, that's what the Lord provided," said Tigard.

"That's what you call a mixed blessing." Rakkim added more gravy to his mashed potatoes. "What are you going to do when the boys go away?"

"These last couple years, James has been shifting us to less labor-intensive crops," said Florence. "More acres of alfalfa, okra, and yams, less of corn and soybeans."

"Better prices too," said Matthew. "The hybrid okra James got us into travels better, which allows us to sell to the Brazilian market, and with beef exports up, the price of alfalfa has tracked the same direction."

"Mom and Dad are going to be okay, Rikki," said James. "Matthew here structured some loan with a bank in Atlanta that's going to allow Dad to buy a couple of robo-tractors. All he has to do is program them and they'll drive themselves to the fields and do whatever is needed."

"Planting, disking, fertilizing, harvesting, you name it," said Tigard. "I don't even have to turn on a darn switch."

Florence patted her husband's thick wrist. "William feels the new tractors make him obsolete."

"A farmer who doesn't get dirt on his hands isn't a farmer," said Tigard.

"Production should increase seventeen percent," said Matthew, "and that includes payment on the loan."

"You still got your pigs, Dad," said James. "Anytime you want to get dirty, they'll be there waiting for you."

"One thing about working on a farm," Tigard said to Leo, "you won't ever go hungry."

"Bill says you're good with electronic things, Leo. Bill's not one to brag, but he fixed our grid antenna so it taps into the Brazilian satellite system. He says their weather reports are much more reliable than anything the Belt provides." She spooned more mashed potatoes onto Leo's plate. "Maybe tomorrow morning he'll show you what he did to it."

Leo looked up from his plate, curious now.

"Farming's a good life," said Tigard. He glanced at his wife. "Everything's sweeter when you're close to the land."

Florence flushed.

"So what do you think?" Tigard asked Leo.

Leo blinked. "Are you talking to me, sir?"

"You're an Ident, aren't you?" said Tigard.

"His contract is already paid for," said Rakkim.

"So I'll buy it out," said Tigard. "Tell the contract holder I'm offering twenty percent above the price he paid."

"Bill . . ." said Rakkim. "It can't be done."

"You want me to work *here*?" said Leo.

"Dad, really, the robo-tractors will make your life so much easier," said Matthew.

"I get four weeks' leave after basic," said James. "I'll be back every chance I get."

Tigard nodded, jabbed at his fried okra with his fork. "I know. It was just an idea, that's all."

"You thought I could cut it working on your farm," said Leo, beaming. "Mr. Tigard, sir, that's the nicest thing anyone has ever said to me."

"Like I said, it was just an idea," said Tigard.

"I could do it too," said Leo. "I'm not very strong, but there's nothing I can't figure out. Tomorrow, before we leave, I'll rig you up a surveillance system so good that if anyone walks up, you'll know the color of their eyes."

"That's real nice of you." Florence spooned more mashed potatoes onto Leo's plate. Added a couple of pork chops. "Maybe when you finish your contract you'll come back for a visit. You're always welcome. Friends are always welcome at our table."

"Yes, ma'am," said Leo. "I'd like that very much."

"What brings you by after so long?" said Tigard. "It's not like we're on the main road."

"I need a favor," said Rakkim.

"You got it," said Tigard.

"That's what I thought," said Rakkim.

"What kind of favor?" said Florence.

"Last time I was here, Bill said he had a cousin in Addington," said Rakkim. "I want an introduction."

"*Addington?*" Tigard peered at Rakkim. "I gave you more credit than that."

"Nice little town, from what I hear."

"It's a nice town if you don't need to breathe. Nice town if you like black lung," said Tigard.

"Nice town," repeated Rakkim, "but they say the folks there keep to themselves."

"They don't like strangers because the only reason folks come to Addington is to try and find the Church of the Mists, and the only people looking to do such a thing are damned fools."

"I've been called worse," said Rakkim.

"Leave Leo here, then," said Florence. "No sense getting this poor boy killed too." She smiled at Leo. "You pick me some blackberries, I'll make you the best pie you ever ate."

"Thank you, ma'am," said Leo, "but I have to stay with Rikki. Somebody has to keep him out of trouble."

Tigard pushed his plate aside with a clatter of silverware. "Trouble is all you're going to find in Addington."

CHAPTER 24

Rakkim listened to the rain beating on the roof as he lay in bed with Sarah, Michael between them. Michael grasped Rakkim's finger, hanging on as Rakkim lifted him up, the three of them laughing. Their laughter faded, changed into something else . . . something ugly.

Rakkim sat up, fully alert now, already out of bed. He'd slept in his clothes. Stepped into his boots. Rain pounded on the roof, louder than the dream. Where was Leo?

Soft sounds from the closet.

Rakkim jerked the door open, dragged Leo out.

"Hey . . . *hey*," said Leo.

Rakkim grabbed the security phone from him and threw it against the wall.

"Hey!" said Leo.

Rakkim dashed into the hall, beat on the opposite door. "*Bill!* Raiders coming!" He heard movement inside, ran back and grabbed Leo by the wrist. "Get out the window," he said evenly, keeping his anger in check.

"I don't hear anything—"

Rakkim pushed Leo through the open window, the kid squawking as he slid down the wet roof, clawing at the shingles. "Rakkim!" Leo clung to the edge of the roof with both hands, eyes wide, blinking in the rain. "Help me!"

Rakkim slid down the roof, landing nimbly on the rocky ground. Just in time to catch Leo in his arms. Rakkim slung him over one shoulder, hopscotched across the pavement to avoid leaving footprints on the muddy ground. He could hear Tigard in the house, calling to his kids.

"Put me *down*," said Leo, squirming, as Rakkim carried him toward the pigpen. "What are you *doing*? I don't hear anything."

Neither did Rakkim. Not yet. What had awakened him was something subtler. A perturbation in the air pressure. Not the storm. Something else. Something worse. Rakkim walked through the horse trough, stepped onto the railing of the pigpen, and jumped in among the squealing beasts.

"What are—" shouted Leo before Rakkim pushed his face into the mud.

Rakkim pulled Leo deeper into the mass of pigs, dodging their hooves and snouts as best he could. "They're going to have thermal imaging," he said in Leo's ear, smearing them both with mud and pig shit, thickly coating their hair.

"*Who's* going to have . . . ?" Leo's voice trailed off as the helicopter floated in over the trees.

The pigs huddled around Rakkim and Leo, complaining at their intrusion into the pen, trying to settle back in the mud.

Rakkim gently eased Leo alongside a huge sow, tucked him against her bulging flank. The sow nuzzled Leo, then reared back, tore at his hair, squealing, starting the others going. Rakkim had his knife poised to drive the tip into the sow's ear . . . then reversed it, slammed the hilt into the base of her skull. The sow sighed, collapsed, breathing heavily. He pushed Leo farther under her body, where he'd be protected by her blubbery flesh, then watched the helicopter hover near the farmhouse. He hoped Tigard had time to get Florence and the boys into the basement shelter.

Figures rappelled down from the helicopter, seven, eight, nine of them in light combat gear, landing gently on the ground. They fanned out around the farmhouse, short-stocked assault rifles swiveling. One of them sauntered through Florence's flower bed, crushing red and yellow blossoms with every step of his combat boots. He glanced at the pigpen, then moved toward the house, directing the others with hand signals.

The helicopter opened up on the farmhouse, its high-speed Gatling miniguns blazing away in the rain, the nitrogen-cooled machine guns disintegrating the walls and ceiling, setting the house on fire. With twelve spinning barrels, and a firing rate of ten thousand rounds a minute, the Gatlings turned the whole place into a kill zone.

The pigs squealed, beating against the rails of their enclosure. Rakkim dragged a pig against him and hung on, banged and bruised, part of the mass of muddy beasts, lost in their heat and panic.

"Abort!" the team leader shouted into his headset. "I repeat, no incendiaries! Goddamnit, I want Jeeter alive!"

The helicopter made a lazy arc over the burning structure, still firing. One side of the house exploded, a fireball rising. As the chopper dipped over the pigpen, Rakkim heard music blaring . . . "Sweet Home Alabama."

Rakkim saw the second story burning, the room they had been in just a few minutes ago crackling. He felt the mass of pigs hunker down into the mud, grunting their complaints as Rakkim crowded them.

The team leader moved closer to the farmhouse, hands on his hips. He removed his helmet, tossed it aside, reveling in the heat. In the light from the fire his red hair was the color of blood.

The chopper hovered overhead, guns bristling but silent now. Its searchlights illuminated the burning house, as if this were an old Hollywood movie premiere.

The back porch collapsed in a wave of sparks, the heat rolling out like a tidal wave. The pigs burrowed deeper into each other, restless in the glow from the burning farmhouse, rain splattering against their broad backs. Rakkim had to grind his teeth to stop himself from shouting. Clutched at the mud to keep from making a move. He could cut his way through the raiders, or at least cause enough confusion to make his way into the basement . . . but there was no way to get away from the helicopter and its Gatlings. Rain dripped down his neck as he buried himself among the pigs, working himself deeper and deeper.

The redhead slung back his machine gun. "Jeeter!" He lit a cigarette. Cupped it in the rain as he watched the house burn. His silhouette was tall and muscular, slouching as he faced the cinders. "Jeeter! You still in there, boy?"

The door to the basement clanged open. Black smoke poured up from below as James and Matthew charged out, coughing, firing their rifles wildly. One of the raiders went down before the twins were caught in a full-auto crossfire, cut to chunks, blood spurting down their chests. James tried to stand and the redhead shot him in the forehead.

Bill Tigard stumbled out, his overalls on fire, carrying Florence in his arms. Her head flopped with every step, half her face blown away. He held her close, his bare feet making sucking sounds in the mud with every step.

The redhead laughed, and Rakkim remembered the file he had read on the Colonel. Remembered comments on his second in command, Gravenholtz, a maniac from the border brigades, a redhead with skin like sour milk and a love of killing, a true infatuation with pain. Now he had come a-calling.

Tigard gently laid Florence among her flowers, then staggered over and grabbed the old scythe from the back porch. The scythe hung loose in his hand, the rusty blade cutting a furrow in the soft earth as he dragged it behind him.

Gravenholtz waved his men back, still smoking his cigarette. "Anyone in the barn?" he said into his headset. He nodded, watching the fire.

Tigard wiped the rain from his eyes, trying to focus.

"Jeeter!" Gravenholtz called to the basement. "Real disappointed in you, Jeeter. Deserting your post sets a bad example. Where would we be if everybody got to make their own rules?" The thought seemed to amuse the redhead. He noted Tigard staggering nearer with the scythe. "Lookee, boys, it's Father Time."

Tigard's hair and beard were burning now. Rakkim could hear the rain sizzle on him.

"You best be careful who you invite into your house next time," Gravenholtz said to Tigard. "A man like Jeeter, man who betrays his comrades' trust . . . no telling what he might have done to you and your family if I hadn't showed up. Hell and rye whiskey, if you had an ounce of respect, you'd *thank* me."

Tigard labored to stay standing. "I know . . . I know who I let in my house . . . *motherfucker*."

Gravenholtz flicked his cigarette into Tigard's face.

Popping sounds from the basement. Ammunition going off. Or Florence Tigard's canned peaches. Whatever it was, it drew the redhead's attention. His and his men's.

"Come on out, Jeeter!" Gravenholtz shouted. "I'll get you a sweet tea."

Rakkim could see Tigard gathering himself. Bracing his one good leg as he glanced up at the redhead. Rakkim silently urged him on. Said a prayer into the burning night.

Tigard stood up, swung the scythe with all his strength.

Rakkim saw the scythe strike the redhead. Saw the blade rake across his chest. The stroke should have cut the redhead in half. Cut him wide open. But it didn't. The redhead howled with pain as he scrambled up, his jacket sliced open, stuffing falling out. Rakkim saw blood, so it wasn't that the redhead was wearing body armor, but it wasn't the mortal wound Tigard's slashing attack should have caused. The redhead seemed more angry than hurt.

"Goddamnit, that stings, you farmer *fuck*." The redhead tore the scythe away from Tigard, snapped the wooden handle like it was a pencil. "Now where's Jeeter?"

Tigard stood there, hair burned away, eyebrows singed.

"Where *is* he?"

Tigard stared at the bodies of his sons. His wife. Turned back to the redhead. "Jeeter . . . he's inside. Guts blown out. Why don't you go check?"

The redhead drove the broken handle of the scythe into Tigard's chest. "Don't tell me what to do, you damned hick." He slammed the handle flat with the heel of his hand, the jagged end protruding from Tigard's back.

Tigard's lips moved silently.

"What?" The redhead cupped his ear. "I can't hear you."

Tigard sank to his knees. Curled up, shuddering, and finally lay still.

"Royce, bring the bird down," Gravenholtz said into a throat mike. He examined his jacket. "That son of a bitch done ruined my flight suit." He turned toward the pigpen.

Rakkim huddled under an enormous pig as the redhead approached. He stroked the sow's belly, calming her. Felt the mud around him warm as the pig urinated into the soft muck.

"Here, piggy-piggy." The redhead put one boot on the fence around the pigpen, made soft sucking sounds. "Here pig-pig-pig."

Rakkim pressed his face into the mud, watching the redhead with upturned eyes, Gravenholtz so close that Rakkim could see the scuff marks on his jump boots. Rakkim tensed, watching the boots. If Gravenholtz pivoted suddenly or shifted back on his heels, it meant he had spotted Rakkim. Time enough for Rakkim to act then. Time enough for him to spring out of the pigpen and gut Gravenholtz before the rest of the squad opened up on him. Perhaps even time enough for Rakkim to enjoy the sight of Gravenholtz trying to push his insides back where they belonged before the bullets chopped him down. Allah was merciful, after all.

The helicopter landed in a nearby pasture. Landed gently and quietly as a dandelion seed. Two raiders dragged the body of their dead comrade into the rear compartment. One lagged behind, a beefy raider tugging the ring off Florence Tigard's finger.

"Here, pig-pig-pig," Gravenholtz grunted, expertly calling to the pigs, and they shuffled and snorted happily toward him. "That's a good piggy." He quickly reached down, grabbed a small feeder pig by the fat around its neck, hauled it out of the pen.

The pig screamed.

Gravenholtz laughed, tucked the twisting pig under one arm as he started toward the helicopter. "Great God Almighty, I dearly love fresh pork." He pointed and the others double-timed after him. "Come on, Nelson . . . rest of you boys, get your ass in the bird. Breakfast's on me."

Rakkim watched them pile into the helicopter. Watched them clap each other on the back, their faces distorted by the flames from the farmhouse. Watched the helicopter lift off. "Keep your head down," he called to Leo.

The helicopter floated high above for an instant, then a missile flashed and the house exploded. The pigs boiled around the pen, grunting and churning up mud, as flaming debris fell from the sky, Rakkim hanging on to the sow to avoid being trampled. The chopper veered overhead, machine guns strafing the pen, sent chunks of meat flying.

When Rakkim looked back up, the chopper was heading north at full speed. Not west. That meant Gravenholtz wasn't interested in the recipient of the call Leo made, he was only interested in the man he thought made the call—Jeeter. Or maybe things were heating up on that mountain in Tennessee and he had no time to waste. Either way, Annabelle and Leanne were safe. For now. Rakkim stood up, bruised and muddy, splattered with blood and not sure how much of it was his own.

Leo stayed on his hands and knees, coughing. No . . . he was crying.

Rakkim walked over to the horse trough, started washing off the mud and pig shit. The cold water sluiced off the filth but didn't cool his rage and frustration. He splashed his face, wanted to tear his hair out, still seeing Tigard on fire, still hearing him tell the redhead that he *knew* whom he'd invited into his home. The words of a dying man . . . and for the life of him, Rakkim wasn't sure if Tigard was telling the truth.

Leo slowly got up. "Why . . . why did they stop? Why didn't they keep on shooting until they killed us?"

"They didn't know we were here." Rakkim couldn't look at him. "If they had known, we'd already be dead."

"So they just shot up the pigs for *fun?*" Timbers in the burning farmhouse collapsed and Leo flinched. "You . . . you think it's my fault, don't you?"

Rakkim didn't answer.

"I . . . I was talking with Leanne. We talked for hours, told each other everything there was to tell and I still couldn't stop. I love her. You probably think that's ridiculous . . ."

Rakkim walked toward Tigard, walked straight into the heat rolling off the farmhouse.

"I checked for tracers," called Leo. "I pulled two tracker chips. There weren't any more." His voice broke. "I didn't want to use the Tigards' phone . . . didn't want there to be a record. I . . . I was trying to *protect* everybody."

Rakkim fell to his knees beside Tigard's body. Wished him a rapid journey to Paradise. As the smoldering farmhouse hissed and popped, Rakkim bowed his head and apologized to Tigard, begged his forgiveness for bringing death to him and his family.

"I wanted to tell Leanne about Mr. Tigard," said Leo. "I wanted to tell her how he offered me a job working on the farm. I wanted . . . I wanted her to be proud of me."

Rakkim moved over and knelt beside Florence Tigard, straightened her limbs. Held her hand, feeling the heat from the burning house against his back. He whispered how sorry he was. It was too late for sorry, but he wasn't saying it for her. He was saying it for himself, and it was too late for him too. Much too late. He folded her hands in prayer.

"I'm going to kill that redheaded son of a bitch," said Leo. "Once we get to where we're going . . . I'm going to find Gravenholtz, and I'm . . . I'm going to kill him."

Rakkim felt the burden of tears lighten by an eyelash. A few days ago, Leo had been horrified at Rakkim taking care of the two Rangers. Now he was filled with the urge for righteous murder. Spider wasn't going to recognize his son when Rakkim brought him back home.

CHAPTER 25

The sun edged above the horizon and Rakkim felt the tug of prayer. Wanted to kneel before Allah, press his forehead into the dust and ask for His blessing and protection. All across the planet good Muslims were rushing to mosque, or prostrating themselves in their rooms, the fields, the desert itself, from General Kidd to the lowliest goatherd. One heart, one faith, one God. Bound together by their devotion, a current running from the Creator to every believer, intimate as a kiss. Rakkim turned his face to the sun. Except for the warmth of first light, he didn't feel a thing.

"I need to sit down for a minute," said Leo.

"You going to throw up again?" said Rakkim.

"No." Leo tossed his shovel aside, flopped onto the ground. Sweat ran down his smooth, beardless cheeks. "I'm just tired."

"I told you, I'll finish," said Rakkim. "Just relax and—"

"I want to help. I *have* to help." Leo sat at the edge of the grave he was digging for James Tigard. He had barely gotten past the topsoil. "I owe it to them."

"It's not your debt. It's mine." Rakkim kept digging, piling the dirt onto the grass; Florence Tigard's grave was four feet deep now. Right alongside the one for her husband. "*I* was the one who brought us here." Another shovelful tossed up. "*I* lied to them." He worked faster, a smooth, steady motion in the soft earth. "*I* used them." Dirt and pebbles flying. "You made a phone call you shouldn't have, but I was the one who got them killed, Leo, not you."

Honor, revenge, hospitality—the three hallmarks of the tribal man, according to one of Sarah's former academic associates, a fussy sociology professor who considered rationalism to be a sign of superiority. Yes, honor was a burden, as was revenge, and Bill Tigard and his family weren't the first or the last to be killed by their own hospitality, but the world was dead without such virtues. A place of musty books and empty promises.

Rakkim shoveled more dirt beside the grave. Almost deep enough now. The two of them had been working nonstop since the helicopter left. They had rinsed off the mud and pig shit, then Rakkim had gone to the bunkhouse, gathered bedsheets from storage, carefully wrapped the four bodies, and carried them over to the hill overlooking the river. A good spot to rest until the Day of Judgment. Leo sobbed quietly as they worked—the shovel was awkward in his hands, and he already had blisters, but he kept at it.

"Why don't you get some wood and wire in what's left of the barn?" said Rakkim. "You make some crosses for the graves, and I'll keep digging."

Leo hesitated.

"The Tigards are good Christians. Can't bury them without a cross to mark the spot."

Leo nodded, ran toward the shed.

Rakkim got back to work, digging steadily at the moist earth, eager to lose himself in the effort. When they got to the next town, he would call the minister at the Tigards' church. Tell them where the bodies were buried, so they could give them a genuine Christian burial. A Muslim and a Jew digging graves for devout Christians, saying their own prayers over the dead . . . say what you want, God might not be merciful, and he had *way* too many rules, but he did have a sense of humor.

Rakkim had half expected the neighbors to show up, but the next farmhouse was four or five miles away, and with the storm and the lightning . . . if the neighbors had heard the guns and the explosions, maybe they just thought it best to wait until morning.

Terrible what had happened to the Tigard family. Beyond terrible. The things he had seen tonight would never be erased, but Rakkim had learned something important from the attack. The stealth helicopter was Chinese built, a Monsoon-class, Model 4. The best bird in their arsenal—fast and maneuverable, with laser-sighted Gatlings, and quiet as a nightmare. It hadn't been the noise of the approaching chopper that had awakened Rakkim, but the minute perturbation in air pressure.

Rakkim took a breather at the bottom of the grave. Deep enough now. He walked up the narrow incline he had left himself, picked Florence

Tigard's body off the ground, and started back down. She was heavy, but he laid her down gently, held his hands out in silent benediction. Then walked back up and started shoveling in dirt.

The Chinese didn't export the Model 4. The president of the Belt himself only had a Model 2, a gift from the Chinese premier on his last official visit. If the Colonel had a Model 4, then the Chinese wanted to do business with him in a very bad way. Which meant they were convinced there was *something* in that mountain, something worth currying favor with the Colonel. The Chinese connection gave Rakkim just what he was looking for. An opportunity. A way in. A cover story that would grant him access to the Colonel. There were problems, of course . . . but after the price the Tigards had paid, there was no way Rakkim wasn't going to act on this new information.

Leo wandered back as the sun started steaming the wet ground, the kid carrying four crosses as Rakkim smoothed a mound of soil over Florence Tigard's grave. Leo had rinsed himself before making the crosses, but his face and hands were still scratched and bruised from his being trampled in the pigpen. He offered Rakkim the crosses that he had made from pieces of white picket fence. "Are these going to be okay? I scratched their names—"

"They're fine. Really nice."

"Honest?"

"They're fucking crosses. Just stick them in the ground. If there's a heaven they're already there. If not . . . it doesn't matter if the crosses are nice or not."

Leo stared at him.

"I'm sorry, Leo. I'm . . . I'm stretched a little thin right now."

"Gee, that's too bad, because me . . . I'm just having a great morning." Leo pushed the cross for James into the ground at the head of his grave. He thumped the cross in with the flat of the shovel, drove it in deeper. "If it doesn't stretch you even *thinner*"—another whack—"I have a question."

"Go ahead."

"Gravenholtz . . . Mr. Tigard slashed him with a scythe, but he didn't die. He didn't even seem hurt very bad," said Leo. "How could that be?"

Rakkim had wondered the same thing. He took one of the crosses from

Leo; meticulously made, the crossbars wired into place, the name and date etched in.

"I *saw* him get cut," said Leo. "He wasn't wearing body armor. He *bled*. Mr. Tigard was strong. The scythe should have cut Gravenholtz in half, but it barely broke the skin."

Rakkim tapped in Matthew Tigard's cross. He could have told Leo the scythe was old and dull. Could have told him that Tigard was weak and dying when he swung the scythe. People believed what made them comfortable. What fit with their preconceptions of how the world worked. The kid would have probably believed him, but Rakkim couldn't lie to Leo. Not today.

"Redbeard told me a story once. A rumor, really." Rakkim tapped the cross in, the sound echoing in the still morning. "We were in his water garden, drinking Coca-Cola. The real stuff, the stuff that gets you thrown in prison for breaking the embargo, not that Jihad Cola shit." The memory warmed him. Redbeard had contempt for substitutes of any kind. Or maybe the State Security chief just liked being bad once in a while. He straightened the cross, gave it a few more taps with the shovel. "Redbeard said that about ten years earlier he got reports that the Belt had started a secret program to counter the Fedayeen. Soldiers of Christ, their own elite warriors, that's what they wanted. Never panned out, or at least we never encountered them. General Kidd said Christians didn't have the discipline for the training required. Or the genetic boosters. Said it was just another tall tale from the Belt, more disinformation, but Redbeard wasn't so sure."

Leo worked a cross into Florence Tigard's grave, listening. He winced, pulled a splinter out of his thumb.

"The subject remained a point of contention between Redbeard and General Kidd, an academic discussion . . . until a Fedayeen forward combat patrol in Missouri lost contact one night. All eight Fedayeen were found murdered the next morning. Beaten to death. Skulls crushed, ribs stoved in. They had followed standard procedures, secured the perimeter. Three contacts from the Belt had been ushered into camp the previous evening, renegades with information to trade. The renegades had been scanned for weapons, but the scanners must have missed something. For three renegades to kill eight Fedayeen, at close quarters . . . nothing like it had ever happened before. General Kidd ordered a full investigation. The ground at the camp was soaked with blood, almost none of it matching the Fedayeen—so they hadn't gone quietly. No trace of drugs in the blood, no genetic anomalies, nothing to indicate how the Fedayeen had been overpowered."

"You think that's what Gravenholtz is?" said Leo. "One of these Soldiers of Christ?"

"I doubt it." Rakkim bent beside Leo, helped him bang in the cross. "If there was some elite warrior program in the Belt, we would have seen it by now. A couple other Fedayeen units disappeared right after that in the same area. Redbeard was investigating clinics in Thailand and Japan that specialized in implanting striking plates in the hands of martial artists, but then the attacks stopped and there were too many other domestic problems—"

"The attacks stopped?"

"Almost overnight. So General Kidd was probably right, it was just more Belt disinformation. Or the Belt ran out of money to fund more than a few prototypes, or maybe they didn't perform as well as anticipated. Gravenholtz is no superman. I think maybe . . . I think he just has some . . . enhancements." He looked at Leo. "You know about that kind of thing, don't you?"

"What's that supposed to mean?"

"I heard you're not off the rack either."

"I have an IQ that's too high to be measured, if that's what you mean."

"I've seen smart guys before. I was told you're something different."

"I . . . I process information very efficiently." Leo licked his lips. "*Really* efficiently."

"Lucky you." Rakkim wiped his hands on his pants. "We should get going. I have to contact Sarah."

Leo glanced at the graves. "I don't think that's such a good idea."

"I'm not calling to ask her to go steady," said Rakkim. "The situation here's changed. The helicopter Gravenholtz used is an advanced Chinese design. Very limited production. If the Colonel has one, it's because the Chinese are courting him. We can use that to our advantage. I need Spider to hack into a very secure database for me." Rakkim was backlit by the remnants of the Tigards' farmhouse, the embers still glowing in the dawn. "If things don't work out, Sarah has to be ready to inform the president. Fuck deniability at that point—he has to be ready to consider all options."

"Like *what?*"

"That's for him and General Kidd to decide. All I know is that with the Chinese backing him up, we can't let the Colonel keep whatever's hidden in that mountain. If it takes a Fedayeen strike force to neutralize the site . . ." Rakkim leaned the shovel against the tree. "Better a diplomatic disaster than an all-out civil war."

"It . . . it doesn't have to come to that. That's why we're here."

Rakkim watched the new day, the morning light soft and golden. He looked around at the farm, noted the fields of alfalfa almost ready for harvest, the neat rows of sweet corn, the peach trees . . . The orchard was Bill Tigard's gift to his wife. Conditions here weren't optimal for growing peaches, not well enough to compete with Georgia and South Carolina freestones, but Florence loved fresh peaches warm from the sun, and Bill loved Florence. The peaches would go to worms and black canker without proper attention, and there was no one to care for them now.

"Rikki?" Leo shivered. "How do you intend to contact Sarah?"

"We had a fallback plan in case things went bad," Rakkim said, still taking in the Tigards' farm, wanting to remember every bit of it. A ladybug landed on his hand. He watched it amble toward his thumb. "I'll transmit a one-second compressed-data packet to a weather station in the Canadian Rockies. The information will move to Sarah—"

"—as part of the regular streaming update of storm conditions." Leo snorted. "Brilliant."

Rakkim watched the ladybug flutter away. Remembered some ancient nursery rhyme about babies on fire.

"If the Chinese are involved with the Colonel, you might as well just send it directly to Beijing," said Leo. "The Chinese have the most sophisticated data-mining operation on the planet. Anything going in or out of the Belt is going to be snagged and decoded faster than you can blink. That's probably what happened to the other shadow warriors—the Colonel probably knew their entry point before the Fedayeen did."

Rakkim stayed calm, evaluating the new information without taking it personally. Leo's expertise wasn't wide, but it was deep. If he said the plan was shit, Rakkim wasn't about to step into it.

"You're not the only one with a backup plan," said Leo. "Spider has an emergency contact in Atlanta. You can call from there."

CHAPTER 26

"Watch your step," said the Colonel.

"I'm no hothouse flower, Colonel," said Baby, dropping to her hands and knees. Her tight jeans scraped the rock face as she squeezed through the opening.

Moseby offered her a hand from the other side. "Ma'am?"

She took his hand, giggling as he pulled her through. "I declare, the Belt has more gentlemen per square foot than anyplace on God's green earth."

The Colonel wriggled through the cleft in the rock, more agile than anyone would have expected for a man his age. He brushed back his hair, dust drifting down. Two of his adjutants waited for him inside the inner passage, two others worked their way through after him. One of them, Trey, a big ole boy from the Kentucky border, almost got stuck, and had to be dragged through, embarrassed and a little frightened.

The Colonel walked around the widened interior passage, his shadow huge in the floor lights. He gingerly touched one of the walls, looked at his fingertips.

Baby pounced on his shadow. Looked around, dirt streaked on her cheek. "Spooky."

"I told you not to come," said the Colonel.

"You know I like a little scare, Colonel," she said, kissing him. "Keeps the blood circulating, that's what my mama says."

"What makes you think this tunnel goes anywhere?" the Colonel said to Moseby. "Jefferson's already checked it out."

"No, sir, he checked out the *main* tunnel," said Moseby. "This is a little feeder line . . . run off the main one to see if it was worth excavating later. The old-timers used to do that a lot when they were chasing coal." For the last few days and most of the nights, he had been walking the tunnels and mineshafts honeycombing the mountain. Examining untouched tunnels and ones that had already been explored, and crossed off from consideration. "My point is, I don't blame Jefferson for not bothering with it, but sometimes folks miss things. They get so focused on what they're looking for that they don't see what's right in front of their nose."

The Colonel walked deeper into the narrowing tunnel, his head almost brushing the ceiling. "I like a man who doesn't take things as they are. Speaks well of you."

Moseby joined the Colonel. "The reason Jefferson was interested in the main shaft was because there's a lot of calcite present, which attracts moisture, and the slope is right to collect it at the bottom somewhere. Like the lake you're interested in. When the main shaft ended in a dead end, Jefferson went on to other tunnels, but this little feeder line has also got the same factors. No reason it might not have a lake down there."

The Colonel shivered. "It's cold down here." He rubbed his hands together. "Some of the other shafts are hot enough to bake bread in."

"Don't get any ideas," said Baby, taking the Colonel's arm. "I can't cook worth a lick. The Colonel's always riding me about his first wife's cooking."

The Colonel leaned close to one of the walls, rubbed his finger over a section and examined it. "What are these sparkly mineral deposits?"

"Schist. It's sparkles because of all the mica in it," said Moseby. "Might be one reason the seam was never fully mined. Schist fractures easily. Causes real problems."

The Colonel rubbed his finger against the wall again. "My information about the lake is sketchy, but there was mention of the passageway down being marked by stars. It was passed off as delusional, but seeing this schist makes me wonder."

"You should have told me earlier," said Moseby.

"You seem to be doing just fine," bristled the Colonel, "and I wasn't sure how reliable the information was. Everything I know I got third- or fourth-hand."

"Colonel, sir?" called one of his adjutants. "Are we almost done here?"

"Why don't you go back into the main shaft," said the Colonel. He turned to Moseby. "My men hate it down here. Can't say I blame them. We're soldiers, not moles."

"That's a rude thing to say to Mr. Moseby," said Baby, tickling him. "If he's a mole, he's a darn cute one."

"Mr. Moseby knows I hold him in the highest regard, Baby, it's just the men and I prefer open sky . . ." The Colonel stopped as the adjutants squeezed back into the main tunnel, taking one of the floor lights with them. The tunnel seemed suddenly smaller, the air thinner. The only way to work this far underground was to keep your mind focused on the task at hand, just concentrate on breathing in and out. Once you let your attention slide, once you noticed how cramped it was, and started to imagine the sheer weight and volume of rock and dirt overhead, you were lost. A man's screams echoing off the walls could start a panic, a blind rush to daylight trampling everyone in the way. "Open . . . open sky is preferable to this entryway to Hades."

Moseby could see the Colonel struggling to overcome his fear—it was one of the reasons he wanted to have this conversation here. He needed all the advantages he could get. The Colonel's eagerness to go back outside might make him tell the truth. At least more than he intended. "It's always difficult finding a specific object underwater, Colonel, but all you've told me is that there's *something* lying at the bottom of an underground lake. Something you evidently want badly enough to commit hundreds of men and I don't know how much money. So what am I looking for?"

"As I've told you before, that information remains classified."

"Colonel, I at least need to know how big this thing is that you want me to find." Moseby walked back to the rocky outcropping that partially blocked the entrance to the main tunnel. "This rock face has been here for thousands of years. Anything or anyone entering this feeder line had to make it past that narrow opening. So, Colonel, is this *thing* I'm looking for going to fit through?"

Behind the Colonel, caught in the light, a single drop of moisture slid down the rock. "Yes . . . yes, I believe it would."

"Is it metallic or organic, because I've got some very sensitive detecting gear? Colonel?"

The Colonel glanced at his wife. "Baby, are you cold? Shall we go?"

"It's all right," said Baby. "I feel safe down here with you two big strong men."

The Colonel jerked as the floor light flickered, the battery running low. "I think we should leave."

Moseby nodded. "Colonel, I've come a long way on your say-so. I left my family with men I don't know, men I don't trust. I was supposed to be able to talk with my wife at least once or twice a week, but Gravenholtz keeps making excuses."

"You know we don't have decent reception up here."

"Gravenholtz left special equipment behind at my house . . . a high-tech phone, supposed to be able to cut through the atmospheric problems. I was assured—"

"There's been a problem," said the Colonel. "I'm sorry, John."

The silence in the tunnel was even more unsettling than the echo of their lowered voices.

"I think you better tell me what the problem is, Colonel," Moseby said softly.

"You giving the orders now, son?" said the Colonel.

Moseby hesitated. "No."

The Colonel pursed his lips. "One of Lester's old comrades, man named Jeeter, was left in charge back at your house. Evidently this Jeeter deserted his post, taking the phone with him. It's quite valuable—"

"What happened to my family?"

"I'm sure they're quite all right—"

"Colonel, right now I don't give a good goddamn if you're sure or not. I want to see my family. I want to be on that chopper in twenty minutes."

"You think you give the orders here, Mr. Moseby?" The Colonel's face tightened, his jaw set. "Give me another order. Go on, Mr. Moseby, please . . . tell me what to do."

They were inches apart, close enough that Moseby could smell the tobacco on the Colonel's breath and the coffee he'd had an hour earlier. Close enough that Moseby could dash his brains out on the rock wall with one quick movement. That wouldn't bring Moseby back to his family, though.

"You two boys shouldn't fight," said Baby. "Colonel, you can't blame John for worrying about his family, it's the most natural thing in the world to do. And John, you should know that if it was in the Colonel's power to let you visit your wife and daughter, he'd do it. Just that there's been too many helicopter trips off this mountain. People in flyover country are starting to wonder what's going on here, and right now we don't need the attention. So just as soon as we can, you're going to be sent right back with your kin. And with your pockets full of money to boot. Isn't that better than standing here mad at each other?"

Moseby and the Colonel stayed squared off.

"I want your word," said Moseby.

The Colonel stuck his hand out, and they shook. "And I want your best efforts, John." He glanced back into the tunnel. "Are we done here? Because I've seen enough of this place to last me a good long while."

"There's a few scrape marks on the floor further on that are rather interesting," said Moseby. "Nothing certain, but—"

"Do what you need to do," said the Colonel. "Baby? Shall we?"

"If you want me to proceed, Colonel, I'm going to need additional help," said Moseby. "There's been a cave-in further down the tunnel. I don't think it was deliberate. No trace of explosives being used. More an aspect of the calcium carbonate that permeates the rock, makes it brittle—"

"Yes, yes," said the Colonel. "Get to the point."

"I need a crew of men to clear the shaft, but it's going to be hard and dangerous," said Moseby. "Round-the-clock work, because we have to chip away the collapsed section into small enough pieces—"

"Anything you need. Just make it happen."

The floor light flickered again.

"I want to select the best men from the other crews working the site," said Moseby. "I already know who I want. The other bosses are going to be pissed off at me grabbing their best—"

"Just *do* it." The Colonel's voice echoed. "Any problems from the bosses, you tell them to take it up with me."

"I'm going to start bunking with the miners, Colonel. Just so you know. You can reassign my bodyguards, I won't need them."

"There a problem?"

"Just trying to make things run smoother."

"Fine. No more bodyguards. Just let me know where your tent is."

"Colonel . . . one more thing. I can appreciate your desire to maintain security, but you're hampering my ability to find whatever it is you're looking for by not telling me the specifics. What's the weight? The size? One container or more? Does it have a magnetic or a radioactive signature?"

"Why do you ask about a radioactive signature?" the Colonel said quietly.

"Because, Colonel . . ." Moseby made sure there was just the three of them in the tunnel. "There's not a whole lot of things small enough to get through this tunnel, but worth enough to justify the scale of your dig. If it's not Fort Knox gold, maybe it's something from New York or Washington, D.C."

The Colonel's shadow waved on the walls.

"*Tell* him, Colonel," said Baby. "One look at Mr. Moseby and you know he's different from the others. He's a finder. You can trust him." She leaned her head on his shoulder, snuggled against him. "Shoot, you owe him the truth. He's risking his life down here at the bottom of the earth."

The Colonel nodded, beckoned Moseby closer. "Somewhere down here, Mr. Moseby, hidden safely away . . . is the Declaration of Independence and the Constitution of the United States, the most sacred documents of the former regime. I intend for us to find them, Mr. Moseby, whatever the cost."

CHAPTER 27

The monorail into downtown Atlanta put even the grand transit system of Seattle to shame. Seattle's elevated train was clean, smooth, and free of graffiti, but even the second-class cars of the new Atlanta monorail had plush seats, soft music, and the scent of magnolias piped in. No telling what first-class amenities were. Rakkim would have liked to find out but Idents weren't allowed in first class. He enjoyed the last of the sun warming the glass of the train.

The outskirts of the Belt capital were the usual shabby apartments and run-down homes with brown lawns, but the people getting on to ride into the city were well dressed, the women in short, frilly skirts and purple anteater-skin boots, the men in suits with high collars and tight pants. They weren't heading into the capital for a night on the town, they were the working poor looking their best for their service jobs taking care of the capital's overclass—making drinks, driving town cars, or serving tiger prawn satay or veal tartare to the sleek civil servants, tech workers, and international-business desk jockeys that were the hot blood of Atlanta.

Rakkim had bought himself and Leo new clothes, spending more than he anticipated on his credit chip, but even so, he felt underdressed. From the glances of the other riders, it was a majority opinion. Even the Idents were fashionable.

"I'm scared," whispered Leo.

"It's okay," said Rakkim.

"I checked the security phone for bugs," said Leo. "I thought I found them all, but I was wrong."

Rakkim stared at his hands. He had a small blister on each of his thumbs from digging graves for the Tigard family.

"I was *wrong*," said Leo. "I'm never wrong about things like that." Leo's knees bounced rapidly up and down. "What happens when we get to the mountain? Maybe . . . maybe I'm not as smart as I think I am."

"Little late in the game for humility, Leo. I liked you better when you were working out the value of pi to a hundred places while pounding it to Leanne."

"Me too." Leo caught himself. "I don't like that phrase, 'pounding it,' in reference to Leanne."

Through the scenic glass Rakkim could see that new skyscrapers had been built since his last visit. A couple of them had to be 250 or 300 stories at least, all titanium and glass, squatty at the base and tapering to fine points. South American money, for the most part, the Brazilian and Columbian conglomerates staking their claim, buying prime real estate in the capital. There were office buildings in Dubai and Singapore over four hundred stories tall, buildings that issued separate weather reports depending on your floor, but these new ones in Atlanta were impressive nonetheless. Nice to see a skyline without antiterror blimps hovering overhead or antiaircraft batteries on the rooftops—for all its flaws the Belt didn't attract the hostility that the Islamic Republic did; its enemies preferred economic pressure and constant territorial encroachment rather than direct attacks.

A young blond Ident across the aisle batted her eyes at Leo—her lids, crusted with glitter stones, flashed rainbows. "Y'all just getting into town?"

Leo nodded.

"He's allowed to talk, isn't he?" The Ident smiled at Rakkim, her grillwork crusted with glitter stones too. She offered her hand to Leo, reaching across Rakkim. "I'm Amanda."

"Leo."

"Leo the lion." She winked at him. "Bet you know how to growl too, don't you?"

Leo looked away.

The monorail raced on, a light electrical hum the loudest sound in the compartment. Leo had phoned ahead after they left the Tigards' farm. Told his contact what had happened, and what Rakkim wanted. Calls within the Belt were generally safe, but the conversation had been in code anyway. Someone overhearing it would have thought it was just casual talk, except for when the man at the other end had said, *Your brother is getting a job offer from Switzerland? You're absolutely certain of that?* The slight change in his tone was a lapse in security, but Rakkim was probably just annoyed for having to use Leo's Atlanta connection.

A few stops later, the trains slowed. Amanda leaned toward Leo. "This is your stop."

Rakkim followed them down the ramp to the street, part of the throng of reverse commuters. At the bottom of the ramp, Amanda kissed Leo on the right cheek, left a lip print, and pointed toward a small cart selling soda. The man selling soda handed Rakkim a couple of RC Colas, whispered an address. Ten minutes' walk later, an Ident led them to the service entrance of one of the largest buildings in the city, Freedom Towers.

Another Ident led them into a private elevator, thumb-coded the control panel. Leo put one hand on the wall, breathing rapidly as the car rose. The doors slid open at the penthouse on the 111th floor. The Ident stepped out, waited for them to exit, and then stepped back inside.

"Good talking with you," said Rakkim.

The Ident didn't change expression.

"*There* you are, dear hearts," said Getty Andalou, fluttering over in a wave of ruffles and silk. The son of the Senate majority leader, he was well over six feet tall, late thirties, slender as a stick, his perfumed hair falling around his shoulders—a real dandy, elegant in cranberry tights and a loose white silk blouse with ruffled sleeves and collar. All he needed was a sword and a floppy hat with a feather in it. He stood with one hip cocked, hands on his hips. "You must be Leo. I've heard *so* much about you."

Leo shifted from one foot to another. "Okay."

"The infamous Rikki." Andalou gave a slight bow. "I'm glad to see you're taking such good care of the lad."

Rakkim curtseyed.

Andalou chuckled. "Ah yes . . . Spider said you were droll." He waved at the expansive living room. "Please, come in. I've had food prepared . . ." His nose wrinkled. "Perhaps you'd prefer to bathe first." He lightly clapped his hands and another Ident appeared. "Please escort our guests to their bedrooms." He looked at Rakkim. "I've taken the liberty of having clothes laid out for you."

"I'm allergic to ruffles and bows," said Rakkim.

"I'm sure you are." Andalou's teeth were perfectly even and white. "I

take a certain pride in anticipating the tastes of my guests . . . although in
your case I had some assistance."

Rakkim followed the Ident down the hall, Leo tagging along after. The
Ident opened a door, bowed, and Leo walked inside. Another door opened,
and Rakkim thanked him. He tried the door after it closed behind the
Ident. It opened easily. He assumed there were cameras. He checked out
the spacious room, its high ceilings and buffed hickory flooring.

Situated at the corner of the penthouse, the panoramic windows
afforded a view of the Congressional Building and the Lincoln Monument. Down the street was Traitors Square, whose embossed floor tiles
noted the names of journalists and politicians who had covertly accepted
Saudi oil money. A trip to the capital wasn't complete until tourists had
tromped all over those names. The Putin Building, the tallest skyscraper
in Atlanta, cast a shadow across the city. Three hundred ten stories, according to what he had overheard on the monorail. High enough to make the
point, but not too high; at 555 stories, the Rio Spire had been the tallest
structure in the world—a ten-thousand-mile view, bragged the publicists—
until it fell over one bright sunny day without a cloud in the sky or a seis-
mic shift underfoot. Just toppled over into the Atlantic like a drunk on the
white-sand beach. Too big to remove, the wreckage, and the twenty thousand dead under it, had become a major tourist attraction.

Rakkim touched a window, noted the anti-eavesdropping filaments in
the armored glass. Nice touch. Some folks would feel safe. The bathroom
was bigger than most apartments in the Belt or the Islamic Republic, all
pink marble and granite, one entire wall a mirror. Probably two-way glass.
He took off his clothes, kicked them into a corner, and walked into the
bathroom.

The ultrasonic shower first sprayed a mist of scented water, then the
ultrasonics kicked in, a barely audible hum that set the water beads vibrating on his skin, tingling him clean. He stayed there for three cycles, enjoying the sensation, then slathered barber cream on his face, his beard
dissolving in the mist. His clothes were gone when he got out, replaced by
blue breeches and a soft buckskin shirt. He had seen similar outfits on the
monorail—a fine outfit, but not so fine as to draw attention. When he
walked out of the bedroom, Leo and Andalou were already waiting for him
in the living room.

Leo waved. He looked like he had lost ten pounds on the mission so far, the new clothes fitting him perfectly—a dark gray suit of some shiny material and a white shirt with a shroud of Turin impression of Jesus on it.

"Feel better?" Andalou didn't wait for Rakkim to answer. "We were just discussing your situation. I notified Spider immediately after speaking with Leo this morning. You know Spider . . . he's already started hacking into the KGB database. Russian security is very good, full encryption and false entry points, but Spider is quite confident. I hope you appreciate the magnitude of your request."

"Cracking the database isn't as hard as you think." Leo sniffed. "Backdating your name into the KGB files, *that's* the tricky part. Probably not more than a dozen people in the world could—"

"My history has to be planted behind at least one wall, two would be even better, and the history has to be *accurate,*" said Rakkim. "From the beginning until three years ago, when I was managing the Blue Moon."

Andalou smoothed his trousers. "I still don't understand why you're—"

"You don't need to understand."

"Such lovely manners." Andalou poured ice tea for Rakkim. "Well, if this little game with your KGB file doesn't work out, I suspect the two-hundred-million-dollar down payment you're offering the Colonel will affirm your good intentions."

Rakkim looked at Leo. "Two hundred *million?* I thought the president didn't want to leave his fingerprints on the operation."

Leo squirmed in his seat.

"The president doesn't know anything about the Colonel's new Chinese friends or the change of plans," said Andalou. "Please . . . try your tea. I hope it's not too sweet."

Rakkim leaned forward. "What's going on, Leo?"

"It's Spider's money," said Leo. "He transferred it into an account at the Bank of Liechtenstein this morning. Left traces of a Russian point of origin."

"That's not what I mean," said Rakkim.

"Rikki wants to know why the president hasn't been updated," said Andalou.

"Why do you think you have to explain things to him?" Rakkim said softly. "Does he seem stupid to you?"

Andalou plucked at the ruffles around his neck, pursed his shiny lips. "Kindly do not threaten me, sir."

"Do you *feel* threatened?" said Rakkim.

"Hey, you two," said Leo. "We're on the same side."

"If you want clarification of my good intentions, sir," said Andalou, "perhaps you should talk with your wife."

"Go ahead, call me *sir* again," said Rakkim.

"Rikki, please," said Leo. "Getty and Spider and Sarah . . . we're working together."

"Nobody told me." Rakkim saw Sarah's face the morning he left . . . he could see she was upset, holding something back. He just thought she was afraid to start crying. *Joke's on you, Rikki. Ha-ha.* "Must have been too important to share with the help."

"Rikki . . . if I may," said Andalou. "I've been in contact with Sarah and Spider for some time now. Sharing information. Building up trust. Diplomacy 101." He shook out his hair, sent perfume wafting through the air. "Sarah wanted to tell you, but I insisted on keeping our little circle small. After all, our lives depend on it." He crossed his legs, the satin trousers rustling, and Rakkim thought of crickets and kudzu and ambushes when you least expected them. "If you want to know the truth, we thought we had more time. This business with the Chinese making overtures to the Colonel has moved everything up, and I'm not at all sure we're ready."

Rakkim waited, enjoying seeing Andalou discomforted. He probably had rehearsed this moment for hours, ready for all the likely responses, but without Rakkim asking *Ready for what?* Andalou didn't know how to proceed.

"You've seen what things are like here now," said Leo. "Mexicans taking back land, kidnapping tourists, diverting rivers. People all over the Belt are losing their jobs, or working for foreigners. Warlords and bandits everywhere, the cops have gone crazy, and the federal government needs press-gangs to fill the ranks of their army."

"My country is dying." Andalou clutched his glass. "My country . . . is *dying*. And so is yours."

"What do you want me to do about it?" said Rakkim.

"Not you," said Andalou. "*Us*. All of us."

Leo brought his pudgy fists together. "Reunification."

Rakkim laughed.

"It's not funny," said Leo.

"It's not possible either," said Rakkim.

"One of the early patriots, Ben Franklin, said we could either hang together or hang separately," said Andalou. "It's as true today as it was then. I'm not the only one who sees things this way. There are others . . . in high office, in business, good folks in the Islamic Republic as well as the Belt. People know things are wrong. Even if they're too young to remember the way things used to be, the evidence is all around them. The bridge in San Francisco . . . New Fallujah, whatever you call it. The bridge is rusting, badly maintained, cables worn through. Another five or ten years, it won't be usable. What happened to the people who built that bridge? The *country* that built that bridge?"

"I'm no traitor," said Rakkim.

"Nor am I," said Andalou.

"I want to talk with Sarah," Rakkim said to Andalou. "Don't tell me you can't do it; you obviously talked to her after Leo called Spider yesterday."

.   The ice in Andalou's drink clinked against the glass. Rakkim wasn't sure if his hand was trembling or if the dandy just liked the sound of it. "It's dangerous," he said.

"A cautious revolutionary? You're not going to get anywhere like that." Andalou nodded. "Indeed."

Rakkim and Leo followed Andalou into one of the other rooms of the penthouse. The bedroom suite. The love nest of a decadent playboy, the bed a round, canopied tent draped in red silk, paintings of fleshy nudes on the walls. Into the walk-in closet, his clothes a rainbow of peacock finery. Andalou pressed a light fixture and a false wall slid back, revealing a small alcove behind a rack of suits. A videophone link was built into a desk. He beckoned them into the cramped interior, the wall sliding shut behind them.

"Landline?" said Leo as Andalou keyed in a number.

Andalou nodded, moved slightly to give Rakkim more room.

"You intersecting through Mozambique?" said Leo.

"Sri Lanka," said Andalou, checking various readouts.

"I'd have gone with Mozambique," said Leo. "They've got faster switches. What's your response delay? Fifteen seconds?"

"Nineteen," said Andalou.

"That's what I mean," said Leo. "Mozambique, you're talking about—" He stopped as Sarah's face flickered on-screen. She looked worried.

"What's wrong?" said Sarah.

Andalou looked at Rakkim.

"Our friend here just told me that you've been keeping secrets," said Rakkim. "When were you going to tell me?"

They waited for the signal to travel the long way around the world to Seattle, a small packet of information among the flood of anonymous words and images. Waited for Sarah's response to make the same journey. Indirect, and slower than satellite feeds, but landlines were safer. Not *safe*. Data mining by both the Belt and the republic filtered all communication channels, searching for useful intelligence, but Andalou must trust his connection. It was his head at risk. Safer, but not safe.

"I know you're angry, but I was waiting for the right moment. Waiting for things to be bad enough. Conditions desperate enough." Her image broke up for a second, reconstituted itself. "I knew how you would react. You have to trust my judgment. It's the only way we're going to survive as a nation."

"What do you think Redbeard would say? Would he trust your judgment?"

"I think . . . I think he saw where things were going for a long time before he died. I think he did his best to make things work . . . to give the nation time to grow, but if he saw what was happening now, he'd say do what you need to do. That's the most basic rule of statecraft. Do what has to be done, regardless of the consequences. If a nation torn apart can't survive, then the nation has to be put back together."

"Who rules this new nation once you put it back together?" said Rakkim.

Her response seemed to take forever to reach him. "A candidate acceptable to both parties. North and South. There will be a vote . . . that's certain."

"So you don't really know," said Rakkim. "You're just hoping it will all work out. You're praying, they're praying, and God, oddly enough, will come down on the side of the one with the most guns and most willing to use them. God always does."

Sarah shook her head. "We don't have time to work out the details. The president came back from Geneva with very bad news. The Aztlán Empire has put in a claim for the whole Southwest and half of Texas. Greater Cuba wants to annex the rest of Florida and south Georgia. The Canadian government, using the Indigenous People's Doctrine, is demanding the return of most of New England, Pennsylvania, Michigan, and Wisconsin. Both the Belt and the republic are being eaten away. Reunification is risky, I don't doubt that . . . but it's our only chance."

Rakkim stared at her on the screen. Wished he were there.

"Rikki?"

"How's Michael?"

"He misses you. So do I."

"You're going to have to tell the president. He's the only one who can sell reunification to the people."

"I know."

"And General Kidd. The president's going to have to work on him. Even Kingsley might not be able to do it, but you won't have a chance without Kidd, and he'll never listen to a woman."

"You sound like you're already convinced." She waited.

"Any word about al-Faisal?"

"State Security concluded he blew himself up rather than be captured. Anthony . . . he's not so sure. Neither am I. You didn't tell me he was a strangler."

"I'm a bad boy. I wish I was there so you could put me to bed without my supper."

"I'd *like* that."

"Kiss Michael for me. Tell him Daddy loves him."

"You tell him." Sarah wiped her eyes. "Come back and tell him yourself."

CHAPTER 28

"So you're just going to stroll into the Colonel's camp?" said Leo. "*That's your big plan?*"

Far in the distance, Rakkim could see the Atlanta skyline in his rearview. They had left Getty's suite after breakfast, driven away in the vehicle he had secured for them—a battered four-by-four Mao safari wagon with rusted door panels and a solid suspension. Reliable, built for the backcountry, but not worth enough to attract hijackers or the authorities. Sarah would have liked it, a car they could use to explore for dinosaur bones in Utah or to take Michael to Mount Rushmore, let him see the dynamited faces of the old presidents, maybe buy him a replica of the original from one of the street hawkers.

"What, I don't deserve an answer?" Leo waited. Little fucker was patient. "*Well?*"

"Yes, I plan to just stroll into the Colonel's camp. Trying to infiltrate didn't work out so well for the other three shadow warriors sent in."

"I hate to break it to you," said Leo, "but in terms of game theory, the opposite of a failed tactic is not necessarily success."

"Thanks for the tip."

"Would you at least tell me why you want Dad to bury your identity in the KGB files? How does that *help*?"

Rakkim watched the road. "Because no one believes what they're told. They believe what they uncover. What they dig up on their own. And the harder it is to find, the more they believe it when they *do* find it."

Leo thought it over. "So you *want* the Colonel to crack your KGB file?"

Rakkim smiled. "If he doesn't, I'm dead."

Leo yawned.

Rakkim kept driving. Traffic had thinned out after their leaving the vicinity of the capital, the roads getting progressively more run down, the ditches overgrown with weeds. A stake-body truck loaded with pianos raced past, changing lanes erratically—battered uprights and grand pianos shifted from side to side, sounding like thunder. Rakkim tailed the truck, moving when it moved. Sometimes outlaws mined the main roads, looting the wreckage. He imagined ivory keys scattered across the asphalt like teeth, wondered what they would be worth.

Carefully cultivated fields of peanuts and soybeans gave way to pine forests and dense underbrush as the miles passed. Rakkim spotted an abandoned car nearly swallowed up by the greenery, creepers twined through broken windows, upholstery furry with moss and mildew. He took an unmarked road toward North Carolina, the car bumping over potholes.

"Could I see the shekel again?" said Leo. "I'll be careful."

Rakkim handed it over. He knew how Leo felt. He found himself fingering it at odd moments, or just touching the pocket he kept it in, reassuring himself that it was still there. Crazy to rely on an old silver coin to win over Malcolm Crews, but they needed Crews and his ragtag army, and faith was the most powerful force in the universe.

Leo cupped the coin in the palm of his hand. "You ever wonder if maybe it's real?"

"'Course it's real."

"No, I mean . . . what if it really was one of the thirty pieces of silver paid out to Judas?"

"You're the math whiz, you figure the odds of that."

Leo rubbed the profiled face on the coin with his thumb, caressed the pitted surface. "Probability's one thing . . . but there's no such thing as zero *possibility.*"

Rakkim took the coin back. It felt warm. He likely wasn't going to have it much longer. Judas probably felt the same way. You could buy anything with money; that hadn't changed in two thousand years. Problem was, what you bought didn't last.

"I liked Getty," said Leo. "He said I could visit him in Atlanta anytime."

"Getty's a politician. You're *supposed* to like him. Doesn't mean you turn the country over to him and trust that he's going to do right."

"Dad trusts him. So does Sarah."

"If Sarah trusted him she would have told me about him before we left Seattle. She thinks she *needs* Getty. Doesn't mean she trusts him."

Leo stretched out his legs. "I still don't know why we don't just go see this Malcolm Crews guy now, instead of taking another detour."

"It's not a detour. I told you, I have business in Addington."

"We got the shekel, what more—"

"The shekel's not enough," said Rakkim. "Every big lie needs at least three parts to be convincing. Three . . . aspects. They don't even have to be mutually reinforcing, they just have to fill in the landscape of the lie."

Leo yawned.

"The shekel's one part. Addington . . . the Church of the Mists, that's the second."

Leo closed his eyes. "What . . . what's the third?"

Rakkim glanced over at him. Leo looked like a big baby, sprawled against the door, mouth hanging open, already snoring. "Me," he said softly. "I'm the third part."

A large wooden cross stood beside the road, JESUS SAVES spelled out in white boulders behind it. Another mile, another cross, this one made from flattened metal cans edged with rust. Another mile, another cross. And another. Rakkim relaxed as the narrow road led him deeper into the foothills of the Appalachians, past small towns cut off from change even before the war, towns given up to ruin and poverty, and their faith all the stronger for it. God's country, that's what the locals called it, disparaging the city Christians for their backsliding and arrogance. During the war, all of the Belt had been God's country, fiercely devout, unified, fighting to the death for what they believed in. The armistice had been in effect for almost thirty years now, time enough for the rot to set in. The same rot he saw in the republic.

Leo sighed, pillowed his head with his arm.

A little after noon, Rakkim stopped for gas at a tiny two-pump station all alone in the woods. No credit chips accepted, just cold cash. The attendant sidled out, a scrawny young guy with a bad complexion and a pistol on his hip—he watched Rakkim fill the tank with a gas-kerosene mixture, the only fuel available. Probably cut with paint thinner as well, from the smell of it. Moonshine even. Rakkim had seen all of them used in this part of the Belt. The attendant lit a cigarette, seemed to enjoy Rakkim's discomfort at the open flame. Rakkim returned the favor, struck a match on the back of his front teeth, and tossed it at the attendant's feet, right next to a splash of spilled gas. The man grinned, ground the match out, then asked Rakkim if he wanted to buy some traveler's insurance.

"Why?" said Rakkim, wary.

"Man like you got a need for some extra protection. Anybody with eyes can see that."

"I'm just another traveler on the road to glory," said Rakkim.

"Yeah, and I'm Willie Jefferson Clinton." The attendant hitched up his trousers, beckoned, walked inside the station.

Rakkim looked around. Followed.

An old desk rested against one wall, under an Osama bin Laden dartboard. The attendant pushed aside an overflowing ashtray, opened a desk drawer, and pulled out a tray of jagged-edged silvery medallions. The medallions were cut out from oil cans, brightly colored geometric shapes—stars and crosses, eagles and rockets and knives, each with a tiny hole at the top strung with clear fishing line. "Hang one of these from your rearview, keep you safe."

"From what?"

"From whatever means to harm you," said the attendant. "You believe in Jesus Christ?"

"*Hell*, yes."

The attendant peered at him and there was blood in the whites of his eyes. "You believe he's coming again, bringing fire and brimstone this time, to smite the wicked and destroy the unrighteous?"

"Who could blame him?" said Rakkim.

The attendant stared. Nodded. "For you . . . ten dollars."

Rakkim paid him, chose a shiny pyramid with an eye at the apex, like from the old money.

The attendant acted surprised. "Drive careful."

"I shouldn't have to drive carefully. Not now. Strictly pedal to the metal." Rakkim spun the pyramid with a flick of his finger. "This thing's guaranteed, isn't it?"

The attendant fired up another cigarette. "Sure, buddy. You got problems, come back and I'll give you a full refund."

Leo was still snoring when Rakkim got back to the car.

The car bucked and backfired for the first few miles, finally smoothed out a bit from the volatile fuel mix. A half hour later, Rakkim drove past a

large sign offering vacation condos along the Carolina coast, happy black
and white children playing in the surf, elaborate sand castles on the shore.

The sign tilted heavily to one side, covered in graffiti and chickweed.
The condos and everything else along the coast had been scoured away by
hurricanes twenty years ago, the offshore islands inundated by rising sea
levels, the former state of Florida eaten away until it was almost an island.
The entrepreneurial Cubans who ruled Nuevo Florida had been building
a dike against the inevitable for the last twenty years, a wall over four hundred miles long, stretching from the Atlantic around to the Gulf. Millions
of tons of concrete were poured every year, raising the wall higher and
higher to protect their orange groves, hotels, and casinos. The Belt didn't
have the money or the will to try to reclaim their coastline. God's will was
the prevailing excuse for giving up. Same excuse they used in the Islamic
Republic.

Rakkim raced past crudely painted billboards daubed with BEWARE 666
and JUDGMENT AWAITS and GOD IS LOVE with the word *love* shot out. The
crosses pounded into the sides of the road came more frequently now,
homemade crosses of all sizes and materials—crosses made of stone and
concrete, crosses made from twists of barbwire, crosses made of white
picket fencing nailed together, a road of crosses rising into the hills, leading him straight toward the dark cloud on the horizon, a boiling mass
blacker than a thunderhead.

Leo jerked awake, blinking. "I . . . I was dreaming of Leanne," he said,
still a little dopey from sleep. He rubbed his eyes. "You think there's such
a thing as love at first sight?"

"We're not going to have another sex talk, are we? Because I'd rather
teach you how to use a knife. I'm better qualified."

"I'm serious. Did you fall in love with your wife when you first met her?"

"Sarah was four and I was nine—the only thing I was in love with at
that moment was a hot meal and a warm bed." Rakkim checked the
rearview, gave the pyramid a spin, the eye going round and round. "With
Sarah and me, love came later."

"The moment I looked at Leanne . . . the very first moment, I *knew*.
She's so . . . amazing."

A brown rabbit darted across the road. Rakkim barely had time to
avoid it.

"I called her last night . . . don't worry, I made sure it was safe. I told her how I felt. I was scared at first, you know, because I didn't know how she would react . . ." Leo smiled to himself. "She said she felt exactly the same way."

"I wish you hadn't done that. I need you focused—"

"You don't think about your wife and son," said Leo. "Does it distract you?"

"Sometimes."

"Well, I'm not like you." Leo pointed at the eye in the pyramid spinning lazily from the rearview. "Where did you get that?"

"You like it?"

"I think you should get rid of it."

The dark cloud ahead of them thickened, rolling above the trees, black and oily. Rakkim could smell it now.

Leo finally noticed what they were heading toward. "What *is* that?"

Rakkim felt his jaws clench. "Addington."

CHAPTER 29

Clyde Winthrop ran a small grocery store and souvenir stand. It didn't take long to find him. The population of Addington, North Carolina, currently stood at twenty-three people, most of them living along a ridge that caught the easterly wind off the mountains, which tended to minimize the smoke from the coal fire outside the town that had been burning continuously, just under the surface, for thirty-one years. Even with the air filter humming, it was still smoky in the store, a dark, irritating haze that made your throat raw. Outside was much worse.

Winthrop, a pudgy black man with short hair and a thin mustache, his eyes rimmed with red, didn't look up from his book as Rakkim walked in. "Howdy."

Rakkim nodded. He could hear the steady thumping of the generator outside.

Leo closed the door after him, coughing, holding a handkerchief over his mouth.

"Got particle masks for twenty-five dollars," said Winthrop, perched behind the register, still reading. "Filters are five dollars each. Last about a half hour." He wrote a note in the margin of the book. "Won't do you much good in the coal fields, but it will make walking around town more tolerable."

Leo stayed bent over, gasping.

"Mr. Winthrop, we're friends of your cousin Bill Tigard," said Rakkim. "I'm afraid I have some bad news for you."

Winthrop put the dog-eared paperback down. *A Short History of Space and Time.*

"Bill and Florence . . . the boys, they're all dead," said Rakkim. "I'm really sorry. Sorrier than I can express."

Winthrop showed no emotion, his face a mask holding itself together by sheer force of will. "Raiders?"

"The Colonel's men burned them out. Murdered them as they tried to escape."

Winthrop cocked his head. "That doesn't sound right. What business did the Colonel have with Bill?"

"They were looking for us," Rakkim said softly. "Me and Leo here."

Winthrop stared at him. "You said you were his friend. Well . . . Bill was always a poor judge of character." He turned away, looked out the soot-grimed windows, and watched the smoke whirl down the street. "I haven't seen or talked to Bill in over ten years. Hardly know what we argued about now . . . except it seemed important at the time." He cleared his throat, spit a black wad into a tissue. "You come all this distance just to tell me the news. That's a long way, even for a guilty man."

"I'm here because I need a favor," said Rakkim.

"Of course you do," said Winthrop.

"I'm looking for the Church of the Mists. I thought you could help me."

"Mister, only reason anybody comes to Addington is to be able to tell their friends that they looked for the Church of the Mists. Everybody searching for that miracle. We get all kinds of college kids and Bible study groups, sometimes soldiers trying to prove to each other how brave they are. Even got a few politicians. Desperate ones, mostly, fearful of the next election and with good cause. They all come to Addington, and they all rent breathing masks and safety gear, go out for twenty minutes or so, and then run back hacking up filth and filled with ghost stories about how close they got. Just another few feet, that's what they say. *I was so close . . . yap yap yap.* Of course, that's the ones that *do* make it back. Plenty of them don't. Least a dozen this year alone. That's why there's a five-hundred-dollar deposit on the gear. Take it from me, mister, hardly *nobody* ever reached the Church of the Mists and lived to tell about it."

"Malcolm Crews did," said Rakkim.

Winthrop looked surprised. Nodded. "He was the only one. Couple years ago, and the fire's gotten even worse since then. Credit where credit is due, though. He did it. Showed me the proof and everything. People look for the church because they think it will change them. Heal them or something. Well, Malcolm Crews found the church, but it didn't do him much good. Turned him clear inside out."

"He's a warlord now up in Tennessee," said Rakkim. "Leader of a bunch called the End-Times Army."

"Yup," said Winthrop. "Crazier than a shithouse rat, just like I said."

"Is the church really surrounded by fire?" said Leo. "A wall of fire, yet it doesn't burn?"

"That's right," said Winthrop. "I attended services there when I was a boy. Nice little church. Nothing fancy, but filled with the Holy Spirit. Addington was a good town, full of God-fearing people making honest wages in the mines. Then the coal fields caught fire and that was that. Tried for years to put it out, but nothing worked. Air just got worse and worse, until everybody up and left."

"Not you, though." Leo still held the handkerchief to his face. "Why did you stay?"

"This is my home," said Winthrop.

"Can't be healthy," said Leo. "Emphysema, lung cancer—"

"I was *born* here," said Winthrop. "That so hard for you to understand?"

"You're sure Malcolm Crews found the church?" said Rakkim. "It wasn't just a tall tale?"

Winthrop's thick fingers clenched the counter. "My daddy helped build that church, mister. I was *baptized* in that church. The front door-knob was special made. Silver, to keep out the devil, and with a raised Jesus on the cross for extra protection. Malcolm Crews stumbled back that day, no safety gear at all, face blistered, tongue swollen so big he could hardly talk, and he had a brand of that crucifix burned into the palm of his right hand from where he threw open the door." He looked at Leo. "The church doesn't burn, it's under God's own protection, but that silver doorknob, it gets hotter than blazes."

"Mr. Winthrop . . . I'd like your help in finding the church," said Rakkim. "You know where the church is. You must know how to get there."

"I know where the church *was*, but everything's different now. You can't just stroll out there. On the best day, with the wind just right, you'll still be blind five minutes in and there's nobody to come get you when you lose your way."

"I'll make it easy for you," said Rakkim. "You want the man who murdered your cousin and his family to die for his crimes, then help me find the church, and I'll do the rest. You want *me* to pay for getting them killed, then send me into the smoke with bad directions. Either way, you win."

"Vengeance is mine, says the Lord," said Winthrop. "According to the Good Book anyway."

"The Good Book also says the Lord works in mysterious ways, so you just sit back and let me do what I intend to, Mr. Winthrop. Think of me as one of those mysterious ways the Lord was talking about."

Winthrop chewed on the idea. "I lied before," he said finally. "Bill was a *good* judge of character. Too good. That . . . that's what we fought over. I was a lesser man in those days. He was right about me then, I imagine he was right about you being worthy of his friendship too. If you're bound and determined to find the church . . . I'll do what I can."

An hour later, Rakkim was lost in clouds of billowing black smoke, his respirator kept clogging, and twice he had broken through a thin crust of soil, flames boiling up around him. The radio connection with Winthrop failed within five minutes, just as Winthrop said it would. Even wearing two-inch asbestos boot protectors, his feet ached from the heat. He kept walking, one hand reaching forward, one hand out to the side—blindman's bluff, seeking the house of the Lord.

The ground was uneven, vegetation blackened, crumbling to dust under his steps. A few gnarled trees remained, leaves gone, but no insects, no birds, no animal life. Just Rakkim, sweating, his clothes soaked. The smoke thinned out slightly along the ground, but the air there was even more toxic, coal gas seeping from the earth. He had no idea how Malcolm Crews had survived, let alone found the church and returned. *Touched by the hand of God or the devil himself*, that's what Winthrop had said. *Maybe that's what it takes.*

Rakkim banged out the filter of the respirator, coughing, eyes and nose burning. He stumbled, fell to one knee and cut himself on something . . . a broken bottle. Orange Nehi. Knee bleeding now, he walked on. Hot wind on his face, flames in the distance, the smoke rippling in the greasy light. The wind howled, shrieking as fire erupted from the earth, a pillar of flame, fire spreading. He stepped back. Stepped around, patting at the eddies of smoke. Taking the long way around.

This way . . . The voice leeched out of the darkness, and he thought of coal gas spurting from fissures in the rock. *This way* . . .

Rakkim stumbled on, head throbbing as he followed the voice. It was coal gas. Or wind caught in the vortex of the flames. Maybe he was light-headed from carbon monoxide or something worse. There was always something worse. He followed the voice anyway. Stumbling, he lurched forward, stepped through a human rib cage. Another step and he crunched through a skull, the bone blackened from the heat, held marginally together by the eroded respirator around its jawbone. Rakkim cried out, disgusted, as the human dust blew around him, and the voice howled in the smoke, laughing now. He hurried on, his breath like fire in his lungs.

This way . . .

He lost track of time and distance. The map that Winthrop had drawn so carefully for him, the map that he had committed to memory . . . it was gone now. What had happened to his sense of direction? The pride of the Fedayeen . . . cover his eyes, his ears, block his nose, suspend him in a warm, saltwater bath so that all sensation is gone. No matter. The Fedayeen will always be able to point to true north. Not today.

A wall of flame rose up before him, higher and higher, twenty . . . thirty feet tall. Sweat poured down his face as he backed away. The flames undulated, stretching out before him, the smoke itself held back by the heat.

This way . . .

That way led to death, he was certain. That way led straight into the flames.

I told you, THIS way . . .

The flames danced in the wind, bobbing along. He felt the rock baking underfoot, thought of the old stories of eggs frying on sidewalks in August, eggs over easy with a side of Rakkim. He staggered back as the flames shot even higher, then flickered, a whole section of the firewall extinguished for a moment before starting to rise again.

Rakkim smiled.

Yes . . .

He backed off from the heat as much as possible, stayed in the smoke . . . waiting. After a few more minutes, the wall of fire shot straight up, even higher than before, then just as abruptly died. Rakkim raced toward the guttering fire, leaped over the rocks and into the smoke as the flames rose higher again. Wisps of smoke clung to him as he stood upright. The fire stirred the smoke as he walked forward. Squinting now. The church . . . he could see the church through the ebbing smoke.

A nice little church, that's what Winthrop said, and considering the decades spent in the middle of a burning coal field, it was still pretty nice. Paint peeling, windows cracked, the steeple singed, but *intact.* Everything else for miles around had burned up, but this little church remained. Rakkim walked closer, felt the heat on his back, but his face seemed cooler. He looked around for some natural explanation, a ridge of wind that kept the flames at bay, a cave bathing the chapel in cool, subterranean air . . . but there was nothing. Just the church.

The wooden steps creaked as he walked toward the door. One of them was broken but he stepped past it. The silver doorknob gleamed in the dim light. Just like Winthrop described it, Christ on the cross embossed on the center. He reached out a hand, felt the heat an inch away. Hesitated. Then grasped the knob, screamed as he opened the door.

He eased inside, groaning, clutching his hand. The door closed quietly behind him, all by itself. No voice in his head now, and though the voice had led him here, he was relieved at the silence. The cool silence. No sound here . . . except the rustle of running water.

Water? He looked around. A small stone fountain lay to the right of the pulpit, water bubbling up and filling the basin, the overflow running down a channel into the floor. He plunged his aching hand into the basin, sighed as the icy water numbed it. He stared at his submerged palm. The crucifix from the doorknob was clearly marked on his skin. No blistering. A clear brand. Definitely a conversation starter when he got back to the republic.

He laughed as he leaned against the basin, exhausted. Finally removed his hand from the water. It still throbbed, but the pain had subsided. He took out the handkerchief that Winthrop had given him, wet it in the basin, and wiped the grit and ash off his face, scrubbed himself clean. Then he splashed cold water on his face, cupped his hands, and drank until he was ready to burst. He rested against the basin for a moment, reveling in the sensation . . . the calm. He was tired. He had barely slept since he and Leo had left Seattle, just snatched a few hours here and there, always skimming the surface of sleep, alert to strange sounds, but here . . .

there was peace in this church. Clean air too; the only whiff of smoke came from his own hair and clothes.

The inside of the church was untouched. The pews in place, the hymnbooks in their holders, the candles ready. Someone had dropped a small paper fan with a picture of Adam and Eve printed on it. Most images he had seen of the first couple showed them shamed by their nakedness, cast out of the Garden by an angry God, but in this depiction they seemed more like young lovers, a girdle of leaves around their nakedness, holding hands—they looked as though they were embarking on some risky but exciting adventure, a honeymoon even. Rakkim wished he could have gone to this church when it was filled with people, would have liked to have heard them lift their voices in song. He walked over to the organ, pressed one of the keys—the sound echoed. The church smelled like sandalwood, still no trace of the acrid smoke that he had been trudging through for hours. He flexed the fingers on his right hand, saw the crucifix move. No pain. A stained-glass image of Jesus beamed down from above the pulpit. Jesus smiling, a lamb beside him. No fire and brimstone for this Jesus. No smiting the wicked. Forgiveness reigned. No wonder they crucified him.

He checked out the back windows, saw another wall of fire. The church truly was surrounded by fire, unburned among the burning. He knelt down in the aisle. Said a prayer of thanksgiving for his arrival at this holy place. Said another prayer asking to be delivered back to Winthrop's store. He offered still another prayer, this one for Sarah and Michael, asked God that they be kept safe until his return to Seattle. Rakkim could take it from there. He almost pressed his forehead against the cool stone floor, but stayed on his knees, eyes closed, as he prayed.

He awoke to the sound of thunder, awoke curled on the floor. Up quickly now. Glanced at his watch. Six o'clock! He had slept for two hours. He looked at his right hand, touched it. No pain. The brand was part of him now. He gingerly reached the doorknob, found it cool to the touch. Which made as little sense as anything else about the church.

He stepped outside as the flame wall started its down cycle, ran straight through the guttering fire and into the smoke beyond. Tripped on some loose rocks, landed hard on his arm, and scooted up. Didn't look back.

The rain started as he walked quickly back the way he thought he had come, the clouds opening up as he ran through the perpetual twilight. Steam rose where the rain landed on the hot rocks, made breathing even harder, but the cool rain soaked his clothes too, and that was a blessing. The storm brought high winds, thinning out the smoke a little, and soon he was seeing familiar landmarks, slabs of rock he had passed on the way in, a discarded camera, a broken water bottle . . . the crushed skull. He hurried on, slipping on the wet ground, splashing through mud, hurrying faster, not sure he would ever find his way out when night fell.

Faster now as the smoke eddied around him. No ghosts, no whispers on the wind. He was sure-footed, effortlessly dodging the flames that still rose all around him. Faster, faster, faster.

He burst out from the smoldering coal fields, rain beating down as he staggered onto the streets of Addington. Through the haze, he saw Winthrop's store in the distance, lights on, the generator thumping away. He ran a hand through his wet hair, wiped at his face, walking slower now. His muddy shoes squished with every step. No one was on the street. The other storefronts were deserted, windows spiderwebbed from the heat.

Leo and Winthrop were drinking coffee when Rakkim walked through the door. Leo knocked over his chair and ran to him, hugged him, crying.

"What's his problem?" Rakkim said to Winthrop as Leo clung to him.

"He's got sense, that's his problem," said Winthrop.

"O ye of little faith," chided Rakkim, squeezing Leo until he yelped.

CHAPTER 30

"I still can't believe I was asleep in there for fourteen hours," said Rakkim, driving with one hand. "I looked at my watch in the church and thought it was six in the *evening*."

"Mr. Winthrop . . . *Clyde* and I stayed up all night waiting for you to come back," said Leo. "Every half hour one of us would walk along the edge of the coal field with a searchlight, calling your name. Clyde gave up on you, said no one could survive that long in the smoke, but I knew if anybody could . . . Well, I figured you might have gotten lucky."

"Thanks, Leo."

"I didn't do anything."

"Yeah, you did."

Leo blushed, the red rising from his neck into his cheeks.

They had left Addington after breakfast, had been driving for almost two hours, right into the Tennessee mountains, the rugged terrain rising steadily as the day wore on, the road hemmed in by pine trees now.

"I read all the briefing notes on the Belt before we left Seattle," said Leo. "Classified and unclassified. Never heard of this Malcolm Crews and the End-Times Army."

"If it's in a briefing paper, it's old news, out-of-date and unreliable. You're going to be fine, just do what we talked about."

Leo shifted in his seat. "Clyde said Malcolm Crews is a total psycho."

"Malcolm Crews believes he's been touched by the hand of God." Rakkim grinned. "I can work with that. I think so, anyway."

"Tell me again about what the church was like." Leo sensed Rakkim's resistance. "Please?"

"It was . . . quiet. No time, no fear. Just an overwhelming sense of peace. Maybe it was because of all the smoke and fire outside, but it was this perfect . . . oasis, this refuge. It smelled good too. I've been in a lot of churches.

Lot of mosques. They're filled with talk of God, but it's just talk. God's nowhere around. This church, though . . . this little church . . . it was like, this is where God goes when he can't bear what's become of the world."

Leo nodded. "What about—"

"I don't want to talk about it anymore."

"Could I see your hand?"

Rakkim showed him. Even with his rapid Fedayeen healing, the burn should have been red and inflamed for a few days. Instead, a raised white scar crossed his palm, the image of the crucifixion clear.

"Did it hurt?"

Rakkim ignored him.

"Before we got to Addington, you said a big lie needed three parts," said Leo. "The Judas coin is one part, and that brand on your palm is the second. So . . . what's the third part you're going to use to convince Crews? I think you started to tell me, but I fell asleep."

"My charm and sparkling personality."

Leo massaged his temples like he had a headache.

Rakkim passed a family van with Georgia plates, the kids in the backseat waving to them until their mother raised the privacy screens. He watched the father pull off onto a side road, the rough-cut cyc in the pyramid spinning slowly from Rakkim's rearview.

"Clyde and I looked over some geologic maps of Addington while we waited for you last night," said Leo. "Addington sits on some interesting terrain. Full of fault lines and pockets of natural gas. Probably never should have mined coal there."

"Little late for that."

The road wound along the foothills. Far below, Rakkim could see a ribbon of blue water rushing over the rocks. In the distance an entire forest had been clear-cut, one whole side of the mountain stripped bare of trees; it was the third one he had seen since leaving Addington. Mountains of stubble now. Shipped to India probably, or South Africa. Mandela City's burgeoning middle class had fallen in love with the dense grain of hickory and ash and hemlock, just as they had fallen in love with lush green lawns and rose gardens; vast tracts of homes now spread across the veldt, each one with hardwood floors and cabinets, their lawns and gardens irrigated from the last of Lake Tanganyika. That great lake might be drying up, but there were still vast swatches of the Belt's natural resources available—Appalachian timber, natural gas from Louisiana and Texas, opals from Arkansas. So much white limestone had been shipped out of southern Georgia that miles of the landscape were uninhabitable, riddled with sinkholes. Dozens of indigenous songbirds were virtually extinct, thanks to a sudden craze for them by the Chinese ten years ago. Everything was for sale.

"I just wish we could get some current satellite imagery for Mr. Winthrop," said Leo, rolling now, anything to get his mind off what was coming. "I sketched out some architectural plans. His computer's circa the early Pleistocene, but I was able to make some rough sketches, trying to use the topography of the surrounding area and a history of prevailing wind currents to redesign the town. Change the whole site. You know, minimize smoke and toxicity. It could be done. Just have to—"

"Why bother? It's not like the Belt is overpopulated. The people who moved out of Addington had the right idea."

"It's their *home*, Rikki. Clyde said the people who left would come back if the air was better, if their kids could play outside. You'd feel the same way if Seattle suddenly became—"

"You're wasting your time . . ." Rakkim's voice trailed off as an empty dump truck roared past them from the opposite direction, bumping along the shoulder, barely staying on the road. He glimpsed the driver's frantic face, saw bullet holes in the windshield. "Leo . . . why don't you slide down in your seat?"

"Why?"

Rakkim pushed him down into the leg space under the dash. He slowed slightly, watching both sides of the road. Something flashed near the top of one of the trees and he braced himself for a bullet to the brain. Nothing happened. He kept driving. The flash was a signal to those who waited ahead. He slipped his knife into the heel of one boot, hid the thousand-dollar gold piece from Stevenson in the heel of the other, the boots deliberately too worn to be worth stealing. The road banked steeply, curving. The perfect spot for an ambush. He slowed, leaned on the horn, the sound echoing off the rocks and trees.

"This is it, huh?" said Leo, voice muffled from his awkward position.

"Let me do the talking. You just speak Jewish."

"*Hebrew*. It's called Hebrew."

Rakkim shrugged. Sounded the horn again.

"What's going *on*?" said Leo.

"I want Crews's men know we're coming. Let them know that we're aware of them waiting for us. That'll make them curious. They'll want to talk before they kill us."

"*Kill* us?" Leo scuttled out from under the dash, banged his head. "I thought they were going to take us prisoner."

"They don't take prisoners." Rakkim slipped the silver shekel into his mouth and placed it behind his teeth on the right side, right up against the inside of his cheek. He could hold a conversation or sing a song and no one could tell it was there. The taste, though . . . two thousand years of sweat and greed filled his mouth. He drove on, horn blaring.

"I should . . . I should have never left Leanne," said Leo. "I should have just stayed with her . . . married her."

"Marry her later." Rakkim saw a car blocking the road as he rounded the corner. One end of the car was stove in, probably from where the dump truck had plowed through. Rakkim waved to the men pointing machine guns at him. "You can tell her all about your dangerous adventures and how you saved the world. Women love that."

Leo's lower lip quivered. "Really?"

"No." Rakkim stopped the car. Rolled down his window.

There was a moment when the two men in front almost opened up with their guns—he saw it in their expression, their posture—then another man, dressed in a black jumpsuit with white bones on it, said something and they half lowered their weapons. The man in the skeleton suit walked toward the car, a pistol at his side.

"Why . . . why is he dressed like that?" whispered Leo.

Rakkim peered at the skeleton man. It was a Halloween outfit. Looked like it anyway. Sarah had shown him pictures from the old days, pictures of people dressed as devils and witches and wild beasts. A holiday or something. Kids and adults both took part. People scared each other and then passed out candy, evidently. Halloween had been banned in the Belt since the war. So what was this guy from the ETA doing dressed like a skeleton?

"Howdy." Skeleton man pressed the barrel of his pistol against Rakkim's forehead. "Any reason I shouldn't kill you?"

"I want to see Malcolm," said Rakkim.

Skeleton man ground the barrel deeper into Rakkim's forehead. "Does Malcolm want to see *you*?"

Rakkim watched the others form a semicircle around the car, a grungy group, half starved, long hair matted. Many of them were bare-chested against the chill, but well armed, torsos draped with belts of ammunition, their automatic weapons clean.

The pistol rapped Rakkim's head. "I can't *hear* you."

"Malcolm's expecting me," said Rakkim. "He just doesn't know it yet."

The pistol eased back slightly as skeleton man considered it.

"You don't want to be wrong, pal." Rakkim spun the eye in the pyramid, the metal flashing in the sun. "I'd hate to be you if you fuck this up."

"Get out."

Rakkim allowed himself to be tripped as he stepped out of the car, his hands jerked behind his back and wired tight. Leo got the same treatment and a few kicks beside. The kid didn't cry out, just muttered something in Jewish or Hebrew or whatever it was.

The two of them were pushed and dragged to a four-by-four panel truck and tossed in the back. They landed on a pile of luggage; leather bags and suitcases, overnight duffels and a red leather makeup kit. The worst was a couple of kids' small suitcases festooned with stickers from Florida Fiesta-Land. Nobody else in the back of the truck, though. No prisoners. Rakkim saw Leo fight back tears at the sight of the happy stickers, saw anger in him too, and was pleased. They were going to need that anger in the coming days.

"You comfy back there?" called skeleton man, turning around in the front seat.

Rakkim and Leo stayed silent and skeleton man turned back. They bounced along in the semidarkness for a long time, at least an hour, while the truck climbed steeply, then careened down a long, twisting slope. Rakkim braced his legs against the side of the truck, but Leo slid back and forth, gashed his face on the edge of a plaid suitcase.

The truck stopped, engine idling roughly before being shut off. The back door swung open and Rakkim blinked in the afternoon light, before the two of them were hauled out and dropped onto the ground.

Skeleton man glared at him. "If Malcolm isn't interested in what you're selling, you're *mine*."

Rakkim got to his feet, looked around. They were on the edge of a large clearing, a stream running down the ridge. Cannibalized cars, new vehicles, and motor homes were scattered across the site, most of them occupied by armed men. Dozens of jungle hammocks hung from the trees, mosquito netting glistening in the damp air. A bullet-riddled school bus lay on its side. He counted nine men wearing skeleton costumes . . . officers maybe, or maybe they had just looted an old store of merchandise and liked what they saw. Guns and ammunition were stacked across the site, small arms, mostly, with a few heavy machine guns. A couple of pickups with antiaircraft rail guns mounted on the back were parked near the edge of the clearing. Men filtered toward them from the woods, their faces hostile and sullen.

Leo had to roll onto his knees to stand up, wobbling.

A tall man strode toward them from the largest motor home, a very tall man, at least six foot six, maybe taller, dressed all in black. Skinny as a blade, thick-bearded, his long hair braided with pink ribbons and yellow marigolds. His eyes boiled with a twisted intelligence . . . the eyes of a starving maniac lost in the mountains after a plane crash and forced to eat the other survivors. And maybe he hadn't been that hungry when he took the first bite. He looked Rakkim over.

"He . . . he said he had valuable information, Malcolm," said skeleton man. "Information you'd want to hear."

"So you brought him here. He and his soft-bellied companion." Crews never took his eyes off Rakkim. "What if he's carrying a bomb? What if he's been sent by the Antichrist to assassinate me?"

"I frisked him myself, Malcolm." Skeleton man sneered at Rakkim. "Besides, seems to me the Antichrist could do better than these two."

"You're an expert on the Antichrist, are you?"

"No . . . no, Malcolm."

A crowd had gathered—hard, disheveled men, faces crusted with dirt.

"What if he swallowed a tracking device?" Crews said lightly. "My enemies might already be on their way, with iniquity in their hearts."

Skeleton man bowed his head. "Forgive . . . forgive me, Malcolm."

"Go and sin no more." Crews drew a pistol and blew skeleton man's brains out. As the sound of the gunshot echoed, skeleton man sat down, then fell backward onto the ground. Crews was fast. Fedayeen fast, maybe.

Leo closed his eyes, trembling.

Rakkim kicked dirt on the body of skeleton man. "Well, one nice thing about hell, there's always a vacancy."

Shouts from the crowd. Demands for Rakkim and Leo to be skinned alive . . . and worse. Crews paid them no mind, his attention on Rakkim. A short man wearing dirty glasses squeezed through, wanded Rakkim with a sensor stick. Then Leo. He looked up at Crews, pushed back his glasses. "They're clean."

"No one's clean," said Crews. "All have fallen short of the glory of God." The breeze made the flowers in his hair flutter. "Any last words?"

"Come closer," said Rakkim. "I've got something for you."

Crews watched him. Wolf eyes under a full moon. All pupil.

Rakkim shifted his tongue, slid the silver coin half out of his mouth.

"Something for the ferryman?" Crews snatched the moist shekel from Rakkim's mouth. His eyes widened slightly as he looked at the coin.

"What is it, Malcolm?" said one of the skeleton men in the crowd. "Malcolm?"

"Untie him," said Crews, still staring at the coin. "Untie the both of them." The short man snipped the wires that bound Rakkim.

Rakkim rubbed his wrists, taking his time. He nodded at Leo, who couldn't seem to stop shaking.

"You surprise me, pilgrim." Crews suddenly embraced Rakkim, kissed him on both cheeks. His breath was foul and the flowers in his hair brushed against Rakkim's neck, their cool, spongy touch like dead fingers. "What's your name?"

"I'm Rikki. This is Leo."

"Walk with me," said Crews. "My flock will take care of Leo."

Rakkim waved to Leo, then followed Crews into the woods, the two of them slipping into the twilight canopy. No one came after them. Crews was either sure of Rakkim or, more likely, sure of himself.

Crews rubbed the coin as they walked. "You always travel with a Jew, Rikki?"

This whole time in the Belt, Crews was the only one who had recognized Leo as Jewish. The South wasn't nearly as anti-Semitic as the Islamic Republic, but there were plenty of good Christians who thought the Jews had got what was coming to them. "I travel with a couple of other Jews too," he said. "Jesus Christ and John the Baptist."

"A good answer." Crews held the coin by the edge. "Did the Jew give you the shekel of Tyre?"

"Now I'm the one surprised," said Rakkim. "I didn't know if you'd recognize it."

"I asked you a question."

"No . . . I didn't get it from Leo. I got it from my grandfather."

Crews smiled. "And you gave it to me. How thoughtful." He led Rakkim deeper into the woods, up a steep, twisting trail, in the increasing darkness. Wind trickled through the trees, cold and damp. Most men would have been exhausted by the climb, but Crews wasn't even breathing hard, seemingly exhilarated by the exertion and their solitude. "So why have you come here, pilgrim?" He flipped the coin, caught it deftly, and held it up for Rakkim to admire. "You and your silver shekel."

"You've heard about the Colonel digging up Thunderhead Mountain?"

"I've gotten reports." Crews scrambled up the slope, all arms and legs, leaping from boulder to boulder. "Verily, it's written that in the last days the wicked will seek to bury themselves in the earth, to hide from the wrath of God."

"The Colonel isn't hiding. He's looking for something."

Crews stopped just below the summit of the path, fixed Rakkim with a red glare in the setting sun. "We're *all* looking for something, pilgrim."

"He's looking for other coins just like the one in your hand." Rakkim climbed up beside Crews. "He's looking for the other twenty-nine pieces of silver."

"Ah, yes, the price for betraying the Prince of Peace, the bounty on God, the blackest of black magic." Crews lightly stroked the raw edge of the coin, watching Rakkim. "Evidently, the Colonel will believe *anything*."

"The Colonel didn't believe me at first either, even after I showed him the coin, but I guess he made some inquiries . . . maybe checked with some people from the old days, folks who might have heard tales of what was buried." He flinched as Crews gripped his shoulder. "The old U.S.A., richest, most powerful nation on earth," he hurried, "and . . . and all that time no one ever asked how it happened, what was the source of that power. My grandpa was part of the unit that moved the coins out from under the Washington Monument during the last days, hid them in the mountain for safekeeping—*Ahhhh!*" He squirmed as Crews dug deeper into his flesh. "My grandpa . . . he was the ranking officer. He stole one of the coins, said if Judas himself couldn't resist temptation, how could he?"

"How could any of us, pilgrim?" Crews relaxed his grip.

"My grandpa said the man on the shekel was a Roman emperor."

"Your grandfather was an ignoramus," said Crews. "That's Melqarth on the coin, the Carthaginian god of the underworld, but I wouldn't expect you to know that." He smoothed Rakkim's hair. "Are you *sure* it's only the rest of Judas's thirty pieces of silver down there? What about a sliver of the true cross?" His eyes caught the last of the sunset. "I heard Ben Franklin himself brought a piece of the cross back from France. A sliver of wood with the power to heal the sick and raise the dead, turn water to wine."

"I don't know anything about—"

Crews gobbed a wad of spit on Rakkim's boot. "Pardon me, pilgrim. Must have been the taste of bullshit in my mouth."

"That's not—"

"I may command a host of inbreds and psychopaths, but I'm an educated man. I was a university professor once, a tenured professor." Crews clutched the coin. "Why would you share such a treasure if it really existed? You *love* me, pilgrim? You have a schoolboy crush on the professor?"

"I'm one man. You've got an army."

"So does the Colonel."

"The Colonel's going to *sell* the treasure," said Rakkim. "You'd use the thirty pieces of silver the way it was meant to be used."

"How do you know what I would do with the silver?"

Rakkim raised his right hand, showed the brand from the Church of the Mists. "Because I'd do the same, exact thing."

Crews looked at his own hand, slowly placed it next to Rakkim's. The brands were identical, the white scars a perfect match. He started to speak, stopped.

"Yeah," said Rakkim. "Ain't that something?"

The wind whipped Crews's hair, scattered yellow flowers.

"I don't know how it was for you, but I must have wandered in the smoke for hours, choking on the stink, about to cough up a lung," said Rakkim, the brand throbbing in the dying light. "I thought for certain I was going to burn up . . . then God led me through the flames to the door."

"The door, yes," Crews said gently. "Were you able to enter, pilgrim?"

Rakkim hesitated, saw something in those wolf eyes. "No . . . no, I wasn't."

Crews relaxed slightly. "Me neither. I beat on that door till my hands were raw, but it wouldn't budge." He showed his sharp, tiny teeth. "Saved by the grace of God, but condemned to forever remain on the doorstep, never allowed inside. That's who we are."

Rakkim nodded.

"Don't despair." Crews fingered the shekel, lost himself in the feel of it. "You can sense the darkness, can't you? Power and dominion over earthly desires . . . the pure *temptation*. Truth be told, I wouldn't have been as interested in a piece of the true cross as I am in this tainted thing. You ask me, Judas got a bad rap." He jabbed the coin at the sky. "There's a battle coming, pilgrim, good and evil, heaven and hell, and no mercy at all, not a bit of it. Perhaps once we drown the unrighteous in a sea of blood . . . perhaps then God will reconsider our exile from Paradise."

"I don't give a shit about Paradise."

Crews laughed.

"The Good Book says God made man in his own image. Look around, Malcolm, and see what we've made of the world. Take a *good* look. What does that tell you about the nature of God?" Rakkim was right in Crews's face, made him take a step back. "I didn't bring you the coin so you could buy your way into heaven. You and I are here to tear down the whole shithouse, set it ablaze, and not look back."

Crews stared at him in the twilight, finally nodded. "Yes . . . I think you and I have a lot to talk about." He started up the path. "Come on, I want to show you something."

Rakkim followed him until they reached the top of the hill. In the distance he saw a small barn made of rough-cut logs and branches. Light leaked through gaps in the walls and roof. A cross was daubed on the door in red paint. The wind was even stronger here, their clothes flapping. He shivered.

"The devil has a thousand names," said Crews, voice rising, "but the name he takes the most pride in is Prince of Lies, because he is such a convincing fraud. Even God himself was fooled by Satan once, so what hope do *we* have to tell what's truth and what's false?" He ran a fingernail down Rakkim's cheek. "Fortunately, God gave us a way to know." He waved toward the ragged church. "Let's go to meeting, pilgrim."

CHAPTER 31

"You look beautiful," said the Colonel, speaking around the lump in his throat.

"Oh, you're just saying that." Baby pirouetted, the wedding dress swirling around her in a corona of white lace. "Doesn't seem right for a girl to only get to wear her wedding dress that one time."

"You . . . you can wear it as often as you like. You look more beautiful now than the day I married you, and I didn't think that was possible."

She spun faster and faster, laughing now, giddy, the dress lifting higher, exposing her long legs, faster, until she lost her balance. She would have fallen if the Colonel hadn't caught her. "My hero." She nuzzled his neck, kissed him, still laughing.

The Colonel kissed her back, gently at first, then deeper as her heat filled him.

Baby fanned herself with her hand. Pulled away from him. "Colonel, suh, you have an erection! What *will* my daddy say?"

The Colonel reached for her, face flushed, but she darted away.

"I bet it's a big ol' purple screamer, isn't it? I heard stories about you."

The Colonel touched a button on the wall, maximized the privacy windows. He could see the last of the sunset, but the sentry posted outside could hear and see nothing inside.

"I know what you're up to, you nasty man." Baby wagged a finger at him. "You're gonna try and put that big ol' thing inside of me."

"Baby, please . . ." Her games made the Colonel uneasy. All the variations, the sheer joy of her play was intoxicating, but he worried that she needed the games to hold her interest. "Baby—"

"Today's my wedding day and I can do anything I want." She lay back on the sofa, lifted her skirt, and the rustle of silk sounded like a roaring fire. "Oh, damnit, I forgot my panties." One hand crept down, lightly stroked her smooth pussy. "What am I ever going to do? Johnny's going to be *so* mad." Her fingers traced their way up her inner thighs. "He thinks . . ." She gasped. "He thinks I'm a little bit of a whore. You don't think . . ." Another gasp. "You don't think I'm a whore, do you, mister?"

"No." The Colonel smiled, started unbuttoning his jacket. "No, ma'am, I don't think you're a whore at all."

She watched him from the sofa, back arched, the wedding dress bunched around her waist. "Johnny, he's a big boy, got muscles on top of his muscles, but I think he's scared . . ." Her fingers flew back and forth. "Scared of my . . . *little . . . pink . . . pussy.*"

The Colonel tossed his jacket onto a chair. "I suspect that Johnny feels like he's the luckiest man in the world."

"I hope so, because I love him . . . love him to death." The moist sound of her fingers filled the quiet room. "That's why . . . why I'm so *worried* about what he'll do . . . when he finds out I'm not wearing panties. He's got a terrible temper."

Thunder rolled off the mountain, shook the house. The Colonel lowered the lights as rain patted the roof, gently at first, then harder. The sentry hunkered down, head lowered. "Rain on your wedding day . . . that's a good sign." He tore open the Velcro snaps of his shirt as he stared at her.

"You have to help me, mister," she cooed.

The Colonel laid his shirt on top of his jacket. "Anything."

"Anything for the bride to be."

"Anything for the bride to be," he repeated.

She beckoned him closer, her finger moving with the lightest touch. "Johnny . . . he's gonna put a whipping on me if he catches me without panties. He's not like you, mister. You like a dirty girl, I can tell, but Johnny, he's just full of rules."

The Colonel knelt in front of her. "Maybe marrying Johnny is a mistake. A . . . dirty girl like you deserves to be with someone who appreciates her."

"I wish I could, I dearly wish I could." She ground her hips. "Johnny, though . . . his family owns everything in our little town. The mill. The grocery store. The bank. If I don't marry Johnny . . . his family's going to foreclose on my daddy's farm. So you can . . . *see* . . . my problem."

The Colonel couldn't see anything else but her. "I . . . I'd be happy to help."

She grabbed his head, slowly moved him closer. "I want you to paint panties on me, mister."

The Colonel looked up at her.

"With your *tongue*, mister. I want you to paint panties on me with your tongue." She pulled his face into her, groaned as his tongue gently probed her softness, teased her. "Anything for the bride to be, that's what you said," she hissed through gritted teeth.

The Colonel pressed her thighs apart, circled her with the very tip of his tongue as she worked against him, and he thought of other intimacies, other women . . . all gone now. Even the memories of them fading like photographs left in the sun. There was only Baby. She twisted against him, tore at his hair, but he held himself back . . . just enough. He always knew when to charge and when to retreat.

She cried out, laughing as her wedding dress floated down over his head.

The Colonel stood up, wiped his mouth. "What time is the wedding?"

"I got to be at Gethsemane Baptist in two hours."

The Colonel unzipped his trousers, let them fall around his ankles. "Plenty of time."

Baby clapped a hand over her mouth, eyes wide. "Well, *look* at you. That's positively fierce, mister." She gnawed on the hem of her dress. "I don't rightly know if I can handle something like that."

The Colonel settled down on her, the wedding dress crinkling around them. He entered her slowly, entered in one long, liquid movement, and she rocked with him, her heat boiling away any doubts. Any thoughts. She held him close as he drove deeper and deeper, whispering in his ear, urging him on, working with him, the two of them panting, fighting for breath as the rain beat on the roof.

It was dark when they awoke, the Colonel's communicator buzzing.

"Don't," said Baby, reaching for him. "Let it be."

The Colonel put the communicator to his ear, listened for a moment, and started getting dressed.

"Zachary?" Her wedding dress rustled against the sheets, the top unbuttoned, her breasts peeking out. "You're no fun," she pouted as he hurried into his pants.

"Moseby called, darling." The Colonel pulled on his shirt, his expression eager as a schoolboy's. "He's found something at the bottom of the tunnel."

Baby examined her nails.

"You want to come look? Moseby sounded—"

"No, thank you, Colonel. I'm just going to lie here and pleasure myself thinking of other men."

The Colonel laughed, grabbed his rain slicker off the peg, and started for the door.

She watched him stride past the sentry, shoulders back, reveling in the storm that raged around him. She sighed in the dim light. Slid her hand down the wedding dress. Rain slanted through the night as she idly stroked her nails across her flat belly.

She was still touching herself when lightning streaked across the sky, flashed on Lester Gravenholtz barreling toward the house in his high boots, soaked, good and angry as usual. The sentry saluted, but Lester ignored him, taking the steps to the front door two at a time.

CHAPTER 32

Malcolm Crews kissed the silver shekel. "I hope you're telling the truth." He pushed open the door to the rickety chapel and ushered Rakkim inside. The men sitting in folding chairs turned around, followed their progress to the front of the room. Most of them wore skeleton costumes. Wind whistled through the dry branches that formed the wall. Howled through the roof woven from twigs. Electric lights propped in the corners cast shadows across the faces. It smelled like an old grave.

"You're not scared, are you?" said Malcolm.

Rakkim looked at the men staring back at him. "Scared of getting fleas."

"You know what you need?" Malcolm picked up a couple of gallon jugs off the floor. He spun the screw top off with a flick of his thumb, the top rolling along the dirt floor. "You need a drink."

"That's okay."

Malcolm nudged him with one of the jugs. "I won't take no for an answer." He waited for Rakkim to take it, handed the other one to a man in the front row. "Bottoms up."

Rakkim sniffed, wrinkled his nose. Tilted back the jug. He spit it out, coughing.

Malcolm took the jug back. Drank deeply, smacking his lips. "Satan can't abide strong drink, 'cause he's afraid he might up and tell the truth."

"It's . . . it's turpentine," said Rakkim.

"Turpentine and rainwater straight from heaven," said Malcolm. "Drink up, pilgrim."

The man in the front row upended the bottle, took a long pull, and passed it.

Rakkim looked into Malcolm's eyes . . . and drank. It flowed down his throat like acid, but still he drank, eyes watering as he fought to keep it down. Wiped his mouth and passed the jug back to Malcolm, who beamed and took another swallow. The jug went back and forth between them, back and forth, the other jug making the rounds of the chapel.

Music started up . . . or maybe it had always been playing. Hard to remember how long he had been standing here among the shadows. Rakkim couldn't tell if the sound came from within the church or outside. It was dark now. Dark out. Dark in. The light from the electric torches guttered as though they were candles. The men stood, swaying as the jug circled the room, around and around. Malcolm and Rakkim had the other jug to themselves, the turpentine burning through them, burning through the lies in search of the truth.

"Feel that?" shouted Malcolm, though they were just inches apart. "That's your sins being eaten away, pilgrim."

Rakkim trembled. It felt like his skin was on fire.

Malcolm preached at the room, arms flailing, talking of the coming battle, the ancient foe, and the cost of redemption. "Matthew ten thirty four: Whoever acknowledges me before men, I will also acknowledge him before my Father in heaven," he shouted, waving the jug overhead. "But whoever disowns me before men, I will *disown* him before my Father in heaven. You get me?"

The crowd amened him, wobbly, bellowing their approval.

Malcolm leaned forward, squinting. "Now don't go supposing I've come to bring peace to the earth, because I come with a *sword*. I'm here to turn a man against his father, a daughter against her mother. A man's enemies will be the members of his own household," he snarled, snapping at the air. "You love your daddy or your mama more than me, you're not worthy of me. You love your son or daughter more than me, you're not worthy of me. Whoever finds his life will lose it, and whoever *loses* his life for my sake will *find* it."

The men cheered, howling with glee, all the dancing skeletons, *bones those bones those dry bones*, and Rakkim felt himself moving too, carried along on a wave of madness, jerking and twisting.

Careful.

Rakkim turned. Circled around at the front of the church, trying to see who was talking. The same voice that had led him through the smoke. Led him through the flames.

"The Good Book and my new best friend says God made man in his own image," said Crews, looking into Rakkim's eyes. "Look around, and see what we've made of the world, my brethren. Take a *good* look. What does that tell you about the nature of God?"

The men howled, baying like beasts, and Rakkim felt sick.

Malcolm lifted the jug to Rakkim's lips. He turned away, but men appeared on either side, skeleton men, holding him up as Malcolm poured the turpentine water into his mouth.

Rakkim choked, sprayed the foul liquid into Malcolm's face.

Malcolm laughed. "Holy water, pilgrim. Much obliged."

Rakkim felt himself tilted back, and the jug banged against his teeth, turpentine pouring down his throat, and he couldn't fight, his legs rubbery. He sat on the ground now, head flopped against his chest as the room whirled around him. Where did all the cobwebs come from? Cobwebs in the corners, hanging from the ceiling. The music was louder. Too loud. He stood up to make it stop, but his legs weren't working so well and the laughter around him was even louder than the music. Rakkim struggled to his feet.

"Let's hear it for pilgrim!" said Malcolm, eyes wild, twitching, and the skeleton men roared their approval. Malcolm hoisted the jug, drank until turpentine dripped off his beard.

Careful.

Rakkim blinked, watched Malcolm's lips, but the warning hadn't come from him.

Two of the skeleton men dragged a covered wicker basket to the front. Electricity crackled from the basket. No . . . no . . . it was buzzing. Hissing.

Malcolm threw back the lid, reached both hands into the basket . . . pulled out a couple of snakes. Long snakes he gripped behind the head. Big, fat rattlers. Tall as he was, the snakes reached almost to the floor. He danced around as the snakes shimmied, mouths wide, showing off their lovely hooked fangs. "Book of Mark, verse sixteen. Book of *Mark.* Verse sixteen."

The skeleton men stamped their feet, cheering.

"Whoever believes," said Malcolm, "whoever *believes* and is baptized will be *saved.*" He shook, rubbed the snakes across his body. "Not just saved *today.* Not just saved *tomorrow.* But for all *eternity*!" He dangled a gray diamondback along his face, the snake lunging at him, a mist of venom blistering Malcolm's lips. "Mark sixteen says *these* signs will accompany those who believe. First off, they will cast out *demons!*"

"Out!" shouted the skeleton men. "Out!"

"They will speak in *tongues!*"

The skeleton men howled at the ceiling, bayed at the moon visible through the slats.

"If they drink any deadly poison, it will not *hurt* them!" said Malcolm as the snakes followed his own undulating movements. "It will *not* hurt them!"

One of the skeletons hoisted the jug of turpentine, finished it off.

Malcolm released the snakes now and they scuttled across the floor. He reached into the basket and pulled out another handful, large ones and small ones, cottonmouths and shiny copperheads. "And those who *believe* . . . they will have the *power* to pick up serpents with their *bare* hands." He seemed to have grown, his head almost touching the roof as he draped the snakes across his shoulders, arms thrown wide as they slithered across him, curled around his neck and down his back . . . and left him untouched.

Rakkim stared at Malcolm as the snakes wriggled past him into the crowd. The taste of turpentine turned his stomach, made his joints ache.

Malcolm reached into the basket, pulled out an enormous timber rattler, six feet long, a beautiful golden brown viper with black bands and huge golden eyes. Malcolm opened his mouth . . . and the snake entered him slowly, poked its head along his tongue and pulled slowly back. Tears ran down Malcolm's cheeks at he turned to Rakkim. He held out the snake.

Rakkim didn't move. The sound of the skeleton men jabbering bounced off the walls, a worse sound than the snakes rattling their warnings.

"The believers shall have the power to pick up serpents . . . and they shall *not* be harmed," said Malcolm, offering the snake to him. "They shall not be harmed, pilgrim."

His hand trembling, Rakkim took the rattler. The snake wrapped around his arm, squeezed gently.

Malcolm swayed, eyes half closed as the music boomed and the rattlesnakes hissed.

The walls moved in time with the music and it looked to Rakkim as if he had been mistaken—the church was not made of sticks and branches, but of snakes, and the serpents were coming alive now, welcoming their brethren. The timber rattler tightened around him and Rakkim looked into its eyes, and they were Malcolm's eyes, pulling him closer . . . closer.

The rattler struck quickly, buried its fangs in Rakkim's upper arm, and he pulled it off him, threw it hard against the floor.

Malcolm nodded.

Dumbass.

Rakkim didn't bother looking. Too busy now tearing at his arm as the fire crawled through him. Too busy . . . too late. He sat down on the floor as Malcolm went back to the basket for more snakes. The more the merrier. The venom turned from fire to ice. His teeth chattered, his fingers already going numb.

You just going to sit there and die? It was one of the skeleton men talking.

"Leave me alone," said Rakkim.

The skeleton man shimmied off his costume. Light filtered through the roof. A slender man with a cocky grin. It was Darwin.

"You're dead," said Rakkim. "I killed you."

I was playing with you and you got lucky. That'll teach me a lesson.

"I had an angel . . . my guardian angel," said Rakkim.

I hate being dead.

The other skeleton men were throwing snakes at each other, talking in tongues, all of it happening in slow motion; Rakkim could actually see the snakes' scales shift in midair. Malcolm glanced over at him but didn't get any closer.

Pay attention. I'm talking at you.

"What do you want?"

I want to be alive.

"I'd just kill you again."

Darwin smiled.

"What's so funny?"

Can't you tell? You would have never said something like that before. Now you're a big, brave killer. Seeing you like this . . . it's almost like being alive.

Rakkim watched the timber rattler that had bit him approach. Then stop, head flicking from side to side. Watched it retreat.

You know what I'm talking about, don't pretend you don't. You should be grateful.

Rakkim waved him away, felt himself drifting. "Go away. I got no time for ghosts."

Ghost? Oh, I'm a lot more than that. Ask Sarah.

"What's that supposed to mean?"

Do I seem different to you? He mimicked Rakkim's voice perfectly. One of the last conversations he and Sarah had had, the two of them in bed, right after making love. *You're more playful lately,* Darwin said, imitating Sarah now. *More fun. Not so serious. I like that.*

Rakkim stared at him.

God, she's a hot bitch. What I wouldn't give to ramrod her all by myself. I'd teach her some tricks. If I had known how tasty she was, I'd have fought my way back sooner.

Rakkim tried to get to his feet. Sat back down.

Don't tire yourself out. Darwin moved closer. *You don't look so good.*

Rakkim thought of Sarah . . . their renewed passion the last few months. "You're not really here."

You know better than that. You've sensed me before now. The thoughts you've had, the things you've done . . . You had to have known. I give you more credit than that.

"You don't give anything. If you're here . . . if you're here it's only because even the worms couldn't stomach you."

Slow your heart down. You need time to metabolize the venom. Slower.

"I don't need your help."

You need something. Pathetic. Darwin shook his head. *I still can't believe you killed me. It's embarrassing.*

It *was* Darwin. No mistaking that assassin smile and those cold eyes. He looked better the last time Rakkim had seen him, mouth wide, Rakkim's blade driven deep into that grin.

What's so funny?

"You." Rakkim kept remembering things. Odd sensations over the last year . . . the unfamiliar memories. They were getting stronger too. "I killed two men in Seattle. Bodyguards for a Black Robe. I . . . I'm not sure how I did it. Was that you?"

Darwin took a bow.

Rakkim tried to move his fingers. A little better now. "Killing the Texas Rangers . . . going out of my way to do it. Was that you too?"

Me? Darwin laughed. It sounded like wasps buzzing. *No, that was all you. Surprised me too. Made me a little proud, I have to admit. All that blood. Kind of intoxicating, isn't it?*

"I'm not like you."

Darwin winked at him. *Don't worry. You're getting there. And those things you told Crews, wanting to burn the whole shithouse down . . . pure poetry.*

"Are you . . . are you in my head all the time?"

Every minute.

Rakkim watched him. "Liar."

Darwin shrugged. *Okay. It takes a lot of work. Not easy being dead. You'll find out.*

"Dead's where you belong." Rakkim tried to stand up. Almost made it this time.

You want some advice?

"No."

Be careful of that redheaded son of a bitch.

Rakkim moved closer. "You know about Gravenholtz?"

I know more about him than you do. General Kidd never told Redbeard, but the Fedayeen lost over twenty men that one summer.

"And then it stopped."

It stopped because I took care of it. About ten years ago, some honcho in the Belt set up a facility turning out Fedayeen killers — hardcore mercenaries with a graphite-composite second skin under their own. Jap jobs, they called 'em, after the gook scientist developed it. Very expensive, but better than body armor. The early models took heavy casualties, but that scientist kept making improvements, changing the recipe. Just a matter of time till he got the batch just right. So Kidd sent me into the Belt. Redbeard didn't know anything about it. Darwin grinned at the memory. *I went through the facility like a fox through a henhouse. Killed twenty-seven in postop. Twice that many still in transition. I'm not even counting the guards. Oh, the fun I had. You're probably the only one who could really appreciate what I did.*

Rakkim rubbed his eyes. Darwin was hazy now. He could almost see through him.

Darwin licked his lips. *You should have seen them, lying in bed, bandaged up from stem to stern, just watching me as I moved in, their eyes getting bigger and bigger. Near the end, I started getting really creative. Professional courtesy. Then I killed the gook scientist and his staff. Destroyed all the records, all the research. Up until I met you, I considered it the highlight of my career.*

"You didn't get Gravenholtz."

Darwin's smile flickered. His lips moved but no sound came out.

Rakkim stood up. "What?"

. . . left something for you to do. Why should I have all the fun? Darwin faded.

Malcolm stepped right through Darwin as though he were made of smoke. "Pilgrim." Sweat poured down his face, streaked through the grime. He grabbed Rakkim's hand, traced the brand in his palm with a fingernail. "Didn't I tell you—those who *believe*, they shall handle snakes with their bare hands and not be hurt? Didn't I say it?"

Rakkim saw men slumped over chairs while others gathered up the last of the snakes. Four of the skeleton men were being carried out.

Malcolm followed Rakkim's gaze. "Not everybody has the faith needed."

"I'm not feeling too good myself."

"Shit, pilgrim, I never heard anybody talk in tongues like that after getting snakebit. You were going a mile a minute, just *flowing*, using these two different voices. Wasn't sure at first if you's possessed by an angel or a devil, but you *survived*, shrugged off that poison like it was a touch of bad pork. You're no Prince of Lies. You're saved to the bone, just like me." Malcolm leaned closer, smiling like Christmas. "Once we get our hands on what's in that mountain, you and me, we're going to bathe the world in blood."

For an instant, Rakkim thought he heard Darwin laughing.

CHAPTER 33

Baby touched the remote and the front door clicked open.

Gravenholtz walked in, stood in the hallway, dripping. "Colonel?"

"In here, Lester."

Gravenholtz shrugged off his wet jacket, shook out his short hair. Same, exact orange-color hair as the kitty cat she had when she was a girl, the one that used to lick milk out of her belly button until her mother caught her.

"Colonel?"

Baby beckoned to him from the bed, lifted one leg slightly, the wedding dress rustling around her bare thigh. "You just missed him, Lester."

Gravenholtz looked around. Checked the sentry through the security window. "Baby, this isn't funny."

"Yes, it is."

Gravenholtz laid an info chip on the coffee table. "Here's my daily report. Give it to the Colonel when he gets back."

"The Colonel's not coming home for a couple hours at least." She stretched, her breasts falling free. "New sentries come on in about ten minutes, so you can slip out the back whenever you want, and they'll have no idea how long you been here."

Gravenholtz couldn't take his eyes off her. Water trickled from his wet hair, hung off his earlobes like pearl earrings.

"Why don't you take off those wet things before you catch your death," she said. "Make yourself comfortable."

Gravenholtz glanced out the window, then back at her. "Baby . . . I can't."

"You say that every time." She slowly, slowly rolled her right nipple between her thumb and forefinger. "But, Lester . . . you always *can*."

• • •

"Sorry to bother you at this time of night, Colonel," said Moseby, "but you told me to call if I found—"

"I'm glad you did, Mr. Moseby. No apology needed." The Colonel waved his aide back to the main tunnel, slipped through the narrow opening into the secondary shaft. Moseby was right behind him. "So, what did you find?"

"I'd rather show you, Colonel."

The Colonel let Moseby take the lead, intrigued by the man's enthusiasm. He shivered in his damp clothes as they walked on, the lights placed at intervals along the tunnels doing little to alleviate the gloom. Couldn't blame Baby for not wanting to leave their bed and tramp around down here. Couldn't blame her for not wanting him to leave either. He smiled at the memory of her in that wedding dress . . . He rubbed the cramp in his hip. She made him feel twenty years younger, thirty years, but that wasn't the same as being twenty years younger. Some nights she damn near wore him out.

"The crews made great progress, as you can see," said Moseby. "You should be proud of them, sir."

"Yes . . . very nice work," said the Colonel, not sure what Moseby was referring to.

Moseby tapped a portion of the wall. "This is where the cave-in was. The men removed all the small rocks and broke down the big ones with picks and chisels. Very delicate work. Didn't want to use explosives or power drills that might collapse the whole structure."

The Colonel glanced up. Shivered as he increased his pace to keep up with Moseby. He didn't like being reminded how deep in the earth they were. How easily the whole mountain could come down on their heads.

They walked on through light and darkness, the electric bulbs spaced too far out for the Colonel's preference. The floor tilted lower, made a sharp turn to the left. The tunnel was wider now, but it didn't help. The Colonel glanced back, kept going, the only sound the echo of their breathing.

"Not much farther, Colonel," said Moseby, his face in shadow.

"No problem." The temperature seemed to be dropping by the moment, and though the Colonel shivered, Moseby seemed comfortable in a light sweater. Another sharp turn and the Colonel stopped. Mouth open.

"I know," said Moseby. "I felt the same way myself when I first saw it."

The colonel looked out on a vast cavern, at the center an underground lake at least a hundred yards across, flat as black glass. Moseby had placed spotlights around the perimeter of the lake, but their beams barely illuminated the inky water. No way to tell how high the cavern was—he couldn't see the top of it, just the rough, rounded outline. "I . . . I had no idea it was going to be this big."

"No way to know how deep it is—not yet, anyway," said Moseby. "I just found it a few hours ago. You're the only other person who's seen it."

The Colonel took a hesitant step forward. "It's . . . it's like a new world, isn't it?"

"You're more of a romantic than I am, Colonel. It's thirty-five degrees, I know that much."

"You have equipment for that?"

"I've got everything I need."

"How soon can you get started?" The Colonel's raised voice echoed back and forth across the cavern, and he shivered again, pushed his hands into his pockets. "You'll need rest, of course," he said, voice lowered, "but obviously, time is—"

"There's something else, Colonel." Moseby reached into his pocket, handed him a small blue enamel pin. "I found this at the waterline, half hidden in the rocks."

The Colonel turned it over. The pin had an eagle etched in gold inscribed on it. He had never seen anything like it.

"I found other things too . . . a valve cut from an inflatable boat, probably sunk after they didn't need it anymore . . . batteries. They were in a real hurry—"

"Who can blame them? What's your point?"

"Sir, you told me I was looking for a box containing historical treasures. The Declaration of Independence, the Constitution, the Emancipation Proclamation. Safely packed away in nitrogen containers, protected by the cold . . . that's what you said."

"That's correct, Mr. Moseby."

"You said they had been taken out of the National Archives during the troubles, taken out months before the atomic attack on D.C. by the federal police, moved here for safekeeping and facsimiles substituted for the originals."

"Mr. Moseby, I don't like your tone."

Moseby turned, and the light glared off his black skin . . . the same color as the lake, his eyes just as cold. "Colonel, with all due respect, I don't like being lied to."

They faced each other in that underground cavern, and the Colonel felt the enormous weight of the earth bearing down upon him, grinding him to dust. He could hardly breathe. Could not even imagine the skill and strength it would take to slip into those icy waters and believe that he would ever come out again. He waited, not trusting himself to be able to lie his way out of it. Angry at himself for feeling the need to. "So . . . so you find a little blue pin and dare to accuse—"

"It's not a pin, sir, it's a badge, and it's not FBI, it's military."

The Colonel tossed the badge or whatever it was back to him. "Obviously, documents of such national importance . . . invaluable pieces of history . . ." One of the searchlights flickered, went out, and he fought to control his panic. "The FBI must have asked for military support—"

"No, sir. That badge is two levels beyond top secret, reserved for a very small, very specific group of professionals. I've never seen one before, but it was described to me once. Grave Diggers, they call themselves. Private joke, because their work involves grave threats to national security." Another spotlight flickered, but stayed on. Moseby closed in on the Colonel. "Grave Diggers do one thing and one thing only—they protect black-ice projects. The good stuff. World busters. The stuff presidents don't trust to other politicians. So, tell me, sir . . ." Their faces were inches apart. "What the *fuck* am I really looking for?"

The Colonel looked out at the lake, waiting for the echo of Moseby's voice to finally fade. "I wish I knew, son," he said softly. "I wish I knew."

Moseby nodded toward the lake. "Are you sure you want me to find what's down there?"

The Colonel felt tired. Beyond exhaustion, or even his age . . . it was an ache, a weariness, a sense of everything he valued slipping away. "Too late now."

"No, it's not, sir. Let's just . . . walk away. Tell the crew it was another false lead. Couple weeks more and you can shut down the whole site and go home. The people love you, sir, not just your men. Your territory . . . it's practically half the state now . . . people know you'll protect them, treat 'em fair and not take advantage. Not many places in the Belt you could say that about. The thing you're looking for in the lake . . . it's going to change *everything*. There's a reason the old regime hid it away down here. A reason they didn't want anybody to find it."

"I know."

"So let's walk off."

The Colonel shook his head. "I have responsibilities. There are certain . . . expectations I'm burdened by." He looked at Moseby. "I'm not the man I used to be, Mr. Moseby, not nearly . . . but I have to pretend. Memory is a ravening beast, sharp of tooth and with a special fondness for the soft spots . . . the tender places." He squared his shoulders. "Tomorrow morning, start searching the lake."

"He's coming!"

"Damn." Gravenholtz pulled out of Baby, yelped as he caught his penis hastily zipping his pants.

Baby laughed. "I was just kidding." Bent over the couch, wedding dress pushed up around her shoulders, she wiggled her bare ass at him. "Come on, cowboy."

Gravenholtz cursed her.

Baby squeezed the back of the couch, bucking back and forth, whinnying softly. She turned her head, slowly rotated her hips against the cushions, showed off her sweet pinkness. She watched as he carefully lowered his zipper, wincing as his foreskin came free. She turned back to the window, gasped as he drove into her. No subtlety from Lester. No finesse. No foreplay.

Gravenholtz grunted behind her, fists grabbing at the wedding dress, crinkling the stiff fabric as he unleashed a string of obscenities.

Baby worked with him, enjoying his passion, directing him to all the best spots. She watched her reflection in the window, excited by her flaring nostrils as he lifted her off the couch with his thrusts. She moved her head back and forth, sent her hair swaying against her shoulders, a light tickle as Lester groaned and snapped at the air.

"You fucking whore," spat Gravenholtz, "fucking . . . fucking whore."

Baby pressed her ass back against him, felt him shudder.

"Fucking . . . *fucking* whore."

Always the same thing with Lester. Men were so predictable. She felt him increase his pace, taking short little breaths. She examined her face in the window, bit her lower lip, opening even deeper for him. Always from behind, that was the best way for Lester. She had caught a glimpse of his penis that first time . . . and that was enough. Ugly, ugly thing, freckled and bent, a blue-veined monstrosity. She half closed her eyes with pleasure, giving in, imagining herself with other men . . . the young sentry outside. He stood there with his back to the glass, rain sluicing off him like a beast in the field. She pressed down on the base of Lester's penis as he lunged into her, held him for a moment, tighter . . . tighter . . . tighter still.

"*Fuck* . . ." Lester burst inside her, a scalding eruption of anger and loneliness. He sobbed for an instant, slid out, and lay on the floor, gasping like a dying fish.

Baby blew a kiss to her reflection, turned around. She picked up his shirt from the couch, wiped herself with it, and threw it on his face. "You didn't ask me if you could shoot that nasty stuff inside me."

Gravenholtz raised himself up on one elbow, still panting, his face like a red balloon.

"Next time you ask *permission*, Lester Gravenholtz."

He stood up, still wobbly. "Someday . . . I'm going to kill you."

Baby shook her head. "Not unless I say so."

Gravenholtz pulled on his pants.

"The Colonel's gone into the mountain." Baby crossed her legs, admired her tiny toes. "Moseby called and said he found something and the Colonel hurried right over."

He shrugged on his shirt, stuffed it into his pants.

"Moseby brings that old-days weapon out from the lake, you best be ready to make yourself useful." Baby tucked her legs under her, watched him finish getting dressed. "You're going to have to move *fast* when the time comes."

"I don't know," he said. "I been thinking . . ."

"That's *my* job." Baby could see the anger bubble to the surface of his face like swamp gas. She should slow it down, take it careful-like, but Baby had given up on slow and careful a long time ago. She had Lester on a choke chain—give him any slack and he might bite a piece out of her, just 'cause he could. "You leave the thinking to me, Lester. You try it, you might pull a muscle."

Gravenholtz balled those big old hands of his into fists.

Baby reached for him, kissed those fists, kissed each and every knuckle while he breathed hot and heavy.

Gravenholtz had to step away from her to find his tongue. "New . . . new weapon or not, I'm not cut out to be what you want me to be."

"Sure you are."

"It's the *Colonel's* command," Gravenholtz snapped. "The men are shit-scared of me, that's not the problem—they seen me break enough heads to jump when I say so, but as soon as my back is turned . . ." He shook his head. "No, they'll charge into hell itself if the Colonel gives the word, but not for me. Me, I'm born to be the hard case, the second in command that gets things done and don't take excuses."

She saw the shiny red hairs sticking out from his shirt collar, and the sight disgusted her. "That *really* all you aspire to, Lester Gravenholtz?"

"Ain't such a bad thing. Colonel could take over the whole damn country with this weapon, and I'd be right there by his side. So would you. We could still—"

Baby sighed. She smoothed her wedding dress down, arranged and rearranged it until it was perfect. She looked up at him, shook her head. "Oh, *Lester* . . . aren't you tired of sloppy seconds?"

CHAPTER 34

"Let's just get *out* of here," said Leo as Rakkim checked out their car.

Rakkim looked up, saw Malcolm Crews walking toward them, a few skeleton men trailing behind. It was late morning, the camp slow to get started after last night.

"Rikki?"

"Not yet," said Rakkim, going back to work. "Can't be in a hurry or you'll ruin everything."

"You don't know what it was like after you tramped off with Malcolm," said Leo, not making eye contact. "I got dragged along while they drove trails, howling and shooting guns . . . jacked up on methamphetamine, smoking whole chunks of it." He scratched his arms. "Just being around them made my skin itch."

Rakkim scratched the inflamed punctures on his arm where the rattler had bitten him. "I wasn't having a picnic myself."

"They . . . they took me to a . . . a body dump," whispered Leo. "*Sinville,* that's what they called it, like it's some big joke. This old satellite relay station in the middle of the woods. Ground antennae was a steel dish fifty yards across and it's filled, Rikki, it's piled high with bodies, hundreds of them, tourists and townspeople, they don't care. They've been adding to it for the last year. I didn't even know what it was at first, because we were downwind and it was so dark, and then . . . one of the jokers . . ."

"It's okay," said Rakkim. "We're leaving soon."

". . . one of the jokers tossed in a white phosphorus grenade, made this big flash, and, Rikki, there were so many crows, I've never seen so many birds in my life, and the sound they made when they flew up . . . it was like the earth screaming."

"Did I hear someone say my name?" said Crews, all in black, fresh flowers in his hair.

Rakkim finished with the car. "Leo didn't appreciate the trip to the body dump."

"Softhearted, is he?" said Crews. "Don't worry, he'll get over it. Come the Judgment, the whole earth is going to be a body dump." He peered at Rakkim. "How are *you* feeling this morning, pilgrim? Seem a little peaked."

"Took a piss this morning and it felt like hot lava splashing into the weeds," said Rakkim.

Crews cackled. "Turpentine *burns*, that's the value of it."

Leo got into the car, but Rakkim lingered. The skeleton men hovered nearby, blinking in the sun. Automatic rifles slung over their shoulders, they stood there listening, clothes caked with mud.

"You trust the Jew?" said Crews, nodding at Leo.

"Enough for now," said Rakkim. "The Colonel wanted a Jew to be there when he found the rest of the silver pieces. He thought there might be some writing along with it, old scrolls or something that might need translating."

"Folks like you and me don't need anything translated, we see things clear. We got the mark, that's all we need to know." Crews waved a well-thumbed Bible, the gilt lettering worn away on its black leather cover. "This belonged to a preacherman I met after my anointing. I was still in shock, trying to understand what had happened, what it meant. You have to remember, I was untutored in the ways of the Lord then. I thought the Church of the Mists contained a treasure, that's why I braved the fires. It *did* contain a treasure, one more precious than silver or gold, didn't it, pilgrim?" He tapped the Bible. "Preacherman tried to tell me that the reason the door wouldn't open was because I wasn't worthy to enter. Said Satan had led me to the door, but God wasn't fooled." He laughed. "That's why I knew you were true. You couldn't get inside either. It was like God telling us, 'I got other plans for you boys.'"

"I can hardly fucking wait," said Rakkim.

Crews whooped it up. "*That's* the spirit. I've been hoping for somebody like you to turn up. There's only so much I can do with these mush-heads."

Rakkim glanced at the skeleton men. "The Colonel has only a fraction of his forces at the site, but they're well equipped. I'll get word to you in a couple days. Let you know if the Colonel has found the silver yet, and where the best point of attack is."

"There's an abandoned Stuckey's on Highway Ninety-nine, not more than a half hour's drive from the mountain. You show up anytime, day or night, I'll know." Crews grabbed Rakkim's arm, turned his palm up. "You ever wonder why you were chosen to walk through the fire and make it back alive?"

Rakkim shook him off.

"You ever ask yourself, Why *me*, Lord?"

Rakkim didn't answer. It didn't matter to Crews.

"It's because we're *special*. We have brains and ambition. Not like the rest of this trash." Crews crowded in on him again. "God needs someone to do the dirty work. He's sick to death of humanity, but he doesn't have the stomach to do what needs to be done. Last time he got fed up, he drowned the whole world. Maybe he can't bear to do it again. That's where *we* come in. God brought you and I together at just the right moment. Think about it, pilgrim. I got hundreds of righteous maniacs with too much time on their hands, and suddenly you show up with a piece of silver Judas himself once grabbed on to. Hell's bells, for all I know maybe there *is* a splinter of the true cross buried under that mountain along with the silver."

"All I know is if God's sick to death of us, who could blame him?"

Tariq al-Faisal tripped on the hem of his brown burka as he walked inside. If he hadn't grabbed the edge of the table, he would have fallen on his face.

Yusef closed the door, dismissed his wife, who had accompanied al-Faisal to their home. "Are you all right, imam?" Credit the man with the good sense to keep his smile hidden.

Al-Faisal threw back the face sack of the burka, sweating. "Someday I'll have one of my wives tell me how she walks in these things."

Yusef pressed his hands in supplication toward a tall, muscular Somali. "This is—"

"I am acquainted with our brother Amir the Fedayeen," said al-Faisal, kissing the man on both cheeks, sensing his resistance. "*Salaam alaikum.*"

"*Alaikum salaam.*" The raised scar on Amir's face was stark against his smooth skin.

"My bodyguard, Sulayman," said Yusef, indicating a huge, bare-chested

Arab with a bristly beard and silver hoops through his earlobes. A scimitar hung from his waistband, doubtless at Yusef's insistence. Yusef was the worst kind of fundamentalist, aping tradition without truly internalizing it . . . and thereby *needing* the trappings of faith. Unlike al-Faisal, who was as comfortable hoisting a stein of bootleg beer as throttling an adulterer, both actions equally in the service of Allah.

Al-Faisal and the bodyguard exchanged greetings.

"And *this* is our brother Bartholomew," Yusef said, beckoning toward the moderate who stood nearby, a rigid young man with a precisely cropped beard, and black shoes shined bright as mirrors.

"*Salaam alaikum,*" Bartholomew hurriedly murmured, head bowed.

"*Alaikum salaam,*" said al-Faisal. "Thanks to you and Amir for coming. Our master rejoices at your faithfulness."

"I am honored," said Bartholomew.

Amir stayed silent.

"Imam, if I may," said Bartholomew. "Is your false attire necessary? I was told the authorities had determined you were dead."

"Are you frightened to be in the presence of a corpse?" al-Faisal said lightly.

"No . . . *no*, imam," said Bartholomew.

"Good." Al-Faisal pulled off the burka, threw it on the floor. He wore the clothes of a modern underneath, with red trousers and a tight white shirt marked with silvery piping, accentuating his lean frame. "Yes, State Security has concluded that I died a martyr's death when I detonated a car bomb, but there is a policeman . . ." He sat down amid the cushions on the floor, waved Bartholomew and Amir to do the same. He waited while Yusef poured them tea. ". . . a fat Catholic who is still making inquiries, poking his snout where it doesn't belong."

"What is this Catholic's name?" Amir said softly.

"I'm grateful for your interest," said al-Faisal, "but I shall talk of this policeman in my own good time, *inshallah*. Besides, Amir, our master values you too highly to see you troubled by such small matters."

If Amir was flattered, it didn't show in his face or eyes.

"May I ask . . . ?" Bartholomew sipped his tea. "You have the device, imam?"

Al-Faisal smiled. The young brother was eager, but his hand was steady, not the slightest rattle of the teacup. All their lives depended on such steadiness. He reached into his jacket, handed Bartholomew the device.

Bartholomew handled the device cautiously, turning it over and over. Metallic, dappled with electronic readouts. No bigger than a child's fist, yet big enough to change the world. "It looks exactly like a standard systems analyzer."

"Performs exactly like one too," said al-Faisal. "You could take it apart, field-test all the components, and you still wouldn't see anything amiss."

"Eagleton made this?" said Bartholomew, still examining it.

"An atheist, and a pervert, but talented." Al-Faisal picked up a sweet from the tray Yusef had put out, popped it in his mouth. "Pity I couldn't allow him to live." He wiped powdered sugar off his lip with a forefinger, sucked it clean. "Still, if you're successful, Allah willing, then we won't have need for such men in the future." He reached for another sweet. "Sulayman? How long have you been in Yusef's employ?"

"Eleven years, lord," said Sulayman. "As soon as I completed my enlistment."

"You were Special Forces, yes?" Al-Faisal nibbled a candied date. "A noble calling, but compared to Fedayeen . . ."

Sulayman glanced at Amir, then back at al-Faisal.

"You *did* apply for Fedayeen?" said al-Faisal.

"Yes," said Sulayman, teeth gritted.

Al-Faisal stood up gracefully, so quick that he was beside Sulayman before the man could react. He traced a fingertip across the bodyguard's bulging biceps. "A bull of a man like you . . . your failure couldn't have been from lack of strength."

"Brother?" Yusef said to al-Faisal. "Surely—"

Al-Faisal pulled down Sulayman's right eyelid. "You're clear-eyed, so you must be intelligent . . ."

Sulayman placed his hand on the hilt of his scimitar.

Al-Faisal patted Sulayman's hand. "Indulge my curiosity a moment longer, great warrior."

Sulayman's eyes blazed.

Al-Faisal stepped back. "How you must have resented those who succeeded where you had failed . . . men like Amir." He peered at Sulayman. "I'm trying to understand why you would have betrayed us."

"I . . . I have *not*," started Sulayman.

Amir was already on his feet.

As Sulayman drew his blade, al-Faisal plucked the silvery piping from his shirt and whipped it around Sulayman's neck. He grabbed both ends . . . jerked . . . and Sulayman's head rolled off his shoulders in a fountain of blood.

Yusef cried out, covered his mouth.

Amir stood beside al-Faisal, his Fedayeen knife in his hand.

"I didn't know," blubbered Yusef. "I had no idea . . ."

"It is done." Al-Faisal tossed the silvery strand of razor wire aside. His white shirt was splattered with red. He turned at the sound of Bartholomew vomiting. "Bring the young brother something to settle his stomach, Yusef, and fetch me a clean shirt."

Amir stared at Sulayman's body. "Who was he working for?"

"Your father." Al-Faisal enjoyed the look on Amir's face. "Not directly, of course, but Sulayman has appraised him of your . . . more questionable activities in the past. I'm sure our new association would be of great interest to the general." It was a lie, of course. Sulayman was as innocent as any man could be. No matter. His death had served its purpose. He nudged Sulayman's head, rolled it facedown so that it lay in a black nest of his beard. "Don't worry. We are brothers now. Your enemies are my enemies."

"Two thousand, three hundred and fifty-seven, with a five percent margin of error," Leo said softly.

Rakkim stood with one foot on the wooden railing, looking off at the gleaming skyscrapers of the small metropolis in the distance. Columbia City. College town, one of the small tech centers in the Belt, exporting gadgets and expertise around the globe. The last time he had been there, he had been amazed at how clean it was, how well dressed and happy the people seemed. Churches on every block, but folks didn't beat you over the head with it. The town should have been a target for every bandit and warlord within a hundred miles, but Columbia had a first-class militia. Every citizen — man, woman, and child — had formal military training and kept up their skills. Best equipment too, and willing to use it. *Eager* to use it. The Colonel had put Columbia under his nominal protection, but they paid him no tribute, which spoke well of them. And the Colonel.

The melting root-beer Popsicle ran down across Rakkim's hand. He licked the sweetness from his fingers. They had stopped for gas about an hour after leaving Crews, bought clean clothes and threw away the others. After all the time spent shampooing their hair in the bathroom sink, scrubbing their hands and faces, scraping the grit from under their nails . . . the stink still clung to them.

He watched the town again, trying to keep his mind occupied. He used to like to quiet his thoughts, stop the words, the anticipation. *The time of no thinking*, that's what the Fedayeen called it. One of the secrets to going days without sleep. Weeks, even. Now, though, Rakkim kept his mind active. Vigilant. Not out of concern of what might happen to him and Leo, some external threat. No, he was afraid that if he quieted his thoughts, he'd hear Darwin scuttling around in there.

"Two thousand, three hundred and fifty-seven, five percent margin of error," Leo repeated.

Rakkim glanced over at him, sucked the last of the Popsicle into his mouth. Made his teeth ache but it tasted good. Leo's own Popsicle had fallen off the stick, untouched.

"I thought . . . I thought calculating the dead would help," said Leo, "but . . . it didn't help."

"I'm sorry, Leo. I didn't know what they were going to do with you."

"The satellite antenna was fifty yards across with a five percent slope to a depth of fifteen feet." Leo's voice sounded distant. "The bodies . . . the bodies were stacked about a foot above ground level. Assuming an average height of five feet ten inches, and an average of three months decomposition—"

"You said it was dark. You said you didn't even know what you were looking at until the white phosphorus grenade went off."

"The grenade lit things up."

"Just for an instant. You couldn't have come up with those calculations."

"That's all I needed. I remember things. Shapes and angles, extrapolations and measurements . . . Archimedes said if he had a lever long enough he could move the earth. Well, I can calculate the exact length of the lever required, and the size and weight of the fulcrum too, and—"

"Who's Archimedes?"

Leo's head slumped forward. "I'm just saying, I wish I could forget the things I saw last night."

"You will. Give it time."

"No, Rikki . . ." Leo's tears fell onto the ground, beside the melted Popsicle. "That's not the way my mind works."

Rakkim put his arm around the kid.

"I . . . I don't want to tell Leanne about this," sobbed Leo. "My father says . . . he says when you love somebody, *really* love them, you can't have secrets, but—"

"That's bum advice. Spider's plenty smart, but he's wrong about that."

"You don't tell Sarah everything?"

Rikki laughed.

They stood there for a long time, Rakkim patting his back, listening to him blubber. Softhearted, that's what Crews had called him. Rakkim liked the kid even more for it.

Leo wiped his nose. "Why . . . why did Crews think you didn't go inside the church?"

"Because that's what I told him."

"Oh. *Oh.*"

"Man like Crews, you can't let him think you're one up on him." Rakkim finished the Popsicle, tossed the stick away. Columbia City gleamed in the distance. "If it makes you feel any better, I'm going to make sure Crews and his men don't make any more additions to the body dump. Say what you want about the Colonel, he's a solid military tactician. If his mountain camp has got any points of vulnerability, it won't matter. I'm going to have Crews and his men charge straight into the killing zone. Let the Colonel wipe them out. I just need Crews to create enough of a diversion so that you and I can take possession of the weapon. Assuming that Moseby has found it by now."

"Sarah said . . ." Leo sniffed. "She said Moseby was very good at his work."

"He's a shadow warrior, what do you expect?"

Leo saw him grinning. "I didn't like you at first, but now . . . now I think maybe I was wrong."

"Don't get carried away. First impressions are usually pretty reliable."

"Not always. I hated the Belt in the beginning," said Leo. "Hated the danger and the violence and the ugly accents. Hated the heat and the bugs and the ignorance . . . then I met Leanne. None of that other stuff matters now."

"You can tell Moseby all about your honorable intentions when this is over." Rakkim watched the sun glinting on the solar panels along the Columbia City waterfront. He wished there was time to take Leo there, give him a sense of the best of the Belt. There wasn't time, though. "Right now, we should get moving."

"What if Moseby doesn't want to help us?"

"Moseby's not working for the Colonel *willingly*. Gravenholtz took him at gunpoint, left a group of armed men holding his family hostage. You think he's going to want to put some new, powerful weapon in the hands of people like that?"

"Not that I blame him, but Moseby went *renegade*. He betrayed his oath and his country. He doesn't owe the republic anything."

"John didn't stay behind in the Belt because he turned against the republic. If he had, I would have killed him when I was supposed to. Moseby was no traitor—he just found someone he loved more than his country."

Leo nodded. "I can understand that."

Rakkim looked over at him. The kid was growing up.

"The church . . ." said Leo. "You said it was real quiet inside. Peaceful."

"That's right." Rakkim smiled. "I couldn't wait to leave."

CHAPTER 35

It was almost 3 a.m. when Rakkim stumbled into the mess tent, head down, the collar of his army jacket turned up against the cold, his assault rifle slung over one shoulder. He stamped his feet, used the movement to case the place. Five soldiers sat on benches facing the electric fireplace. A potbellied cook with a dirty apron leaned against the counter reading a magazine, HITCHENS stitched on the breast of his uniform. Ashes drifted down from the cigarette in the corner of his mouth.

"I need a couple pots of coffee and some cups for the Colonel's guards," said Rakkim.

The cook looked up from a well-thumbed *Political Insider Quarterly.* "What am I, the fucking welcome wagon?"

Rakkim shrugged. "I'm just following orders, chef."

The cook raised an eyebrow. Pleased. Probably the first time he had ever been acknowledged by that term. He picked up a dented coffeepot from the back burner. Hefted it and handed it over. "This should be plenty for those assholes. Grab some cups off the rack."

"Thanks." Rakkim hooked a couple of cups with his thumb. Started to leave.

"I'm serving French toast at oh-six hundred," the cook called after him. "I'll save you a double order for five minutes, then it's up for grabs."

Rakkim took a right outside the tent, walked over the rocky ground. Good light discipline from the troops; only starlight illuminated the landscape. Plenty for Rakkim to make his way.

It had been almost two days since Rakkim had left Malcolm Crews, and the memory was still raw. He and Leo had reconned the area, hanging out in cafes and main-street shops, picking up news and rumors, trying to decode which was which. Most folks in the area thought the Colonel was opening up the coal mines again, others thought there had been a secret strike of gold or silver or diamonds, whatever their imaginations could come up with. Everyone was happy for the military presence nearby. The Colonel paid his bills immediately and in full, his men obeyed the laws and respected the women. No complaints, other than the occasional traffic jam when the rock- and earth-moving equipment inched along the local roads.

Rakkim had left Leo back at a small motel in the busiest part of the nearest town, made him promise not to call Leanne, no matter how safe it seemed. Maybe the kid would keep his word. Rakkim had other worries at the moment.

The Colonel's base camp was two thousand feet up the mountain, a few hundred tents and outbuildings spread out along a rocky plateau, the camp reachable by at least a dozen trails and a two-lane blacktop from the small town below. At the edge of the trailhead, jeeps, trucks, and mining equipment were parked beside a skein of logging roads that led higher up the mountain. As Rakkim had figured, the major access points were well protected, armored personnel carriers and machine gun emplacements ready for any attack from the north, south, or east. The westerly approach to the camp was straight up a sheer wall.

Up ahead, Rakkim watched three irregulars standing around a heater, passing a bottle. He walked toward them carrying the cups and coffeepot, with the tired, steady cadence of soldiers everywhere, neither hurrying nor lollygagging. "Hey."

"Hey, yourself," said one of the irregulars, hiding the bottle under his coat.

"I'm all turned around," said Rakkim. "Which way is the Colonel's bivouac? I just got in from Murfreesboro and they sent me to fetch and carry and I can't hardly see shit."

One of the irregulars pointed. "Keep going past the outhouses, then make a left and go . . . maybe another hundred yards." He spit tobacco juice. "It's a nice clapboard house. Used to be a park ranger station."

"Obliged." Rakkim kept walking.

Good directions, he thought fifteen minutes later when the house came into view. He circled the Colonel's place at a distance. Two sentries, one in front, one in back. Wide awake, from the way they carried themselves. Cold too, the icy wind howling off the mountain. He made plenty of noise as he approached, pretending to stumble, cursing, banging the heavy ceramic cups against each other.

"Who goes there?"

Rakkim stared at the barrel of the shotgun pointed at his chest. "I love you too." He hoisted the coffeepot. "Hitchens sent this over. One of you two must have blown him or something, because I never seen that sumbitch do a favor for anybody."

"Amen to that." The sentry lowered the shotgun. "Had to been Meeks, 'cause I don't get along with Hitchens a-tall." He took a cup, waited while Rakkim filled it. Blew across the top before he drank. "Thanks."

"I'll hit Meeks with a cup, then come by again in a couple hours."

The sentry toasted him, then pulled his neck deeper into his coat.

Rakkim walked slowly around to the back of the one-story house, noting the windows, the side door. The cellar door wasn't visible from either sentry position, but the back side would be particularly blind because the rear sentry had his back turned to the wind. He clattered along toward the rear.

"Halt!"

"Jesus H., Meeks," said Rakkim. "You want coffee or not?"

The sentry smiled in the starlight, a faint Cheshire grin.

Rakkim handed him the cup, filled it.

"Is it Christmas already?" said Meeks.

"I figure either Hitchens seen the light or maybe the Colonel told him to get off his fat ass and do something for real soldiers."

Meeks took a swallow of coffee. Winced. "Tastes like he put pennies in the pot."

"What did you expect? Only thing worse than Hitchens's cooking is his coffee."

"Ain't seen you around before," said Meeks.

"Let me top that off for you," said Rakkim, filling his mug. "Stay warm." He walked toward the side of the house.

The Colonel struggled to wake from one of his recurring dreams—he was fourteen or fifteen, wearing shorts and a flag T-shirt, standing on the sidewalk sweating as he watched the Fourth of July parade make its way down

Main Street. Floats from the car dealerships draped with bunting moved slowly past. Slim Johnson, who owned both dealerships, and cheated everyone equally, tossed plastic-wrapped peppermint candies to the kids in the crowd. Probably left over from Halloween. The high school drill team followed, pretty girls in short skirts and white boots with tassels, high-stepping to the *rat-a-tat-tat* of the drumline. The crowd stirred and the Colonel tossed in his bed, caught in the cobwebs of time. The dream went silent, no birds, no drums, no sound at all as the main float inched forward. The Colonel's hand flew over his heart. Veterans of the Gulf War II stood at attention on a flatbed truck, waving listlessly to the crowd . . . no, the crowd was gone. The crowd was always gone. It was just the Colonel standing on the sidewalk and the vets melting in the heat. The Colonel awoke with tears streaming down his grizzled cheeks. He was not alone.

"It's all right," said the man standing beside the bed, his face lost in the dimness.

The Colonel turned his head. Baby slept beside him, her night breath sweet as fresh hay.

"Hate to interrupt your beauty sleep, Colonel," the man said softly, "but I thought it best this way."

The Colonel nodded. Mississippi, that was the accent. Gulf Coast. He wondered if it was one of Moseby's crew come to take him home. Moseby seemed the kind of man to inspire that kind of loyalty, and this fellow, he was a cool, hard customer, just the type to dive for baubles in New Orleans. "You mind if I sit up?" he asked, one hand snaking under the pillow for the pistol he kept there. Dark as dust in the bedroom, but the man saw what he was up to.

"No need for that, Colonel. I don't mean you any harm."

"Of course you don't." The Colonel kept his hands in sight. Just as well. His shoulder was stiff for the first hours after getting up. Dying was bad enough—getting Baby hurt because he wanted to play the hero was worse. "How much did you pay my guards? I'm just curious what my life is worth."

"Your guards are tried and true, Colonel, and only God knows what your life is worth."

"I see. My guards are steadfast but incompetent."

The man had a nice laugh. Sincere. Confident. "That's one possibility, sir."

Baby rolled over in her sleep, one bare leg sliding out from the covers.

"Why don't we go in the other room and you can finish things," said the Colonel.

"If I wanted things finished, you'd already be dead," said the man. "Let's stay right here for now." He pulled over a straight-backed chair. "May I?" He sat down.

The man wore the uniform of one of his irregulars and smelled of campfires and tobacco. He sat beside the bed, seemed utterly at ease, as though he were going to tell the Colonel a bedtime story. Who *was* he?

"I apologize for giving you a start, Colonel, but I wasn't sure if the Chinese fellah was still in camp. I've got a business proposition and I wanted to keep things private."

The Colonel didn't respond, stunned at the mention of the Chinese liaison. This man's information wasn't perfect—Ambassador Fong had never been at the camp, had contacted him through the church in Jackson where the Colonel was a deacon—but the mere fact that he knew of a Chinese connection was unnerving. Had to be that damn chopper. Monsoon 4, state of the art, but a giveaway to someone who recognized it hurtling overhead. Word must have leaked out. The Colonel had almost refused when Fong offered the Monsoon as a sign of good faith, not wanting to obligate himself to the Chinese. *Almost.* He gave himself a dozen reasons not to, then he had accepted the chopper, thanked that little Chinaman, and toasted him with sour mash. The Monsoon 4 was some sweet ride, but it wasn't a world changer. No, the world changer was at the bottom of the underground lake, waiting for Moseby to find it.

"Zachary?" Baby yawned, stretched, one strap of her pink slip sliding down her arm. "What's going on?"

The man bowed slightly. "Sorry to disturb you, ma'am, but me and the Colonel have some talking to do. Hope you don't mind."

The Colonel patted Baby, as always, aroused by the warmth and electricity of her firm flesh. "It's okay, darling. Go back to sleep."

"You want me to make you boys some coffee?" said Baby.

"That's all right," said the Colonel.

"Actually, ma'am, if it's not too much trouble . . ."

"No trouble at all," cooed Baby, sliding out of bed.

The man averted his eyes as Baby put on the silk robe the Colonel had given her for their first anniversary. A gentleman. He held out his hand. "Rikki."

The Colonel shook hands. "Zachary Smitts." He nodded toward his uniform hanging in the corner. "You mind if I get dressed . . . Rikki?"

"It's your house, sir."

The Colonel dressed quickly. He could easily throw something through a window, send the guards running to help, but the evident ease with which this Rikki had strolled into his bedroom unnerved him. No matter what the Colonel had said, he knew his guards were not incompetent. He heard Baby bustling around in the other room, the coffeepot already sputtering.

"I can zap some biscuits if you want," said Baby as they walked. She flicked on the gas fireplace. "I made them this afternoon."

"That sounds fine, ma'am," said Rakkim, sitting down at the table like he didn't have a care or concern in the world.

The Colonel thought of pulling the flat gun from the pocket of his uniform and blowing his brains out, but the man made him curious. One of those steady types who seemed to exist in a state of utter calm. Best sniper the Colonel ever knew had the same stillness about him. The Colonel had asked him once how he was doing after his wife left him for another man. *I'm serene as a head shot, sir,* the man answered, then laughed. Sniper joke, he had explained, although the Colonel never saw the humor in it. He sat down across from Rikki. "You said you have a business proposition for me. Who do you represent?"

Rakkim glanced at Baby.

"Go ahead," said the Colonel. "I don't have any secrets from my wife."

"I heard you were a brave man, sir, but I had no idea," said Rakkim.

Baby laughed, trailed her fingers across Rikki's shoulder. "I like this one, Zachary." She shook out her hair, sleepy eyed, so beautiful it made the Colonel's chest ache.

"I'm working for the Russians, Colonel." Rakkim picked up his coffee cup, letting his statement sink in. "It's pretty simple. The Chinese want what's in your mountain. My Russian clients want it too, and I think you'd rather do business with them." He sipped his coffee, looked at Baby. "This is delicious, ma'am, thank you very much."

The Colonel stared at Rikki. "Why did the Russians feel the need to hire some Belt ghost to do their negotiating?"

"They didn't want to advertise their interest by sending in one of their own," said Rakkim. "And they have a certain trust in my ability to get into places where I'm not supposed to be."

Baby laughed and they both turned to her for a moment.

"I've taken assignments from them before and I guess they liked the outcome," continued Rakkim. "I should also correct your misapprehension, Colonel. I'm not a Belt ghost." He added sugar to his coffee, stirred, the spoon not making a sound. "No offense, sir, but ghosts aren't worth a wormy turd. Me, I'm a former Fedayeen shadow warrior."

Baby put down the plate of biscuits so hard it rattled.

Rakkim broke a biscuit in half. "Ex-Fedayeen, Colonel. I'm strictly apolitical. The Belt or the republic, it's all the same to me. The last few years I've been freelancing for the Russians in Africa and South America, did a little action in Malaysia too." He slathered peach preserves onto the biscuit halves. "Good work. I enjoy it."

"The Russians thought I'd do business with a goddamned *Muslim?*" said the Colonel.

"Well, I'm not much of a Muslim, and besides, it's not really me you're doing business with. I'm just the go-between." Rakkim bit into the biscuit. "So you can choose to work with the Chinese, atheists who deny the very existence of God, or you can work with the Russians, who are Christians, just like you." He licked jam off his fingers. "You ever been to Russia, Colonel?"

"No," the Colonel said stiffly. "Can't say I ever have."

"Oh, you'd like it." Rakkim spooned jam onto another biscuit. Stretched his legs out toward the fireplace. "Strong families. Plenty of kids. Crosses everywhere. There's more churches in Moscow than there are in Atlanta. That's no lie, sir."

"Zachary . . . you always said the Fedayeen were the best soldiers you ever saw," said Baby. She chased a crumb on the table with a moist fingertip, plopped it in her mouth. "You said if you had a division of Fedayeen you could—"

"I know what I said, Baby, but this man's our enemy."

"That's pretty much a technicality, sir," said Rakkim, wolfing down his biscuit. "And at least the Muslims believe in one God, like you, and they honor and revere Abraham and Jesus, like you. Russians are the same way.

The Chinese? Sir, you go to Beijing, you're going to see more pictures of Richard Nixon than Jesus Christ."

Baby bent over the table, staring at Rakkim. "Zachary . . . he doesn't look like an enemy."

Rakkim stared back at her. She had that effect on men. The Colonel had seen it before. Heck, he was the same way himself.

"Oh . . . I almost forgot." Rakkim rooted around in his field jacket, pulled out a pad and pen. He wrote three series of numbers on the pad. Shoved it across the table to the Colonel. "The first number is a private account at the Bank of Liechtenstein." He picked up another biscuit, put it back down. "The second and third numbers are passwords that allow you online access to the account balance, which currently stands at one hundred seventy million Swiss francs. Approximately two hundred million Belt dollars at the current exchange rate. Consider that a down payment. A sign of my client's seriousness. You get another . . ." He eyed the pile of biscuits on the plate. ". . . another three or four billion, depending on how useful the weapons system turns out to be. If it's a total bust, plans for a car that runs on chocolate syrup or something, you still keep the down payment. Russians are generous people and they treat their friends accordingly."

"Go on, Rikki, have another one," said Baby. "I *know* you want it."

Rakkim reached for the biscuits. "Been a while since I had home cooking."

The Colonel blinked, trying to keep the numbers in focus. Two hundred million dollars as a *down payment*? The Chinese weren't offering anything even close.

"I got an Ident wizard stashed nearby, real smart Jewish kid," said Rakkim. "He'll go over whatever you find in the mountain, see what it's worth, and then give you and the Russians his evaluation. The weapons system won't ever have to leave your possession until you decide to make the deal."

"I never met a real Jew," said Baby.

"He's something, that's for sure. I still don't understand half of what he's talking about, but he's honest." Rakkim turned to the Colonel. "Another thing you should consider, the Russians are willing to share the technology with you once their scientists get done with it. The Chinese may talk that shit—pardon me, ma'am—but once you turn the weaponry over to the Chinks, that's the last you'll see of it *or* them. You want parts or resupply for that fancy chopper of yours, they're going to give you a million excuses, but you're never going to get what you need. Once you make a deal with the Russians, it's like you're family. Putin-class choppers aren't as good as the Chinese Monsoons, but you just have to put in an order, and the Russians will keep you up and running as long as you want."

"How noble of our Russian brothers," said the Colonel.

Rakkim shrugged, pushed his plate away. "Nobody does anything for nothing, agreed, but you have to realize, the Russians want the Belt *stronger*. The old USA was the only real counterbalance to the Chinese, and now that we're all busted into a million pieces, we're not doing anybody any good. Atlanta is useless, and that new president of yours is a total joke. Reminds me of one of those red-tailed baboons baring their ass to the world hoping to avoid trouble. Russians think you've got spine, Colonel. They respect that." He slurped his coffee. "Just an opinion. You do what you want." He stood up, nodded at Baby. "Thank you very much for your hospitality, ma'am."

Baby yawned, her pink mouth a perfect O. "Anytime."

"I'll check back with you in a couple days, Colonel," said Rakkim. "You can let me know what you decided. I promise I'll knock first."

"You must have a lot of faith in your charm," said the Colonel.

"No, sir, I have a lot of faith in *you*. If you were going to kill me, you would have already pulled that flat gun out of your pocket and started blasting away."

The Colonel inadvertently touched the pocket holding the gun.

"You're still thinking things over right now," said Rakkim. "You'll run a check five minutes after I leave, see if that account in Liechtenstein is valid, and you'll start wondering what you could buy with the down payment. What you could buy when you actually find something. Three or four billion dollars pays for a lot of food and equipment, health care if you want it, just any kind of expertise. It's all for sale. You've already got half the state under your authority—why stop there?"

The Colonel didn't respond. He didn't like it when people predicted his responses, particularly when they were right. He *did* have someone who could check out Rakkim, him and this bank account, a contact in

Columbia City, a gifted young woman with access to the best encryption technology and the brains to use it.

"It all comes down to who you want to be in bed with, the Russians or the Chinese," said Rakkim. "Who can you really trust, people of faith or people who don't even believe in God?" He shook hands with the Colonel, a good strong grip with nothing to prove. "It's an honor meeting you, sir. I studied your wilderness campaigns at the Academy. Absolutely brilliant. I'm just glad the Belt didn't have a dozen more like you."

"How many wives do you have, Rikki?" asked Baby. "I hear Muslims have just a boatload of females willing to do all sorts of nastiness."

"I'm not married, ma'am. I guess, unlike the Colonel, I never found the woman of my dreams."

"Maybe you should look for a Christian girl," teased Baby. "We know how to keep a man from thinking he needs more than one wife to make him happy."

"Baby, please, let the man be," said the Colonel.

"I'm just saying," said Baby, "this man's no more a real Muslim than Lester is."

CHAPTER 36

"Don't worry." Anthony Colarusso switched off the police cordon around Eagleton Digital Entertainment, the electrical field crackling as it went down. "Rakkim's *fine*."

"If he was fine he wouldn't have gone to the doctor." Sarah stepped over the threshold after the deputy chief of detectives. "He wouldn't have asked for all those tests."

Colarusso closed the door after her. Checked the street. The Zone wasn't busy on a Thursday afternoon, just a few well-dressed moderns on their way to the Tarantino retrospective, and a band of Catholic workmen heading into the Kitchy Koo Klub across the street. He waved a hand and the defense blinds clicked into place—Eagleton had good security in his shop, able to protect against a determined burglar or a suicide bomber in the street. But his security hadn't protected him from al-Faisal's knife thrust.

Sarah pushed back her hood. She was dressed casually: jeans and sweatshirt, looking just like the college kids who frequented the Zone. Except she looked older and more tired, her hair needing a good brushing. Other than that . . .

He pointed at the blackened bloodstains on the floor. "This is where it happened, obviously. I've been all over the crime scene, but I was hoping a fresh set of eyes—"

"I'm worried about him, Anthony," said Sarah.

"He seemed perfectly healthy before he left."

"That's what the medical report showed," said Sarah. "In fact, he's better than healthy. The Fedayeen doctor checked his current reaction times against when he graduated from the Academy. They're *faster* now. The doctor said he's never seen it before. That's how I found out. The doctor called and wanted Rikki to come in for a retest."

"I'd like to get quicker reflexes as I get older." Colarusso patted his substantial belly, his baggy gray suit spotted with dried egg yolk from breakfast. "I'm fast with a fork, but not as fast as I used to be."

"Don't patronize me. Rikki wasn't due for a checkup. He went in and asked for his DNA to be tested."

"So he was worried about his genetic boosters."

"He asked the doctor if it was possible to get cross-contamination from being cut with a Fedayeen knife. Not his own. A Fedayeen knife—"

"I know, it's made with the owner's own DNA."

"The doctor told Rikki he was looking at things backwards—it's all about the *blood*, not the blade. You can get hepatitis or plague or any number of diseases any time there's blood, but DNA doesn't get passed on," said Sarah. "Rikki insisted on being tested anyway."

"And the tests cleared him, right?"

Sarah nodded.

"Rikki never mentioned his concerns to you?"

"Does sharing his *concerns* seem like something Rikki would do?"

"Well . . . if his leg was cut off he might ask for a Band-Aid, but that's about it." Colarusso spread his arms around the small shop. "I need your help. I kind of hit a dead end here."

"I thought the investigation had been completed. Al-Faisal and his bodyguard blew themselves up at the roadblock on I-90. Case closed."

"That's State Security's version. Me, I'm a stubborn old Catholic."

"I heard you're a stubborn old Catholic who almost got himself taken into custody at the I-90 site."

"I found something there, something State Security missed."

"I didn't hear that. What did—"

"An ear."

"How nice for you."

"Yeah, it was," said Colarusso, annoyed. "The shape and whorls of an ear are as good as fingerprints for making an ID. The bodyguard was ex-Fedayeen, every hair on his head's in the files. The ear's not his. The surveillance footage from the shop gave us a good view of al-Faisal's ears—"

"So was it his ear or not?"

Colarusso shrugged. "The ear was in pretty bad shape. Forensics said it was an unlikely match, but that was as far as they would go."

"What did State Security say when you told them that?"

"I didn't bother. I think al-Faisal is alive and well, that's all that matters." Colarusso handed her a thumb drive. "I've got all my files here. Full photo array. I wanted you to walk the scene, look around, see if you spot something I missed." He nodded at her. "Redbeard's niece . . . between the two of us, something's got to pop."

Sarah slowly circled the room. Bins of electronic components, laser-etching tools, high-magnification glasses, nanocircuit boards, all of it neatly organized. One side of the room was filled with children's toys—antique mechanical cars and airplanes, an Etch A Sketch, new handheld games, and zero-grav dioramas. She picked up a faceted Fly's-eye viewer, looked through it. The whole room was broken into a thousand identical pieces. Colarusso waved at her, his face upside down and right-side up and all around. She put the viewer aside.

"All I know for sure was that it would have to take something *big* to get al-Faisal up here," said Colarusso. "It's just too risky for him."

Sarah walked over to one of the identical nonconductive metal tables that lined the walls. "Is this Eagleton's main work area?"

"Yeah. How did—"

She pointed to the floor. "More scuff marks here than by the others." She sat down in the elevated chair, fitted her hands into the remote-control gloves Eagleton had used to manipulate minute objects—a good glove stud could tie a double-loop bowline hitch in an eyelash. She removed her hands, wiped them on her pants. "Was this the height the chair was set at?"

"Yeah."

She swiveled the chair from side to side. Redbeard always said if you wanted to know what a man was thinking, check the view from his favorite spot. The facing wall was covered with images: sexy, pretty girls, sexy, pretty boys, sleek Japanese electronic gear, Italian sports cars. A publicity photo of a Russian astronaut who had died last year, hit by a tiny piece of debris while on a space walk. A postcard from a surfing beach in South Africa.

"Had he visited South Africa recently?" said Sarah.

"Not according to the State Department or Border Control. It was evidently a fantasy of his, according to the bartender at the Kitchy Koo. He was going to emigrate, surf all day, and live on coconuts."

"There're no coconuts in South Africa."

"He didn't surf either. I guess that's why it was a fantasy."

She removed the photos and postcards. Nothing on the back. She tilted each one in the light. No bumps. No microdots. Nothing. She replaced them exactly where they had been. Then she turned to the one untouched card, a five-by-seven holographic display card placed in the upper-right-hand quadrant of the wall. Key spot, according to Redbeard. The place where the eyes wandered during a pleasurable reverie. Most men would have put up a photo of their wife or sweetheart there, maybe their kids or a sports figure. Eagleton had a pornographic image of himself with his penis jammed deep into a woman's mouth. Eagleton's back was arched, his head turned to the camera. Leering.

Colarusso cleared his throat. "Yeah, that . . . that one's a real prize."

A very expensive holo, the image amazingly crisp. Flawless. She took it down from the wall, touched the controls on the side: 360-degree view and every inch of it high-definition. So clear she could see the reflection in the young woman's eye. She zoomed in on the reflection, hoping to see something . . .

"That thing's been checked out by experts," said Colarusso. "Experts and nonexperts. Everybody wanted to take a peek."

The reflection filled the screen . . . a small, half-lit room, night sky visible through the window.

Colarusso looked at the screen. "Never saw that before."

Sarah rotated the image, zoomed farther in, trying to see what was out the window of the room. Just lights . . . a line of yellow lights. Freeway . . . or airport runway maybe. She zoomed back out to the main image, aware of Colarusso shifting from one foot to the other beside her. She looked past Eagleton's triumphant expression, stared at the young woman's face. Noted a small blemish on her cheek, pushed out from the pressure of Eagleton's penis. She touched a tab, sent the image into full motion, Eagleton grinding slowly away for the camera, holding the young woman's head in place with both hands.

"I seen enough," said Colarusso.

Sarah kept her eyes on the screen. "I met him once. Did I tell you that?"

"Eagleton?" Colarusso looked shocked. "No . . ."

"I was seventeen or eighteen. The Zone was exciting and nasty, and I wasn't supposed to go anywhere near it." She watched as Eagleton wiggled his scrawny hips, tiny black hairs covering his thighs. "I went to his storefront to buy a satellite descrambler. He had the best, that's what my girlfriends said. I was the only customer that day. He didn't know who I was, of course. I remember . . . I remember him showing me how to install the descrambler, standing right behind me, and I suddenly realized he had his penis out and was rubbing his erection against me. I slapped him so hard my whole arm went numb, ran out the door. I remember looking back at him, and he was watching me like nothing had happened, just stroking himself and smiling."

"You never told anybody?"

Sarah shook her head. Switched off the full-motion mode.

"No offense, but you might have gotten off easy," said Colarusso. "Cops working the Zone told me this perv was as sick as they come."

"He needed to be one up on everyone." Sarah swiveled back and forth in the chair. "That was his real perversion. Fooling me into thinking he was helping me . . . that's what really got him off."

"Didn't stop the Black Robes from coming to him for help when they wanted something," said Colarusso. "Guardians of public morality—"

"You take photos of everything on this wall?"

"They're in the thumb drive."

"I'm going to take this holo home with me."

"I don't think that's a good idea."

"I do." Sarah touched the desk. "Where's the computer console? Had to be one here."

Colarusso grimaced. "Eagleton had it booby-trapped with magnesium switches. Soon as our techs attempted a download, the whole thing went up. Almost burned the police lab down."

The Old One dismissed his acolyte with a wave of his hand, stared out through the observation deck of the *Star of the Sea*. Better to watch the approaching storm than another pink-cheeked novice back away, head bowed, eager to impress him with his piety and manners. The Old One distrusted piety in the young and was bored to his very bones with proper manners. Times like this he missed Darwin. The assassin reeked of death, reveled in his bloody impulses, but he was a *man*. No excuses. No regrets. No fear. Contemptuous of everyone, regardless of status or station, Darwin wore his insolence like a badge of honor, a mark of his rejection of good and evil. No God, no devil . . . just death and Darwin as far as the eye could see.

Now Darwin was gone and the Old One felt the loss as a dull ache. Phantom-limb pain. The world was different without the assassin. Without spice or savor. Darwin was the only man who dared to laugh at the Old One. And the only one who had made the Old One smile. No . . . there was another. Rakkim. The Old One had offered Rakkim the world and Rakkim had turned it aside with a laugh, said what value was there in the world if it cost him his soul? Give him time, the Old One had thought, and let Rakkim live. All these long, *long* years and just those two had deeply touched him—and Darwin was dead and Rakkim was missing. But perhaps not for long.

The Old One's increased surveillance in Seattle had paid off. Five days ago, Sarah had been spotted at a Saint Sebastian Day fair dressed as a modern. Consorting with Catholics, doubtlessly planning more trouble. She wore a gauzy veil at the fair, but there had been an altercation with a Black Robe in his employ, and her features were momentarily exposed. A blessing, to be sure. The whore, a child, and another, older woman had managed to elude his men, disappearing into a nest of abandoned buildings in an industrialized part of the city. His men continued the hunt.

Dark clouds rolled toward the *Star of the Sea*, black thunderheads across the Pacific, pushing him closer to the coast of North America. The promised land. To have been so *close* to success. The bitch would have undoubtedly led his men to Rakkim, or failing that, her capture would have drawn Rakkim from hiding. Instead, she had somehow disappeared into the crowd, clutching a small boy. A *child*. That was good news. She would stick close to home now, wherever that was. Good luck and bad, as though Allah himself could not decide whether he favored the Old One at this most crucial hour.

The Old One braced himself, knees slightly bent. The massive luxury liner could weather any storm, but old habits died hard. He had been caught once in a sudden squall off Djibouti, caught in a leaky boat, the small sail of the dhow ripped to shreds as he rode the waves . . .

Still no sign of Rakkim. Whether he was in hiding or on a mission, the Old One didn't know. Even his most trusted spies, men planted twenty years earlier and privy to the most intimate secrets, remained in the dark about Rakkim. And so did the Old One. It rankled. No, worse than that, it made his joints ache, as though he had slept badly, restless as a woman. Once before Rakkim and Sarah had upended his plans. Ruined decades of work. The Old One had been cautious in those days, slowly moving men into position, believing in the inevitability of his ascension. A one-world caliphate under the green banner of Islam, the Old One's destiny at last complete. Yet those two had ruined his plans, and these last two years, the Old One had found himself hurrying, taking chances. He knew now that even *he* could run out of time.

The Old One felt light-headed for an instant at such a thought—it felt like champagne bubbles rising, toasting a New Year's Eve a hundred years ago. He might as well have been a mayfly, doomed to die with the dawn, a small, buzzing creature unaware of tomorrow. He and the rest of his companions had counted down the seconds until the New Year, mindless pleasure seekers, fallen from grace. All of them gone now. Long gone. Returned to the dust, no wiser than when they became flesh.

He put such thoughts away, tucked them into a quiet corner of his mind with the rest of his ancient memories. Wives and children gone, fortunes won and lost, friends abandoned. Nothing remained now save his goal and his purpose, the path lit by glory, his footsteps guided by God. A solitary path to be sure, but the Old One had long since gotten used to that.

The Old One felt the *Star of the Sea* shift slightly as the edge of the storm reached it, and wondered yet again if he should have had Rakkim killed when he had the chance.

"How are *you* doing?" asked Colarusso. "Everything going on, I forgot to ask."

Sarah ignored him. She had a line of welts across her back where the Black Robe had flailed her last week, and even worse, a nagging suspicion that she had been seen, her presence noted. She had used every precaution getting back home from the Saint Sebastian Day fair, even had her mother take Michael a separate way so that she could observe them approach the house and see if they were followed. They weren't, but the welts on her back still burned so badly she could hardly stand to take a shower. She would have liked to have stayed and given the Black Robe a few jolts from the stunner. Set it to max and made him sizzle. She shook her head, amused. Such *language*, Sarah. The price one pays for keeping company with infidels.

"Sarah?"

"I'm good," said Sarah, finishing her walkabout of the shop. She had taken plenty of her own photos. "Keeping busy."

Colarusso peered at her, probably noting the bags under her eyes. He took her hand, ran a thumb over her chewed-short fingernails. "I don't think so. I mean, I'm a gentleman and all, housebroken after twenty-eight years of marriage, but, Sarah . . . you don't look good."

She swatted him. He laughed but it didn't help. It didn't help either of them. "I miss him, Anthony." Her voice shook slightly. "I hate going to bed alone. I hate waking up alone. I *miss* him. And I'm scared for him."

"He's good. He's the best."

"Those other shadow warriors who disappeared . . . they probably thought they were the best too."

Colarusso held her, the two of them standing there, just breathing.

"You're his friend, his best friend," said Sarah, hanging on, her voice muffled against his beefy chest. "He asked me . . . before he left, he asked me if I thought he was different lately." She pressed her cheek against him, hiding. "I lied to him, Anthony. I love him, but he's not the same now and I don't know why. I couldn't tell him. Not when he was leaving for the Belt. He's got . . . he's got so much to worry about."

"Marriage changes a man," soothed Colarusso. "Most ways for the better, but there were times after Mary Elizabeth was born, I'd get off work and couldn't decide whether to drive to Canada and not look back, or just drive off the nearest dock."

"It gets better, though, doesn't it?"

"Sure."

"He's not going to be like this forever, is he? I'm sorry, Anthony . . . I don't have anyone else to ask."

"He loves you, girl, that's all I know. You just hang on a little longer. You'll see. He'll be his old self again. Then, being a good wife and all, you can complain about that."

They finally broke the clinch. Sarah wiped tears from her cheeks, still feeling Colarusso's comforting, bearlike heat.

"No sign . . ." Colarusso cleared his throat, embarrassed. "No trace of explosives in the shop, but plenty of exotic materials and metals, titanium, Carborundum, lithium, palladium . . . man could have been building anything."

"Did you run a radiation scan?"

"Jesus, lady, you got a dirty mind." He grimaced. "State Security must have checked, but I'll get right on it and make sure."

"We should go. I'll let you know if I have any ideas."

"How about coming for dinner tonight?" Colarusso rubbed the back of her arm. "Bring your mom and the boy and we'll have a barbecue. Marie's a lousy cook, but even she has a hard time screwing up a steak."

Sarah smiled. "Thank you, Anthony, but I'm working late again."

"The president?"

She sighed, half closed her eyes. Wished for a moment she was back home . . . not her home now, but her home when she was a girl. Home with Redbeard, her uncle . . . her protector after her father was murdered. The head of State Security, Redbeard was harsh but loving. Always demanding, turning every incident from spilled milk to a misplaced book into a damned learning opportunity. The training never ended in that house. *People like us can't afford to be surprised, Sarah. We don't have the luxury of making mistakes or being caught unaware. We have to sense who's on the other side of the door before they knock, and we have to know if they're a friend or enemy.* Then Redbeard would kiss her hair . . . or get down on the floor and play dolls with her, until he was called away on business.

"Sarah?"

Sarah put her hood up. "The official state visit to Mexico City is a nightmare. *Amistad por Siempre!* Friendship forever, my ass. Every senator up for reelection is begging for a spot on Air Force One and the president wants to minimize the political footprint. He'd leave the vice president here if he could, but it's best to have a Mexican-American beside you when you're groveling before the Aztlán Empire."

"It's that bad?"

"It's worse. The president's using the visit to try to negotiate a compromise—giving Aztlán all gas and mineral rights from Southern California,

Arizona, and New Mexico, in return for them renouncing all claims to the territory itself."

Colarusso stared at her. "That's the *best* we can do?"

"That's the best we can hope for. It's going to take all of Kingsley's skills and Mendoza's folksy barrio stories to convince the Mexicans to accept the deal. They don't need to compromise. They could take the territory if they really wanted to."

"What about General Kidd? His forces—"

"The Fedayeen are already stretched thin. We have to choose our battles."

Colarusso gnawed at his lower lip. "Plane full of politicians . . . president and vice president . . . seems to me that's just asking for trouble."

"Air Force One is safer than the Presidential Palace. Redbeard used to pack Rakkim and me along when he rode with the president," said Sarah. "Amazing technology. The freeways may be crumbling, but Air Force One gets every security upgrade. Microwave chaff generators, triple redundancies, complete system assessment prior to takeoff . . ."

"I had no idea."

"You're not supposed to." Sarah opened the door. "Raincheck on the dinner invitation? Rakkim and I will come by as soon as he gets back."

"Just bring your antacids."

CHAPTER 37

Rakkim was peeling potatoes when Moseby walked into the mess tent, looking exhausted, and started moving through the chow line. He didn't notice Rakkim stuck in the back, working through a pile of spuds.

Rakkim tossed his apron aside. "Taking a break."

The cook grunted, stirred the pot of chili he was working on.

Rakkim had been working in the miner's mess since he slipped out of the Colonel's house early yesterday morning. Just wandered in and told the morning cook that he had been assigned as his line monkey until the rest of his unit came up from Murfreesboro. The cook didn't question the orders, grateful to have the help. Rakkim got a cot next to the cooler, a hideout where no one would think to look for him, and sooner or later, Moseby had to show up. Midafternoon on the second day, there he was.

The miners, covered in dust, tended to congregate together even when there was room, sitting so close they were constantly banging elbows. Moseby was off in a corner by himself, digging into his chicken steak and greens like he hadn't eaten in a month, when Rakkim tapped him on the shoulder.

"Get you some gravy, suh?" said Rakkim, standing behind him.

Moseby recognized his voice immediately, fingers tightening on his knife.

"What *is* it with you people?" said Rakkim, sitting beside him with a cup of coffee. "You think I've got nothing better than to go around all day killing folks?"

Moseby kept his grip on the knife. Not that it would do him any good. "How'd you find me?"

"*Please.*" Rakkim put two heaping spoons of sugar into his coffee. Stirred. "You think you're the only finder in the world?" He sipped his coffee. Added another spoon of sugar. "Annabelle sends her best. Leanne too. Smart girl. Must have got that from her mama."

Moseby didn't move. Barely breathed. "Are they all right?"

"They are now." Rakkim sipped his coffee. "I moved them out of New Orleans. They're staying at her cousin's place in Arkansas."

Moseby relaxed slightly, lowered his shoulders. "Good. Her kin may not like me but they'll do what's right."

Rakkim rested his head on his elbow, looking past Moseby, checking out the rest of the room. "Annabelle's worried about you. I promised her I wouldn't let anything happen to you, but I'm not sure she trusts me."

"Thanks." Moseby set the knife down. "I owe you."

"I know."

"It's never free, is it?" said Moseby. "You always keep a running tally."

"A man can never have too many friends." Rakkim finished the coffee. "How's the treasure hunt going? Must have been four or five crews through here in the last day, and that's all they talk about. Some say it's at the bottom of an underground lake, others say it's buried under a filled-in mineshaft. They're not even sure what they're looking for—gold, silver, Billy Clinton's crocheted jockstrap—but they're all convinced they're the lucky ones. Me, I'd put my money on you anytime." He reached over, took a roasted potato off Moseby's plate, popped it in his mouth. "So . . . did you find anything?"

Moseby watched him chew.

"Interesting indentations around your eyes—looks like a face mask," said Rakkim, going back to Moseby's plate. "You been scuba diving, John? Probably no crawfish around here, but I bet there's some mighty tasty freshwater crabs in that river I saw on the way up here. That it? You find yourself a good spot for a little R and R?"

Moseby stood. "There's a rusted-out logging truck broken down near the trailhead to town. Meet me there in fifteen minutes."

Rakkim slid Moseby's plate in front of him as the man walked off. Picked up the fork and started in on the rest of the chicken.

Rakkim was sitting in the driver's seat of the logging truck when Moseby showed up ten minutes later. He brought company, of course. Rakkim couldn't blame him.

"Nice sawed-off you got there," said Rakkim as Moseby slid into the passenger side. "Nothing like a wide field of fire. Say what you want about full-auto, a scattergun—"

"Stop talking." Moseby centered the shotgun on Rakkim's midsection. No matter how fast a man was, there was no avoiding a load of double-aught at that range.

"Sure." Rakkim kept both hands on the wheel. "Why destroy the peace and quiet of a summer day? I bet if we sit here for a few minutes we'll hear all kinds of birds."

"I'm serious."

"Me too. Honest." Rakkim peered through the cracked windshield, cranking the steering wheel back and forth, making *vroom-vroom* sounds.

"What's *wrong* with you?"

Rakkim went silent. Sat back in his seat. Looked at Moseby. "I don't know," he said softly. "I don't . . . I don't seem to be myself lately." He started laughing, couldn't stop.

"Are Annabelle and Leanne really okay?"

Rakkim shook with laughter.

Moseby nudged him with the sawed-off. "Did you hurt my family, Rikki?"

"No." Rakkim wiped his eyes, serious now. "You know me better than that."

"I thought I did. Now . . . I'm not so sure."

Rakkim took his hands off the wheel, stared at his fingers like they didn't belong to him. He wiped his palms on his pants. "I'm sorry, John. Didn't mean to worry you. Annabelle and Leanne, they're fine. Both of them."

Moseby stared at him. Nodded. "I believe you."

"If you believe me, you best put away the gun. One of us could get hurt."

Moseby slid the sawed-off back into his jacket. "You should go back where you came from. There's nothing for you here."

"You like living in the Belt, John?"

"It's my home now."

"Met a lot of good people here myself. Lot of sick, twisted fucks too, but you find that anywhere. You wouldn't believe New Fallujah now—I've seen slaughterhouses with better ambience." Rakkim drummed on the wheel, not sure if he even knew what the word *ambience* meant. "Yeah, I like the Belt."

"What do you want from me, Rikki?"

"You know what I want."

"I'm not going to put some black ice into the hands of the republic."

"You'd rather put it into the hands of the Colonel?"

"The Colonel's a good man."

"I know. I've met him." Rakkim let that sink in. "You give the weapon to the Colonel, though, you're giving it to Gravenholtz too. Maybe that's what you want. After all, he was so kind to your family. Me, all I did was get them out of harm's way."

Moseby didn't answer.

Rakkim inhaled. The logging truck smelled of rust and mildewed leather and cracked plastic. He pumped the brakes, his foot thudding on the floorboard. "What if the weapon didn't end up back in the republic?"

Moseby shook his head. "Once something like that's been found, you can't just make it disappear."

"I'm not talking about that." Rakkim picked up two pinecones off the seat, held one up. "You've got the republic. Kingsley's not going to live forever, and even if he did, the country—what's left of it, anyway—is just one step ahead of a fundamentalist takeover." He held up the other pinecone. "Then there's the Belt, which, other than a few pockets of affluence, is a backwater dumping ground, owned and operated by foreign corporations." He tossed both pinecones out the window. "Neither the Belt nor the republic can be trusted with the weapon."

"You got another pinecone?"

Rakkim smiled. "I've got another option. We all do."

"The Colonel doesn't even know what the weapon is," said Moseby. "All he knows is that it's in a graphite canister small enough for a strong man to carry . . . and it's got a marking on it. Seventy-two-slash-one-oh-six."

"Seventy-two-slash-one-oh-six? What does that mean?"

"No idea." Moseby grinned. "Maybe it's the phone number for some general's mistress."

"Why does the Colonel think there's black ice buried here anyway?"

"Dying man told him. Tobacco farmer outside of Daystrom. Don't laugh. Farmer said the canister was hidden in the mountain by a special commando unit. Six men went into the mountain, only one came out. The farmer was the grandson of that man. This farmer reached out to the Colonel when he was on his deathbed. He had his grandfather's medal, a commendation from the head of the black-ice program to back up his story. He just didn't have the exact location of the lake they dumped it in."

"Not really a lot of proof."

"I found a Grave Digger ID badge beside an underground lake."

"*Damn.* I was half hoping it was all bullshit."

"Me too." Moseby ran a hand across his skull, wiped sweat on his trousers. "So fuck the republic and fuck the Belt. What's the other option?"

"My wife's a liberal. Sarah's Redbeard's niece, raised moderate, but she might as well be a Catholic. She's the one who uncovered the truth behind the suitcase nuke attacks."

Moseby's eyes widened.

"I know, I know," said Rakkim. "I should have married a good Muslim girl who'd rub my back and never ask me how my day was, but I fell in love."

Moseby's black skin made his smile seem even brighter. "That makes two of us."

"Sarah's been working with people, both in the republic and in the Belt—Christians, Muslims, Jews—all of them evidently putting aside their differences for one goal. Reunification."

Moseby didn't laugh. Just watched him.

"You act like . . . like you're not surprised," said Rakkim.

"It's the only logical alternative."

"To you, maybe. To me . . . it was sort of a shock. My wife the traitor."

"Is that the way you feel?"

Rakkim let it lie for a moment. "No. I think if I didn't trust her on this, if I didn't do everything I could to help her . . . then *I'd* be the traitor."

"So this group, the ones trying to reunify the country, they want the weapon?" Moseby looked out the window. He didn't need an answer. He shook his head. Turned back to Rakkim. "The Belt's got plenty of problems, I know that better than you do . . . but I'm not about to let you turn the weapon against it."

"It's not about that," said Rakkim. "It's using the weapon to stop the Belt and the republic from getting nibbled away by our neighbors."

"*Our* neighbors. I like the sound of it. Wish it wasn't just you saying it." Moseby kept chewing things over. "You ask a lot of your friends, Rikki."

"I know."

A truck full of young soldiers rolled past them, kicking up dust, the soldiers hooting and hollering.

"I'm not asking you to do anything I'm not doing myself," said Rakkim. "The president expects me either to bring him the weapon or destroy it, and I'm going to lie to him. I'm going to give the weapon to people who want to change things in a big way. I don't know how it's going to turn out. That's Sarah's job. I'm just going on faith and her say-so that I'm doing the right thing."

"You might be wrong. She might be wrong." Moseby watched the troop transport until it was out of sight. "*I* might be wrong."

"True enough, but, John . . . how long do you think either country is going to last split in two like it is?"

"I've got to go, Rikki."

"One of the people working for reunification . . . I brought him along. His name is Leo. Young kid. Probably too smart for his own good. Jewish, so he's not about to do anything with the weapon that's going to make the mullahs happy." Rakkim hesitated. "I think he's in love with Leanne. Nothing's happened," Rakkim hurried, seeing the heat in Moseby's eyes. "More of a puppy love kind of thing. I was going to let Leo tell you, but it would probably take him an hour to get the words out."

"What does Annabelle think of him?"

"You figure out what women think, you let me know."

Moseby put his hand on the door.

"Will you do it? If you find the canister . . . ?"

"You think you're going to waltz in, throw it across your back, and just walk out again?" Moseby snorted. "You're good, but you're not that good."

"I'm working on it. In a day or so the Colonel is going to introduce me to you, so play nice. You'll meet Leo too. I'm warning you, that could be a bit of a jolt."

Moseby watched him and Rakkim had no idea what he was thinking. Whether he would go along when the time came, or whether he would betray them. Moseby kept accounts too. He owed Rakkim. The question was whether he owed him enough.

"So will you do it, John? If you find the weapon . . . will you let me know?"

Moseby opened the door to the truck, the rusted hinges screeching like something in pain. "Already found it."

CHAPTER 38

Rakkim heard footsteps approaching, heard whispers and someone circling around to the rear of the tent—plenty of time to get away or turn the
ambush back on them, but he recognized the Colonel's old-fashioned
pine-tar soap and the gruff whisper . . . yes, that would be Gravenholtz.
Best to let them think they had surprised him.

Gravenholtz passed by, breathing heavily, and Rakkim thought of Florence Tigard with her clothes on fire, her sons shot to pieces in front of
her . . . thought of Bill Tigard dying as he tried to defend his family.
Rakkim saw it all over again, the flames and gunfire, the look on Gravenholtz's face as Tigard's scythe barely broke the skin . . . he remembered
that look and almost reconsidered his decision to let himself be caught
napping. *Let's see if that second skin of his works against a Fedayeen blade.*
Rakkim imagined a hundred different ways to kill the redhead as he barged
into the tent, each more painful than the last, more interesting . . . Instead,
he lay back on his cot, forced the images out of his head. It was harder
than he expected. Darwin's face curled at the foot of his bed, wispy as a
nightmare, his smile fading now, fading . . . Rakkim closed his eyes as the
footsteps stopped just outside.

"Peekaboo!" Baby peered through the tent flap.

Rakkim yawned. He hadn't picked up on Baby—her light footsteps over-
shadowed by the Colonel and Gravenholtz. He sat up in bed. "Morning."

The Colonel stepped into the tent, bending his head to clear the can-
vas. "Hope you don't mind the interruption," he said, pleased with himself. "Turnabout's fair play."

"You're a hard man to find," said Baby. "The Colonel's been looking
high and low."

A bowie knife slashed open the back of the tent, the blade just inches
from Rakkim on the downstroke. Gravenholtz muscled his way in.

Rakkim swung his legs out of bed, fully dressed. "Thanks, Red, it was getting kind of stuffy in here."

"*Lester*, that wasn't necessary," chided the Colonel. "This is Lester Gravenholtz, my second in command."

Rakkim saw the challenge in Gravenholtz's eyes as he sheathed the bowie knife in his boot. Double-barreled machine pistol. Blousy cammie trousers and a big-weave thermal T-shirt that showed his taut musculature. Dressed for intimidation. Rakkim had to admit, close up the Jap job was impressive. Gravenholtz moved naturally without any hint of the eighth-inch polycarbon-fiber sheathing under his skin. The redhead balled his fists. The knuckles would be reinforced, strike plates inserted along the sides of his hands. In spite of the advanced technology, Rakkim found the idea repugnant. Fedayeen genetic boosters dramatically improved one's natural gifts, but without discipline and training the boosters were pointless. A Jap job led to arrogance and dependency.

"What are you looking at, cocksucker?" said Gravenholtz.

"Grandma, what big *teeth* you have."

Baby laughed.

"Peace in the valley, you two," ordered the Colonel. "This isn't really a social call, Rikki. I had you checked out . . . there's two hundred million dollars in the overseas account, just as you said. The money transfer bounced around the world before landing in the Bank of Liechtenstein, but my contact traced the point of origin to a bank in Moscow. It seems your story is accurate. That part of it anyway."

"I wish you'd hurry up and decide who we're in bed with, Zachary," said Baby. "That Chinaman you told me about sounded like a real stickbutt, wrinkling his nose at our food and asking if the water was safe to drink. Besides, how can we trust an atheist to keep their end of the bargain?" She eyed Rakkim. "I vote for this one."

The Colonel kissed her gently on the cheek. "You don't have a vote, darling."

"Have you found the weapon yet?" Rakkim said to the Colonel. "The Russians are eager for their technical expert to get started."

"I'll let you know when the time comes," said the Colonel. "Don't want to get ahead of yourself. In the meantime, I'm interested to know how you penetrated our security cordon. The sentries guarding my home have already been debriefed. Clever, bringing them coffee."

"I still say we should have shot the sons a bitches," said Gravenholtz.

"I don't waste *men*, Lester." The Colonel pulled down the jacket of his uniform, maintained his perfect appearance. "Reassignment and loss of a month's pay is sufficient to spread the message that we have to remain vigilant." He held open the tent flap and they all filed out into the morning. "I'll give you a tour of the camp, Rikki, although I doubt you really need it."

"You boys have fun," called Baby. "I'm going horseback riding."

"Take a couple men with you," said the Colonel.

Baby waved and kept walking.

"She's not going to listen." The Colonel watched the tight seat of her jeans as she strode down the line of tents, her blond ponytail swinging with every step. "She'll do exactly what she wants." He kept watching her. "Are you married, Rikki? No, that's right . . . you already told me you're a bachelor. My first wife was killed during the war. Wife and all three children. An accident, not your people. I never thought I'd remarry. Wasn't like I didn't have enough to occupy me . . . and there's a certain freedom to a life without emotional entanglements, as I'm sure you know. Then I met Baby a few years ago . . . and everything changed." He sighed as she disappeared behind a cluster of machinery, absently touched his dyed black hair. "I know she's too young for me . . . but I couldn't imagine life without her."

"You're a lucky man," said Rakkim.

"Yes, I am," said the Colonel.

The three of them walked past a line of seven-ton trucks being worked on. Men bent over the open hoods with wrenches and socket sets; others had removed the tires and were checking and replacing brakes. Too busy and too greasy to salute, the men acknowledged the Colonel with polite greetings and nods of their heads. He returned their greetings, acknowledging them by name.

"Maintenance and resupply are the backbone of any military," said the Colonel. "It's not glamorous, they'll get no parades, but if a truck full of munitions or gasoline breaks down, a battle can easily swing in the wrong direction. Keep your mechanics and drivers happy, that's one of the keystones of victory."

"My experience is mostly with very small units." Rakkim noticed a couple of the Colonel's personal guards had fallen in behind them, keeping their distance, but ready to defend him if need be. "We kept a low profile and lived off the land."

"Guerrilla operations do require different tactics," agreed the Colonel. The sun came out; every button on his uniform gleamed. "Now, how *did* you get into camp? We had motion sensors along the perimeter, all of them in good working condition."

Rakkim smiled. The Colonel had lulled him into talking about himself. "It was a dog, Colonel. A large brown mutt."

The Colonel turned, raised an eyebrow. "A *dog*, Rikki?"

"I figured you'd have a perimeter established so I picked up a stray in the nearest town," said Rakkim. "Picked up a bag of hamburgers too. Cute pooch, but underfed. That night I started up the south slope. Every twenty or thirty yards, I'd toss a bit of hamburger up ahead, let the dog go bounding through the brush after it. Eventually he tripped the sensors and set off the alarm. Lights came on, sentry came out. He saw the dog, patted him on the head. Lights went out. I shadowed the sentry past the sensors and kept going." Rakkim shrugged. "Wasn't that hard, really."

The Colonel laughed. "No wonder the Russians hired you."

"That Fedayeen razzle-dazzle is overrated," said Gravenholtz.

"Lester has a point," said the Colonel. "We've intercepted several of your former compatriots. Of course, that makes Rikki's success even more laudatory."

"More like *lucky*," said Gravenholtz.

"Don't take it personally, Rikki, Lester doesn't like anyone."

"Let him take it personally," said Gravenholtz. "Fine by me."

They kept climbing. Had to give the Colonel credit, he maintained a fast pace while giving a running commentary about troop rotations and local politics, the unique hazards of a mountain bivouac, and the necessity of his periodic trips to put down bandits and keep the peace.

"What do the men think you're looking for in the mountain?" said Rakkim.

"The lost gold of Fort Knox," said the Colonel. "Barrels of diamonds. A vein of platinum that goes clear to the center of the earth. I've heard it all bandied about. Besides you, Rikki, the only ones who know the truth are myself, Baby, and a very special fellow from New Orleans, a finder named Moseby."

"I'd like to meet this Moseby," said Rakkim.

"Soon." The Colonel pointed out the Monsoon 4 under a camouflage tarp. "I imagine that's how the Russians realized something important was happening here."

"I don't know how they found out," said Rakkim. "Not my department."

"Still, we have to use the bird judiciously," said the Colonel. "The Russians aren't the only ones who might want to poke their noses into our business."

"What's the point in having it if we can't *use* it?" said Gravenholtz. The Colonel glanced at him and Gravenholtz backed off. "I'm just saying . . ."

Deeper in the woods, Rakkim saw a small encampment, the tents pitched haphazardly, wet laundry hanging off nearby tree branches. Men stood around in the shadow of the pines, watching them pass by. No salutes to the Colonel, no greetings. They were different from the troops in camp, different from the miners too. Sullen brutes, unshaven, arms draped across the rifles slung across their backs. They looked like scarecrows.

Rakkim recognized one of them, and another one too. He had seen them at the Tigards' farmhouse, howling with glee as they unloaded rounds into the burning home. He was about to make an excuse to get closer when Gravenholtz tugged on his earlobe and the men melted back into the forest.

The path forked. The Colonel started down the low road.

"What's up there?" said Rakkim, pointing toward the other path.

It was close to noon, sun beating down directly on them; even the birds were retreating from the sky. "Just a view," said the Colonel.

"Okay," said Rakkim. "If you're tired . . ."

The Colonel's mouth worked.

"Don't you want to head toward the lake, sir?" asked Gravenholtz. "It'd be cooler, and there's been some rock slides along the ravine; I don't think it's safe."

The Colonel hesitated, shook his head. "I haven't been to the rift in a while—besides, I want to get Rikki's opinion on using the area for antiaircraft coverage. If I decide to deal with the Russians instead of the Chinese, Beijing may be less than happy."

"It's a mistake, sir," said Gravenholtz. "You're giving this towelhead way too much credit."

"Hey, Lester, let's keep it civil," said Rakkim. "I mean, I could call you a pasty-faced, freckle-assed, thimble-dicked mother—"

Gravenholtz swung on him. Rakkim slipped the blow, but slowly, not wanting to reveal his own speed. Might have been a mistake. One of Gravenholtz's fists just barely grazed him, but drew blood and laid a welt along the side of his jaw.

"That's *enough*, Lester," said the Colonel. "Now, I'm showing Rikki the ravine. You can either accompany us or find something else to vent your spleen on."

Rakkim walked beside the Colonel. Touched his fingertips to his jaw. Now he had a good idea of how fast Gravenholtz moved.

"I warned you," muttered the Colonel. "Lester's a dangerous man to provoke."

Rakkim heard Gravenholtz start after them, the redhead slipping on the loose rocks.

They climbed on for another ten minutes, one switchback after another, when Rakkim heard it. The other two kept climbing, oblivious. A few minutes later, when they reached a large, flat area near the summit, even they could hear it. The call to noon prayer, the voice weak but insistent.

"Lester?" The Colonel glared at Gravenholtz. "God*damn* it, Lester, you try my patience." He stalked into the woods, Rakkim and Gravenholtz following. The Colonel's two guards trailed behind. The forest was sparse, the soil rocky and poor, the ground littered with broken whiskey bottles and empty cans of beef stew and Spam and creamed corn. The call to prayer was coming from a lean-to the size of an outhouse. A grimy man dozed beside a nearby tree, an assault rifle resting on his knees.

"Open the door!" the Colonel barked as the grimy man woke up.

The man got to his feet, fumbled in his pocket, and stuck a key in the padlock on the lean-to.

The Colonel pushed him aside, opened the door. He looked back at Gravenholtz.

"I can explain, sir," said Gravenholtz.

"No, you most certainly cannot," said the Colonel. He extended his hand into the lean-to, helped a man inside stagger out, the man half blinded by the light, blinking, his arms bound behind his back. "Give me your canteen," the Colonel ordered.

The grimy man reluctantly handed it over.

The Colonel held the canteen to the prisoner's mouth, water pouring down the man's chin in his eagerness. "Easy, soldier," urged the Colonel, giving him time, making him slow down. They stood there, the two of them, until the Colonel finally tossed the empty canteen aside. "I gave orders before I left last week that this man was to be executed," he said to Gravenholtz.

Rakkim recognized the prisoner—a Fedayeen named Hodges, first in his shadow warrior class two years ago. Rakkim had been at the small graduation ceremony as a guest of General Kidd. It was Hodges, but his face was wrong . . . the planes of his cheeks were misaligned, his jaw unhinged, one eye swollen shut, his chin caved in. So broken he could never be made whole again.

The pain must have been agonizing, but Hodges stood there calmly, legs spread slightly, to the limit of the short chain around his ankles. His arms were strapped behind his back, bound at the wrist and elbow. At the Academy, Rakkim had seen a Fedayeen commando tied hand and foot like this, watched him jump and snap his knees into an instructor's forehead. Knocked the instructor out. Nice move, but the commando didn't have a broken ankle. Hodges did. Rakkim made eye contact with him, saw a glimmer of acknowledgment, a moment of relief, then resignation. Hodges had to have guessed what Rakkim was doing here. There was nothing Rakkim could do for him without jeopardizing the mission. They both knew it.

The Colonel's two guards had joined them, their weapons trained on Hodges.

"You disobeyed my direct order, Lester," said the Colonel.

Gravenholtz's face was the color of a rotting orange. "Well, sir . . . the boys get so little entertainment, stuck up here, that I decided to do what I could to lighten their load."

"*Your* boys, not mine," said the Colonel. He gently turned Hodges's head, noted the filth and scars along the side of it, the places where his broken bones had not healed properly. He unbuttoned Hodges's shirt, saw his busted ribs sticking out like pick-up sticks. The Colonel buttoned him back up. Smoothed his blood-crusted hair. "You have my apology, soldier."

"He's a damn *spy*, Colonel," said Gravenholtz.

"Yes, he's a spy. That's why I sentenced him to be executed," said the Colonel, his eyes still on Hodges. "He's also a soldier operating under orders and one *hell* of a brave man, which is why he deserves to be put in front of a firing squad and executed with full military honors, not abused for the pleasure of cowards."

Gravenholtz's voice was a raspy whisper. "Sir, you got no call—"

"You disobeyed my order, and you disgraced yourself," said the Colonel. "Torturing a man like this . . . If I didn't need you, I'd put you down like a rabid dog, Lester." He rested his hand on his sidearm. "You're dismissed. Take this piece of shit with you."

Gravenholtz gave a sloppy salute and ambled off, the grimy man following.

"Shall . . . sir, shall I put the prisoner back?" said one of the Colonel's guards.

"Let him bathe first. You know where the freshwater spring is. Let him take all the time he wants, but don't get too close and keep your weapons on him at all times. Every moment," said the Colonel. "After he's clean, give him time to pray and then bring him back here. We'll put him out of his misery." He stepped closer to Hodges. "Are you ready to meet your maker, soldier?"

Hodges nodded.

"Sorry I don't have your holy book so you could read—"

"No need, sir," croaked Hodges, "I've memorized the holy Quran."

"It would be defiled by my touch anyway. That's the way it works, right?"

Hodges looked straight ahead.

Rakkim watched Hodges limp away, the two guards following behind, weapons ready. The wind rose up from the lowlands, and he smelled pine and cedar, clean smells, earth and eternity. He hoped Hodges filled his lungs before he died. Strange business. Rakkim had been warned that the Colonel had become a ferocious Muslim-hater, preaching vengeance and genocide, but it wasn't true. The Colonel had no qualms about executing his enemies, but there was no cruelty in the man, only a harsh justice. Gravenholtz was a beast—even worse, he slipped his leash from time to time.

The Colonel looked out over the hills and valleys below. The breeze blew through his long hair, his eyes squinting, as though waiting for some phantom army to appear, the heavenly host in all its glory.

Rakkim remembered seeing the new president of the Belt on TV in the diner. A grinny-Gus, that's what the hunters at the Piggly Wiggly Diner had called him, forks scraping over their plates as they mocked the president. You would never hear anything like that in Seattle, not in public anyway, but politicians were the same everywhere. Most of them weak, preening word merchants eager to accommodate whoever was in front of them. Lip service. It sounded obscene. Even President Kingsley wasn't immune to making the most repugnant compromises, playing off the conservative ayatollahs against the modern technocrats, watering down a proposed travel ban on unmarried females and trumpeting it as a victory. Maybe it was. All Rakkim knew was that if someone had to rule, he preferred a leader who was hard but honorable, with spine and a sense of decency. A man like General Kidd. Or the Colonel.

"Who were those men we saw on the way up?" said Rakkim. "The ones whose tents were falling down around them."

"Those are Lester's men. He brought them with him when he joined up about five years ago. Border raiders, one step ahead of the noose. Scum for the most part, and no field discipline, as you noted, but fierce fighters. Like Lester himself. He lacks charm, and he's got a mean streak, but when the bugle blares . . ."

"It's when the bugle goes silent that I'd worry, if I were you."

"Lester's a good ol' boy." The Colonel looked past him. "I think the prisoner recognized you."

Rakkim was impressed. So much so that he didn't trust a lie to go undetected.

"We were introduced the last time I was at the Academy."

"Seeing you here with me . . . he must realize you've gone renegade," said the Colonel, face turned to the wind. "'Bout to break his heart, I imagine."

"A Fedayeen has to travel light, Colonel. A heart would be an unnecessary burden."

The Colonel looked at him. "Betraying your country might not have been all that hard for you, but I suspect there's plenty like that young prisoner who would never consider it. Not for love or money. The Russians are God-fearing people, just like you said, so I'll consider doing business with you, mister, but make sure you stay downwind of me."

It was an hour later when the two guards brought Hodges back, freshly scrubbed now. His clothes were rinsed clean, still wet. His chains clinked with every measured step, his hands bound in front of him.

"You ready, soldier?" asked the Colonel.

Hodges pulled back his shoulders as the wind rippled around him.

The Colonel waited until the guards walked Hodges over to a wall of rock. He gestured and they pointed their weapons, facing the Fedayeen.

"Colonel?" said Hodges. "Might I ask a favor?"

"Don't worry," said the Colonel. "You'll be buried with the other Muslim war dead at the cemetery in Jackson Ridge by noon tomorrow. I know your procedures."

"That's not it, sir." Hodges nodded at Rakkim. "I'd like to request that *he* be the one to execute me."

The Colonel stared at Hodges. "You want a *renegade* to carry out the sentence? You mocking me, soldier?"

Hodges came to attention. "Sir, with all due respect, I would prefer to be executed by a renegade Fedayeen than a couple of pork-chop-eating kafir bastards."

"With all due respect?" The Colonel laughed. Shook his head. "I will *never* understand you people." He glanced at Rakkim. "You have a problem with this?"

Rakkim looked at Hodges. "It would be an honor, sir."

The Colonel took out his sidearm, removed the magazine, left a single bullet in the chamber. He held it out to Rakkim.

Rakkim ignored the gun. He walked slowly over to Hodges, his Fedayeen knife concealed in his hand.

"Thank you," Hodges said, barely moving his lips.

Rakkim watched him, saw no fear in the man. None at all. Hodges didn't ask for Rakkim to revenge him. Didn't ask for reassurance that their mission would be completed. He didn't need to. "I'm sorry," Rakkim said softly.

"Don't look so sad, brother," said Hodges. "Today I shall lie upon a golden couch in Paradise."

Rakkim stabbed him in the heart, withdrew the blade before the man had time to blink.

CHAPTER 39

"Shouldn't we be hiding or something?" said Leo.

"The idea is for Malcolm Crews's men to find us."

Leo ducked into the shadow of the abandoned Stuckey's, the former restaurant and tourist stop now a collection of burned cinder blocks, broken windows, and a collapsed yellow roof. A rat scurried around in the dark interior and Leo quickly joined Rakkim.

"Why don't you sit down and relax?" said Rakkim. "I'll let you know if I see anybody coming."

"I'm tired of sitting down," said Leo. "You spend three days on the mountain having fun, while I'm stuck in that lousy motel listening to trucks race past my window."

"You should have gone for a walk, gone to a movie."

"People looked at me funny every time I went out. 'Where you from, buddy? What kind of accent you talking there, pard?'" he mimicked. "Nothing for me to do all day except sit in my room, watch TV, and think about Leanne."

Rakkim walked past the gasoline pumps, looked down the highway. No lights anywhere. The Stuckey's had been abandoned even before the war, left behind by the tourists and the new interstate. He looked up at the sky, saw only stars and a thin slice of moon.

Leo unwrapped another candy bar, gnawed at the end. "What did Leanne's father say when you told him about me? Was he impressed?"

"Oh, yeah, I definitely sensed tumescence."

"Ha-ha, very funny."

The kid had screwhead priorities—merely nodded when Rakkim had told him that Moseby had found the black-ice canister, more interested in Moseby himself. A half-hour drive to Stuckey's and all he talked about was Moseby and what did he think about Leo's offer of marriage, and was Leo's religion a problem, because if it was . . . *and did you tell him how much Leanne and I have in common and how we really, really love each other? Well, did you, Rikki? Yeah, I told him you were regular soul mates*, Rakkim had said, which didn't even slow the kid down; he went right back to the questions. Did Moseby think they were too young? Should Leo pretend that he and Leanne had never made love? The kid never shut up.

"I'm taking you back up the mountain with me when we're done here tonight," said Rakkim. "You ready for that?"

"Yes."

"I made it easy for you. I told the Colonel you're an arrogant Jewish odd-ball who can look at the weapon and tell us what it is, and if it works and—"

"I said *yes*."

Rakkim squeezed through the entrance of the tourist trap. He let his eyes adjust to the dim light, then moved forward, glass crunching underfoot, past the overturned racks of singed postcards. He bent down, picked up one that showed a leering crocodile biting a half-naked woman on the ass. TASTES LIKE CHICKEN, read the postcard. He tossed it aside. Christian humor.

"Hey! I thought we were supposed to stay out here," said Leo.

Rakkim listened to the rats scurrying over debris. Mushrooms sprouted in the corners where the rain got in.

"I don't like being here by myself," called Leo.

"Then come inside."

"I don't like it in there either."

Rakkim's laughter echoed among the melted bottles of suntan oil and shattered bisque lawn jockeys. He heard Leo cursing as he darted inside, tripped.

"Where *are* you?" asked Leo.

"Right here," said Rakkim.

"Right here," said Malcolm Crews at the same time.

Rakkim turned slightly as Crews detached himself from a darkened corner of the structure, dressed all in black, a shadow among the shadows, his own darkness deeper than any natural phenomenon.

"Surprised?" said Crews.

"Very," said Rakkim.

"Rikki?" said Leo, hands outstretched as he stumbled forward. "Who's there with you?"

"Malcolm Crews." Crews clicked his heels.

Rakkim looked around, half expected a dozen skeleton men to emerge from the gloom.

"It's just me," said Crews. "My flock can't keep quiet to save their necks, and truth be told, they *weary* me."

"How long have you been waiting?" said Rakkim.

"Since yesterday." Crews stretched, his arms extending until they almost touched the ceiling. "Just kind of hibernating until you arrived."

Leo held a butane lighter up, the tiny flame flickering as he found his way beside Rakkim. "Why . . . why don't we talk outside?"

"Your Ident buddy's afraid of the dark," said Crews.

"I think he's more afraid of you," said Rakkim.

"Ah, well . . . who can blame him?" Crews settled back into the shadows, his back against the wall. "Sit down, I prefer talking in here."

Rakkim picked his way over the debris to Crews, his knife back where it belonged, resting against the inside of his right forearm.

Crews reached out, pretended to pluck something from Rakkim's ear. Showed him the shekel of Tyre. "Has the Colonel found the rest of these yet?"

"No, but we know where they're hidden," said Rakkim. "They're at the bottom of an—"

"Underground lake." Crews enjoyed Rakkim's surprise. "Word's leaked out that he's searching for something, but we're the only ones who know what it is." He shoved his hands in his pockets, strolled around under that sliver of moon. "It's peaceful here."

Leo tripped over something, the lighter sliding across the floor. He fumbled around on his hands and knees looking for it.

"There'll be a new moon in four days," said Rakkim. "The Colonel will have brought up the shekels by then. You and your men should attack from the south—it's a tough climb, but the Colonel's defenses are thin in that area. You don't have to launch a full-on assault, he's too dug in for that—forty or fifty men should do it. Just a raid . . . something to distract them long enough for me to grab the pieces of silver. I'll slip through the lines during the firefight and meet you back here."

"My own little homing pigeon," said Crews.

"Where else am I going to go?" said Rakkim.

"Indeed . . ." Crews stared at the brand on his hand. "Does your mark burn?" He looked up at Rakkim. "Mine does. Sometimes it hurts so bad it wakes me up at night."

"No . . . it itches a little, that's all."

Crews smiled in the darkness. "Give it time."

Rakkim rubbed his hand, stopped himself. "Can you have your men in position in four days?"

"They'll do whatever I ask." Crews stepped back, seemed to settle deeper into the darkness. "What about you, Rikki? Will you do what I ask?"

"I want what's in that underground lake just as much as you do."

"That's not what I asked." Crews leaned his head back, faced the sky. Lost in the immensity. "I was a full professor once upon a time. Chairman of the department. Hard to believe, isn't it, considering the company I keep these days. Don't think for a moment I'm not aware of that." His head bobbed. "American literature, that was my specialty. *Huck Finn. Moby-Dick. The Amazing Adventures of Kavalier and Clay.* Ah, the stories I could tell you, the depth of my insights . . . Do you read much, Rikki?"

"Not lately."

"You should make time. I've . . . I've neglected my own studies too, for this . . . higher purpose." Crews's mouth twitched as though circled by worms. "Many are called but few are chosen . . . but they don't tell you what you're chosen *for*," he snarled, his right hand sweeping aside a display of souvenir key chains. "Look at us. Called to the Church of the Mists, but left on the doorway . . . Locked out. Unfit. Unworthy." He leaned forward. "Says *who*? We'll show *him*, Rikki. You and I. Who dares stand against us?"

Rakkim belched.

Crews shook his head. "I like you." He detached himself from the corner, eased closer, and Rakkim let him come. "This tale of the thirty pieces of silver, the ultimate blood money . . . lost and now found." He cocked his head. "Is it really true? Or are you Judas himself, come to betray me? Judas betrayed Jesus with a kiss. Is that who you are?"

"Don't get your hopes up," said Rakkim. "Four days, Malcolm. Don't be late."

"'On a moonless night, I shall lead the army of darkness into battle,'" said Crews, taking a deep, theatrical bow, arms spread wide. "That's Christopher Marlowe."

Rakkim shrugged. "Don't know this Marlowe guy, but it's the title of an old horror movie too. *Army of Darkness*. Woman I know is a real fan of that stuff."

"You'll have to introduce me," said Crews.

"Not a fucking chance."

Crews glared at Rakkim.

There was only the sound of crickets rising and falling, the same sad note over and over coming through the broken windows.

"We . . . we should go," said Leo.

"Yes, you should," said Crews, not taking his eyes off Rakkim.

Rakkim led Leo out through the overturned display cases and soggy cardboard boxes, Leo lumbering along, keeping close, until the two of them were outside in the fresh air, the crickets even louder now, filling the night.

"I hate that guy," whispered Leo.

"I've met worse."

"*Where?*" Leo didn't expect an answer, wouldn't have believed Rakkim anyway. He looked toward the car. "Do I meet the Colonel tonight?"

"Tomorrow."

"Did Mr. Moseby really find the canister?"

"It's still at the bottom of the lake, but he's seen it. He'll bring it up when the time is right."

Leo tore cobwebs off his hair, swatted at bugs that may or may not have been there. "The sooner the better."

"It'll be chaotic when Crews attacks the base camp—we'll have plenty of opportunity to slip away with the weapon, once you tell me if it's worth taking. I've picked at least eight potential escape routes—" The crickets stopped chirping and Rakkim grabbed Leo, hustled him into the car. Drove off at full acceleration, throwing up gravel from the tires as they shot down the road, lights off. Rakkim steered by starlight, as relieved as Leo to be away from the place, away from Crews.

Leo waited in vain for the headlights to come on. "Can you really see in the dark?"

"It's not dark."

"That must be useful." Leo cleared his throat. "FYI, we won't need to take the weapon when we escape, I can already tell you that."

"I thought that was the whole idea. Take the weapon from the Colonel so he doesn't destabilize the Belt or use it against the republic . . . maybe even turn it into a tool for reunification, show people in both countries that we can cooperate . . . *What?*"

"That *is* the idea, it's just that once I get my hands on . . ." Leo's grin threatened to crack his face. "How big did Mr. Moseby say the canister was?"

"He didn't . . . not exactly. He said one man could carry it, that's all."

"See, a canister that small, it can't have a full-size weapons system in it. It's got to be almost pure data—computer cores, thumb loads, maybe even hard copy. Whatever was state-of-the-art information storage back in the old days. Point is, it's all *data*." Leo happily chattered on now, unable to contain himself. "Information . . . data, that's my business."

"We'll *still* need the downloads and whatever—"

"We won't need a thing. When Crews's army attacks, I'll wipe the cores clean and we'll get away, just like you said. What we leave behind will be useless, but it will look like we didn't get anything either." Leo grinned again. "But we'll have *everything*. All of it." He tapped the side of his head. "Right here."

"You have a photographic memory?"

"Don't insult me. Memory only works if you've actually *seen* the data, experienced it in some way. That would take months and we only have, what . . . a few hours? Memory . . ." Leo shook his head, giddy. "Oh, I'm *way* beyond that."

"Before we left"—Rakkim checked the rearview—"Sarah said you had been modified."

"I prefer the term *maximized*." Leo held up his hands. "My fingernails are permeated with organic silicone, converting them into ion traps. Just a little genetic manipulation, plus some nanotechnology. It's my dad's design, although he didn't do the work himself. He's more of a theoretician . . ." He saw Rakkim's expression. "It means I can access any data-storage system there is with a near-instantaneous transmission rate. By *touch*. And brainpower, of course. That's the most important component. Without brainpower . . . You have no idea what I'm talking about, do you?"

"You're some kind of biocomputer."

Leo shook his head. "*You're* a biocomputer. I'm a quantum computer." He wriggled his fingers. "With these, I don't need to memorize what's in the cylinder. I can download the whole thing while you're singing 'Onward Christian Soldiers.'"

Rakkim drove for another mile before he said anything. "Have you ever done this before? Downloaded massive amounts of data with just . . . your fingertips?"

"I've been *tested*."

"But you've never done it under field conditions?"

Leo stared out the windshield into the darkness, pouting. "My maximization wasn't completed until recently. I . . . I have total faith in myself."

Still no headlights in the rearview. "I do too, kid."

"Really?" Leo rocked happily in his seat. "Most people only use five percent of their brains. *I'm* what happens when you use the other ninety-five. That doesn't usually make the five-percenters happy." He stretched his long legs. "This canister Mr. Moseby found . . . what's it made of?"

"Graphite."

"No metallic signature that way, pretty standard stuff." Leo sniffed. "Any markings on the outside? Symbols or warning—"

"No. Just a serial number or something."

"What's the number?"

"Ah . . . Seventy-two-slash-one-oh-six."

"You're *sure*?"

"What's wrong?"

Leo let his head flop back. "Wow. They actually *did* it."

"Did what?"

"Seventy-two-slash-one-oh-six isn't a serial number. It's the atomic structure of hafnium. Seventy-two protons. One hundred six neutrons. Those old-time scientists . . . you have to give them credit. So far beyond us, in some ways. Pure research, a culture of intellectual inquiry and unlimited budgets . . . must have been nice." Leo rubbed his nose, sniffed. "It wasn't even supposed to be possible. Oh, maybe in a purely theoretical sense, of course, but not—"

"Is it some kind of a bomb?" said Rakkim. "Like a hydrogen bomb or a neutron bomb?"

"No . . . not like that." Leo giggled. "Hafnium bomb . . . it's *much* more powerful."

CHAPTER 40

Late morning and the camp rippled with activity, an increased focus Rakkim hadn't seen before. Nothing definite, but the squad of troops moving from their tents to a nearby staging area had an extra kick to their step, trucks rumbled past more often than usual, and soldiers sat around outside the mess hall cleaning weapons that were already maintained. Rakkim wasn't the only one who noticed. The miners leaned against their machines, bleary-eyed and covered in dust, watching the proceedings.

"What's happening?" Rakkim asked a sergeant barreling past.

The sergeant barely glanced at Rakkim and Leo, both of them in civilian work clothes, and walked on.

"Does the Colonel know we're here?" said Leo.

"I sent word." Rakkim spotted Baby on horseback at the edge of camp, ran toward her, waving his hands to catch her attention. She must have seen him, because she turned her horse, a huge white stallion, and trotted over, her movements graceful, perfectly attuned to the stride of the horse.

"There you are, handsome," said Baby, tall in the saddle, the reins in one hand as she patted the horse's neck with the other. The sun turned her blond hair bronze. Her boots creaked in the stirrups. "Colonel's looking for you."

"What's going on, Baby?" said Rakkim.

"Oh, trouble somewhere in the kingdom, like always," said Baby. "Never a dull moment. Bores me to tears, if you want to know, but the Colonel's sending off some boys to settle things down." She nodded at Leo. "Who's this big fellah?"

"I'm Leo, ma'am," said Leo, stepping away from the horse. Probably allergic.

"Nice to—" Baby pressed a finger to her earpiece, listening. "I'm talking to him right now, sweetie." She looked down at Rakkim. "Colonel says to meet him at the east lookout and double-time it." She patted the horse's back behind the saddle. "I could give one of you a ride, but I'd be hard-pressed to choose." She spurred the horse, dirt kicking up around them.

"Wow," said Leo. "That's the most beautiful girl I ever saw . . . except for Leanne."

They found the Colonel peering through binoculars down the east access road. A half-dozen guards stood nearby, assault rifles tracking Rakkim and Leo as they approached.

The Colonel turned, beckoned them closer.

"Colonel, this is Leo—smartest man you'll ever meet, just ask him," said Rakkim. "Leo's the Ident tech wiz that the Russians hired to check out your weapon."

"You make me feel old, son," said the Colonel. "You started shaving yet?" He glanced at Rakkim. "Still haven't found the weapon. Still haven't decided if I'm going to share it with the Russians when I do."

"Come on, Colonel, you didn't win all those battles by overthinking every decision," said Rakkim. "You're going to do what your instincts tell you, and most of the time, you're going to be right."

"You're just saying that because I took a liking to you," said the Colonel, bright blue eyes sparkling in the morning light. "So did Baby, and I usually trust her judgment. Only thing that prevented me from throwing in with you that first night was I can't abide a man who betrays his country, even the republic." His eyes crinkled. "Turns out you're not a traitor."

They turned and watched a couple of loaded troop transports roll past, the Colonel's expression serious for a moment before his good humor returned.

"You *told* me you had betrayed your Fedayeen oath when the Russians made you a large enough offer. Nothing special, just another tough guy gone outlaw." The Colonel wagged a finger. "Not so."

"Heck, Colonel, if you only deal with honest men, you're going to be awfully lonely."

"Let's just say I like to know who walks in my house. So I had some folks do a full workup on you." The Colonel tugged at one of his sideburns. "Turns out you're not just another outlaw, you're Rakkim Epps. Orphaned at nine, raised by Redbeard himself, a Fedayeen shadow warrior until you abandoned your calling to consort with lowlifes in the Zone. *Damn,* you must have been a disappointment to Redbeard, 'cause I know it would tear me up to see a pup I raised to hunt end up with his snout in garbage." He seemed amused. "I put a hacker on you, real smart lady in Columbia City—she dug up your true background." He inclined his head toward Rakkim. "It seems sometimes one *can* find a needle in a haystack."

"You reach into a haystack, be careful you don't draw blood," said Rakkim.

"You've been playing a role since you were a child," said the Colonel. "You're not a renegade, and you're no Muslim either. You're a *patriot*, a Russian sleeper agent." He gently turned Rakkim's wrist, touched the crucifix burned into his palm. "Born-again Christian too. I wondered about that the first time we shook hands."

Rakkim felt the breeze off the mountain wash over him, felt clean to the bone, pleased. Spider had done his job, planted the false background so deep that only another top hacker could find it. Best way to make certain the lie would be believed.

"Nine years old and set out on the street," said the Colonel, shaking his head. "Hell's bells, boy, you're the deepest sleeper I ever heard of. Gave up your childhood for Mother Russia."

"Wasn't like I had a choice." Rakkim shrugged. Offered his hand. "We have a deal?"

The Colonel shook his hand. "Screw the Chinese."

"Screw the Chinese," said Rakkim. "How did you find out about me?"

"Evidently there's some kind of back door at a KGB database that this little gal in Columbia City discovered. She only found it because of some new wormware developed last year."

"Lucky girl," said Rakkim.

"God*damn*, the boys in Moscow must have been proud of you." The Colonel clapped Rakkim on the back. "I'd love to know what it was like growing up with Redbeard. Most of them running the show in the republic are useless as tits on a bull, useless as our own politicians, but Redbeard . . . he seemed like a real man."

"Redbeard didn't cut slack, Colonel, not for himself or anybody else, but the things I learned from him saved my life more often than I can count. You and Redbeard . . . I think you would have liked each other."

"I take that as a high compliment." The Colonel leaned forward. "Did he ever have any idea . . . ever get a hint of who you really were?"

Rakkim shook his head. "Not that there weren't times I wanted to tell him."

"Probably just as well. Head of State Security nursing a Russian spy to his bosom, teaching him all his tricks . . . might have been too much to bear."

"We all make mistakes."

"That we do." The Colonel looked down the road below. "I even made a few myself."

"You waiting for something, Colonel?"

The Colonel kept his face turned away. "Got word yesterday of some bandit activity in Hattiesburg and Marston, ugly business. Last night I sent Alpha Company to bolster the local defense units. That left me with just two companies, which is a little shorthanded, but things have been quiet. Until now." He turned to Rakkim. "You ever hear of a gang of trash called the End-Times Army?"

"Some kind of hopped-up maniacs, right?"

"That's them. Run by a fellow called Crews. Calls himself a preacher"—the Colonel spit—"but him and me must be reading a different Bible. He's outside my authority, but I've been meaning to pay him a visit anyway, and clean out the whole nest. Couple hours ago I got a report of End-Timers around here. Nothing credible. Rumor mostly. Still, it made me wonder if the attacks around Hattiesburg and Marston were just feints to get me to split my force." He smiled but there was no humor in it. "Maybe this Crews figured he'd get to me before I got to him. Always somebody wants to find out if the old dog still has teeth."

"Might not be you Crews is after," said Rakkim. "Maybe he wondered what you were digging for these last few months."

The Colonel looked into his eyes. "Hard to keep a secret, isn't it?"

Rakkim looked away from the path up the mountain, focused on the treeline in the distance. You could hide a whole division there and no one would know. Or there could just be trees. Hard to imagine that Malcolm Crews could have gotten his men into position so quickly. *They'll do whatever I tell them to do,* that's what Crews had said last night, already knowing that the Colonel had divided his forces. He had agreed to attack in four days, on the night of the new moon, but Crews had made other plans, because either he didn't trust Rakkim or he didn't trust his own men. Either way, they were on Crews's timetable now. Not bad for an English professor. Rakkim had never intended for Crews to be a threat to the Colonel's forces, never thought that Crews had that sizable a force—he just needed a diversion so that he and Leo could escape with the weapon and take Moseby with them.

"Might be time to send up that Chinese bird," said Rakkim. "Thermal imaging should be able to tell you what you're up against, and there's more than enough firepower in the Monsoon—"

"Chopper's down for maintenance. Temperamental piece of shit." The Colonel touched his ear, listened. "On my way." He looked at Rakkim and Leo. "Come on, boys, let's see what Moseby found in the lake."

The three of them piled into a nearby jeep. The Colonel raced up the mountain road, skidding on gravel, leaning on the horn to blast laggards out of the way.

Leo hung on with both hands, eyes squeezed shut.

"The information you must have fed to your people when you lived with Redbeard—" The Colonel banged against Rakkim as he hit the brakes, sent the jeep into a controlled spin around a switchback. "When you were in the Fedayeen. Why did the Russians want you to give up your commission?"

"They didn't. I decided to be my own man."

"Dangerous decision." The Colonel bounced off the seat as they hit a pothole too fast. "But I expect they weren't too surprised. You got the look of a man who has to dance to his own tune."

"You fortifying the eastern slope in case you're attacked, Colonel?"

"It's the easiest approach. Got to figure that's the way Crews's men would come. From what I hear, his men are poorly trained . . . it's the dope that gives them courage. Dope and some crazy-ass snake-handling mumbo-jumbo."

"Don't neglect the southern route either," said Rakkim.

"Too rugged," said the Colonel. "I've got to place my forces at the most likely choke points."

"I studied every engagement you ever fought, Colonel. Battle of Big Pines, the rest of the Belt commanders concentrated their men at the shallows of the river, where it was easiest to cross. You—" Rakkim almost flew out of his seat as the Colonel accelerated. "*You* sent your men downstream, where the river was deepest, and fastest, and enough of them survived the crossing to circle behind the Second Army of the Republic. You surprised them . . . then annihilated them." He hung on. "I'm just saying, maybe I'm not the only one who studied your strategy."

The Colonel drove on, his knuckles white from gripping the steering wheel. He touched his earlobe. "I want you to move four squads along the southern approach. Heavy machine guns . . . Do it, Lester. God*damnit*, Lester, you disobey another one of my orders, I'll shoot you myself."

Another ten minutes and the Colonel parked outside the entrance to one of the many tunnels into the mountain. He got out, saluted the guards inside the entrance, and kept walking. Rakkim and Leo followed. The tunnel was barely lit, rock debris everywhere. It smelled like sweat and engine grease.

"Hang *on*," said Leo, voice reedy as he struggled to keep up.

Neither the Colonel nor Rakkim slowed his pace.

Leo was gasping for breath when he finally caught up with them a hundred yards later, the two of them waiting for him outside a cleft in the rock. He clung to the wall, bent over. "I . . . I'm claustrophobic," he wheezed, shaking his head.

Rakkim grabbed Leo by the hair, dragged him into the opening.

"Intellectuals," snorted the Colonel as Leo banged his head against a rock outcropping. "Always a reason they can't do something. The porridge is too hot, the porridge is too cold, but it's *never* just right."

Rakkim dropped Leo on the other side. "Careful, Colonel, he'll give you some fancy math problem, then laugh at you when you can't solve it in your head."

"I wouldn't waste my time," said Leo, scrambling after them. "Might as well try to teach a chimp particle physics." The kid did okay. He kept up, even though he'd put his shirttail over his mouth, trying to cut down on the dust they were breathing.

It took longer than Rakkim anticipated to get there, the barely lit tunnel gradually sloping, down, down, down, until even he found himself slowing his steps, feeling the weight of the mountain closing in on them. The Colonel felt it too.

"Almost . . . almost there," said the Colonel, his voice too loud.

They rounded the bend and there it was . . . the lake. Even with the floodlights spread along the rocky shore, the surface was the color of an oil slick. They approached cautiously, stood blinking as they looked out.

"This is what the hour before creation must have been like," Rakkim said quietly. "Darkness moved across the face of the water . . ." He took in the oxygen bottles littering the shore, the single thermal blanket. "You let him dive alone?"

"Moseby insisted," said the Colonel, not taking his eyes off the black lake. "I told him to wait . . . he's been pushing himself for days and—"

"I see something." Leo wiped his nose. Pointed.

Rakkim saw a light deep below the surface, coming closer . . . brighter now.

A diver burst out of the water, sent spray into the air. He paddled toward shore, almost invisible in a full black dry suit and black dive hood. Only the flickering halogen penlights on either side of his face mask made his position clear. The diver paddled crookedly, exhausted, his gloved hands barely clearing the water. He left a wake . . . he was towing something.

Rakkim splashed into the shallows, immediately felt his legs go numb from the cold. He stayed there, took another step. "Moseby!"

Moseby turned his head awkwardly, barely able to stay afloat.

"This way!" shouted Rakkim, teeth chattering as he moved to deeper water. "Here!"

Moseby swam toward him, arms flopping as he kicked himself forward.

Rakkim reached for him, dragged him closer; then he fell backward, head underwater for just an instant, but his ears felt like they were going to burst from the cold. He scrambled up, pulled Moseby partway onto the shore, slipped on the wet rocks. He tore off Moseby's face mask. "J-John . . ." he gasped, shivering. "It's . . . it's okay now."

His eyes bright red from exploded capillaries, Moseby tried to speak but couldn't. He just lay there, trembling like a hooked fish.

Leo ran over, looked down at both of them, unsure what to do.

The Colonel bent down, grabbed Rakkim and Moseby by the collar, and pulled them farther up onto the stones, then sat down beside them. The sound of their breathing echoed off the rocky cavern. Echoed. Echoed.

Rakkim raised himself up and stared at the gray graphite canister resting along the shoreline, "72/106" stenciled on the side. He was looking at both the past and the future, and it gave him no pleasure. None at all.

CHAPTER 41

Rakkim hit the front door with his shoulder and carried Moseby inside.

The Colonel and Leo followed him in, the Colonel hefting the graphite cylinder. A dozen guards took up positions outside the Colonel's house, squinting in the midafternoon sun.

Rakkim gently laid Moseby onto the sofa. Worked the dry suit off him, Moseby shivering uncontrollably, eyes fluttering and unresponsive, his lips blue. Water dripped off his short hair, beaded along his chest—diving that far underground had increased the pressure exponentially, far beyond the limits of the suit, allowing the frigid waters of the lake to seep in.

The Colonel put the canister on the floor, Leo elbowing him aside to get at it. The canister was smaller than Rakkim thought it would be, maybe four feet long, and twice the diameter of Moseby's oxygen tank. Sixty, seventy pounds tops.

Rakkim rubbed Moseby's bare arms, his legs, the skin cold and rubbery—he cursed the man for his stubbornness and bravado. There was a deep tear along the back of the suit where he had brushed up against something sharp. Moseby *had* to have known the suit was compromised, yet he had stayed down in the icy depths, feeling the numbness spread until he could barely breathe. It must have been the Colonel's decision to split his troops that had forced Moseby to continue—he had realized the danger they were in and gone after the canister without waiting for Rakkim.

"Go on about your business," said Baby, bustling in with fresh thermal blankets, ignoring Moseby's nakedness. "Shoo, Rikki." She slipped heat socks onto Moseby's feet, patted his bare thigh before covering him with a thermal blanket. "I've got water boiling for tea," she said to Moseby, as though he could hear. "You're going to be just fine, John."

Moseby jerked, teeth chattering.

"I've seen Baby just about raise the dead, boys," said the Colonel.

There was nothing Rakkim could do for Moseby. He turned away, watched as Leo studied the canister, wincing as the kid tapped it with his knuckle.

"That thing's safe to have here, isn't it?" The Colonel rested his hands on his hips. "Got to say it looks kind of disappointing after all the trouble we went through to find it."

"It's not the package, it's the toy inside that counts." Leo pressed his fingertips against a small panel at the end of the cylinder, eyes closed, intent as a safecracker.

"What's he up to now?" said the Colonel.

"No idea." Rakkim lied. Leo said he could directly access computers using the natural conductivity of his skin, plus those genetic maximizers . . . an epidural interface, he had called it, which sounded like something Sarah had gotten when Michael was born. He smiled at the memory. The first time he held Michael, he'd started crying. Sarah had laughed, exhausted, said if he felt that way, they could always trade Michael in for a baby more to his liking.

The Colonel walked over to the sofa, watched as Baby slid heat packs under Moseby's covers.

Baby looked up at him. Her hair curled around her face, her expression as angry as it was tender. "I hope whatever you boys got there is worth practically killing this poor man." She placed her slim white hand on Moseby's forehead.

The Colonel touched the communicator on his earlobe. "Son of a *bitch*." He started pacing. "Tell the men to get ready because we're sure as shit going to get hit tonight. Any updates from the scouts?" He checked his ivory-handled pistols, slid them back into their holsters. "Send out another team and then set the perimeter for maximum sensitivity, thermal as well as motion detection. I don't care if we get false readings, I'd rather be wrong than surprised." He turned off the earpiece with another touch.

"I'm armed and dangerous, sweetie, so you go do what you have to," said Baby, still smoothing Moseby's hair. The top two buttons of her blouse had come undone and Rakkim could see a tiny birthmark between her breasts. She looked up and caught him staring. It didn't seem to bother her.

"You should go to the bunker, Baby," said the Colonel.

"What kind of Christian would I be if I did that? God hates a coward. You *scoot* now."

"What's happening?" Rakkim asked the Colonel.

"I hoped Alpha Company might get back before morning, but the bridge over the Hatchie was dynamited a few hours ago. Next crossing is forty miles of bad road in the wrong direction, so no reinforcements until tomorrow. Looks like we're on our own." The Colonel's expression turned wistful. "Wish that Moseby had found that canister a few days sooner. Lord knows what's inside that thing—I've heard stories about black-ice projects on impenetrable force fields and sound waves that throw men into a panic. Be nice to have something like that right about now." He straightened his shoulders. "Guess we'll have to kick ass the old-fashioned way."

"Old-fashioned works just fine for me," Baby said softly.

The Colonel kissed her. He glanced at Leo bent over the canister and shook his head. The door closed after him.

Through the window, Rakkim saw the Colonel give orders to the guards outside. He got down beside Leo. "Can I help?"

"Yeah, try not making me laugh with dumb questions," said Leo, eyes half closed. "It's distracting."

Rakkim stayed on the floor, watching Baby hold Moseby's hand. He touched his own ear link. The Colonel's officers used a dedicated frequency, but their links had lousy security filters compared to the Swiss link he had.

"... this is Tiger Six, I want your men dug in along the west ridge," said the Colonel, "and tell the miners to soldier up. We're going to need every one of them."

"Affirmative."

"Scout team D missed their check-in . . ."

Rakkim drifted along on the com links, heard nervousness among the buzzing voices. Nothing worse for a soldier than being hunkered down, waiting to be attacked. No idea where the assault would be launched, or how many of the enemy there were. The young ones pretended to be tough, cursing and watching their comrades out of the corner of their eye, looking for a reflection of their own fear. Old warriors dozed before a coming battle, or took a last, comfortable crap.

"There we go," said Leo, grinning, eyes wide. His fingers danced over the buttons on the end of the canister, and there was a hissing sound as if pressure was being released. He unscrewed the top as easy as if it were a pop bottle.

Rakkim leaned in closer.

Leo reached into the cylinder, pulled out a clear, insulated pack filled with computer cores. He set them carefully down, reached farther in. Finally tipped the cylinder so that a long, rectangular box slid onto the floor with a thunk. Dinged the wood floor, it was so heavy. The box was sealed with lead and stenciled with various official Defense Department seals and the same number marked on the outside of the canister: 72/106. Leo looked at the box and went back to the computer cores.

"That's it?" said Baby.

Leo opened the insulated pack, gently pulled out the first computer core. He placed his fingers on the download inputs and closed his eyes. He breathed heavily now, laboring at something. His eyes darted back and forth under his closed lids.

"Leo?" said Rakkim.

Leo sat frozen, head twisted at an odd angle, barely breathing now.

"Something wrong with him?" said Baby. "Looks like he's thrown a fit."

"He's just . . . thinking," said Rakkim.

"How long is he going to sit there thinking?" said Baby.

Rakkim shook his head.

"I can't tell if he's smart or slow," said Baby. "Seems to me if the Russians want to pay billions of dollars for that weapon thing, they could have hired somebody who does more than sit there and drool."

Ten minutes later, Leo opened his eyes. Picked up another computer core.

"You want to talk?" said Rakkim.

Leo moved his jaw a few times. Probably grinding his teeth while he was . . . gone.

"Is it working?" Rakkim shook him. "Leo?"

Leo stared at him.

"Leo! Are you in?"

Leo slowly nodded. "Tenth . . . tenth-gen security hash logarithm, but I am in . . . in like sin," he whispered. "Massive gamma radiation . . . far beyond anything the Tether program anticipated," he said, voice trailing off. He was in there somewhere, but not anyplace Rakkim could reach.

Rakkim watched him go through five more of the cores, no longer responding to questions from Rakkim or Baby. Not responding to anything outside the interface. It was getting dark now, the ear-link chatter more frequent.

"Go on, Rikki," said Baby. "I can tell when a man's restless. Can't blame you either. Leo's a sweet boy and all, but I sure don't see him doing any honest work."

Rakkim got up and bent down beside Moseby, placed a hand on his cheek. "Hey, John, how are you doing?"

Moseby didn't respond but his breathing held steady and his skin was warmer.

"Go shoot somebody, handsome, I got things under control here," said Baby. "Go. I been taking care of sick men my whole life."

Rakkim said good-bye to Leo, but got no response.

Bartholomew finished his morning prayers, carefully rolled his prayer rug, and placed it in his cubby. His position had been slightly off during his devotions, his spine not perfectly straight. He begged Allah to forgive such sloppiness. The most minute error could have catastrophic consequences, that was both his professional and personal creed.

Through the window of his office, he could see Frank, his personal secretary, waiting patiently for him to compose himself before knocking. A slender, beardless modern with a too-ready laugh, Frank had been a difficult hire. Most of the other inspectors refused to work with moderns, viewing that as un-Islamic and unclean. *Let him go to work making pornography or serving beer in the Zone,* his colleague Nicolas had said after they finished the interview. It had been two years since Bartholomew hired the modern. Two years and Nicolas still refused to go to mosque with him, but Bartholomew knew what he was doing.

When an opening in the elite security detail was announced, Bartholomew was the one who got the promotion. He was not so arrogant as to believe his new duties were solely the result of his superior test scores and performance evaluations, though he ranked in the upper 1 percent of certified aircraft inspectors. The president surrounded himself with moderate Muslims, moderates not just in dress or demeanor, but in behavior

as well. Hiring Frank was considered a clear sign of Bartholomew's char-
ity and tolerance; he was just the sort of professional the presidential staff
trusted and wished to encourage.

Bartholomew checked his reflection in the glass. He smoothed his hair.
Picked a minute spot of lint off the lapel of his black suit. The bows in his
knotted shoelaces were the exact same size and length. He finally beckoned to Frank, acknowledged the gratitude in the modern's eager face.

Come the change Bartholomew would have the apostate beheaded.

The Colonel's base camp was perched on a scraggly, rocky plateau mid-
way up the mountain. It should have been easy to defend except there
were too many access points from the valley below—two-lane logging
roads from the north, a series of gravel paths from the south, and dozens
of trails cut through the surrounding trees along the western perimeter.
While a mechanized force would be limited to attacking from the north,
lightly armed men like Crews's End-Timers could assault the camp from
the south and east as well. Holding the high ground was still an advantage,
but if the End-Timers were willing to ignore their mounting casualties and
keep coming . . .

Rakkim imagined skeleton men drifting through the woods as he
passed lines of empty tents, hurrying to where he had parked his car after
coming back from Stuckey's last night. Four-wheel-drive trucks with
heavy machine guns mounted on back roared past, some so close he had
to dive for cover. By the time he got to the motor pool he was covered in
dust and the sun was setting. In New Detroit and Philadelphia, the
muezzin would be calling the faithful to prayer, the man's strong voice
undulating in the crisp air. Instead of bowing to pray, Rakkim was nodding to a young soldier guarding the vehicles. He slid under his car and
pulled his rifle from a hidden compartment. Grabbed a handful of
ammo clips too, and stuffed them in his pocket. He probably wouldn't
have gone to mosque anyway.

Scout team D . . . still hasn't checked in.

Disperse . . . ammo, said the Colonel. . . . *don't want . . . lucky round . . .
set it off.*

Rakkim cradled the weapon, a sleek sniper rifle made by a gunsmith in

Greenville, the next town over—simple, rugged, and accurate. "You seen the Colonel?" Rakkim asked the soldier.

The soldier pointed.

Rakkim found the Colonel and Gravenholtz striding down a gravel path, the Colonel pointing out gun emplacements and natural cover to the redhead.

Gravenholtz eyed Rakkim's rifle. "This ain't your fight."

"Fight?" Rakkim fell in beside them. "I thought we were hunting turkeys for Thanksgiving dinner."

In twilight now, the Colonel seemed determined to walk the whole line, stopping every few minutes to talk to the men, reminding them to stay alert and not waste ammunition, and promising that God was watching over them. The same suggestions and assurances that good commanders had offered their men since time began.

. . . oil pressure still not where it should be, and the rotors are noisy.

The Colonel pressed his ear link. "I don't care *what* the oil pressure is, Royce, you get that damned bird airborne."

Tiger 6, still no word from scout team D.

Gravenholtz threw a light punch at Rakkim's jaw, but he caught the redhead's fist and pushed it aside. "Maybe when this is over, you and me can have some fun," said Gravenholtz, embarrassed at being thrown off balance. "Ex-Fedayeen, you must have *some* skills. Unless they kicked you out for cowardice or queerity."

"Queerity?" Rakkim laughed. "You making up words now, Lester?"

"This isn't the time for school-yard nonsense," chided the Colonel. "Lester, make sure your men have secured the northern access points. I want them dug in along the logging roads in case—"

"My boys don't take to scraping in the dirt, sir." Gravenholtz sucked at a tooth.

"That's an order, Lester," said the Colonel.

Gravenholtz tugged at a lock of red hair. Glowered at Rakkim. "How about you and me make a date for when the fireworks are over."

"No queerity, Lester," said Rakkim. "You'd be marching crooked for a month."

Gravenholtz stalked off.

"I wish you wouldn't provoke him," said the Colonel. "I've got enough trouble keeping him in line. His men are even worse—they've been through hell and back so often they think they're fireproof. No fear. No discipline. If we get through this night, I'm going to disband them, send them back to whatever swamp they call home."

"They may not go without—"

"Baby?" The Colonel turned away from Rakkim. "You doing okay?"

Don't you worry about me. I'm just tending to John Moseby and watching Leo play with his toys.

"Love you, Baby." The Colonel turned to Rakkim. "I'm going to the western perimeter; you're welcome to come."

"I thought you'd never ask," said Rakkim.

"I'd like to hear more about Redbeard," said the Colonel as they strolled along, the Colonel realizing that the troops were watching him for any sign of panic. "Did he really die of a heart attack, or was he helped along by his enemies?"

"It was a heart attack. If he had been murdered, he wouldn't have any enemies left. I would have seen to that."

CHAPTER 42

Tiger 6! The cry came from a dozen voices over the ear link, a squawking cacophony as gunshots erupted from all sides of the camp. *Tiger 6, we got action . . . multiple hits . . . everywhere . . . sector B reporting heavy activity . . . overrunning . . . need men . . .*

"Baby," said the Colonel, "get in the bunker *now.*"

. . . not afraid, darlin' . . . you do what you have to . . .

Rakkim and the Colonel scuttled along the west ridge, crouched over, hearing the crack of small-arms fire in the distance. The wind kicked up as the temperature dropped; chilled by their own sweat, they slipped through the scrub and took up positions with a commanding view of the dozens of access trails running up the slope.

The Colonel sat with his back against a rock, flipped open a palm display of the battlefield, at least that part with perimeter sensors. The northern and southern sectors had moderate activity, but the treeline fronting the steep, western approach to the camp was a mass of red dots. Crews's main force was heading right toward the Colonel; scores of fighters passed through the sensor array, immediately replaced by others charging up the slope. Rakkim had suggested that Crews launch a limited attack, fifty or sixty men, but this was a full-out assault involving hundreds of End-Timers, more men than Rakkim even thought Crews had under his command.

. . . movement northeast perimeter . . . fire for effect . . . shit, shit, shit . . .

Rakkim eased himself flat against the ground, arms supported by a rise of dirt, the sniper rifle peeking out between the rocks. Machine-gun fire bombarded the perimeter. Wasteful. The seduction of raw firepower in the darkness, spray and pray. Rakkim kept both eyes open as he looked through the scope of the sniper rifle, saw men moving through the brush below, their movements jerky in the darkness, wired up on bathtub crank and death. He waited . . . finally saw a skeleton man emerge, the white bones stark in the night as he gesticulated at his men. Rakkim put a single shot through his mouth, the back of his head exploding.

Rakkim turned, hearing a faint laugh . . . but there was no one except the Colonel and it wasn't his laugh.

"Bulldog Two, lay down suppressing fire at a sixty-degree arc along the clearcut," the Colonel said evenly. "Mustang Three, maintain your position . . ."

Rakkim shot an End-Timer with a necklace of dolls' heads through the throat, the man standing there with a look of surprise before he collapsed.

The Colonel glanced at Rakkim, then back at the palm display. "Eagle Two, you got that chopper ready? We could use those Gatlings. Shitbirds are stacked up along the perimeter."

. . . almost there . . .

"Almost my ass," said the Colonel. "You get that thing airborne."

Rakkim shot another End-Timer. Another. Another. Breathe and fire, breathe and fire. The living stepped over the dead and kept coming.

"You want a night scope for that sniper rifle?" the Colonel asked Rakkim.

"No thanks." Rakkim took down another skeleton man. "Things are going to be lit up soon, and night scopes will be worse than useless. I'll stick with the eyes God gave me."

"Thought Fedayeen got special eyes from corpses," said the Colonel. "Implants or something so you can see like an alley cat in the dark."

"When I was a boy they told us Christians liked the taste of pork so much they fucked pigs every chance they got," said Rakkim. "I grew up, though, and learned better."

The Colonel grinned, then looked over as the Monsoon 4 lifted off, he and Rakkim shielding their eyes from the dust it kicked up. *"That's* better . . ." His face fell as the chopper set back down hard, bouncing on its skids. The Colonel talked over his com link to his other officers, trying to coordinate their actions.

Return fire from the End-Timers kicked up dirt around them now, pinged off the rocks. One of the colonel's men must have been hit, howling in pain. Rakkim scrambled to another position about twenty yards away.

. . . taking casualties . . .

. . . keep killing them, but . . . just keep . . . who are they?

The Colonel's men fired a barrage of mortar rounds, balls of fire erupting in the trees below. Rakkim blinked, kept shooting. Mortars were a lousy tactical trade-off—the blasts wouldn't deter fanatics like Crews's End-Timers, and anyone on the plateau wearing night goggles would be blind for minutes. He slapped in another magazine.

The Colonel moved nimbly over the rough terrain. "Never did talk to you about that Fedayeen prisoner. I felt bad that you had to be the one to put him out of his misery."

"He was ruined," said Rakkim, watching the underbrush beside the trails. "It was the only kindness I could give him."

"Right through the heart." The Colonel shook his head. "Happened so fast I didn't even see it. None of us did." The wind stirred the grass. "Red-beard must have been—"

. . . overrun here, Tiger Six, southwest perimeter . . . multiple penetrations . . .

"Fall back, son," the Colonel said gently, "gather your men and rally along the heavy-equipment depot. I'll send a reaction force."

Rakkim sighted on a skeleton man he remembered from Crews's church, ugly bastard waving a copperhead. Before he could get a shot off, the man ducked behind an outcropping of rock. Rakkim held the shot, finger curled on the trigger, sight centered on the last place the man had been.

. . . bandits in the wire!

Rakkim squeezed off a round as the skeleton man peeked from behind the rock, sprayed the boulder with pink.

Heavy gunfire roared from the heights around him as the End-Timers launched waves of attacks, dozens and dozens of them clawing their way straight up the slope. The machine guns on the heights opened up, swept back and forth across them, and the End-Timers broke and fell back, disappeared into the trees. Some of the Colonel's men started after them, but the Colonel quickly put a stop to that, said he'd shoot anyone dumb enough to leave the high ground.

. . . still looking for those reinforcements, Tiger Six.

The Colonel raced ahead of Rakkim, the two of them sprinting across the camp. The Colonel stopped three times to check on his men, offering encouragement, giving orders. At the heavy-equipment depot, they dove behind a twelve-ton earthmover, bullets slamming into the sides, then crawled to a gigantic bulldozer that the ranking officer had turned into a command post.

The southwest perimeter was a mess, men strung out without regard to the fields of fire. The lieutenant and both sergeants were dead. A big blond corporal with pimples and a belly wound had assumed command and was directing the holding action against the End-Timers. He had dug his men in, sent runners for ammunition; from the shelter of the bulldozer he directed return fire, and did his best to secure the perimeter before he bled to death. According to the Colonel's palm display, over a hundred of Crews's men were KIA, but at least that many were still putting pressure on the unit.

"Sorry . . . sorry, sir," gasped the corporal. "We keep killing 'em, but . . . they don't care."

"No cause for apology," said the Colonel, gently applying a pressure bandage to the corporal's wound. Blood continued to leak out the sides.

Rakkim set himself up behind the blade of the bulldozer, started taking down End-Timers who ventured into view. They seemed more cautious now, eager to hunker down and seek cover. Precisely the wrong tactic. Once they had cracked the Colonel's defense perimeter they should have launched an all-out assault. If the southwest perimeter collapsed, the whole camp was at risk of being overrun; the Colonel's remaining forces would suffer attack from inside and outside the line. Yet the End-Timers seemed listless and burned out, either awaiting orders from Crews or a resupply of bathtub meth.

I sent four of my boys to your house, Tiger Six, said Gravenholtz. *Figured the missus might need a little extra protection.*

"Appreciate it." The Colonel sent runners to redirect the troops to a drainage ditch, allowing them to put the End-Timers in a cross fire the next time they charged the yard. They waited, listening to the sound of scattered gunfire and war whoops, and the groaning of the wounded. "I know your secret, Rikki," said the Colonel.

"Yeah?"

"It's my secret too." The Colonel moved closer. "The secret of every warrior who ever lived. Battle is a frightening thing, a *terrible* thing, but once you develop a taste for it . . . nothing else comes close. Men like us weren't meant to die in bed."

"Well, I was kind of hoping," said Rakkim.

The Colonel rested his hands on his pistols. "You're a fine young killer, destined for better things. Don't look so glum . . . I meant it as a compliment."

"We winning, sir?" said the corporal.

"We're holding our own," said the Colonel. "Thanks to you."

An hour passed. Then another. It was almost 2 a.m., darker than ever.

Rakkim slid into the brush, listening; he worked his way deeper behind enemy lines, trying to see if the End-Timers were massing for another rush. They lay clustered under the shelter of the trees, must have been over a hundred of them, passing around jugs of moonshine or turpentine, waving their weapons. He got a glimpse of Crews, striding among the trees with reinforcements; the men cheered, fired into the air, and in the sudden flash of gunfire, he saw the shekel of Tyre on a chain around Crews's neck, the coin swinging back and forth with every step. Rakkim raised his rifle, but Crews stumbled as Rakkim squeezed the trigger, the skeleton man beside him knocked backward. Rakkim got off three more shots, but Crews cowered behind a tree as his men opened up on Rakkim's muzzle flash, leaves drifting down around them from their concentrated fire. Rakkim retreated back to the heavy-equipment yard.

"Crews is leading a force of around a hundred and fifty men," Rakkim said to the Colonel, "but they're more of a mob than a military unit. Give me a dozen men, Colonel, and we'll infiltrate the woods and circle behind them."

The Colonel shook his head. "Can't risk it."

"I just need—"

"I said *no*." The Colonel jabbed a finger at his palm display of the battlefield. "We're getting more pressure from the north and south. I may have to shorten our skirmish line here and send reinforcements to the other sectors." He glared at Rakkim. "And don't tell me what I would have done when I was younger. This is *now*. And I have to protect the weapon."

"COLONEL!" The amplified voice boomed out of the forest. "MALCOLM CREWS HERE. YOU GOT SOMETHING BELONGS TO ME, YOU HEATHEN FUCK."

The corporal raised himself up on one elbow, frightened. The Colonel eased him back down, then ordered another mortar barrage into the forest, trees exploding in all directions, until one by one the mortars fell silent, out of ammunition.

Crews's laughter echoed from the forest. A single shot boomed out, a 50-caliber rifle from the sound of it. *Boom. Boom. Boom . . .*

One of the eight-ton trucks used as a barricade exploded. Then another, as Crews's 50-caliber marksmen found their gas tanks, the heavy slugs cutting right through their light armor. Rakkim fired back at the muzzle flashes, silenced a couple of the shooters, but there were too many of them. A bulldozer lifted six inches off the ground as its tank went up. A front loader blew up, fell over on its side. Crews's men had the range now, set off two trucks to the rear of the Colonel's line of troops. A backhoe erupted next, sent flames high into the sky. They were surrounded by flames now, illuminated by the spreading fires, perfect targets. A few of the Colonel's men broke ranks, headed for the darkness, but were cut down before they went more than a few feet.

"TIME TO CALL IT A NIGHT, COLONEL. YOU AND YOUR MEN WILL BE WELL TREATED, I PROMISE. CROSS MY HEART." Crews couldn't keep from laughing.

Rakkim reloaded, feeling the heat on his face from the fires that burned around them. Gunfire cracked steadily into the heavy-equipment vehicles, trying to find the right spot. The Colonel finished giving orders over his ear link, told Baby he loved her. His mouth moved silently in prayer.

"COLONEL, LAST CHANCE TO GIVE IT UP BEFORE—"

The End-Timers charged from the forest, guns blazing, spraying everything in front of them, not even trying to aim. The front row were hit multiple times by the Colonel's men, but they kept coming, crawling forward, and there were so many more . . . Crews must have brought his whole army. Rakkim took them down, one shot, one kill, slapped in another magazine. The rest of the Colonel's troops held their ground, firing steadily, making the shots count. The Colonel took shelter behind the tread of the bulldozer, firing with both hands, unhurried and unafraid, a strange smile on his face.

The men the Colonel had positioned in the drainage ditch opened up, caught the End-Timers in a cross fire, and this time they went down screaming, faces contorted in the glare from the burning trucks.

"Damn!" The Colonel rolled over, his right hand bleeding, shot clean through.

More troops arrived from the rear, called in by the Colonel. They dug in along the overturned vehicles and returned fire.

The Colonel got down beside the wounded corporal, wincing as he held the boy's hand, blood running down his fingers. "Take it easy, you're going to be just fine."

"THOSE PIECES OF SILVER BELONG TO THE MAN WHO KNOWS HOW TO USE THEM, COLONEL."

"What's he talking about?" the Colonel asked Rakkim.

"I'm scared, sir." Every time the corporal took a breath the pressure bandage rippled.

"That's okay, I am too." The Colonel beamed. "You know the Twenty-third Psalm, don't you?"

The corporal nodded.

"'The Lord is my shepherd, I shall not want,'" recited the Colonel. "Come on, son, say it with me. 'He makes me lie down in green pastures. He leads me beside the still waters. He restores my soul.' That's it," he said as the corporal moved his lips. "'He leads me in the path of righteousness for his name's sake.'"

A group of End-Timers slipped through the cross fire, opened up on the bulldozer, bullets clanging against the heavy metal. Rakkim shot all four of them. Three fell but the fourth staggered forward, fire reflected in his eyes as he leveled his shotgun at the Colonel. Rakkim shot him in the head, and he fell face-first in the dirt.

The Colonel looked over at Rakkim, nodded in gratitude. "'Yea, though I walk through the valley . . .' Come on, son, don't leave me now, I need you here, come on . . . 'Yea, though I walk through the valley of the shadow of death, I will fear no evil, for you are with me . . .' Son?" His hand shook as he reached over and closed the corporal's eyes.

"I'm . . . I'm sorry," said Rakkim.

"What have you got to be sorry about?"

Rakkim started to answer, turned back to the battle. He heard bugles in the distance. The fires burned higher now, illuminating the whole line. He spotted Crews at the edge of the trees, a wraith in black, watching him. Bullets slammed into the bulldozer inches from Rakkim's head as he fired—Crews was lucky, or touched by God; the bullet merely sliced open his cheek.

Crews howled, stepped back into the woods. "YOU LIED TO ME, RIKKI."

"Rikki, what . . . ?" The Colonel held the pistol in both hands, dropped it. "I can't keep you straight in my mind," he said, trying to pick the gun up, his fingers slippery with blood. "One minute you're a Fedayeen traitor, the next you're a Russian patriot . . . now . . . now I don't know what to think."

Rakkim gently took the pistol away from him.

The bugle calls were louder, coming from the south and north too, the perimeter under attack from all sides. More gunfire, heavy machine guns, cheers and charges.

"BACK, BACK, BACK, YOU DUMB BASTARDS."

The End-Timers raced back into the woods. The only sound left was the crackling of the fires, and the wind whipping the flames higher.

"ROAST IN HELL, RIKKI."

"Who are *you*, Rikki?" whispered the Colonel.

Rakkim didn't have an answer.

Eagle Two, this is Woodpecker Five, we're good to go here, said Gravenholtz..

The Colonel looked confused. "What's Lester doing calling Royce?"

Alpha Company reporting for duty, Tiger Six. Cheers over the com link.

"Zebra Five?" The Colonel stood up. "How did you get here so fast?"

Locals ferried us across the river in every boat, barge, and skiff they had. We didn't even have to ask them. We're here, Tiger Six, and we've got them on the run.

The helicopter lifted off with a rush, flew low over the camp, hovered quietly overhead.

"Good job, Eagle Two," the Colonel said to Royce. "Light up the woods. Just be careful you don't hit Alpha Company."

The chopper banked gently, then zoomed back across the camp. Rakkim watched, saw where it was headed.

"Eagle Two! Where are you going?" the Colonel shouted into his throat mike. "Eagle Two! Get back here."

That's a hearty fuck you, Tiger Six, said Royce.

Rakkim was already gone, racing full out toward the Colonel's house.

CHAPTER 43

Eight of Gravenholtz's raiders ringed the Colonel's dimly lit house, lean, capable men with cigarettes bobbing in their mouths and rifles at the ready. The same hard core that had attacked the Tigards' farmhouse. The chopper idled nearby, whisper quiet, blades slowly turning, landing struts grazing the ground. Red and yellow landing lights spun erratically from the sides of the chopper, the colors sliding back and forth across the raiders as they waited. It reminded Rakkim of the dance floor of the Blue Moon back home, dancers swaying under the kaleidoscope. No music here, though, just the sound of distant gunfire and shouted commands as the Colonel's men continued to force back Crews's End-Times Army.

Rakkim approached obliquely, unhurried, keeping to the shadows. To anyone watching, the house never seemed to be his destination, yet he kept getting closer and closer. The raiders kept glancing at the helicopter, eager to escape. Regular troops occasionally raced past the house on the way to the front, looked over, and were waved on by the raiders. Rakkim never drew attention.

He spotted two uniformed bodies stuffed under the front porch, Baby's guards, who hadn't yielded their posts, or perhaps had been suspicious of the raiders' suddenly taking over. He wondered what the inside of the house looked like, if Moseby and Leo were piled in a corner or stuffed in the crawl space. Baby would be fine for now—Gravenholtz would keep her as insurance, in case the Colonel was tempted to mount a full-scale assault. It was obvious what had happened. The Colonel trusted Gravenholtz too much. The redhead knew about the black-ice weapon. Knew what it was worth. The Colonel had forgotten that for a good Christian to survive in this world, he needed to be able to think like a devil.

Woodpecker Five! What's going on at my house? said the Colonel.

Just taking care of business, drawled Gravenholtz.

I want Eagle Two put under arrest for insubordination and failure to obey, said the Colonel.

Rakkim heard laughter as Gravenholtz broke off his com link.

A team of soldiers approached the house, serious fuckers too, the Colonel's best, full-auto and fresh from the line, faces dirty, body armor scored with numerous hits. The lieutenant told the raiders to stand down and surrender their weapons, *now*, said the Colonel had ordered him to take control of the house and the chopper and the raiders too. The lieutenant's men squinted in the flashing lights from the chopper, looked like they just wanted Gravenholtz's team to give them an excuse to let loose.

A beefy raider leaned against the front porch, staring up at the stars, barely listening. Rakkim remembered him . . . had seen the man tear the wedding ring off Florence Tigard's finger that night. Nelson, that was his name. Gravenholtz had yelled at him, said, *Come on, Nelson, get your ass in the bird.* "Okay, Lieutenant, sir." Nelson insolently set his assault rifle down, waved at the other raiders to do the same. He smiled at the lieutenant, flicked his cigarette at him, but it landed short, scattered sparks across the officer's boots.

The chopper rose a few feet into the air, its spotlight pinning the lieutenant and his men. Then its Gatling machine guns opened up, and the soldiers looked like marionettes dancing on invisible strings, hit so hard and so fast they couldn't even fall over until the guns finally stopped firing.

Rakkim put three shots from the sniper rifle into the windscreen of the chopper, but it was armored acrylic, bulletproof. The spotlight wasn't.

Blind in the sudden darkness, Nelson and the other raiders stumbled around, tripping over the dead. The helicopter moved higher, its motion erratic as Royce, surprised by the attack, overcompensated.

Taking fire! shouted Royce.

Rakkim put his next bullet through Nelson's left eye. Shot four more men before the last three tumbled through the front door of the house. Rakkim raced to the porch, squatted beside Nelson's body. The chopper's thermal imaging system would be confused by the double image. For a few moments anyway.

Royce, what's going on out there? said Gravenholtz, using the man's name now, abandoning all com discipline.

Rakkim darted around the side, shot out the electrical relay, and the lights inside went out. As he rolled under the house, the chopper's guns blasted away, tearing up the ground and the siding, shattering a window.

Motherfuck, Royce, you trying to kill us all?

Somebody's making a move on your position, but I can't see for shit, said Royce. *You got some kind of radiation inside that's fucking up my sensors.*

I'll handle it, said Gravenholtz. *You just be ready to get us out of here.*

Rakkim heard footsteps approaching overhead, the floorboards creaking. A chair was knocked over in the darkness, and Gravenholtz cursed. He heard Baby's voice and others too, but not Leo or Moseby. Rakkim scooted farther under the house, the crawl space littered with mouse droppings, cobwebs veiling his face.

No visuals yet, said Royce. *He might be under the—*

Bullets tore through the floorboards, the raiders inside emptying their automatic weapons, then reloading and firing again and again. A couple of near misses but the only blood drawn was where a shard of wood cut his arm. He smelled gunpowder and heard coughing from inside the house, voices complaining they couldn't breathe and couldn't see, while Gravenholtz told them to shut the fuck up. Rakkim waited. Flashlight beams filtered through some of the gunshot holes in the floor, dust motes dancing in beams of golden light.

A boot stomped on a section of floor that had been chewed up and weakened by gunfire. Kept on stomping until the boot crashed through and was quickly withdrawn.

Rakkim bellied over toward the opening. He had left his sniper rifle outside—no room to use it under the house—but his knife was in his hand.

"Do it," said Gravenholtz.

Mumbles from above. A flashlight beam flickered across the broken floor. Another round of gunfire tore chunks out of the floorboards.

"Fucking *do* it," said Gravenholtz.

Rakkim lay in the darkness beside the hole, ears ringing, waiting. A spider crawled over his hand and continued on its way.

A flashlight jiggled in the opening, then a pistol. A man's head and shoulders followed.

"See anybody?" said Gravenholtz.

The flashlight swept under the house, its beam reflected back by sheets of cobwebs hanging from the old wooden supports. "No . . . not yet."

"Keep looking," said Gravenholtz.

Rakkim lunged out of the dusty shadows, jammed the knife into the side of the man's neck, and pushed forward. The man died in silence, any last words lost in a gush of blood. Rakkim took the flashlight from his hand, tossed it toward the front of the house. He tucked the pistol into his belt, even though it wouldn't be of any use against Gravenholtz, and he preferred the silent killing of a blade anyway. The personal touch it offered.

Groups of the Colonel's men are converging on the house, said Roycc. Machine-gun fire echoed in the distance. *Doing what I can to slow them down.*

"Well?" Gravenholtz demanded of the dead man. "Is somebody there or not?

Rakkim retreated into the deeper darkness. He had heard Baby's voice, surprised at how calm she sounded, but still nothing from Leo or Moseby. Gravenholtz would keep Baby alive to use as a bargaining chip, but he didn't need them.

"Hey?" Gravenholtz jerked the man back out of the opening. "I asked . . . *Fuck.*" The man's body hit the floor. No one fired his weapon. No one made a sound. Listening.

Their initial surprise and disorientation had passed; they were ready now. Rakkim heard fingers snap. Heard footsteps move cautiously toward where he had thrown the flashlight. The opening in the floor was dark now as the raiders gathered near the other end of the room, thinking he was using the flashlight to find his way.

As the raiders blasted the floor with gunfire, Rakkim slipped up through the hole, lost in the noise. He moved low across the floor, the air thick with gunsmoke, almost impenetrable in the faint light from their flashlights. Slumped in the middle of the room were two bodies . . . Leo and Moseby.

"Is he dead?" One of the raiders peered through the holes in the floor. "His light's off . . ."

All units not engaged, close in on my house, said the Colonel, his voice tired. *My wife is in there, so avoid hostilities. Repeat, my wife is in there.*

Royce, get your ass down here for dust-off, said Gravenholtz.

One of the raiders again unloaded his weapon into the floor.

Baby put her hands over her ears.

Through the security windows, Rakkim could see the flashing red and yellow position lights as the helicopter descended.

Gravenholtz grabbed Baby's wrist, pulled her toward the front door.

One of the raiders hoisted the canister from the underground lake onto his shoulder.

Rakkim started after Gravenholtz. He didn't make a sound, but Baby turned . . .

"Rikki!"

Gravenholtz whirled in the open doorway, raised his assault rifle one-handed, sprayed the rear of the room until he emptied the clip.

The helicopter touched down in the yard, tracer rounds from somewhere dinging off the canopy as the pilot struggled against the turbulence. Maintaining low ground clearance was the hardest part of any chopper pilot's job.

The raider carrying the canister raced past Gravenholtz and across the dirt, dove head-first into the passenger compartment of the chopper.

The chopper rose six feet off the ground, Gatlings spinning as it tore through the Colonel's men, then settled back down. The yellow and red position lights rotated slowly on either side of it, overlapping circles of concentric color.

Gravenholtz hesitated, one arm around Baby as he glared at Rakkim. "I should have known it would be you. I've been wanting to—"

"Lester, let's *go!*" shouted the raider from the passenger compartment.

Gravenholtz scampered toward the chopper, easily carrying Baby over his shoulder.

Cease fire! said the Colonel. *That's Baby!*

Rakkim caught up with Gravenholtz halfway to the chopper, lunged at him, but the redhead used Baby as a shield and Rakkim backed off. They capered around each other, Gravenholtz's free hand balled into a fist, while Rakkim circled, trying to find an opening.

Royce fired the machine guns in bursts, keeping the Colonel's men back as the chopper lurched and jerked.

Rakkim slashed Gravenholtz's shoulder, drew a cry of pain, but it was a light wound, Gravenholtz's second skin stopping anything but a direct thrust.

Gravenholtz shifted Baby to his other arm as he retreated closer to the chopper.

Rakkim came in again, blinded for a moment by dust kicked up by the chopper's rotors, and Gravenholtz swung at him. The blow barely grazed his jaw, but Rakkim felt his teeth rattle, his mouth filling with blood. A look of awful triumph distorted Gravenholtz's face in the swirling red and yellow lights.

"Lester!" bellowed the raider in the passenger compartment, his sweating face caught in the auxiliary lights of an approaching jeep. Bullets slammed into the compartment, and the raider screamed. The chopper pitched.

I said, cease fire! said the Colonel, visible now at the edge of the yard, waving his arms.

Gravenholtz snarled at Rakkim, hurried the last few feet, and threw Baby into the chopper. Put his hands on the edge of the open door and lifted himself up . . .

Rakkim launched himself as the chopper started to rise, holding on to the metal door frame with one hand, stabbing Gravenholtz again and again. Most of his thrusts were deflected by Gravenholtz's armored skin, but he heard the redhead groan at least twice.

"Lester, you in?" shouted the copilot.

Sprawled inside the chopper, Gravenholtz punched at Rakkim—he missed, but his fist shattered an unbreakable plastic jump seat. Rakkim again slashed at Gravenholtz, half severed his ear and the redhead screamed, rolled back inside. The chopper lurched about fifteen feet off the ground, rising slowly.

"Lester?" called the copilot. "Deeks, what's going on back there?"

Rakkim put his knife away. Standing on the chopper's skid, he held out a hand to Baby. "Come on."

"Baby!" the Colonel called from below, dirt swirling around him. "Let Rikki help you!"

"Come *on.*" Rakkim could see Gravenholtz struggling to get upright, blood pouring down his neck from his ruined ear. He beckoned to Baby. "Give me your hand."

The chopper kept rising.

"Trust me." Rakkim grabbed Baby's arm, drew her closer. He could see her pulse pounding at the base of her throat. "It's okay, I've got you."

Baby kneed him in the face and Rakkim flew backward, landed heavily on the ground. He lay there, not moving. Above him the helicopter rose rapidly as Royce regained control. Still dazed from the fall and the shock, he saw Baby looking down at him from the passenger compartment, her long hair billowing in the breeze.

"Baby!" The Colonel stood over Rakkim, looking up, and the sadness and longing in his voice carried clear to the stars. *"Baby!"*

Baby waved to him.

The Colonel sobbed. His troops clustered around the house seemed to take a step back, the night's silence broken only by the rapidly diminishing sound of the chopper heading over the treetops, and the Colonel's soft weeping.

Rakkim rolled over, gasped. Slowly got to his knees, then his feet. It hurt to breathe. "Colonel . . . ?"

The bandage on the Colonel's right hand was soaked with blood. "Joke's on you," he said gruffly. "Looks like you paid me two hundred million dollars for nothing."

"It was something," said Rakkim, holding his ribs.

The Colonel jabbed a thumb at the chopper and blood flew from the bandage. "There goes your something."

Rakkim watched the chopper disappear from view.

"Why did you do it?" The Colonel looked at him. "You brought that End-Times scum here, and then you fought beside us instead of stealing the canister. You lied to me, then you saved my life. *Why?* Are you stupid or just confused?"

"It's worse than that," said Rakkim. "I fell for my own cover story. Started seeing you as more than an honorable enemy—as an honorable man. The way you treated the Fedayeen, burying him with full honors . . ."

"What are you talking about?" said the Colonel.

Rakkim watched two of the Colonel's men helping Leo and Moseby out of the cabin. "It doesn't matter now. The weapon is on its way to the highest bidder. The Chinese probably . . . maybe the Brazilians. There's going to be all kinds of trouble coming."

"There's *always* trouble coming, and always people willing to face it." The Colonel stared at the spot over the trees where the helicopter had disappeared. "Right now, I'm trying to decide which of us is the bigger fool. *You* for changing your mind and standing beside me, or *me* for thinking that Baby loved me the way that I love her."

"I'd have to go with you, sir," said Rakkim. "Unless, of course, you decide to execute me, in which case *I'd* be declared the winner."

"We're going to have to have a long talk," said the Colonel, still watching that patch of night sky.

CHAPTER 44

Rakkim sucked at the strawberry malt as the high-speed train raced across the Canadian Rockies and tried again to figure out why Baby hadn't killed Moseby and Leo back at the house. It had to have been her decision—Gravenholtz would have killed them on general principles, beaten them to death just to hear their bones crunch. The maglev train rode smoothly four inches above the guideway, its magnetic propulsion system almost silent, but Rakkim felt a steady hum in his ears that gnawed at him, deepening his bad mood. So, why had Baby let them live?

On the other side of the compartment, Leo snored peacefully as he had for the last three days, ever since he'd tried accessing the computer cores detailing the construction of a hafnium bomb. Three days, waking only to stumble to the bathroom or push food into his mouth. He barely spoke, and what he said was a soft muttering in some other language. They had been on the train for the last day, hurtling along at 285 miles an hour. While Leo slept, Rakkim thought about Sarah and Michael; he thought about Malcolm Crews backing into the forest, and the Colonel's tears and the sight of Baby looking down at him from the ascending chopper . . . Most of all, he thought about his own failure.

His mission had been simple. First, find the weapon. Then, steal the weapon from the Colonel and either bring it back or destroy it. Better to bring it back where it could be used to intimidate the Mexicans and the Mormons. Or even better, use it to establish trust between the republic and the Belt, start the reconciliation both nations needed. As a last resort, he was to destroy the weapon, so it couldn't be used against them.

Yesterday, he had contacted Sarah from Montreal. Told her that he had failed. Failed to secure the weapon, failed to destroy the weapon, failed to kill Crews or Gravenholtz. Other than that, the mission was a total success. Sarah said she was just glad he was alive. Glad Leo was alive too. He told

Sarah that his best guess was that the hafnium weapon was probably on its way to a research center in China, and Baby and Gravenholtz were richer than anyone needed to be. Baby, anyway. No way would she stick with Gravenholtz after she no longer needed him. Sarah said she'd alert the president to the changing global paradigm. He wasn't sure exactly what that meant, but he suspected the president wasn't going to order a parade in his honor or give him another of those *a grateful nation thanks you* private dinners.

All Rakkim had managed was a mild concussion and three teeth reseated back into his jaw by a dentist in Boonesville who smelled of clove oil. Even Stevenson's shekel of Tyre was gone. He rubbed his right hand, checked it again. Yeah, the crucifix branded onto his palm was definitely fading, being reabsorbed. He could barely tell what the image was anymore.

Beautiful landscape through the windows, snowcapped mountains and blue vistas, but Rakkim wasn't interested in sightseeing. He just wanted to be home.

He looked over at Leo lying there, mouth open, a trickle of drool crusted along his chin. Another of Rakkim's great successes. When they'd left, Leo was the pride of his family, a human computer, a vast step up the evolutionary ladder. At least according to Leo. Now . . . now he was a glorified gort, one of those lobotomized clones that Swiss billionaires kept on ice for organ transplants.

Moseby had recovered fast, probably as much from Baby's efforts as his Fedayeen recuperative powers. Another question Rakkim wanted to ask her someday. Moseby looked after Leo, sat beside him, praying, night and day. It couldn't hurt. Moseby didn't have much to say to Rakkim, too many bad memories between them maybe, but Moseby did have questions about Leo and his daughter. Not the kind of questions Rakkim would have anticipated, nothing about appropriate or inappropriate contact, of family honor violated. Moseby wanted to know if Leo was a good man. An honest man. He wanted to know if he made Leanne laugh. If he understood her when she said things like numbers were God talking to us in his own voice. He wanted to know if Leo made her happy. Then he drove off in Rakkim's old car, drove off to join his family, giving the eye in the pyramid hanging from the rearview a spin for good luck.

Rakkim and Leo left the next day. The Colonel had actually embraced Rakkim at the airport in Nashville. Hugged him hard, said he wished all Muslims were like him, the world would be a better place. Rakkim didn't have the heart to tell him it wouldn't make any difference. Probably make things worse. The Colonel never said a word about Baby the whole drive to the airport, Leo bundled in the back of the armored personnel carrier while they rode up front. Not a word. They talked about Malcolm Crews, and the likelihood of wiping out his remaining forces. They talked about Leo and what various doctors might be able to do for him. They didn't talk about Baby. Not until Rakkim was about to walk onto the plane, pushing Leo, who sat sleeping in a wheelchair. The Colonel laid his hand on Rakkim's shoulder.

The Colonel tugged down his gray uniform, his posture perfect. "Young people . . . young women particularly . . . they're easily led astray," he said, not making eye contact.

It would have been easy to nod his head and agree, go along, but Rakkim respected the Colonel too much for that. "I'm sure that's true, sir, but I don't think there's a man or woman alive who could lead Baby any-place she didn't want to go."

The Colonel nodded. A sad smile on his face. "Yes . . . I always loved that about her." He turned on his heel and stalked across the airport lounge.

The flight from Nashville to Montreal took the plane in a looping curve out into the Atlantic and then north over Canadian airspace. Service was only once a week, and space was reserved months in advance, but the Colonel had made a phone call. Rakkim and Leo had fake Belt passport chips, and a couple of Belt bank accounts—the flight went smoothly, the plane packed with businessmen, most of them foreign nationals intent on staking their claim to the Belt's resources.

The Colonel said the new president had been selling concessions to the highest bidder since his inauguration, auctioning off chunks of prime real estate and mineral rights. There was even talk of turning the sunken city of New Orleans into a tourist destination. Japanese honeymooners were considered a particularly lucrative market. That's what happens when you elect your presidents every few years, Rakkim had told him, turns politicians into shortsighted whores. You people and your president-for-life are just as bad, the Colonel had answered—what happens when Kingsley dies? The next one might be a despot, *then* what are you going to do?

The train hummed along, floating above the guideway, no noise, no friction, no pollution. Sarah said Canada used to be considered the little brother of the United States, slower paced, slightly backward. Today it was a leader in applied technology and research, a pristine ecological storehouse blessed with one of the highest standards of living in the world, ironically fueled by the wealth of its oil sands and natural gas deposits. Rakkim stared out the window as a vast herd of caribou champed listlessly at the tundra.

He kept expecting to hear Darwin's whisper break the silence. *Where's the gratitude, Rikki?* Maybe turn his head and see the assassin standing among the whirling dust motes or lying there when the bed opened up in the train cabin. He was alone, though, just he and Leo. Rakkim had sensed his presence a couple of times, thought of an enormous crab scuttling along the ocean depths . . . He rubbed the crucifix branded into the palm of his hand. *That* was real. It was fading by the day, but it was real. It had happened. Leo had asked why Rakkim was allowed into the Church of the Mists and Malcolm Crews left outside. Rakkim still didn't have an answer.

A bell chimed softly and a small gate in the wall lifted. Rakkim pulled a tray out of the auto-waiter, set it on the table in the compartment. Lunch was beef bourguignonne, sourdough rolls, and green salad. Full-size, heavy silverware. English china plates. Linen napkins monogrammed with the crest of the Canadian Rail System. He had ordered a vanilla milk shake in a cold-pak for Leo, in case he woke up later, and another strawberry malt for himself.

He lifted the silver lid off the plate, inhaled the fragrant steam.

Leo sat up. Yawned. "That smells good." He rubbed his eyes. "Where are we?"

Rakkim put his fork down. "Canada. Just past Calgary. Are you . . . really awake?"

"What are we doing in *Canada*?"

Rakkim waited for him to lie back down and drift off again.

"What do you keep looking at me for?" Leo slid the plate of beef bourguignonne closer, picked up Rakkim's fork. "Did you already tell me why we're in Canada?"

"We're going home."

Leo stuck a chunk of beef into his mouth. "What if I don't want to go home?"

Rakkim put a hand on Leo's arm, stopped the fork halfway. "Leo, do you have any idea what's happened?"

Leo shook his head. "All I know is I'm on a train in Canada and I'm really, *really* hungry."

Rakkim let Leo eat, the kid gobbling down the beef stew until it was all gone, sopping up the remains with the sourdough rolls. He left the wine and the salad untouched.

"I'm smarter too." Leo removed the vanilla milk shake from the cold-pak, flipped up the straw. "Smarter than anybody's ever been, I bet."

"You've been asleep for the last three days," said Rakkim.

Leo gave up on the straw, spooned up the milk shake. "Processing. Not sleeping, processing. *Big* difference." He chased down some errant crumbs with his pinkie, plopped them in his mouth. "Where's the hafnium isotope?"

"The canister? It's gone."

"Not the canister, the *isotope*." Leo looked back at the auto-waiter. "Can you order me some more food?"

"It's all gone. The canister and everything in it."

Leo knocked over the glass of wine. Didn't seem to notice. "That's *bad*."

Rakkim tossed a napkin on the spilled wine. "I know."

"You *don't* know." Leo blinked rapidly. "Without . . . without the hafnium isotope, all . . . all . . . all the information from the computer cores is *useless*. It would take years to refine more—"

"It's worse than that. Baby and Gravenholtz took the canister. Probably sold it to the Chinese. They have everything—"

"They don't have *everything*." Leo stood up. Ran a hand through his wild hair. "I have to pee."

Just as Rakkim was about to knock on the door, see if Leo was okay, the kid came out. He walked over to the auto-waiter, scrolled through the menu.

"What did you mean, Baby and Gravenholtz didn't have everything?"

"Have you had the fried chicken? I kind of got hooked on that stuff—*Hey!* Lay off."

"I asked you a question," said Rakkim.

Leo rubbed his arm. "You should learn to appreciate me." He punched in his food order. The computer beeped: SORRY, UNAVAILABLE. Leo snorted, accessed the main control panel as his fingers flew over the touchscreen: ORDER RECEIVED. He turned to Rakkim. "I think a little respect is in order, that's all. I mean, I did *my* job."

"I said Baby and Gravenholtz had the canister." Rakkim picked up the fork, spun it around two fingers. "You said they didn't have everything." He pressed his fingers together, bent the fork in half. "So, Leo . . . this is the time for you to use that big brain of yours, look into my eyes, and tell me what the *fuck* you're talking about."

"Sure." Leo nodded. "No need to get all macho opera about . . . okay, okay. Gravenholtz and Baby have the isotope, which is a huge loss for us, granted, but without the data on the cores, they can't make a hafnium bomb. The isotope might as well be cat litter."

"I told you, they *have* the cores."

Leo handed Rakkim the fork. "Could you straighten this out for me, please?" Leo waited. "They've got the cores, but they don't have the *data* on the cores." He beamed. "I changed all the critical formulations while I downloaded them. The data is so tangled up they'll never be able to untie it."

The auto-waiter chimed.

Leo jumped up, retrieved his double order of fried chicken.

"You . . . encrypted the data while you were downloading it?" said Rakkim.

"Not exactly encrypted it, quite a bit more secure than that actually, but in your terms . . . yes." Leo crunched into a fried chicken leg. "I'm good. I'm even better than my dad thought."

"You've been in a coma for the last three days. That's how *good* you are."

Leo wiped grease off his chin. "I'm not perfect. *Yet.*"

Rakkim watched him eat. "So, it's a draw. We can't use the information in your head without the isotope, and the isotope is useless without your information."

"That's what I *said.*"

"So, it's a stalemate?"

Leo gnawed at a thigh, the fried skin crackling off in chunks. "I despise a stalemate. That's for gutless grand masters afraid to lose. It's an insult to the game. I really wish you had been able to hang on to the isotope. No offense."

Rakkim glanced at his watch. He'd have to message Sarah at their next stop so she could update the president with the good news.

"What about Mr. Moseby?" said Leo.

"He had a rough time, but he's going to be okay—"

"I don't mean *that*. I mean what did he think of me? Was he impressed?" He licked his fingers. A bit of chicken was stuck to the corner of his mouth. "I intend to ask for his daughter's hand in marriage, so I hope I made a good impression."

"Oh, yeah. He was . . . just totally . . . overwhelmed."

Leo grinned, head bobbing. "I get that a lot."

Rakkim watched him. "Leo . . . are you really okay?"

"I'm way beyond okay." Leo belched. Reached for a chicken wing. "I heard these two guys talking back at the Colonel's camp . . . they said the best aphrodisiac in the world is where you beat a raw egg into a lukewarm Coca-Cola." He gestured with the chicken wing. "Got to be a *fertile* egg and a lukewarm Coke. Then you eat a raw oyster and wash it down with the egg'n'Coke and wango. They didn't say aphrodisiac, of course. They said 'blue-steel hard-on,' but—"

"Kid, the last thing you need is an aphrodisiac."

"I wasn't talking about me." Leo slid his teeth over the wing, stripped the meat away in one smooth movement. "I meant you. I'm not even at my sexual peak yet, but *you*, I mean you got to be over thirty years old." He chewed with his mouth open. "Fedayeen, big deal, you're still on the downward slope."

Rakkim smiled at him. "Just *one* raw egg in the Coke?"

"That's all it takes. According to these two guys." Leo peered out the window, watched the barren landscape whip past. "I've been thinking about Baby. She . . . she was really something, wasn't she?"

Rakkim remembered the last time he had seen her, Baby pulling Gravenholtz into the chopper, her face lit up, triumphant.

"I think she liked you," said Leo. "I think maybe you kind of liked her too." He drew an intricate geometric figure on the glass with his fingertip. "I notice things, Rikki. People think I don't see what's going on, but I do."

"Baby's beautiful. So is a cobra. I wouldn't want to take either of them to bed."

Leo shook his head, continued with his drawing, one of those multi-sided shapes that Leanne had made out of paper. "The problem isn't that I noticed, Rikki. That problem is that *she* noticed too."

Rakkim stayed silent for a few miles, listening to the whoosh of air as the train raced on. "Leo?"

"Uh-huh."

"What happens when the Chinese realize the data cores are useless?"

"It might take them a while," said Leo, making minute additions to the geometric figure he had drawn on the window.

"But when they *do*?"

Leo looked over at Rakkim. "Well . . . they'll probably be annoyed at Baby and Mr. Gravenholtz."

"Definitely annoyed, but that won't stop them Chinese. You've got the data that they need in your head. *You're* the key player now."

"You're just realizing that?"

"It's not necessarily something to be happy about. It puts you in danger."

"I'm not scared."

"Then, Leo, you're not as smart as you think you are."

CHAPTER 45

Gravenholtz hated Miami. He had been waiting three days to meet Fong, the Chinese ambassador to Nuevo Florida, and still no word from Baby when it was going to happen.

Miami was hot and sticky, and everyone spoke too fast in this mixed-up language, part Spanish and part English, so that he couldn't understand but every second or third word. Fuck 'em. He understood well enough that a redhead who burned, but didn't tan, was at the low end of the totem pole. Even the white people were brown as coconuts, and they were the ones giving him the dirtiest looks. Hard to imagine it was once part of the US of A. Shows you what can happen if you let folks push you around. Meanwhile, Baby acted as if she were right at home, speaking the lingo as well as anyone, which was weird for a country girl born and raised in Dickson, Tennessee. He shouldn't have been surprised. Everything about Baby turned out to be different from what he supposed. Shit, the Colonel wouldn't have believed it, but Gravenholtz had seen the proof.

Three days ago, Royce had set the Chinese chopper down in the middle of the Everglades, right where Baby said to, and before the blades hardly slowed, all these Asian guys with guns stepped out of the palmettos.

Royce was about to open up with the Gatlings and blow these gooks to ground chuck when Baby patted his hand, said, *Don't worry, they're Fong's men.* Deeks and Cunningham were relieved, but Gravenholtz was still pissed about having to caravan to the embassy, and worried about his wounds getting infected. Fuck the ambassador and his fear of creating a diplomatic incident, Gravenholtz didn't like the idea of landing in a god-damn swamp. He scratched the blood crusted along his back and side, patted the bandage on the ear that Rikki had half sliced off. If there was a God above, which he fucking doubted, Gravenholtz prayed for another chance to go one-on-one with that guy. He'd hold himself back and make Rikki suffer—pounding out his teeth, beating his bones to jelly, leaving the vital organs for last.

The flight from the Colonel's base camp had been a real ass-clencher. Royce kept the chopper at treetop level, the ground a blur as Deeks puked his guts out into his boot, while Royce and Cunningham laughed their asses off, yelling, *One more time!* Baby swatted them for teasing Deeks, changed the dressing on Deeks's hand, and told him he was going to be just fine, which was bullshit, since two of Deeks's fingers had been shot off by groundfire leaving camp. When they stopped for fuel at a little airport in Georgia, Cunningham tried to make amends, killed the gas attendant for his boots. Real nice boots too, hand-tooled and everything, but Deeks just complained the rest of the way that they were too tight. You can't win with some folks.

The chopper smelled like throw-up, and Royce's and Cunningham's cigars didn't help, but Gravenholtz had to admit, the chopper's avionics and stealth tech worked perfectly—they zipped right across the border into Nuevo Florida and never tripped the radar or anything else. Smooth ride until they set down in the Glades.

Baby stepped onto the saw grass, the back of her neck shiny with sweat, told Gravenholtz to bring the canister. He was about to tell her to stay put, wait until he checked things out, when she looked back at him with that fuck-me-*please* look and he grabbed the canister and hopped down, showing off his muscles.

Royce hesitated, his hands on the controls for the chopper's machine guns, but by then the Asian guys had slung their guns and were dragging coolers of iced beer out of the weeds. Deeks and Cunningham whooped it up, jumped down—Royce slipped out of the pilot's harness, swatted at the mosquitoes that drifted around him.

You go ahead, I'll be right there, Baby said, letting Gravenholtz walk ahead of her.

Gravenholtz saw her out of the corner of his eye . . . saw her reach for something, and then she shot Royce and Deeks and Cunningham, shot them in the back of the head, *bam-bam-bam,* as if she were swatting flies. She put away the pistol, grabbed Gravenholtz's hand, and kissed him.

Whoeee, she said, *I've been wanting to get rid of those three since Alabama.*

Gravenholtz stood there for a second, trying to decide what to do.

Royce and Deeks and Cunningham had been with him since the border wars . . . proud rednecks, no weakness, no mercy, but he was in the middle of nowhere, facing down a dozen armed men. The armed men were no big deal; it was Baby beside him making happy sounds as if he was balls-deep on a rainy afternoon that sealed it. Gravenholtz held up a hand, caught the cold beer one of the Asian guys tossed him.

Nobody said a word on the ride into town, which was fine with him, because he was damn tired. And sore too where Rakkim had stuck him. Never been cut like that before, even by a Fedayeen blade. Enough to make most men doubt themselves, but Lester Gravenholtz wasn't most men. He figured they were going to the Chinese embassy, but, nope, instead they drove up to a private entrance of the fanciest hotel Gravenholtz had ever seen. Fit-for-a-king swanky, and right on the beach. He didn't like the change of plans, and *really* didn't like the idea of him and Baby getting separate rooms, but he held his piece, said, sure, later will be greater, and gave her a wink.

He barely had time to check out the suite before there was a knock on the door, and these four doctors walked in as if they owned the joint. Indians or Arabs they were, skinny little gooks with white jackets and cases of surgical instruments. More gooks wheeled in an operating table and lights and machines with dials and hoses. Doctors seemed real impressed with him, yammering away as they examined him, touching his red hair, gently probing his wounds while he ground his teeth. He guessed stitching him up was real tricky, what with his second skin impervious to their scalpels, but they did this microsurgery thing with lasers, using the existing knife cuts from Rikki to get inside. Real smart gooks. They stitched his ear back up, then filled him full of antibiotics and probably something else, because all he did for practically the next three days was sleep.

Once, he woke up and saw Baby looking down at him, same expression she had just before she blew away Royce and Deeks and Cunningham.

A few hours ago he woke up feeling good. Supergood. Then Baby called, said get ready, because she had a surprise. He asked if they were finally going to the Chinese embassy, but she just laughed. Now here he was, walking with Baby down a marble hallway, barefoot, wearing these gauzy white pants and shirt, a fruity-ass outfit that made him almost glad Royce wasn't here to see him.

Baby kissed him just before they came to an ornately carved door. "I'm glad I kept you," she whispered.

Gravenholtz didn't like the sound of that, not at all, but the doors swung open. Two men inside led them deeper into the room, young guys, dressed all in white like Gravenholtz.

Another set of doors opened and the two young guys stayed outside while Baby and Gravenholtz walked in. An older man turned away from a window overlooking the beach—they must have been forty or fifty stories up.

Baby bent down on one knee, which was the weirdest thing Gravenholtz had ever seen her do, weirder even than killing his three raiders. She tugged at Gravenholtz's leg but he stayed standing.

"That's all right, my dear," said the geezer, smiling as he walked toward them. Spring in his step too, as if he was enjoying himself. "He'll learn manners soon enough."

Baby stood up. "Father, this is the man I've told you about. I'd like to present Lester Gravenholtz. Lester, this is my father."

Gravenholtz went to shake hands, but the man's expression made it clear that shit wasn't happening. He had a neatly trimmed beard, smooth brown skin, and black eyes so intense Gravenholtz felt he could see clear through him. He looked around. The three of them were alone.

"You're feeling well . . . Lester?"

"Full of piss and vinegar."

"How lovely for you," said the old man, his mouth tightening slightly. "Thank you for assisting my daughter in securing the black-ice canister. My scientists are still analyzing the contents. I expect their evaluation any moment—"

"So I guess I'm not getting my share of the money," said Gravenholtz. The old man cocked his head.

"I told Lester that we'd be selling the weapon to the Chinese," said Baby.

The old man nodded. "Of course." He sat in a plain, high-backed chair. Crossed his legs, one knee over the other. "I'm offering you something of infinitely greater value, Lester."

"Ain't nothing more valuable than money," said Gravenholtz.

"Do you believe in God?" said the old man.

"Jesus H., that's just what the Colonel asked me the first time we met."

The old man smiled. "The Colonel worships a false god. I am servant of Allah, may his name be praised."

Shit, oh dear. Gravenholtz should have known. All that bowing and scraping . . . only ones who did that other than the gooks were the towelies.

"You look in pain, Lester," said the old man. "Should I summon a physician?"

Gravenholtz turned to Baby. "This is your father? I seen you in church, girl. I seen you take *Communion*."

"You've seen me do a lot of things," purred Baby.

Lester felt his skin grow warm.

"I have many daughters," said the old man. "Hundreds. The sons I keep close, the infant daughters I spread like seeds across the earth. Raised carefully, they marry rich men, powerful men, politicians and military officers on the way up. Sometimes I aid the process . . . a wife dies suddenly, and a young woman is there to comfort the grieving widower, or a diplomat too busy for love finds it easier than he had imagined, and finds a bride more skilled in statecraft than himself. Yet, even with all my efforts, most of my seeds fall on barren ground, but some"—he smiled at Baby, and she lowered her eyes—"some bear fruit beyond my wildest expectations."

"So . . . is that why you brought me here?" Gravenholtz said to Baby.

She burst out laughing.

The old man sighed. "No, Lester, you are not the prize of which I speak. I was referring to Baby's marriage to the Colonel, which allowed her to bring me the weapon. You, Lester, you are . . . a *bonus*."

Gravenholtz took in the elegant surroundings, the exquisite marble and hardwoods, the artwork . . . the view. Beaucoup bucks here. Plenty of power too.

"May I see your hand?" said the old man. He waited, snapped his fingers. "Your *hand*."

Gravenholtz offered his hand. Reacted at the lightness of the old man's touch, the sense of entitlement. Ownership.

"Yes, yes," mused the old man as his hands wandered over Gravenholtz. "I didn't want to get my hopes up, but he's just as you said, Baby . . . just as the doctors confirmed." He crooked a finger. "*Closer*."

Gravenholtz did as he was told before he was even aware of the command.

The old man lightly thumped Gravenholtz's chest . . . his stomach . . . his ribs. "Very nice."

Gravenholtz backed away.

"Look, Baby, he's *shy*," said the old man.

"Not the last time I looked," said Baby.

"Professor Yamato's great experiment . . . in the *flesh*." The old man peered at Gravenholtz. "I thought all of your kind were dead."

"My kind . . . ?" Gravenholtz had never spoken of his history to anyone. Would have lied had he been asked. But the old man wasn't asking. "I'm my own kind. The others, the ones you might have heard about, they're dead. Me, I was away at the time. Sent out on a test-drive. Solo. The others . . . they were made to be part of a team. Like I said, me, I'm different."

"A *solo* model." The old man clapped his hands with delight. "Lovely." He reached out, touched the bandage on Gravenholtz's side. Examined the tip of his finger. Showed Gravenholtz the spot of blood. The blood spread out on Gravenholtz's white shirt too.

"That's nothing," said Baby. "Russian agent got lucky. He was working with the Colonel, trying to buy the weapon —"

"Doesn't look like a bullet wound," said the old man.

"My sheathing's thin in places where I need to move fast." Gravenholtz rubbed his neck.

"It doesn't *look* like a bullet wound," repeated the old man.

"Bullet wouldn't have done shit. Guy stuck me with a knife —"

"Rikki . . . the Russian agent," said Baby, "he was ex-Fedayeen."

"*Rakkim*." The old man stroked his beard. "You should have told me, Baby."

"There wasn't time . . . Father." Baby lowered her eyes. "I was barely able to get you news of the weapon, and this Russian . . . this Rakkim —"

"I fought Fedayeen before and never got cut this bad," said Gravenholtz. "He just got lucky, found a weak spot."

The old man shook his head. "No, Lester, *you* got lucky."

"Bull*shit*," said Gravenholtz.

Baby prostrated herself. "What have I done, Father?"

The old man beckoned her to rise. "Rakkim is no Russian. He's Fedayeen. Undoubtedly sent by the president to retrieve the weapon for the republic." He gazed at Baby with what passed for affection. "You should be proud of yourself. Rakkim is . . . dangerous. Yet you stole the weapon right from under his nose."

"What about me?" said Gravenholtz. "I had a little something to do with it too."

"It's true, Father," said Baby.

"Do you believe in God, Lester?" said the old man.

"You already *asked* me that," said Gravenholtz, balling his fists. Didn't matter if there were machine guns behind every wall, he could crush the old man's skull like a Concord grape before he was brought down. Break Baby's neck too . . . same moment he broke his own heart. "Get it straight. I ain't no Muslim."

"And I believe you," said the old man, unconcerned with the flush rising in Gravenholtz's face, the bloodstain spreading out on his white shirt. "Let me tell you a story, Lester, a true story. Sultan Murad, the first ruler of the Ottoman Empire, was a practical man. Surrounded by mortal enemies, he had tens of thousands of soldiers, but real warriors, then as now, were in short supply. The sultan created a small group of elite fighting men, totally loyal, uniquely skilled—called the janissaries. Though, of course, the sultan was a Muslim, many of the best janissaries were dhimmis . . . infidels. The sultan would finish his late-night prayers, then sleep peacefully until dawn because there were Christians outside his door, weapons at the ready, *eager* to do his bidding."

Gravenholtz found it hard to meet the old man's eyes. Felt like the old man was rooting around in his skull.

"Do you understand my story, Lester?" The old man leaned forward in his chair. "Sultan Murad was a true believer, a devout Muslim, but he was also a practical man. And, Lester . . . I too am a practical man."

Gravenholtz nodded. "Yeah . . . I get the message."

An aide hurried in, bowed.

The old man waved him closer. Listened as the aide whispered in his ear. The old man's expression didn't change but his eyes hardened on Baby. He waited until the aide backed away before speaking. "It seems you and Lester were misled," he said to Baby. "It's *Rakkim* who deserves to be proud of himself at this moment, not you."

Gravenholtz could see Baby tremble. Could see her trying to speak.

"The data cores for the isotope are useless," the old man said quietly.

"It's only due to the skill of my acolytes that their flaws were discovered. We might have wasted weeks, months—"

"So fix them," said Gravenholtz. "Reboot 'em or recode 'em, or whatever it is the math wizards need to do to make it work. We gave you prime goods—"

"*Silence,*" whispered the old man.

Gravenholtz felt his jaws snap shut.

"The data cores are ruined. My engineers have no idea how they were corrupted or how to make them function. Without the data—"

"*Leo,*" said Baby.

The old man glared at her.

Baby lowered her eyes. "Leo was Rikki's companion. Jewish fellow. Practically a boy. He was the only one who had access to the data cores." The old man nodded, eyes so bright Gravenholtz couldn't look at him.

The Old One strolled across the anteroom barefoot after Baby and Gravenholtz left, humming a tune he hadn't heard in a hundred years, excited as a schoolboy. He dug his toes into the carpet with every step. After so much time and so many setbacks, the Old One's plans for the republic were finally coming to fruition, his ascension to power assured. At this precise moment, with the Old One about to spin the world again, Allah had signaled his approval through two most unexpected blessings. Not only had Baby shown up with Professor Yamato's wondrous and terrible creation, but Sarah and Rakkim, the last of the Old One's . . . *vexations,* were about to be delivered to him.

Sarah and Rakkim had exposed his deepest machinations, caused the Old One to flee like a common criminal. He had searched for them without success . . . until two weeks ago, when Sarah had been spotted at a Catholic street festival, she and a male child, and a woman believed to be her mother. They had been followed by one of the Old One's operatives, but Sarah managed to lose him at the last minute, disappearing in a warren of abandoned buildings. No matter. The Old One's men would pinpoint her location soon enough. Al-Faisal, his chief operative in the republic, had begged for the chance to snatch her up. Even better, now Rakkim was coming home, with his new friend, Leo, the Jew who held the secrets. All the Old One had to do was close his hand.

The Old One had little regard for superweapons—they were usually oversold by their makers, or as risky to their owners as their targets. The Old One valued *tools*, like this beast Gravenholtz, people whose abilities or contacts could serve his ends. Not that he would turn down such a weapon as this hafnium bomb. Yes, Baby's sudden arrival had presented new opportunities. Glorious opportunities.

First . . . he would squeeze this Jew of his secrets like a ripe pomegranate, then cast him aside. He still had hopes for Rakkim, wanting one last chance to turn him. Rakkim was too unique a talent to simply discard. Under the Old One's tutelage . . . *anything* was possible. Sarah was different, as dangerous as her husband, but indifferent to the Old One's temptations. Blame that on Redbeard's blood coursing through her veins—the high-minded State Security chief had blocked the Old One for years, then had the rank audacity to die peacefully. Insult to injury. Sarah was the last of Redbeard's bloodline, she and her son. The Old One would gladly snuff them both out, but they might be useful in bending Rakkim to his will. Love enslaved more men than all the conquerors of history, a lesson the Old One had learned at great cost. He basked in the memory as sunlight poured through the one-way window, feeling the heat stir his bones.

The Old One snapped his fingers, summoned one of his courtesans, the Yemeni with the coarse black hair and a mouth that tasted like honey. He inhaled, already smelling her perfume.

Al-Faisal had actually offered to see if there was some way for the Old One to watch the president's face while he died, every panicked twist and contortion. The Old One had declined, concerned that any such capability might jeopardize the plan, but he appreciated al-Faisal's initiative. The Black Robe had been invaluable in the past, would be even more important in the future. Last year, al-Faisal had snapped the neck of a meddlesome police captain during noon prayers, done it so quickly that the policeman's fellow worshippers had thought the man died of a heart attack, and al-Faisal, who was leading prayers at the time, never raised his voice. Such devotion . . .

The door to the anteroom swung open and the Yemeni entered, bowed low, her thick black braids flying around her shoulders.

"Flower of Allah, how *lovely* you are," said the Old One.

CHAPTER 46

Sarah winced as she stared at the images projected onto the wall of her office. All the pretty girls and boys, foreign advert models in forbidden swimwear, African kids with tiny white seashells stark against their skin—the view from Eagleton's desk chair. In the upper-right quadrant of the wall was the original five-by-seven holographic card, Eagleton looking back at her while he forced his penis down the throat of a young woman. Sarah imagined him sitting at his desk, building God only knew what while his imagination ran free. The wall was a puzzle, the holo card the key. One of Eagleton's games, hiding his intentions in plain sight to prove how superior he was to everyone else. She shook her head. At this moment, he *was* superior, because every moment she spent looking seemed like a violation, and she still had no idea what he was hiding.

She should have been spending her time on better things. Plenty of other items on her agenda, from the president's upcoming state visit to Aztlán, to the fact that Rakkim was still unaccounted for. The last she had heard was a call from Getty Andalou a week ago. The Colonel had reached out to a woman in Columbia City and she had hacked the KGB file Spider had created. Take a bow. No worries, Getty had said. Maybe for him. She turned, hearing Michael's laughter through the open door, and her mother laughing with him. Yes, there were much better ways for Sarah to spend her time than trying to help Anthony Colarusso with a case that everyone said was already closed. Al-Faisal had blown himself to pieces, and whatever he had bought from Eagleton had been destroyed with him. Still . . . She got up and quietly closed the door.

The images of the latest Japanese electronic gear and Italian sports cars on the wall somehow had the same unsavory sheen. In fact, all the images the tech engineer had on his wall had a similar cool, ironic feel, from the mass-produced photos of political and religious figures, to the touristy postcard from the surfing beach in South Africa. Even the in-memoriam card honoring the Russian astronaut killed by a speck of space debris had a tiny hole burned into it at the exact spot the poor man had been struck. Ha ha.

She had tried downloading various screens onto the hologram. Hundreds of screens. Different colors, different filters, all kinds of high-resolution screens that someone like Eagleton would have liked. She ran the holo at high speed and low speed. She spent hours following various parts of the image through 360 degrees of rotation, with particular emphasis on the reflection in the young woman's eye. Nothing. Once she thought she had broken the code, crying out with delight as a South African diffraction screen showed a string of minute, mirror-image words beyond the reach of the woman's lips, a ring of words around the base of Eagleton's penis. When she made the necessary adjustments, the words read, *Wish you were here.* She felt just as she had the day she ran from Eagleton's shop, turned back to see him stroking himself and smiling at her.

Loud cries from the other side of the door, Michael shrieking. She jumped up before she realized they were cries of joy. She reached for the door, curious now. The door opened before she could get to it . . .

Rakkim stood in the doorway, holding Michael in his arms. He shifted the boy, made room for Sarah as she threw herself on him.

She winced as he embraced her, the welts on her back from the Black Robe's beating fading but still tender.

"What is it?" said Rakkim.

Sarah held him tighter. "Nothing," she breathed into his neck. "Nothing, *now*."

Hours later, the call to late-night prayer echoed through the streets, and Sarah turned her head. She had no idea that so much time had passed.

Rakkim smiled down at her. "Yes, it's late. Good thing you're already in bed."

She clamped herself around his cock, made him laugh, and the vibration ran through both of them. He eased himself deeper inside her, and she locked her legs around his waist. "Now I've got you," she whispered. "You're trapped."

"Just where I want to be too." He kissed her, and she held the kiss as he rocked deeper and deeper, the two of them working back and forth against each other, grinding away the time lost and the miles between them, the differences and the doubts, until their cries echoed louder than the call to prayer.

Sarah buried her face in his chest for a moment, then lay back on the sheets, the two of them still holding hands. He had cooled the bruises on her back with kisses, the Black Robe's fury a fading memory. For her, anyway. She had heard the change in his voice when he saw the marks, gently asking her for details about the man's appearance. There was a time when she would have demurred, said the Black Robe had paid enough, that there was already too much violence in the world and no need to add to the tally. Not now. She remembered every detail of the man's face, his crooked teeth, the shape of his beard, the red dots on his earlobes, signifying his high rank . . . the scar on his right wrist wielding the flail. Rakkim would see to the rest of it.

Rakkim kissed the sides of her mouth.

She inhaled him, eyes half-closed. "Your sweat smells different. Steamy . . . ripe. You smell like the Belt. It's not bad . . . just different." She slid a hand along his thigh. "Not bad at all."

A light knock on the door. "Am I interrupting?"

Sarah pulled the sheet over them. "Come on in, Mother."

Katherine opened the door, walked in with a tray of sliced fruits and cheese, a pot of tea. "I thought you might need some nourishment after your . . . exertions."

"Thanks for interrupting," said Rakkim. "I think your daughter's trying to kill me."

Katherine allowed herself a small smile. "Runs in the family." She set the tray down at the foot of their bed.

"How's Michael?" said Rakkim.

"Sleeping peacefully. He has bad dreams when you're away." Katherine pushed back her long, reddish brown hair. More gray in it every day now, the lines deepening around her mouth.

"Are you all right, Mom?" asked Sarah.

Katherine waved away the question. "It was easier when I lived in the nunnery. I liked it better when I was insulated from the constant barrage of news, the endless threats and counterthreats."

Rakkim sat up. "Did something happen?"

"Something is *always* happening, that's why it's a burden. Go on, enjoy your picnic, I'm going to sleep."

Rakkim waited until the door closed behind Katherine. Reached down and poured them tea. "Katherine looks tired."

"She's worried about President Kingsley." Sarah added a spoonful of honey to her tea. "We all are. His trip tomorrow is billed as a goodwill visit, but El Presidente Arbusto is interpreting it as a sign of weakness, a prelude to surrendering the Southwest."

"It *is* a prelude to surrender."

"When you're in a weak position, getting the best deal possible is a victory." She sipped her tea, enjoying the sweetness. "Kingsley has been playing the game for almost forty years. We have to trust his judgment."

"I wish I could have brought the weapon back. It might have made a difference—"

"It's *done*. The president still has faith in you. He recognizes how difficult the mission was. At least after what Leo did, no one can use the isotope." Sarah tapped the edge of her teacup with a fingernail. "Perhaps after the president returns from Aztlán we could make some back-channel overtures to the Chinese—"

"You're good at that sort of thing, aren't you?" said Rakkim.

"Are you referring to Getty Andalou?"

"I don't like him. And I like it even less that you had dealings with him without telling me . . . *or* the president."

"Getty doesn't like you either, but he's willing to work with you again. That's why it's called *diplomacy*." Sarah's mouth formed a thin line. "And I'll tell the president when I think the time is right."

"When *you* think it's right?"

Sarah set her teacup into the saucer so hard it almost broke. "For a man who gets indignant about my failure to disclose information, you're keeping a secret of your own."

"What's that supposed to—?"

"Your doctor called while you were gone. Why did you want him to test your DNA?"

Rakkim reached for an apple slice. "What did he say?"

"He said you were fine . . . better than fine. He said your reaction time is faster—"

"What about my DNA?"

She shook her head. "Perfectly normal. No change. Were you worried about your genetic boosters? Have you had some kind of . . . problem?"

"No problems."

"Talk to me, damnit. You're worried about something or you wouldn't have gone to the doctor. I'm your wife, Rikki. What's going on?"

Rakkim stared at the ceiling. Started to speak. Stopped. When he finally spoke, his words were a whisper and his eyes stayed on the ceiling. "Ever since I killed Darwin, I've had some . . . strange thoughts. I know things I shouldn't know. Assassin craft. I *am* faster, Sarah, faster than I've ever been—"

"You think Darwin . . ." She bent over him, cupped his face. "Even if his blood *infected* you or something, DNA isn't transferable like that. Even if there was cross-contamination, you wouldn't suddenly develop his skills or his—"

"I *saw* him."

"Darwin's dead."

"Tell him that." Rakkim felt his face flush. "He's . . . in my head. I think he gets lost sometimes, or pushed to the edges, but he said he can—"

"Is he here now?" She looked around the room. "Can you see him?"

Rakkim shook his head.

She lay down beside him, drew him to her. She felt his heart beating.

"There are times . . . Sarah, there're times that I'm not sure who I really am."

"*I* know who you are." She stroked his hair. "I've loved you since you were nine years old. You're the same person now that you were then. Strong and brave and kind . . . scared too, sometimes, but it didn't stop you. No matter what the cost, you never backed away." She laughed. "It used to drive Redbeard crazy. He said you always picked the hardest path, the most difficult route."

"I love you. I want you to always remember that."

"I won't have to remember it." She kissed him. "You should have told me."

"I didn't want to admit it to myself."

She kissed him again. "No more secrets. Deal?"

Rakkim kissed her back. "What kind of marriage would that be?" He stroked her belly, serious now. "We should move."

"Shhh."

"You said you'd been spotted at the street fair."

"I said I *might* have been spotted, but here we are, safe and sound." She kissed him. "Besides, I like it here."

"So do I. That's why we should move. We're too comfortable. Sooner or later, we're going to make a mistake. I'll ask Spider tomorrow if he knows of a place. He's already got Leo stashed away—"

"I think that's an overreaction."

"Spider didn't think so."

"What did Leo think?" said Sarah.

"He thinks Spider and I are treating him like a two-year-old, which we're not. We're treating him like someone with information in his head that a lot of people would kill for."

"What about you?" Sarah tapped his forehead. "What have you got in there?"

Rakkim grinned. "Not a thing."

Sarah kissed his ears, his cheeks, his nose, kept on kissing him, afraid to stop and not knowing why. "That's . . . the way . . . I like my men. Strong and stupid." She kissed his eyes shut. "Go to sleep. You're home. You're with your family. No one can hurt you now."

She hummed softly as they lay tangled up in each other. Michael's favorite lullaby, the mockingbird song. Rikki's favorite too—their house-keeper, Angelina, used to sing it to them at bedtime. Sarah sang it now until Rakkim drifted off to sleep. A strange lullaby from the old days, about a baby getting one gift after another, each one needing to be replaced. A mockingbird that didn't sing, a diamond that turned to glass, a dog that wouldn't bark, a looking glass that broke . . . Rakkim said that it showed that love wasn't perfect. All Sarah could think of was that the little baby sure had bad luck.

CHAPTER 47

Bartholomew stepped into the security dock, stood quietly while the machine completed scanning him. The machine beeped and a guard waved him through. His electronic gear took much longer to be cleared, each tool and gauge minutely examined by a Secret Service agent. His heart rate and skin-conductivity index were probably also being monitored, so he concentrated on images of Paradise and the blessings that awaited him.

Give good news to those who believe and work righteousness that they will have gardens with flowing streams, and pure spouses therein. They abide therein forever.

"Master Inspector," said the Secret Service agent, beckoning him over.

"Yes, Officer?" said Bartholomew, stomach churning.

The agent was a small man with a cleft chin and a spotless blue uniform with the presidential seal over his heart. He held up one of Bartholomew's handheld resonance meters. "*This* is not on the approved list."

"It's the latest model," sputtered Bartholomew. "Just came in last week from Lagos. That's why it's not on your list."

The agent slipped the resonance meter into a plastic bag. Pursed his lips. "You can pick it up on the way out."

Bartholomew bowed, seething, his cheeks flushed. He had practiced his reaction for weeks now, clenching his jaw muscles to bring color to his cheeks. *Give the agent something easy to reject, something to justify his authority—that way they won't look too closely at the rest of your things,* that's what al-Faisal had said. As always, the Black Robe was correct.

Peterson clapped him on the shoulder as they started up the corridor to the presidential jet. "Don't worry, Bartholomew, last week they made me remove a decal of the Kaaba from the inside lid of my toolkit, an innocent souvenir from my hajj."

Bartholomew shook his head. Peterson was the other aeronautical inspector on the flight, a redundancy like everything else on the presidential jet, human and mechanical, designed to ensure maximum security.

"You been to Mexico City before?" said Peterson, a slender modern with a thin strip of beard running along his jaw, a beard in name only. "Oh, you've got a *treat* in store for you. Stick with me, I'll show you some places you won't want to tell the imam about."

Bartholomew smiled. This time he didn't have to fake the color in his cheeks.

"Does having a baby . . . does it, you know, change things?" said Leo.

"*Things?*" said Sarah.

Leo glanced at Michael, the toddler playing with wooden blocks, then back at Sarah. "Things. *Sex.*"

"Well, you don't have as much time for sex, but the—you tend to appreciate it more. Don't look so glum, you and Leanne have plenty of time before you think about having kids."

"Tell that to Leanne."

Sarah looked up. "Is she pregnant? Oh, Leo, that's *wonderful.*"

"No, no, I was just asking, because . . . with my brainpower and everything, I probably pack a real punch down there too." Leo's face reddened. "You know . . . sperm-wise."

"How romantic."

Sarah and Leo sat on the floor of Michael's bedroom, watching as he built tall towers of blocks. Leo had been visiting for the last hour, working up to asking questions about marriage. Sarah was glad for the company, eager to take a break from trying to figure out what Eagleton was hiding on the holographic display card. Tired of watching him star in his own pornographic movie. Even a shower didn't make her feel clean afterward.

Being with Michael allowed her to breathe again. She watched as he balanced a red block on top of a yellow column, then looked up at her and giggled. He reached for another block. Always pushing the limits, angry when the pile collapsed. Just like his daddy.

"What if Leanne loves the baby more than me?" said Leo.

"You're getting a little ahead of yourself." Sarah patted Leo's arm. "Is this why you dropped in? I heard Spider had you locked away for safekeeping."

"Spider doesn't think I can take care of myself. Neither does Rikki."

Sarah knew what Leo meant. Rakkim said they needed to move, so that's what they were going to do. She hated the idea. This apartment was their nest. Familiar and spacious. She would argue with him, but eventually Rakkim would get his way. He deferred to her judgment on most issues, but when it came to security, his was the only voice heard.

"You want me to help you with the holographic card?" said Leo.

"No, thanks."

"You sure?"

Sarah watched Michael banging two blocks together, laughing at the sound. It would have taken more than money to tempt Eagleton to climb in bed with the Black Robes. He must have known the risks, the risks if he failed, the even greater risks if he succeeded. Colarusso's forensic accountants had traced over $30 million deposited into Eagleton's overseas account in the last five months. Plenty for him to buy his way out of the republic and retire to that South African surf beach. It couldn't have been just money that drew him in. The challenge . . . that would have been the ultimate attraction. To do something . . . enormous, *and get away with it.* His little secret. The best of all worlds.

The tower of blocks suddenly collapsed, and Michael bellowed. Threw one of the red blocks across the room. Bounced it off a shelf of other toys. He looked up at her.

"You threw it, *you* go get it," said Sarah.

Michael heaved himself up, walked over to the shelf, and picked up the block.

Sarah stared at the shelf loaded with toys. Mechanical toys, computerized dragons, plastic soldiers, knights and warriors, paint sets and coloring books. Like the shelves of toys in Eagleton's back room. She got up, kicked aside some blocks in her haste.

Michael watched her approach, mouth open.

"What is it?" said Leo.

Sarah picked up the Digi-Sketch off the shelf. A gift from her mother. Supposed to encourage artistic expression in babies, but Michael had ignored it after five minutes and never played with it again. It was a small, flat holographic unit, light enough for an infant to hold, with knobs and buttons to draw numbers and colored images on the monitor. Twelve screen options were available with a touch. Eagleton had three of them in his shop, plus a few antique Etch A Sketches. She carefully removed the control chip from the side of the Digi-Sketch. "Leo, would you play with Michael for a little while?"

"You figured it out, didn't you?" said Leo.

Michael raised his hands toward the control chip. "*Mine.*"

Typical male, thought Sarah, closing the door to her office behind her.

"I hardly recognize Leo," chastised Spider, bundled up in spite of the sun on his face.

Rakkim and Spider sat in sagging lawn chairs atop the flat roof of a house in the Catholic sector. Spider's latest home, run-down from the outside, but wireless surveillance technology was deployed throughout the structure. Anthony Colarusso sat at the kitchen table downstairs, eating roast chicken and arguing football with Spider's twelve-year-old daughter, who had evidently memorized every game in the history of the sport. Dogs chased each other, ran through wash hung out to dry. Kids played ball in the crumbling streets, rode bikes through the alleys, whooping and hollering. After years living underground, Spider said he was happier here than anyplace else he could imagine.

"He's *different,*" said Spider. "You were supposed to look after him—"

"All that stuff he downloaded into his brain, no wonder—"

"I'm—I'm not talking about *that,*" sputtered Spider. "Leo's more than capable of massive data transfers, it's the rest of him that's different. You saw what he was like when you two left. Naïve, full of fear and bluster—"

"He was a pain in the ass," said Rakkim, squinting. "I spent the first week pissed off at you and Sarah for saddling me with him, but the Belt . . . it changes people. When we left he was a burden . . . but, he grew up on me. He saw things there, good things, beautiful things, and terrible things too . . . he *did* things, Spider, things neither you nor I would have believed him capable of. I've seen it happen fast before. I've seen it happen overnight. In a single moment—"

"He wants to get *married*. He wants to move to the Belt and marry some girl he spent less than twenty-four hours with."

"Leo's a man now, and he made a man's decision."

"Easy for you to say." Spider slumped in his chair, wrapped the blanket tighter around himself. "Wait until Michael grows up and wants to marry a stranger."

Rakkim turned his face toward the sun. Not a cloud in the sky. "That's a long way off."

"Not as far away as you think."

Rakkim heard a dog barking, the sound setting off others. "Where is he? Have you checked on him today?"

Spider started to speak. Stopped. Waiting for the shakes to subside. His eyes were clear now. "He's at your place, talking with Sarah. I thought you knew."

Rakkim straightened up. "I thought we decided he was to stay put."

Spider's hand twitched. "I can't stop him anymore. He's a man now, *remember?*"

Al-Faisal checked his watch for the hundredth time, glanced out into the cloudless sky. A beautiful day. From the minaret of the Grand Saladin mosque he could see the whole city spread out before him, helpless as a kafir on Judgment Day.

He had met last night with Amir Kidd, reassured the Fedayeen that today's actions were in complete accordance with the Quran. That obedience to the Old One superseded all of his previous oaths and commitments.

Pigeons circled the minaret, wheeled off to more inviting perches in nearby buildings. Filthy birds, may Allah strike them from the sky and shatter their eggs in the nest.

Al-Faisal had sensed uncertainty in Amir last night. After all this time, the young officer still felt the gossamer strands of loyalty to his father, the Fedayeen commander. Such weakness disgusted al-Faisal. He had spent over two years getting close to Amir. Two years of the most gentle persuasion . . . a comment uttered by a trusted fellow Fedayeen, a sermon by a battlefield imam, a rumor shared by a concubine during a night of lust that questioned the president's judgment. Al-Faisal had waited a long time before making direct contact with Amir. He had played the youth masterfully, appealing to his youthful idealism, his passion, his faith and courage . . . and, most of all, to his mixed feelings about his father. Love and ambition were dangerous weaknesses, and al-Faisal had exploited them mercilessly.

So this is the famous Lion of Boulder, al-Faisal had greeted him, kissing Amir on both cheeks, after his Fedayeen unit beat back the Mormon attack into Colorado. Amir had dismissed the phrase, credited his men for the victory, but al-Faisal could see it pleased him.

Even after Amir swore allegiance to the Old One, he insisted that his father not be harmed. His father was no apostate, he assured al-Faisal, but a noble warrior whose piety was beyond dispute. General Kidd's only failing was that his devotion to the president had left him blind to the man's deficiencies. Against al-Faisal's counsel, the Old One himself had decreed that General Kidd's sin would be overlooked, and the warrior allowed an honorable exile in his native Somalia with his wives and estates.

Two years al-Faisal had worked on Amir. The Old One had spent even longer turning al-Faisal from the Black Robe's hierarchy. Al-Faisal had no regrets. He would stand at the right hand of the Old One in this life and the right hand of Allah in the next. The Old One had assured him that nothing would be denied the righteous warrior. Al-Faisal glanced at his watch. Turned his face into the blinding sun. A glorious day, *inshallah.*

Sarah touched the remote, did a rapid turn behind Eagleton's straining thighs, then darted out the open window. Nothing. The line of headlights had been transformed to a line of flaming torches, Eagleton's leering face was a cubist nightmare, but there was still no hint of what had drawn his attention for all those hours as he sat at his desk.

The control chip for the Digi-Sketch was compatible with Eagleton's holo display card, of course, and one of the twelve screens from the Digi-Sketch keyed perfectly to the card's program. It was a whole new porno show. Some joke. Sarah had been chasing her tail for days trying intricately engineered screens to search for clues, but the answer had been in the opposite direction: using the simple, basic graphics chip of a baby's toy. Somewhere in hell, Eagleton was amused.

Since downloading the Digi-Sketch screen, Sarah had spent a half hour scanning the card without success, looking in all the corners, inside out and upside down. The screen showed Eagleton with a barbed penis, a monstrous member that drove through the back of the young woman's skull, spurting flowers from the tip. She followed each bud of the flower, expanding the frame farther and farther, until she was certain there was no useful information there.

"Is everything all right?" called Leo through the closed door.

"Not now." Sarah's fingers hovered over the control pad. She needed to slow down. Unpleasant as it was, she had to think like Eagleton. She let the image run, Eagleton's barbed penis pistoning back and forth.

She closed her eyes, opened them, taking in the whole wall that Eagleton had looked at, the porno card the most important part, but not the only part. High-gloss cars . . . motorcycles . . . speed and reflected light . . . a surfing beach, waves stacked up . . . a young man with his eyes rolled back in pleasure . . . a college girl with a charm bracelet. The bracelet was the first thing she had gone over, looking for some symbolic meaning in the charms. It was just a photo, her innocence the basis of her appeal. She forced herself to relax . . . looked down, then up. Eagleton was supremely arrogant. What would confirm his sense of superiority? What could he see on the wall that no one else would notice? It would have to be obvious. Everyone would have to be proven a fool for Eagleton to be as brilliant as he knew he was.

She went back to the holo card, looking for patterns, light and dark. The young woman's face drew her attention . . . but she had already studied it from every angle. She looked at the face again, forced herself not to stare, but just *look*, the way Eagleton had. What was *that*? Sarah tilted the holographic image, saw a tiny gold gondola among the strands of the woman's hair. Just like the gold gondola on the college girl's charm bracelet. It had been a bead of sweat on the original, without the toy screen. Sarah's excitement faded as she inspected the gondola without seeing anything.

There. Another gold charm in the young woman's hair, this one a tennis racquet. A car. A heart. An airplane. A seashell. A rose. All of them in the exact order as the charms on the college girl's wrist. All of them so artfully placed among the hair that Sarah hadn't noticed them before. She zoomed in on them one by one, blowing each of them up until they filled the screen, turning them over and around, making sure no surface was unexamined. Halfway through the hidden charm bracelet, she came to the gold airplane.

"Oh . . . *shit.*"

Bartholomew held his systems analyzer in the palm of his hand, tapped into the main terminal of the aircraft while a dour Secret Service agent peered over his shoulder. His fingers flew over the keys, making minute adjustments, aligning the computer interfaces. There were fifty-one individual electronic systems on Air Force One. Seventeen separate systems with triple redundancy. Any failure immediately initiated a backup. In the rare event that the backup failed, there was the third system. It had never been needed. He monitored the readouts on the systems analyzer, a Beck-Dibden DB9. If he hadn't known better, he would have sworn it was his own.

Bartholomew had no idea how Eagleton had done it, but the man had made an exact match of Bartholomew's DB9, even down to the serial numbers etched into the microscopic components. Same wear patterns as his old one. Same digital history. His own DB9 had been a gift from his father upon his graduation from advanced training five years ago. Cost enough to buy a house, enough to put his father in debt for years, but his father never looked happier than when Bartholomew opened the box. Bartholomew had prostrated himself in gratitude before his father, his tears soaking the carpet. A week ago . . . a week ago, after getting this one from al-Faisal, he had taken the ferry to Bainbridge Island and tossed the gift from his father overboard halfway across the Sound.

The DB9 beeped. Bartholomew showed the screen to the Secret Service agent, then disengaged the unit. He bowed to Peterson, then sat in the jump seat, while the other inspector did his own check, watched over by another Secret Service agent. Peterson wouldn't find anything amiss. Allah willing.

Bartholomew belted himself in, then looked out the window at the refueling trucks on their way back to the terminal. He was astounded at how calm he was. From the other side of the curtain, he could hear the president telling a joke to the assembled reporters. Their laughter disgusted Bartholomew. He turned back to Peterson. The man was utterly serious. Focused. He might be an idolatrous modern looking forward to the sins available in Mexico City, but at this moment he was a dedicated, superbly trained professional.

Peterson showed his DB9 to the Secret Service agent and sat down in the jump seat opposite Bartholomew. He clasped his seat belt. Nodded at Bartholomew as the plane started moving.

Bartholomew watched the tarmac roll past, faster and faster, the big jet rapidly gathering speed. He felt as though he were beginning his ascent into Paradise.

Rakkim pointed and Spider turned, the two of them watching the president's jet rising above the city. Not a plane in the sky other than Air Force One and the six fighter jets providing an escort. People in the surrounding houses walked out into their backyards, shading their eyes with their hands. Most of them crossed themselves. Even with all that had happened, the constant religious tension and steady decline in the quality of life, President Kingsley was the only politician that drew support across all classes and faiths.

Rakkim clasped his hands toward Air Force One. "*Salaam alaikum.*"

"Shalom," said Spider.

"Mr. President!" Sarah pressed a finger against her ear link. Static. "Sir!" She was one of only a dozen people who had a direct link to the chief executive. Day or night she should have been able to reach him on this emergency frequency. She stared at the holographic image of the gold airplane on the screen. "Sir!" The gold airplane's cockpit was filled with fire, and the frightened pilot looked just like the president. "Mr. President?" Static. Sound of electronic snow drifting higher and higher.

Bartholomew stared out at the city below, the neat grid of streets and skyscrapers, the lush green parks . . . the golden dome of the Great Mosque. It was never more beautiful than now. The great engines of the jet thrummed all around him, the power of man, dwarfed only by the will of Allah.

He slipped off his watch. Time was irrelevant now. He saw Peterson watching him and turned again to the window. Faint static filled the air, every electronic device in the plane overwhelmed by the chaff—Air Force One generated a stream of jamming frequencies across the spectrum on take-off and landing to prevent a missile attack.

Bartholomew thought of his mother and father down below . . . in a small house off Green Lake with a neatly trimmed yard and a rusting basketball hoop over the garage. He hadn't lived at home for years, but his father kept the hoop up anyway. Said he liked to look at it as he left for work in the morning. Bartholomew was their only son, their greatest joy. He hoped they were not looking up in the sky right now, following the president's progress. He should have been proud of his handiwork, his small part in the vast design, but Bartholomew was weak. He hoped his parents were busy with other things.

"Mr. President!"

"Sarah?" More static. "—that you?"

"Mr. President, thank God." Tears rolled down Sarah's cheeks. She could see her mother in the doorway, holding Michael in her arms. Leo stood beside her. "Mr. President, order your plane to land, *now.*"

"Sarah . . ." Static crackled, then cleared. "What's wrong?"

"Please order your plane to land, sir. I don't care where, just put it down."

"Yes . . . yes, of course."

Sarah heard the president order the pilot to land, his voice steady. Then she heard . . . silence. All the static of the transmission was gone. All that remained was the president's voice, perfectly clear, saying, "That's odd." And the pounding of her heart, getting louder.

"Mr. President? What's happening, sir?"

The president cleared his throat. "It seems . . . we seem to have lost power."

Bartholomew listened to the nervous whispers from the rear of the plane. The prayers.

A Secret Service agent jerked him from his seat, pushed him toward the main console. "*Fix* it."

Peterson was already at work with his DB9, trying to make a connection.

Seventeen separate networks, triple redundancy. Yet, exactly eighteen minutes after Bartholomew had run his preflight diagnostic, every system went dead. Irrevocably dead. The secret was a molecular timer inserted with Eagleton's DB9. Perfectly normal until eighteen minutes later, at which point the whole system fried.

The floor of the plane tilted down. The pilot performed brilliantly of course, but he had no stabilizers, no engines, no wing flaps, no communications. He had nothing . . . but a heavy piece of metal, and gravity was calling. The floor tilted farther . . . farther.

The Secret Service agent kicked Bartholomew in the ass. "Do something."

Bartholomew fell to his knees, pressed his forehead against the cool carpet, and offered his devotion and praise to Allah, and the Wise Old One who served him.

> And as for him who was outrageous and preferred the life of
>   this world, verily, hell is the resort!
> But as for him who feared the station of his Lord, and prohib-
>   ited his soul from lust, verily, Paradise is the resort!

"I saw . . . I saw it on TV," panted Colarusso, out of breath. "You know what's going on?"

Spider shook his head, focused on the small, silver shape that was the president's plane. He watched as it rolled over, spinning slowly as it fell.

Rakkim ran down the stairs.

"It's quite all right, Sarah." The president sounded relaxed. At peace.

"Send out a Mayday—"

"We have no communications at all." The president chuckled. "It's just you and I, dear girl."

Sarah could hear weeping in the background. "The ejection pod—"

"A total systems failure, according to the pilot," said the president. "There may be some mechanical explanation . . . or it could be our enemies have finally succeeded."

Sarah's mother had turned on the television, stared at the image of Air Force One dropping out of blue, blue sky. She sobbed, trying to distract Michael with a stuffed bear.

"Pay attention, Sarah," chided the president. "With the vice president and I gone . . . Sarah, please, don't cry . . ."

Sarah heard the background noise from the plane getting louder through her ear link, heard people shouting and the rush and rattle of wind.

"Sarah . . . tell Rakkim—"

Sarah's earpiece went dead.

Leo covered his mouth as the television showed a fireball . . . the tail structure of Air Force One scattered among the fields of red tulips just north of the city . . . then cut back to the studio news anchor, a handsome man with gray hair and a neatly trimmed beard. He couldn't speak, lips trembling, finally shook his head, and walked off camera.

Assalaamu Alaikum. A state of national emergency is now declared, said a deep voice, as the other anchor and the weatherman exchanged stunned glances. *Until further notice, all forms of communication within the capital are now blocked in the interests of national security. Please go to your homes and await further word from the Office of the President.* The screen went to an image of the flag billowing over the Presidential Palace.

Sarah heard pounding at the front door. She wiped her tears, checked the security monitors. Yelled to Leo and her mother.

CHAPTER 48

Rakkim's throat tightened as he saw the security shutter to their apartment half-raised. "Stop the car."

"What's the—?" started Colarusso, but it was too late.

Rakkim had already rolled out the door of the moving vehicle, sprinting toward the abandoned storefront below their apartment, terrified at what he would find inside.

The raised security shutter was Sarah's signal for danger. With communications down throughout the capital, even the presidential com link, he hadn't been able to get through to her, and she hadn't been able to reach him, but she was still able to warn him. She had time for that. Maybe time enough for her to grab the baby, for her and Katherine and Leo to escape through one of the emergency exits. Time enough to reach their rally point, their prearranged meeting place. *Maybe.*

Redbeard's dictum: Plan for the day when all your plans fail, when those you trust betray you, when your certainty cracks like a rotten egg and you are alone in the storm. That's the place he was right now. The president dead, the government in turmoil, helicopters buzzing over the city, and the Fedayeen on high alert. None of that meant a thing right now.

Rakkim kicked the boarded-up door open, still running, breathing hard. He took the rickety wooden stairs two at a time, three at a time, kicking up dust as he accelerated. His foot broke through one of the termite-ridden steps, but he pulled it free, kept running, the knife in his hand. He turned off at the sixth-floor landing, raced down the deserted corridor, tearing through cobwebs.

The door to Rakkim and Sarah's closet looked like part of the plasterboard wall. He pressed a recessed button along the floorboard, looked into a knothole for the iris scan, and the section of wall slid noiselessly back.

He could smell Sarah's perfume on her clothes, saw them bunched underfoot where they had been ripped from their hangers. He felt the softness of her pale blue dress brush against his face as he peered through a gap in the doors. Sounds from the other rooms. Glass breaking. Furniture being knocked over. Loud voices, as though they didn't care who heard them. He eased the doors apart, padding forward. Their bed had been slashed apart, Sarah's antique dresser kicked to pieces, all her pretty things scattered. His heart beat quietly now, steadily, calm as milk as he closed in on the strangers in his home.

Michael's room was empty. A few toys scattered, his rocking horse decapitated. Sarah's office ransacked. The bathroom door tilted open, the lock broken. Someone had taken refuge behind that door. He moved closer, looked inside. Oh, *Katherine* . . . He stepped inside, bent down beside her on the floor, shaking his head, aching. Her eyes bulged, the whites red with burst capillaries. Her neck was swollen and purple, her blackened tongue extended. A strangler had killed her slowly, painfully. Her crucifix had been torn off. He found it resting at the bottom of the toilet and retrieved it. He returned to Katherine, gently turned her head. Two slight indentations were on the back of her neck, two indentations where the strangler had knotted his killing cord, a signature. Rakkim had seen two indentations in exactly the same spot in the photo of Eagleton's body. Al-Faisal's calling card on his return from the dead.

Rakkim stroked Katherine's hair. Closed her eyes. Did you run in here as death closed in? Did you call out to the killers, buying time for the others to escape? Did you beg for mercy as they beat at the doors, a smile on your face? *Please, we're all alone in here. Take what you want, just leave us in peace.* Is that what you said? May God wrap you in his loving embrace for telling such a beautiful lie, Katherine. He kissed her forehead and stood up. He eased into the living room.

Two men in moderate street clothes ransacked the room, clearly ex-Fedayeen from the determined way they moved. The reinforced front door hung by one hinge, the door frame chopped away. The two Fedayeen cut into the walls with their knives, looking for hidden compartments, slashed open the sofas. A Black Robe examined the books on Sarah's bookshelf, stroking his fine, dark beard, disgusted. A fourth man stood with arms crossed monitoring the security screens—circular drive, underground

garage, the two elevators, the main entryway. Army Special Forces according to the notch in his right nostril. Fedayeen, Special Forces, and Black
Robe, a classic strike team, a mixed crew of professional killers in his living room, waiting for Rakkim to show up.

No sign of Sarah or Michael. Or Leo. No sign of al-Faisal. Just these
four men. Al-Faisal must be with the rest of the strike team, in pursuit of
his family . . . or in possession of them. Rakkim felt his heart turn to ice—
no fear, no forgiveness. He moved slowly across the living room, *very*
slowly, a half glide to avoid alerting the Fedayeen.

The transition was instantaneous. One moment Rakkim barely moved,
the next he had driven his blade into the ear of the first Fedayeen, killed
the second with a single thrust under the jaw. Special Forces rushed over
from the security screens, just missed him with a low strike, an assassin tactic to bleed out the femoral artery. A good move, but the man hadn't
learned his lessons well enough. He should have rolled as he slashed at
Rakkim's thigh, come up fighting from a tuck position. Rakkim dodged
the strike, sliced the man's carotid with a flick of his blade. Rakkim didn't
wait to see him die, instead chased down the Black Robe, who scampered
toward the front door in a billow of black fabric. The cleric almost reached
the doorknob before Rakkim threw him back into the living room.

Rakkim stared at the tiny red crescent on each of the Black Robe's earlobes, a sign of his elevated rank. A tall, scrawny man with a sharp nose . . .
and a mouth full of crooked teeth. Just as Sarah had described the Black
Robe who had beaten her at the Saint Sebastian street fair.

The Black Robe scuttled to his feet, grappled with him, but Rakkim
dashed the man against a decorative pillar, beat him down.

Rakkim walked into the kitchen. Came back a few moments later with
a couple of Sarah's carving knives. The Black Robe saw the look on his
face, got halfway up. Rakkim pushed him back with a foot, sat on the man's
hips. The Black Robe slapped at him, but Rakkim held him by the right
wrist, drove the carving knife through the palm, pinning him to the hardwood floor.

The Black Robe arched his back, screaming.

Rakkim held the left hand down, drove in the other knife.

The Black Robe groaned, bit his gristly lips shut. Blood welled in his
palms.

"Where's my family?"

The Black Robe spit in his face.

Rakkim wiped his face. "Does al-Faisal have my family?"

The Black Robe's eyes widened, surprised at Rakkim's mention of the name.

Rakkim flicked the handle of the knife pinning the Black Robe's right hand, the blade vibrating in the pooled blood. "I'm in a hurry."

The Black Robe ground his teeth. "Do you think I fear death, apostate? Whatever you do to me, this day I shall be in Paradise."

Rakkim sliced open the man's robe, cut away his undershirt. His flesh was hard and sinewy, mottled with self-inflicted wounds—another masochist convinced that Allah took pleasure in the mortification of his divine creation. Brutalizing him for the truth would be fruitless; the Black Robe considered suffering a badge of honor.

"You see the marks of my faith?" preened the Black Robe. He tugged at the knives holding down his hands, deepening the cuts. "Go ahead. I'll show you how a good Muslim dies."

Rakkim blotted sweat from the Black Robe's forehead with the edge of the man's hood. "When did al-Faisal and the others leave?"

"If you hurry, perhaps you can catch them. Al-Faisal will welcome you."

"Be careful what you wish for." Rakkim traced the man's smile with the tip of his knife. "You see how easily I killed these three."

"See how well you do against twice that number." The Black Robe clamped his mouth shut at what he had revealed, but quickly recovered, his bravado returned. "You should see what al-Faisal's capable of when he has time. You'll feel the cord slowly tighten around your neck until you'll piss yourself for a single breath—"

"My family is everything to me." Rakkim lightly ran the tip of his blade down the man's nose, brought a drop of blood to the tip as the Black Robe squirmed. "Duty, honor, country . . . those are just words. I'd burn down heaven for my family." The knife sliced one nostril, the Black Robe's panting breath setting the membrane flapping. "There's nothing I wouldn't do to protect my family. Nothing I wouldn't *do* to someone trying to hurt them. Do you understand me?"

"You're a weakling." The Black Robe reveled in the pain the blade brought him. "Suckling at a woman's teat for comfort—"

"What about you?" Rakkim said idly, his face just inches above the Black Robe's. "What do you care about?"

"*Allah*," sneered the Black Robe. "Allah is all I care about, all that I love. The rest is dust. Go ahead, flay me, you kafir filth, skin me alive and set me ablaze. I fear only God."

"I'm glad to hear that," said Rakkim, genuinely pleased.

The Black Robe gasped as Rakkim lightly cut a five-inch line down his chest.

Rakkim looked into his eyes. "Does al-Faisal have my family?"

The Black Robe stayed silent, knowing any answer might reveal the truth.

Rakkim cut another line into the Black Robe's chest, this one forming a V with the other one. "Does he?"

The Black Robe's eyes fluttered in ecstasy, "Yes . . . no . . . yes . . . no." The Black Robe giggled, turned his head from side to side with every answer. "Yes, no, yes, no."

Rakkim turned, hearing sounds from beyond the bedroom.

"Troop? Where are you?"

"Anthony! This way. Walk through the closet." Rakkim could see the Black Robe's heart pounding in his bare chest, blood filling the cuts.

"Troop, we've got to leave. There's all kinds of . . . Jesus, Rakkim! What are you *doing*?"

Colarusso looked around at the dead men scattered around the living room, blood pooling on the hardwood. "Where's Sarah and—?"

"That's what I've been asking my friend here," said Rakkim.

"Rakkim?" Colarusso was beside him now, his voice soft. "You want me to arrest this prick, fine. Heck, you want him to have an accident coming down the stairs, bust a few bones, I can live with that too, but the whole country's coming apart. We need the law more than ever now. I'll take him in for questioning. I won't go easy—"

"I don't have time for the law, Anthony." Rakkim watched the Black Robe. "Not the time, or the inclination. You go on now, I'll be fine."

"You can't torture a man. I don't care what he's done."

"He doesn't mind pain, Anthony." Rakkim tapped the flat of his blade under the Black Robe's silky beard. "Isn't that right?"

The Black Robe jerked at the knives pinning his hands, tearing his own flesh. "For every *minute* of pain I suffer, I shall be rewarded with a thousand years of pleasure."

"I have to get to the financial district," said Colarusso. "Christians are breaking windows and burning cars, shit-scared of who's going to replace the president—"

"Al-Faisal's alive," said Rakkim. "He murdered Katherine. The Black Robes may be behind the assassination of the president."

"We don't know there's been any assassination . . . Al-Faisal's alive?" Colarusso scratched his belly. "That is important. All the more reason to bring this one in for questioning."

"You can come back for him when I'm done." Rakkim slit a straight line across the V carved on the Black Robe's chest, connecting the two arms of the triangle.

"Rakkim . . . this is *wrong*," said Colarusso, as the Black Robe gasped. "This isn't you."

"Don't tell me who I am, Anthony."

"Look . . . I'll help you find Sarah," said Colarusso. "Fuck the financial district. I can call in some cops I know to join us, hard-ass Catholics—"

"Hard-ass Catholics?" cackled the Black Robe. "Al-Faisal will nail their blackened tongues to the nearest church."

"You should go," said Rakkim. "I appreciate the offer, but I'll take care of this myself."

"Rikki . . . ?"

"Go serve the law, Anthony. This man has something to tell me, and I can't wait to hear it." Rakkim waited until Colarusso had left, then walked over and picked up a piece of broken mirror. He sat back on the Black Robe, held the mirror over the cleric's chest, and showed him the triangle cut into his flesh. "Do you see where I'm headed?"

The Black Robe squinted at the mirror.

Rakkim cut another line into him, this one bisecting the top angle of the triangle. Held up the mirror. "Do you see it yet?"

The Black Robe craned his neck.

Rakkim cut another slanted line that bisected one of the two lower angles of the triangle.

The Black Robe stared at the mirror. Eyes wide now . . . *wider*.

"You see it now, don't you?"

The Black Robe thrashed against Rakkim, straining to pull his hands free.

"Allah is all you care about. All you fear." Rakkim's knife hovered over the Black Robe's chest. "One more stroke of the blade, and you'll have a Jewish star carved into your flesh. No chance for Paradise then. You might as well show up before God wearing a pig's head."

"I beg you, *no*."

Rakkim's knife popped the skin on the Black Robe's pale chest. "Burning forever without being consumed. And when you beg for a drop of cool water for your scorched tongue . . . you shall be given boiling oil to quench your thirst. That's what you teach, isn't it?"

"Please . . . ?"

"One lie from you and I'll complete the star. One lie . . . and I'll know." The knife edged slowly across the Black Robe's skin. "Does al-Faisal have my family?"

"No! We . . . we heard the old woman's voice . . . thought they were all hiding in the bathroom." The Black Robe grimaced. "Al-Faisal . . . he was furious. He kept demanding that she tell him where your wife had gone, but the old bitch just *laughed* at him."

"Does al-Faisal have any idea where my family has gone?"

The Black Robe shook his head, his eyes on the tip of the knife resting on his bleeding chest.

"Al-Faisal and the others . . . they're out there, aren't they? They're waiting for me to lead them to Sarah and Michael, aren't they?"

The Black Robe looked up at him. "How . . . ?"

"It's what I would have done." Rakkim stropped the knife against the Black Robe's hairless chest. "Did the grand mullah have the president assassinated? Al-Faisal wouldn't have done that on his own."

The Black Robe tried to flatten himself away from the knife. "Al-Faisal is *obedient* . . . as am I."

There was something in the man's tone, some hidden knowledge. "Who sent you for Sarah and Michael?" The blade started toward the last arm of the star. "Why them, why today of all days?"

"Michael . . . ?" The Black Robe looked confused, dry balls of spit popping from his mouth. "I . . . I was told the Jew's name was *Leo*."

"Leo?" Rakkim grabbed his hair. "Is *that* who you were after?"

"You think you're so clever . . ." The Black Robe thrashed, jerked against the kitchen knives that held him down. "But the truth . . . the truth won't help you at all."

Rakkim leaned into him, their faces inches apart. "I asked you a question."

The Black Robe tried to look away, but couldn't.

"*Who* sent you?"

"Your f-face . . . ," said the Black Robe, teeth chattering as though he were freezing. "Your face . . . it's different, b-but I recognize those eyes. I *know* you."

Rakkim had never met the Black Robe before, he was sure of it.

"What . . . what is this game?" said the Black Robe, still trembling. "Do you *test* my loyalty?"

"Who sent you?" demanded Rakkim, the knife skating across the Black Robe's chest.

"I serve the Old One." The Black Robe tore one hand free, grabbed Rakkim's wrist, and plunged the blade into his own throat, blood spurting from his neck like a fountain as he wriggled in pain. "As . . . do . . . *you,* Darwin."

CHAPTER 49

Rakkim watched Redbeard's ruined villa from the nearby woods. Spotted Sarah's car half-hidden under a collapsed section of roofing and allowed himself to breathe. No other cars, no helicopter hovering in the distance — just her unregistered getaway ride, a beat-up German import with a high-performance engine and rugged frame. He skirted the property just inside the trees, approaching the villa from the blind side, away from any roads.

The villa was a sprawling, one-story retreat outside the city, the house uninhabited since the State Security chief's death almost three years ago. Many of the white stone walls had been battered down, the rest blackened by fire, marred by obscene graffiti. Sarah and he had grown up in that house, knew every hallway and hiding spot, shared memories of late-night suppers with Redbeard and afternoons studying in the water garden. All gone now, the villa useful only as a rally point, a last resort if they were ever separated. It was enough.

He had been followed after leaving the apartment, a gray sedan with smoked windows — Rakkim driving his own emergency vehicle garaged blocks from his home. He had lost the gray sedan after a series of risky maneuvers, but didn't believe it. He gave al-Faisal too much credit for that. He avoided the rioting in the downtown core, raced to an underground mall parking garage, and changed cars — Rakkim stole the worst vehicle he could find, a three-wheeled halal-meat delivery van, finding the driver's cap behind the seat for good measure. Still no phone or communication, but judging from the smoke rising from other parts of the city, and the swarms of police helicopters, the rioting had spread. He drove the delivery van a few miles, switched to a nondescript family wagon from a looted used-car lot, and headed out of town. Once he exited the freeway, he waited twenty minutes to see if he had been followed, then continued on, taking backroads, checking his rearview. He had made the final approach on a logging road not on any map, left the family wagon on the other side of the woods. It had taken him almost two hours, but he knew he hadn't been followed.

The only thing pursuing Rakkim were the Black Robe's final words, the cleric driven mad by pain and fear, in his desperation seeing Darwin in Rakkim's eyes. No . . . Rakkim knew better. It wasn't madness that gave the Black Robe such a vision. Today's terrible events had stirred Darwin from his slumbers and brought him closer to the surface, rising on a tide of blood. Rakkim could feel the assassin under his skin, could hear him calling out, the dead man's whisper like the rustle of dry leaves. Rakkim ignored him as best he could, and Darwin fell silent, just another ghost along for the ride.

The passenger-side door of Sarah's car hung open. He imagined her slipping from the driver's seat, Michael in one arm, while Leo jumped out the other side, looking around, too scared to close the door. Sarah would have been calm . . . as calm as she could be with Michael there, as calm as she could be knowing what must have happened to her mother.

Rakkim loped through the trees, staying clear of the blackberry bushes sprouting thorns and the morning-glory vines. He hadn't played in these woods in fifteen years, the trails were overgrown and eroded, but he could have found his way in the dark.

Al-Faisal was working for the Old One, not the grand mullah of the Black Robes. Rakkim cursed himself for his stupidity. It should have been obvious once the president was killed. With both the president and vice president dead, the next in line of succession was Peter Brandt, Speaker of the House. Brandt was a youthful, charismatic politician and a solid moderate with a modern wife. The last person who the Black Robes would want to replace President Kingsley. The Old One didn't care about lines of succession. He thrived on chaos and uncertainty. The worse things got, the more likely it was for someone of his choosing to seize the reins of power. Rakkim prayed that Speaker Brandt . . . *President* Brandt was in a secure bunker somewhere. And General Kidd . . . no way he would be anywhere but in the thick of the conflict, but he would also have to be a target. If the Fedayeen were compromised . . .

He increased his pace. A chipmunk observed his progress, scampered deeper into the woods. Rakkim had expected an attempt on his and Sarah's lives sooner or later—they had too many enemies for someone not to make a move, but he'd never considered that *Leo* might be a target. He remembered the look on the Black Robe's face as he pushed the knife deeper into his own throat . . . as though the man had won some prize. Maybe he had. The prize of silence. Being beyond Rakkim's questions. It didn't matter. Rakkim had all the answers he needed. If the Old One wanted Leo, it was because he already had the isotope for making the hafnium bomb. The Big Bang. Hard to imagine the Old One reaching out to Baby and Gravenholtz, but if his operatives could penetrate the Black Robes hierarchy, State Security, and the Fedayeen, they might even have compromised the Colonel's own household. Baby might not have put up much of a fight either.

Rakkim knelt at the fringe of the woods, ready to make his final approach. This close, the villa was in even worse shape than he remembered. Two years ago during Ramadan, vandals and successive mobs of fundamentalists had swarmed the site—what they couldn't carry away, they broke or burned. Even the water garden hadn't escaped their fury.

The water garden was Redbeard's favorite spot, more *him* than even his office, a lush acre protected from the cold by a clear plastic dome. Filled with towering tropical trees and plants, waterfalls and streams. A good place to pray, the water garden was as close to Paradise as existed this side of death, that's what Redbeard had said. Even at their worst moments, arguing over his studies or his insolence, even when Redbeard didn't speak to him for a week after Rakkim told him that he was joining the Fedayeen, they still sat together beside one of the waterfalls, just the two of them, listening to the water splashing over the flat stones. He and Sarah had first kissed in the water garden, surrounded by flowers, laughing as a bluejay interrupted their innocent ardor with its angry squawks.

He darted out of the woods, stayed low through the high grass, keeping the late-afternoon sun behind him to screen his movements from the main house. He slipped into the garden through a section where someone had crashed a stolen car through the dome, the car abandoned, covered with moss and yellow oleander blooms. Sweat rolled down his back in the sudden warmth and humidity. The mobs two years ago had uprooted plants, torn branches from the trees, and broken apart the fountains with picks and sledges, but the garden had reseeded itself, spreading out. It was much wilder now than when Redbeard lived here, a raw tangle of vines and bushes, more jungle than garden, the bamboo brushing the top of the dome.

He heard laughter behind him, turned, but no one was there. Weeds rustled . . . whispers through the fronds. Still no one there, but he wasn't alone. He listened for something, some sound beyond the water bubbling from one of the freshwater springs. He looked into the small pond . . . and Darwin looked back at him, pleased, a knowing smirk on his face.

Let me out to play, Rikki. Look how I helped you with Fareed . . . the Black Robe. Not a bad fellow, but limited . . .

The water rippled, Darwin's face shimmering, struggling to maintain its outline. Something wolflike in the tilt of his head, the angular cheeks and large eyes . . . the hunger in his gaze.

It helps when you cooperate, Rikki. Come on, let me out, I'm better at this than you are.

Then why are you dead . . . and I'm alive? Rakkim said silently.

Maybe . . . maybe there really was an angel on your shoulder. I'm sure of one thing, though, there's no angel here now.

I don't need an angel anymore, said Rakkim.

You still need me. I worked with the Old One for over ten years . . . I know the way he thinks, the little tricks he uses. The moment you're feeling good, feeling safe . . . the moment you know you've won, that's the moment you've lost.

Go away.

Listen to me. If you die, then I'll really be dead. Al-Faisal is good, Rikki. You never went up against a strangler. You've got to do something he doesn't anticipate . . . something unexpected. Darwin's image shifted as the sun slanted across the surface of the water, breaking up. *Show some gratitude, I'm trying to help you. You're like the son I never—*

Rakkim plunged his knife into Darwin's face. Is that unexpected enough? When the water smoothed out, he saw his own face looking back at him. He moved quickly through the water garden, following the path that Sarah and Michael and Leo had taken, brushing over their footprints. They had tried to be careful, but they were hurrying, and Leo kept stepping off the rocks. The sound of the waterfall got louder and louder as he approached, Rakkim circling around, leaving no trace. He eased himself through the thicket that covered the small waterfall, no more than a five-foot drop to the jagged stone below, but room enough underneath . . . He leaned over the side, the cold water misting his face. "Sarah?"

"Papa!" squealed Michael.

Rakkim quickly slid under the rushing water, managed to stay partially dry as he scrambled onto the mossy ledge under the falls, a tiny grotto they had discovered one day when they were teenagers. A secret spot to tell stories by candlelight, an innocent spot, never a hint of anything inappropriate, but *their* spot, private.

Michael threw himself into Rakkim's arms, clutched him.

Rakkim saw Sarah in the twilight, face damp, trying to smile. She was thinking about her mother. He nodded, and Sarah closed her eyes for a moment . . . crossed herself. He raised an eyebrow at that, and she embraced him, the two of them banging their heads against the rock ceiling. They held each other, their clothes damp, hair dripping as they kissed. He gently bit her lips, and she drove her mouth against him, the two of them sharing their heat, warming themselves with their joy and their relief.

"Nice to see you too," muttered Leo.

Rakkim saw Leo curled up in the corner, shivering and filthy, hardly any room to move.

"I'm claustrophobic and freezing to death, but what the heck, it's just Leo, right?"

"I know somebody who would be happy to trade places with you," snapped Rakkim.

Leo stared at him. "S-sorry." He glanced at Sarah. "Sorry."

"It's okay." Sarah turned to Rakkim, her arm still around his waist, Michael between them. "Now what do we do?"

"I don't want to spend the night in here," said Rakkim. "We can try working our way back to the city. Com links are down, a lot of roads are blocked off, but if we can get back to Spider's house, we should be safe." He felt Sarah shiver, rubbed her shoulders.

"The men who broke into our apartment . . . who *were* they?" said Sarah.

"Al-Faisal . . . and a strike team."

"I thought he was dead," said Leo.

"He was after you, Leo," said Rakkim. "Sarah and I were a bonus."

"Great." Leo pressed himself deeper into the corner, folding his legs up against his chest. It was getting darker outside, less light filtering through the waterfall, but Leo's eyes were large and shiny. "Somebody found out about the data cores, didn't they?"

Rakkim nodded. "The Old One."

"This is bad," said Leo, trembling. "This is really, *really* bad."

"Rikki and I have faced off with the Old One before," said Sarah. "We're still here."

"Yeah, but look where you are," said Leo.

Rakkim and Sarah laughed, and Michael laughed too, clapping his hands.

"It's not funny," said Leo.

Sarah felt Rakkim's back. "What *is* this?"

Rakkim twisted, reached around and felt the small of his back. Felt a small metal button. "Oh . . . shit." He peeled it away, held the button in the palm of his hand.

"We're dead," moaned Leo, holding his head in his hands. "That's a model seventeen. Got a thirty-mile range."

Sarah picked up a rock. "Put it down. I'll smash it."

"Bad idea." Rakkim kissed Sarah. Kissed Michael. "Stay here. No matter what happens, you stay here for as long as it takes. Don't move until I come for you. Understand?"

Sarah kissed him. "Go get 'em."

Rakkim slipped out the side of the waterfall, stayed on the rocks. He took off his wet jacket as he started walking, keeping to the hard places, the overgrown spots where he wouldn't leave a trail that could be backtracked. The Black Robe at the apartment . . . he had grappled with Rakkim in the first few minutes. He had thought it simple desperation at the time, but now he knew better. The Black Robe had gladly sacrificed himself to plant the tracking button. The three men from the strike team probably had no idea they were being used to sell the trap. Rakkim stuffed his wet jacket deep into a blackberry thicket, trotted over to the edge of the water garden's dome. He waited over three minutes, fighting back his impatience. The tracking device would indicate the general location of where he had been, how long he had stayed there. He had to make it appear as though he were wandering around the villa, not staying long in any one place. If he had let Sarah break the device, the grotto would have been pinpointed.

For the next ten minutes Rakkim moved around the villa, stepping over piles of burnt furniture, broken masonry, and crushed, empty cans from spiced meat and Jihad Cola. He sat for a few minutes in Redbeard's old office, remembering standing before the great man, Redbeard often angry at him for some real or imagined offense, sloppily executed prayers or a complaint from one of his teachers. It didn't matter. Redbeard loved him, they both knew it. He walked over to where one of the roof supports had fallen, got down on his belly. The flooring had buckled, left a gap between the hardwood and the subbasement. Rakkim tossed the tracking button into the narrow opening, heard it clatter. He got up and started running toward the front of the house.

Good timing. Two gray sedans were slowly coming down the winding driveway from the small private road leading to the villa. They didn't hurry, just drove on steadily. They knew he was trapped. He and Sarah, Michael and Leo. Rakkim smiled, stepped deeper into the shadows. The strike team was trapped too.

He watched as the cars stopped, and six men got out—three ex-Fedayeen, two army Special Forces . . . and al-Faisal. The military men moved with precision, fully alert, machine pistols at the ready, shock sticks on their belts. Al-Faisal could have been at a picnic, unarmed, dressed casually in loose-fitting pants and a dark-checked shirt. He strolled around the outskirts of the villa, hands in his pockets, picking up pieces of broken tile and bits of burnt wood as though they were treasures. He looked like a man with nothing to fear.

Rakkim retreated deeper into the villa as the men separated—two of them fanned out around the north and south sides of the villa, while three of them accompanied al-Faisal in the direction of Redbeard's office. The Fedayeen leading the way had a handheld locator keyed to the tracking button.

"I'm not scared," said Leo.

Sarah pressed her finger against her lips. Michael did the same.

"Rakkim and I . . . we've been through worse," said Leo.

Sarah watched the waterfall cascade a few inches in front of them, the garden dark and diffuse through the rushing water.

* * *

Rakkim decided to kill the tall, blond Fedayeen first. He was part of the strike team working the perimeter, spread out by necessity. Their intention was to form a loose cordon around the site, preventing escape, while the other four worked on the current location of the tracking button. A reasonable plan . . . but it left the perimeter guards vulnerable to someone who knew every inch of the villa. Besides, al-Faisal's men were combat warriors, fine enough for overpowering an objective, but marginally effective when stealth was demanded.

Rakkim scooted ahead of the blond Fedayeen, not making a sound as he scrambled over the loose rubble. He flattened himself against an interior wall, listening as the blond Fedayeen approached. He heard the man stop. Operational training called for a sneak-and-peek around such a corner, a quick glance in and out. Rakkim timed it perfectly, stabbed him in the eye as he jerked his head in for a look. He lowered the blond Fedayeen to the ground. Went after the next one on the other side of the villa, taking a shortcut through the old laundry room. As he slipped through the house, he could hear them in Redbeard's office, banging around.

The Special Forces man with the shaved head was more cautious—Rakkim could see that just by the way he moved, the care he took before every step, testing the ground before putting his weight on it. Rakkim circled in front of him, lay flat under a pile of wallboard as the man walked by, close enough that Rakkim could see his own reflection in the man's polished boots. He waited until the man passed, then eased out from under the trash and cut the man's throat as he had one foot still poised in the air.

Rakkim took the machine pistol from the dead man. Checked it out. Guns were loud and sloppy things, but when you needed to kill a lot of people fast, and from a distance, they were just what was needed. He approached Redbeard's office. Heard someone saying, "Goddamnit, come out of there or somebody's going to get hurt." Rakkim stayed low, found a collapsed section of wall he had noted earlier. A glimpse was all he needed to pinpoint the positions of the four men. A full-auto spray and Sarah and he could grab Michael and Leo and get out of here. He held up his knife, checked the reflection in the blade. He saw one man in the office, just inches away, only one, the Special Forces operator talking to himself, nervous, his own weapon pivoting from side to side.

Rakkim killed him, then ran toward the water garden, ran as fast as he could.

Sarah heard them coming before she saw them through the waterfall. They kept their voices low, and the water was loud, but she heard them anyway, tramping through the flowers, crunching through the bushes. They walked past the waterfall once. Then twice. The third time they stopped.

This time they lowered their voices until she could barely hear them as they conferred. Three of them . . . one clearly in charge.

Michael squirmed but didn't make a sound.

Leo looked as if he wasn't able to take a breath, his chest heaving.

Sarah pushed Michael to safety on the far side of the shelf and picked up a rock.

A man peeked through the middle of the waterfall, water streaming down his face. He blinked for a moment before he saw her.

She bashed him as hard as she could with the rock. He fell facedown and she hit him again. And again. Somebody dragged him away by the feet.

Another man lurched into their hiding spot, cursing. She didn't see the knife until it was too late. Leo surprised her. It wasn't just that she couldn't imagine him throwing himself in front of the blade, it was that she couldn't believe he could move that fast.

"*Ouch.*" Leo stared at the knife sticking out of his stomach. His mouth worked. He touched the handle, jerked back. Blood seeped down the front of him. He looked over at her as though expecting her to chastise him.

The man who'd stabbed Leo was jerked backward by a thin, cream-colored cord that snapped around his neck and jerked him off his feet.

"I told you, I wanted them taken alive." A man peered in from the side of the waterfall. "Look what you've done. You cut the *boy.*"

Sarah heard gagging from outside, someone trying to breathe.

A hand slipped through the waterfall. "Come on out. All of you." The fingers beckoned. "We'll get Leo some medical attention, but you're going to have to come out. Please." His tone was friendly, but a sharp edge was just under the surface, like broken glass on the beach. "I'm Tariq al-Faisal,

Sarah. I'd hate for anything to happen to you and the baby. I honestly wouldn't want that on my conscience."

Leo looked at her, one hand on his stomach. He shook his head no.

As Sarah hefted the rock, a cord whipped through the waterfall, wrapped around her throat, and jerked her into the base of the waterfall. She came up coughing, trying to pull the cord from around her throat. The man she had hit with the rock lay facedown in the shallow stream, a scum of blood eddying round and round.

"Haskins, you get Leo out there, and slap a pressure bandage on him," al-Faisal ordered the man who had stabbed Leo. "If he dies, I'm going to hang you by your balls until they explode."

Sarah clawed at her throat as the man went under the waterfall, but the knotted cord seemed made of some unique material . . . a four-foot whip when al-Faisal wanted it, but a garrote that adhered to itself when he twisted it.

Al-Faisal watched her, an arrogant man in his thirties with a long face and small, dark eyes. "What, Sarah?" He tugged gently at the cord. "I can't hear you."

Sarah fell to her knees, the edges of her vision going dark.

"Nice dirty doggy," said al-Faisal, continuing to tug at her. "*Heel.* That's what the Catholics say, isn't it?"

Sarah heard Michael crying, but she couldn't seem to move. She was dimly aware of Leo on the ground, the other man hovering over him.

"Carlson?" Al-Faisal spoke into his wrist. "Any sign of him?"

"Yeah, he's in the water garden," said Rakkim.

Al-Faisal turned, saw Rakkim beside a nearby copse of bamboo trees, the machine pistol leveled at him.

"Let her go," said Rakkim.

"Guns are for cowards." Al-Faisal jerked the corded leash, sent Sarah sprawling. "Put it down or I'll snap her neck."

"You'll be dead," said Rakkim.

"We all die, Rakkim. Some of us go to Paradise."

Sarah clawed at the stones, breathing through a pinhole.

"Haskins, you keep working on Leo. Rakkim and I can handle this between ourselves."

Rakkim tossed the gun aside. His knife was already in his hand.

Al-Faisal made some small movement of his fingers and the leash fell away from Sarah's neck.

Rakkim leaped at him, one hand raised to protect his neck, but al-Faisal whipped the cord around his knee, wrenched it. Rakkim flopped on the ground, grunting in pain—he got up quickly, but his left leg no longer fully supported him.

"Hurts, doesn't it?" said al-Faisal, circling, the cord wriggling from his hand. "It's okay, I can help you with that."

Sarah took deep gasping breaths, her throat so swollen she couldn't speak.

"The Old One wants you alive," said al-Faisal. "Still . . ." The cord snaked out and back, Rakkim half-stumbling to avoid it. "I could turn you over to him paralyzed from the neck down . . . You'd still be alive, right? Just snap the third cervical vertebrae—"

"Why do guys like you always have to *talk* about what they're going to do?" said Rakkim.

Al-Faisal laughed. "Guilty." The cord whipped out, flicked Rakkim in the side.

Rakkim gasped. Felt as if one of his ribs had cracked.

"*Strangler* really doesn't do justice to what I can do, does it?"

Sarah heard Michael crying inside the waterfall grotto, but she left him. He knew to stay put. The Fedayeen called Haskins continued to work on Leo, turning him slightly. He tossed away a bloody bandage, applied another one. Leo stared at Sarah, but she wasn't sure he could see her. She concentrated on breathing, and crawling toward the dead Fedayeen lying in the stream.

The knotted cord flicked out again and again, and each time it struck Rakkim, something cracked. Something went numb. His ribs. His shoulder. His leg. His face. One eye was swollen shut and he could barely stand. He kept lunging at al-Faisal, but the man was fast, and Rakkim's sprained left knee slowed him down.

"I'm bored," said al-Faisal. "I was expecting more from you. My master . . . he spoke so highly of you."

"S-sorry."

Al-Faisal feinted another low strike, flicked the cord out around Rakkim's neck, and *jerked*.

Had Rakkim pulled back, which was the natural response, his neck would have broken at precisely the third cervical vertebra . . . but he didn't resist. Instead, Rakkim launched himself forward and drove his blade into al-Faisal's chest. Al-Faisal exhaled in shock, and Rakkim smelled rotting peaches, the end of every summer there ever was.

Al-Faisal kept pulling the cord tighter, his grip still strong, but Rakkim just pressed himself against the strangler, ignoring the spots in front of his eyes.

"Did you *enjoy* hurting my wife?" Rakkim whispered in al-Faisal's ear as he worked the knife deeper and deeper into the man's chest. "Did you smile hearing my son call for his mother?" His head throbbed as the knotted cord dug into his neck. "Were you going to feed off the memory for years . . . savoring their cries . . ."

Al-Faisal struggled harder now, let go the cord, pushing against Rakkim with both hands. Blood ran down the sides of his mouth as he tried to scream.

"Don't go," said Rakkim as al-Faisal's eyes started to roll back. "Stay just a little longer." He slowly moved the blade in small circles, the knife cutting through the rib cage.

Blood bubbled from al-Faisal's mouth as his bones gave way one after the other.

They stood together for a moment, then Rakkim threw al-Faisal's body aside. Rakkim swayed, trying to breathe, collapsed. He lay against the cool earth, lay there in the blackness, listening . . . No sign of Darwin. No trace. Just . . . Rakkim.

Haskins pushed Leo aside, stood up.

Rakkim pulled weakly at the cord still twisted around his neck.

The pressure bandage soaked with red, Leo grabbed at Haskins's pant leg.

Haskins ignored him, raised his machine pistol toward Rakkim.

Rakkim clawed at the cord with his one good hand.

Leo buried his face in the grass at the sound of gunfire. He looked up as Haskins crashed down beside him.

Sarah lay in the stream, the other Fedayeen's machine pistol in her hand. She sat up slowly, soaking wet, hair in her face.

Rakkim waved.

Sarah threw down the gun. Went back into the grotto to get Michael.

EPILOGUE

"You look good," said Rakkim.

Leo tried to laugh, started coughing, the IV tubes in his arms twitching.

"Thank you, Leo," said Sarah.

Leo sat up in the hospital bed. "You . . . you're repeating yourself."

"Seeing you like this"—Sarah touched her throat, still bruised purple from al-Faisal's cord—"brings it back . . . what you did in the garden. You saved my life."

Leo nodded. "Weird, huh?" He looked over at Rakkim. "Surprised you, didn't I?"

"Yeah, I thought you could bend steel with the power of your mind," said Rakkim.

"I know your secret now, Rikki," said Leo.

"Oh, yeah?" Rakkim winced as he moved closer, one eye still swollen from the fight with the strangler, his body covered in welts. "Which one?"

"Risking your life for someone . . . being a hero, it changes a person," said Leo.

Rakkim rested his hand on Leo's shoulder, the only part of the kid's torso that wasn't bandaged.

"I wasn't really awake much these last few days," said Leo, "but I was still thinking. Can't turn it off even if I wanted to, you know? Like when I overloaded my brain in the Belt. You thought I was unconscious, but I wasn't. I was just . . . someplace else." He grabbed Rakkim's wrist, held on. "I know all kinds of things now. Things you wouldn't believe. I'm a lot smarter than I was before. A *lot*."

Sarah stood beside the hospital bed. Smoothed the sheet. "You should rest."

"I'm not bragging," said Leo. "It's the truth."

"Just get better," said Sarah.

"I didn't do it on purpose. Jumping in front of the knife . . . I didn't mean to do it. I just . . . did." Leo glanced at Rakkim. "That still counts, doesn't it?"

"It still counts," said Rakkim.

"I remember being so surprised." Leo shook his head. "I remember lying there and thinking that I was going to die. Me . . . *dead*, and all the things I knew, all the things I was *going* to do, the discoveries I was going to make, the breakthroughs . . . they were never going to happen." Tears shimmered in his eyes. "And I thought that was so sad, so . . . tragic, but I heard your voice, Sarah, and you were talking to Michael, and I thought . . . maybe it's okay, *dying*, you know, maybe it's not the worst thing that could happen."

"I'm glad you're here to tell us about it," said Sarah.

"Me too," said Leo. "The world caught a lucky break."

"Yeah, there's celebrations going on all across the planet," said Rakkim. "Haven't you heard the fireworks?"

Leo smiled, lips cracking. "Michael's okay?"

"Fine," said Rakkim. "He's with your mother and father."

"We have to go," said Sarah. "The presidential inauguration is this afternoon."

"Is that safe?" said Leo.

"Don't worry. Go back to sleep . . . or whatever it is you do," Rakkim said. "The hospital is secure, but as soon as you're well enough, Spider has a new facility he wants to move you to. The Old One isn't going to stop looking for you."

"Let him," said Leo. "He doesn't know who he's dealing with."

Three hours later, Rakkim and Sarah were in the gallery above the great hall of the Congress, watching Peter Brandt take the oath of office. The president-designate tall and assured, one hand resting on the Quran. Only the second president in the history of the republic. The hall was silent except for Brandt's solemnly repeating the words spoken by the grand ayatollah, the senators and representatives assembled below leaning forward in their seats.

General Kidd and Amir sat in the front row in their plain blue uniforms. The overhead lights gleamed off Kidd's stark black cheekbones, his eyes locked deep into their sockets. With the nation still in turmoil and the army in disarray, more than ever the Fedayeen were the key to the nation's security.

"It's my fault," Sarah said softly. "If I had gotten through to President Kingsley ten minutes sooner—"

"You did better than any of us."

"That day at the apartment," said Sarah, "Leo asked if I needed help . . . and I told him I could handle it. He asked me . . . and I turned him down. Bright as he is, bright as I *knew* he was . . . I turned him down."

" . . . in the name of Allah, the merciful, I do solemnly swear," intoned Peter Brandt.

"I didn't want help," Sarah said angrily. "I'm Redbeard's niece, I didn't *need* any help. Now . . . now the president's dead."

The grand ayatollah closed the Quran, bowed before President Brandt as the senators and representatives jumped to their feet, shouting, "*Assalaamu Alaikum!*"

"And now there's a *new* president. You make mistakes, people die, you move *forward*. Perfect people accomplish nothing." Rakkim noted the fundamentalist legislators glowering at the podium, Black Robes not even bothering to hide their hate. "We're lucky Brandt was next in line. A solid moderate, just like Kingsley."

The gigantic screen behind the podium filled with a close-up of Brandt's handsome face framed by his tousled, sandy hair. Tears streamed down his cheeks as he acknowledged Kingsley's widow.

General Kidd and Amir stood with their hands folded in front of them as the politicians applauded wildly, and everyone else seemed smaller and dirtier by comparison.

"Brandt's flexible too, and well traveled," said Sarah. "We're going to need that."

"You trying to convince yourself?" said Rakkim.

Sarah fingered her mother's small, gold cross as the new president basked in the applause. She had been wearing the crucifix under her blouse since the funeral three days ago, had wept when Rakkim presented it to her. He kept waiting for her to take it off.

"I've read the dossier on him," said Sarah. "He's the best we could have hoped for. The Old One wanted chaos and insurrection, but he didn't get it. We won. He lost."

Rakkim stayed silent.

Brandt walked down from the podium, kissed his wife, drawing a gasp from the Black Robes, who fled up the aisles and out of the hall. Brandt continued his progress through the hall, gracefully accepting the prayers of the most powerful legislators. He looked as if he was enjoying every moment of it, his easy manner reassuring the country, the people desperately wanting a smooth succession.

"Camelot," murmured Sarah.

"You think this is Camelot?" said Rakkim. "What, am I supposed to wear a suit of armor and *joust?*"

"It's a historical allusion . . ." Sarah squeezed his hand. "Never mind."

Amir must have felt Rakkim's eyes on him, turned and found Rakkim in the gallery. He pressed his palms together in greeting. Rakkim returned the salutation. Amir had performed nobly during the rioting after the president's death—directing Fedayeen units to secure vital facilities, initiating contacts between his father and various foreign governments, and personally protecting Brandt and his family. Kidd had promoted him to his senior staff; Amir now the heir apparent. Rakkim had called to congratulate him, their bad blood of weeks ago forgotten.

Rakkim watched as the president approached General Kidd. The president embraced Kidd warmly, kissed him on both cheeks, but Rakkim knew the general well enough to see that Kidd was keeping his distance.

The president stepped over to Amir, kissed him also, kissed him even more eagerly, then whispered in his ear. They broke the embrace, the president and Amir smiling into the cameras, side by side, the new guard, the hope and future of the republic.

Applause thundered across the hall, louder than ever, the sound rolling and echoing off the marble, building on itself like a storm growing in power and intensity. Hardened politicians wept with joy, sensing this opportunity, this last great chance for the nation to regain its former grandeur.

"*Allahu Akbar!*" shouted Rakkim, his voice lost in the roar. "*Allahu Akbar!*"

Sarah stood beside him, beating her hands together as loudly as he did, eager to believe, swept up by the moment and the glorious possibilities ahead. God was indeed great.

ACKNOWLEDGMENTS

I would like to thank my daughter, Dani, for coming up with the title for this book, after myself and a team of highly trained professionals tapped out.

Others to whom I am indebted include: Carolyn Reidy for being in my corner and having the good sense to tell me the fight wasn't over yet; Colin Harrison, my editor, for his encouragement and keen instincts for what I was trying to accomplish; Karen Thompson, editorial assistant to Colin, for a very smart first read of the manuscript; Karen Richardson and Steve Boldt, for their alert and insightful copyediting; Susan Moldow, my publisher, for her courage and creativity; and Mary Evans, my agent, for her steadfastness, brains, and good cheer.

I would also like to credit Rhino Records' set of Southern gospel CDs, and a stack of rare bluegrass and country 45s from my pal Carl Waluconis, which together formed the soundtrack by which *Sins of the Assassin* was written.

Thanks to Calvary Presbyterian Church, a Holy Ghost tabernacle full of sweat and miracles—forty years later and I can still feel the floor shake.

ABOUT THE AUTHOR

ROBERT FERRIGNO is the author of nine previous novels, including *Prayers for the Assassin*, *The Wake-Up*, *Scavenger Hunt*, *Flinch*, and the bestselling *The Horse Latitudes*. He lives with his family in the Pacific Northwest.

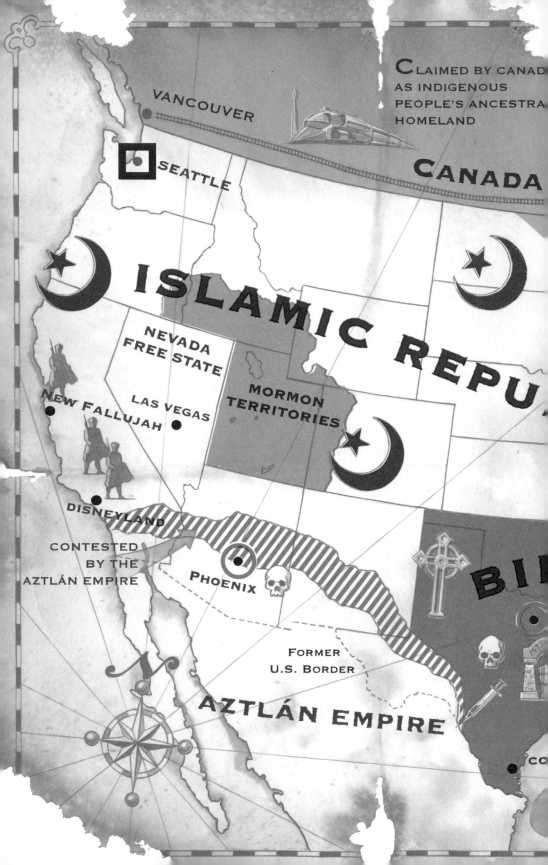